'Theodor Adorno said that to write poetry after Auschwitz was barbaric. To which I would say, yes, but you can still write an excellent novel. *A Man Lies Dreaming* is that novel.'

Philip Kerr, author of *January Window*

'A Holocaust novel like no other, Lavie Tidhar's *A Man Lies Dreaming* comes crashing through the door of literature like Sam Spade with a .38 in his hand. This is a shocking book as well as a rather brilliant one, and it treats the topic of genocide with a kind of energetic unseriousness . . . The book manages to provide both the guilty pleasures of a fast-paced violent pulp and the more thoughtful moral depth of a genuine engagement with what the camps meant . . . *A Man Lies Dreaming* is a twisted masterpiece.'

Guardian

'Uniting sci-fi counterfactual history with pulp noir and literary intensity . . . *A Man Lies Dreaming* makes you realise again the enormity of the Holocaust, while doing so with the darkest of wits and the most ingenious of conceits . . . Something exceptional.'

Scotland on Sunday

'Poetic and terrible . . . As riveting as it is disturbing . . . There is eloquence and gravitas in the sparseness and brevity of noir fiction when it is good, and Tidhar's is quite incredible. He examines the Holocaust in the light of what he knows — imagined alternative narratives of survival, fictions based on possibilities and potential.'

Tor.com

'This is a brilliantly original examination of the Holocaust.'

Catholic Herald

'Lift your eyes at all and you notice the shadow of history pressing in, feel the terrible, crushing, annihilating weight of it. *A Man Lies Dreaming* seems to me a brilliant and potent thought experiment.'

Herald Scotland

'Tidhar is a masterful writer . . . perhaps the UK's most literary speculative fiction writer, and we should celebrate *A Man Lies Dreaming* ... more a masterful work of literary fiction than of speculative ...

...Horizons

Also by Lavie Tidhar

Osama

The Violent Century

LAVIE TIDHAR

A Man Lies Dreaming

HODDER

First published in Great Britain in 2014 by
Hodder & Stoughton
An Hachette UK company

First published in paperback in 2015

1

A CIP catalogue record for this title is available from the British Library

ISBN 978 1 444 76294 5

Printed and bound by Clays Ltd, St Ives plc

Hodder & Stoughton policy is to use papers that are natural, renewable and
recyclable products and made from wood grown in sustainable forests. The
logging and manufacturing processes are expected to conform to the
environmental regulations of the country of origin.

Hodder & Stoughton Ltd
Carmelite House
50 Victoria Embankment
London EC4Y 0DZ

www.hodder.co.uk

A Man Lies Dreaming

'He had gone beyond good and evil, and entered a strange landscape where nothing was what it seemed and all the ordinary human values were reversed.'

Hugh Trevor-Roper,
report for the Secret Intelligence Service

'Clichés, stock phrases, adherence to conventional, standardised codes of expression and conduct have the socially recognised function of protecting us against reality.'

Hannah Arendt, *The Banality of Evil*

In another time and place, a man lies dreaming.

In another time and place a man lies dreaming.

I

Extract from Wolf's Diary, 1st November 1939

She had the face of an intelligent Jewess.

She came into my office and stood in the doorway though there was nothing hesitant about the way she stood. She gave you the impression she had never hesitated a moment in her life. She had long black hair and long pale legs and she wore a summer dress despite the cold and a fur coat over the dress. She carried a purse. It was hand-threaded with beads that formed into the image of a mockingbird. It was French, and expensive. Her gaze passed over the office, taking in the small dirty window that no one ever cleaned, the old pine hatstand on which the varnish was badly chipping, the watercolour on the wall and the single bookshelf and the desk with the typewriter on it. There wasn't much else to look at. Then her gaze settled on me.

Her eyes were grey. She said, 'You are Herr Wolf, the detective?'

She spoke German with a native Berliner's accent.

'That's the name on the door,' I said. I looked her up and down. She was a tall drink of pale milk. She said, 'My name is Isabella Rubinstein.'

Her eyes changed when she looked at me. I had seen that look before. In her eyes clouds gathered over a grey sea. Doubt – as though trying to place me.

'I'll save you the trouble,' I said. 'I am nobody.'

She smiled at me. 'Everyone is somebody.'

'And I do not work for Jews.'

At that the clouds amassed in her eyes and stayed there but

she remained calm, very calm. Her hand swept over the room. 'I do not see that you have so much choice,' she said.

'What I choose to do is my own damn business,' I said.

She reached into her handbag and came back with a roll of ten-shilling notes. She just held it there, for a long moment.

'What is it about?' I said. At that moment I hated her, and that hatred gave me pause.

'My sister,' she said. 'She is missing.'

I had two chairs for visitors. She pulled one to her and sat down, crossing one leg over the other. She was still holding the notes between her fingers. She didn't wear any rings.

'A lot of people are missing nowadays,' I said. 'If she is in Germany I cannot help you.'

'No,' she said, and this time there was tension in her voice. 'She was leaving Germany. Herr Wolf, let me explain to you. My family is very wealthy. After the Fall our assets were seized, but my father still had friends, some even amongst the Party, and he was able to transfer much of our capital to London. I myself, and my mother, were both allowed to leave the country legally, and my uncles continue the family's continental operations in Paris. Only my sister remained behind. She is young, younger than me. At first she was beguiled by their ideology; she had joined the Free Socialist Youth before the Fall. My father was furious. But I knew it would not last.' She looked up at me, with a half-smile. 'It never does, with Judith, you see.'

All I could see was the money she was holding between those long slim fingers. She moved the roll of notes back and forth, idly. I had been penniless before, and poverty had made me stronger, not weak, but that was in my former life. My life was different now, and it was harder to be hungry.

I said, 'So you arranged for her to leave.'

'My father,' she said quickly. 'He knew men who could smuggle people out.'

'Not easily,' I said.

'Not easily, no. Not cheaply, either.' Again that half-smile, but it flickered and was gone in a flash.

'How long ago was that?'

'A month. She was meant to be here three weeks ago. She never appeared.'

'Do you know who these men were? Do you trust them?'

'My father did. As much as he could be said to trust anyone.'

Something jogged my recall, then. 'Your father is Julius Rubinstein? The banker.'

'Yes.'

I remembered his likeness in the *Daily Mail*. One of the Jewish gangsters who grew rich and fat on the blood of the working man in Germany, before the Fall. His like always survived, like rats abandoning a sinking ship they fled Germany and re-established themselves elsewhere, in clumps of diseased colonies. They said he was as ruthless as a Rothschild.

'Not a man to cross,' I said.

'No.'

'Your sister . . . Judith? She could have been captured by the Communists.'

She shook her head. 'We would have heard.'

'You think she was brought to London?'

'I don't know. I need to find her. I *must* find her, Herr Wolf.'

She put the roll of notes on my desk. I left it there, though whenever I looked at her the notes were in my field of vision. The Jews are nothing but money-grubbers, living on the profits of war. Perhaps she could see it in my eyes. Perhaps she was desperate. 'Why me?'

'The men who smuggled her here,' she said, 'are old comrades of yours.'

There was nothing behind her eyes, nothing but grey clouds. And I realised I had misjudged Fräulein Isabella Rubinstein. There was a reason she had picked me, after all.

'I do not associate with the old comrades any more,' I told her. 'The past is the past.'

'You've changed.' She said that with curiosity.

'You do not know me,' I said. 'Do not ever presume to think that you do!'

She shrugged, indifferent. She reached into her purse and brought out a silver cigarette case and a gold lighter. She opened the case with dextrous fingers and extracted a cigarette and put it between her lips. She offered me the open case. I shook my head. 'I do not smoke,' I said.

'Do you mind if I do?'

I did mind and she could see it. She flicked the lighter to life and wrapped her half-smile around the cigarette and drew deep, and blew smoke into the cold air of my office. A draught came in through the window and though I was dressed in my coat I shivered. It was the only coat I owned. I looked at the money. I looked at her face. She was nothing but trouble and I knew it and she knew I knew. I had no business hunting for missing Jews in London in the year of our Lord 1939. I once had faith, and a destiny, but I had lost both and I guess I'd never recovered either. All I could see was the money. I was so cold, and it was going to be a cold winter.

When the Jewish woman departed, Wolf sat there for a long moment staring at the money. The smell of her cigarette hung in the air, rank and nauseating. He could not abide the smell of tobacco. Outside the window it was already dark. The cold clawed at the windowpane. Below he could hear the market shutting, the sound of whores sashaying into the night. His landlord's bakery on the ground floor had already closed for the day. He stared at the money.

He pushed the chair back, stood up and took the roll of notes and put them in his pocket. He set the chair back and went round the desk and stood looking at his office. The painting on the wall showed a French church tower rising against the background of a village, a field executed in a turmoil of brushstrokes. Three dark trees grew out of a tangle of roots rising in the foreground of the church. On the bookshelf, a personally inscribed copy of *Fire and Blood*, Ernst Jünger's memoir of the Great War, sat next to J.R.R. Tolkien's *The Hobbit*, Madison Grant's masterpiece of racial theory, *The Passing of the Great Race,* a collection of Schiller's poetry, and a row of Agatha Christies.

There was no copy of Wolf's one published book. He stood looking at the shelf. He had saved only a handful of the collection of books he had amassed before the Fall. Their loss ate at him. But he had already lost so much. He went to the hatstand and put on his hat. His shadow fell on the wall like a dirty coat. Wolf opened the door and went outside.

Berwick Street, Soho, on a cold November night. Electric lights cast the pavement in a gloomy glow. The dirty bookstore was open. Whores loitered outside. He stood under the awning of the bakery when his landlord came out of nowhere like a Jew in the night.

'Herr Edelmann,' Wolf said.

'Mr Wolf,' Edelmann said. 'I am glad I caught you.'

He was a short, pudgy man with hands and a face as pale as flour. He had a furtive manner. 'What is it, Herr Edelmann?' Wolf said.

'I hate to bother you, Mr Wolf,' Edelman said. He wiped his hands at his sides as if he still wore his apron. 'It is about the rent, you see.'

'The rent, Herr Edelman?'

'It is due, you see, Mr Wolf.' He nodded, as though confirming something to an unseen audience. 'Yes,' he said, 'it is due some days now, Mr Wolf.'

Wolf just stood there and looked at him. The baker hopped from leg to leg. 'Cold, isn't it,' he said. Wolf watched him in silence.

'Well,' Edelman said finally, 'I hate to ask, Mr Wolf, really I do, but it is the way of things, isn't it, it is the nature of the world.' His whole stance seemed apologetic, but Wolf wasn't fooled. There was a flash of steel underneath the baker's quivering exterior. Wolf didn't deign to reply. He reached into his pocket and pulled out the wad of money and peeled off two ten-shilling notes, watching the baker's eyes all the while. He returned the rest to his pocket. He held the money in his hand. The man seemed hypnotised by the money. He licked his lips nervously. 'Mr Wolf,' he began.

'Will this do, Herr Edelmann?' Wolf said. The man made no move to take the money, waiting for it to be offered. 'It is the nature of the world that evil exists,' Wolf said. 'It is not money that is evil but the means to which it is put to use. Money is an instrument, Herr Edelmann, it is a lever.' He held the money steady in his fingers. 'A small lever to move small people,' he said. 'But give me a large enough lever and I would move the very world.'

'That's very interesting, Mr. Wolf,' Edelmann said. He was still looking at the money. 'Do you wish to pay for a month upfront?'

Wolf handed him the notes. The baker took them and secreted them about his person.

'I would require a receipt,' Wolf said.

'I will put one through your door.'

'Make sure that you do,' Wolf said. He touched the brim of his hat, lightly. '*Guten abend*, Herr Edelmann.'

'Good evening to you, too, Mr Wolf.'

Wolf walked off and the baker disappeared into the darkness like a shadow. There had been too many dark streets and too many shadows, melting into the night, never to be seen again. Wolf thought about Geli. There had not been a day gone past when he had not thought about Geli.

The whores were gathered in Berwick Street. They stood light as shadows, mute as stone. Wolf hesitated as he passed nearby. With his approach the girls grew lively, and raucous laughter welcomed Wolf's approach. In a passageway between buildings a fat whore was squatting with her back to the brick wall, crapping. He caught a glimpse of her pale loose flesh, her garments round her ankles. 'Looking is for free,' someone nearby said. A girl no older than sixteen flashed him a smile. Her lips were red, set in a white, made-up face. Her teeth were small and uneven. 'Hey, mister,' she said. 'You want a quick one?' She spoke English with an accent he knew well and with a vocabulary learned from reading cheap novels.

Wolf said, 'I've not seen you here before.'

The girl shrugged. 'What about it,' she said.

'You are Austrian,' he said, in German.

'What about it.'

In the alleyway the fat whore farted loudly and laughed as her bowels emptied steaming onto the cold flagstones. Wolf averted his gaze.

'You should find another line of work,' he told the girl.

'Go to hell, mister.'

Underneath the streetlights a few johns were already passing, eyeing up the girls. In a few hours trade would be brisk. Another whore approached them. She was someone Wolf recognised, Dominique, a half-caste girl. 'Pay no attention to him,' she told the new girl. 'It's just Mr Wolf's way with us. Isn't it, Mr Wolf?' She smiled at him. She had light brown skin, red lips and cool eyes. The new girl looked at Wolf uncertainly. He knew the expression in her eyes. Trying to place him. When he had first come to London many had known his name. Now there were precious few who cared. 'Fräulein Dominique,' he said, politely.

'Mr Wolf.' She turned to her sister in trade. 'Mr Wolf never goes with one of us.' Her smile was mocking. 'Mr Wolf only ever looks.'

The Austrian girl shrugged. There was a dull look in her eyes. Wolf wondered how she had come to London, what she had escaped from. He could imagine it well enough. He bore the scars of such a departure himself. 'What is your name?' he said.

'It's Edith.'

He touched the brim of his hat. 'Edith,' he said.

'You can fuck me for ten shillings,' the girl said.

'What Mr Wolf wants,' Dominique said, 'it would take more than a ten-shilling whore to satisfy.'

Wolf didn't answer back. There was never a point, with prostitutes. In Vienna before the War he had seen them on the

Spittelberggasse, each girl behind a lighted window, some young, some old, some sitting, some standing, some doing their hair or smoking cigarettes. For a long time he had walked past the low one-storey houses, with his friend, Gustl, watching them, and the men who came to use their services, how the lights in the rooms would be turned off once a deal was concluded. One could tell by the number of darkened windows how trade was going.

The fat whore – her name was Gerta – had emerged from the alleyway pulling up her undergarments. She waved at Wolf cheerfully. He repressed a shudder of revulsion. The young girl, Edith, had lost interest in him. A couple of men on the other side of the street were looking at her with interest, cattle traders examining livestock. They called to her and she was gone, into the shadows. The half-caste Dominique was suddenly very close. She was taller than Wolf. Her lips were by his ears. Her breath warm on his skin. 'I know what you want,' she said. 'I can give it to you.'

There was a strength about her; he feared and desired what she could sense in him. Her hand reached down and pressed painfully on the front of his trousers. 'Yes,' Dominique murmured, 'I know. And I would enjoy doing it to you, too.'

For a moment he was frozen; she had snared him with lust; what the Jews called the 'evil inclination', the *yetzer hora*. But he was stronger than her; stronger than that. He removed her hand. 'I'll thank you not to touch me again,' he said. Dominique looked him down and up. Her lips curled and then she too was gone, into the night. Wolf walked on.

Wolf's Diary, 1st November 1939 – *contd.*

At night the fruit and vegetable market closes and a different type of market springs beyond my office window. Whores. How I hated whores! Their bodies were riddled with syphilis and the other ills of their trade. The disease was but a symptom. Its cause was the manner in which love itself has been prostituted.

I did not feel pity for the young girl, Edith. No. Instead I felt a cold anger, the sort of anger that had once driven me to oratory, when it had burned bright and strong. To see a Germanic girl prostituted in this way, in a foreign land, was a reminder to me of my own failure, of the way the land itself had been prostituted. Once Germany bled like a soldier; now it bled like a whore. It was a slow death; it was a death of love. I walked past the girls and in the night I felt unseen eyes watching my passing; but there are always eyes watching in the night. A mystery is not when one's action goes unobserved. Rather it is an action to which no witness is willing to come forward.

I know what Isabella Rubinstein feared. I made my way down through Walker's Court onto Rupert Street, passing the White Horse and the Windmill cinema onto Shaftesbury Avenue. Theatreland. The lights burned bright here and theatregoers strolled along the avenue mingling with pickpockets and dollymops. At the Apollo Theatre on the corner the electric signs advertised Patrick Hamilton's *Gaslight*. A pair of coppers I knew by sight went past me, eyeing the whores openly. I nodded to them and went on.

Gerrard Street was full of little clubs and dusty alcoves. At this time of night gentlemen were heading out to supper with their wives, and young men of a literary bent were debating the merits and faults in the poetry of W.B. Yeats, Ezra Pound and Modernism in general. On the corner with Dean Street I saw a group of Blackshirts standing together in a dark mob, eying the passers-by with sullen hostility. On a wall I saw a placard for Mosley's election campaign. Oswald's handsome British face stared out at me with its dapper moustache and ironic smile. I saluted him, crisply. Then I went into the Hofgarten.

It lay at the bottom of a narrow staircase behind a grey wooden door that bore no plaque. It was not a members-only club but then it was not *not* a members-only club, either. It was a place for like-minded people to meet and talk of the past. I abhorred it for all that it represented and all that it wasn't, and couldn't be. I pushed the heavy door at the bottom of the stairs and went in.

It was dark and smoky inside. The smell of heavy Bavarian beer hung in the air like a peasant woman's thick skirts hanging to dry. I could hear laughter, men's drunken talk, the tap-tap-tap of chess pieces against a chessboard. A small piano stood in the corner, but no one was playing. It was too early and years too late for anyone to be playing the Horst Wessel Song.

I could feel eyes on me. Heard the pitch of conversation change. In years past I would have revelled in it. Now I set my jaw and bore it. I hung up my coat and my hat and made my way to the bar counter.

'What could I get you, sir?'

'I would like a herbal tea,' I said.

He was a big ugly brute of a man; a fine Aryan. The face he turned on me began to open its maw in a display of mockery or outrage, revealing a wealth of gold. He truly was a man who carried his valuables on his person. He never did finish, though. He took me in and his face changed and his mouth closed without voicing whatever wisdom it was he had been about to impart.

'Tea, sir?'

'If you would be so kind.'

'But of course. Of course. Herr—'

'Wolf,' I said.

He rubbed his hands together, as if he were cold. 'Wolf. Of course.'

'Has Herr Hess come in yet?' I said.

At that he all but stood to attention. 'Not yet, sir,' he said.

I gestured to an empty table in the corner. 'I shall be sitting over there,' I said. 'Please be so kind as to bring me the tea when it is ready.'

He nodded that great big head of his. A farmer boy from Austria, of the kind I had grown up amongst. Salt of the

earth. I wondered if he was smarter than he looked. I made
my way to the empty table and sat down. I was glad of the
darkness of the room. Too many familiar faces, too many
reminders of a past the world had already forgotten and I was
trying to. I fingered the roll of money in my suit pocket. I had
not been to the Hofgarten in three years.

'Our fight is for the soul of this country, and the soul of the
world. We must struggle, for nothing comes easily to men
such as us, who will change the world. We, the Blackshirts,
have been called, and we shall lead this nation to a new and
higher civilisation. There is a cancer growing in our midst, the
cancer of Judaism. This is our revolution. We shall be baptised
in fire. Remember, you have a voice. You have a vote. Vote
Mosley. We shall triumph in adversity—'

'Turn the God damned radio off,' someone said.

His shadow fell on the table before I saw him. I may have
dozed off. The cigarette and pipe smoke hurt my eyes. My tea
had been cooling on the table for some time.

'Hess,' I said. He had thick wavy black hair and thick black
eyebrows. His smile was genuine but cautious. I didn't blame
him.

'Wolf,' he said. For a moment, I thought he might try to
hug me. I rose from the chair and shook his hand, formally.

'It is good to see you again,' he said.

'You, too,' I said. I looked at him. He bore up well. London
had been good to Hess. His hair looked luxurious and shiny.
His jacket was styled in black with the lightning bolt of the
Blackshirts on the lapels. It looked tailor-made. He wore
riding boots and a paunch. Hess had grown fat in this foreign
city, after the Fall.

'You are doing well,' I said.

He patted his belly. 'I get by,' he said.

I gestured at the chair opposite and sat down again. He
followed. 'Can I get you anything?' he said. I shook my head.
'You never come to the Hofgarten,' Hess complained. 'Never

come to see me. I wish you'd let me help you, at least. Money—'

'I do not want your money.'

He sighed. 'I know,' he said. He signalled to the barman. The lad brought over a small brandy and placed it at Hess's elbow. Hess swirled it around, sniffed it appreciatively, and sipped.

'Good?' I said.

'Wonderful.'

I slapped the glass out of his hand and it smashed to the floor, the brandy spilling on Hess's hand. I heard chairs scraping back, saw three men rise and marked them. Hess shook his limp hand then sucked on his fingers. He stared at me mournfully. 'Bring me a napkin, please, Emil,' he said. He gestured at his men and they sat down again. 'You have an escort, these days,' I said.

'These are dangerous times,' Hess said. 'A man needs must take precautions.'

The big barman brought over a silk handkerchief. It was embroidered with RH. Hess wiped his hand clean fastidiously and gave it back. 'Thank you, Emil,' he said.

I stared at him across the table. 'I meant no disrespect,' he said.

'I'm sure that you didn't.'

'What is it?' he said.

'I need information.'

He nodded. 'I heard you were working as a private investigator,' he said.

'You heard correctly.'

His eyes grew as soft as his face. 'They called you the Drummer,' he said.

'I have always fought,' I said. 'But I have always fought for order.' I took a sip of my cold tea. 'There must be order in all things.'

'Yes,' he said. 'Of course.' He loosened his tie. 'What do you need to know?'

'I am looking for a girl. She would have been coming from Germany, to London.'

'I see. Without papers, naturally.'

'Yes.'

'Such a thing is not impossible, for a price,' he said.

'Tell me, Rudolf,' I said. 'Do many people disappear, en route from Germany?'

'Disappear how?'

I said, softly, 'She was a Jewess.'

He stared into my eyes. 'Wolf . . .' he said. 'Don't.'

'For the sake of my love for you,' he said. 'Don't ask me.'

'I need to know.'

'There are doors which are best left closed,' he said. He pushed his chair back and stood up. 'For the sake of our friendship.' He looked at me curiously. 'What do you care what happens to a Jew?'

'I don't.'

'Come and work for me,' he said, impulsively. He saw my face. 'With me, I mean. There is money to be made, power. I am someone here, Wolf. I am a man of influence.'

'Hess,' I said, 'you are a pimp and a thief. You have traded your honour for cash.'

'Don't use those words.'

'What words would you have me use?'

He laughed at that. 'Perhaps I've merely outgrown you,' he said.

'You have been reduced,' I said. 'While I remain the same. My integrity cannot be purchased so cheaply.'

'You are a shadow of what you once were. A ghost.' He laughed again, a sad, bitter sound. 'You died in the Fall; what is left of you makes a mockery of what you once were.'

I stood up too. He was taller than me, but he had always been the smaller man. 'Please,' he said, again. 'Do not go asking such questions, mein freund.'

'Give me a name,' I said.

Hess sighed. He reached into his breast pocket and threw down on the table a *carte de visite*. I picked it up. Printed on thick, expensive paper, it contained an address in the East End and nothing more. On the back, a symbol I had not seen in some time: it was a swastika.

The night was full of eyes, watching. Wolf made his way out of the Hofgarten. At the end of the street the same group of Blackshirts was beating a man lying on the pavement. The man had curled in a foetal position, his hands uselessly covering his head. The Blackshirts wore thick-soled boots and they were kicking the man savagely. A pair of policemen were watching from the sidelines without expression. The air was scented with the smell of men's sweat and blood and violence. It was a smell Wolf knew well, had in fact delighted in. Two white teeth lay on the ground beside the victim. Wolf paused as he walked past them. One of the Blackshirts wiped sweat from his face with the hem of his shirt. 'What are you looking at,' he said. Wolf shook his head. He walked on. Behind him the victim was whimpering in a broken voice. Oswald Mosley stared down at Wolf from the public walls, smiling winningly. Wolf walked on.

There were eyes in the night, watching. He felt shadows gathering about him and he stopped and started, dawdling in front of shop windows, trying to catch a reflection, a clue as to the unseen watchers' identity. Perhaps there was no one there. But he could scent them, hunters in the night. He had used the name Wolf in the 1920s and now he used it again, in London. He had always felt himself to have an affinity with wolves.

The *carte de visite* was in his suit pocket. He did not like seeing Hess again, did not like being reminded of what had passed. How Hess had risen while he himself fell. There was a dull ache in his left leg. It had broken in the camp and never healed properly, and ached in the cold. He had been there three days short of five months when he escaped. Sometimes he missed Germany with a powerful ache, with every fibre of his being. He knew he was unlikely to ever see her again.

The '40s were coming. Christmas was in the air and along Charing Cross Road early decorations were already going up. A man behind a cart was selling roasted chestnuts. He had the swarthy complexion of a gypsy. The city was filled with refugees from the Fall, but the borders were closing, and tensions were mounting everywhere. Wolf bought the evening edition of the *Daily Mail* and glanced at the headlines as he walked. 'Duke of Windsor in Support of Mosley' said the front page. Well, no surprise there. The abdicated king had been a keen supporter of Wolf's own politics, too, back when Wolf still had politics. He was a fool to marry the American woman, though. Love was a weaker force than hate, and Wolf could not help but despise the former monarch for that.

There. Was that a shadow moving behind him? Wolf ducked into an alleyway. A man in a black suit with an unremarkable face. But the man continued past, seemingly oblivious. Wolf emerged from the alleyway. He found himself by Collet's Bookshop, still open at this hour, coffeehouse revolutionaries conspiring amidst leftwing pamphlets and communist propaganda. The man in the black suit had disappeared. Wolf walked on, stopped by Marks & Co. to browse the books outside. Popular fiction, books thumbed and marked. Dashiell Hammett's *The Maltese Falcon*. A row of P.G. Wodehouse novels. Another copy of *The Hobbit*. A review copy of Anthony Powell's *From a View to a Death*. But Wolf had little love for the weakness of the English tongue. German had a martial tune; it was neither tarnished nor afraid. He walked on.

Oxford Street coming up, Wolf walking aimlessly, checking his reflection in shop windows. He had black hair receding at the temples, a high forehead, a strong chin, ears sticking out slightly. No moustache. He could no longer abide the moustache.

There!

He turned suddenly and rapidly and began to walk with purpose the way he'd come. A second youngish man in a black suit and tie like an underemployed undertaker had begun to turn the other way, too late. In moments Wolf was on him, grabbing the man by the lapels, slamming him against the brick wall. He pressed his face close into the stranger's. 'Who are you?' he said, speaking low. 'What do you want?'

The man didn't struggle. 'Excuse me, pal,' he said, 'I think you got the wrong idea there.'

Despite his diction his accent came across loud and clear and American. Wolf released him. The man had not struggled though he looked like he could have put up a fight, had he wanted to. Under the cheap suit was a body kept trim and in shape. 'Why are you following me?' Wolf said. The man looked embarrassed.

'Do you know the way to the British Museum?' he said. 'This damn city can be confusing. I think I lost my way somewhere.'

'Yes, you did,' Wolf said. He stared hard at the man. 'The museum is closed.'

'It is?'

There was a twinkle in the man's eyes. Wolf's hands tightened on the man's lapels. The man still didn't struggle. He seemed to regard Wolf with some irony. It was not a quality Wolf possessed, or much appreciated.

'Where is your friend?' Wolf said.

'Excuse me?'

Wolf spat. His phlegm hit the brick wall over the man's shoulder and slid down, slowly. 'I won't give you and yours a second warning,' he said. He turned just as abruptly and walked off. He did not watch to see if the other man was following him still.

★　　★　　★

In Berwick Street the whores were busy at their trade. The watcher in the dark had seen the detective exit his office and speak to the young German whore and to the coloured one, and seen him leave, but he remained behind. He had time. All the time in the world. He eyed the whores.

He was wrapped in shadows. He was like a ghost, or H.G. Wells's invisible man. In his invisibility there was power. He felt the knife under the coat. The smoothness of the grind versus the sharpness of the point and edge. How good it felt. He watched the whores, watched a sailor talking to the young German, or was she Austrian, he understood only hazily the difference but it didn't matter. The sailor took her by the hand and they vanished into the shadows. He felt the knife, stroking the metal. They couldn't see him, nobody could. All he had to do was choose. He felt so hard, painfully so, but it was a good pain: it was a pain of anticipation. Soon. He had no need to rush. Waiting was half the pleasure, though perhaps he did not see it that way. It was just a fantasy. He wouldn't do anything. Not yet. But he could imagine it, standing there, watching the women, holding his knife. The things he would do to them. They didn't even see him. But he saw them.

Later he saw the detective come back. A small figure, so unremarkable. But you couldn't be deceived by appearances. It was for the detective that he was doing this. He watched the man's weary steps. The detective passed so close to him, nearly brushing against him, and he held his breath, but the detective didn't even notice him. No one ever did. Once the detective was past he pressed his back against the bricks and watched the whores again, his hand in his pocket. He was so hard and then he was soft and there was a pleasant warmth. He wasn't going to do anything. Not yet.

But soon.

*   *   *

In another time and place Shomer lies dreaming.

When Wolf returned it was late. He climbed the steps slowly. He rented a small bedsit next to his office. When he pushed the door open he found an envelope on the floor where it had been pushed through under the door. It was a heavy cream paper. His name was written on the back in a beautiful hand, in black ink. He picked it up and hefted it. There was no postmark. It must have been hand-delivered. He thought he knew the handwriting. He carried the envelope across the room.

Wolf's accommodation consisted of a bed and a desk and a kitchenette. The only decorations were the books. They lay everywhere, on the floor, on the windowsill, on the desk. A sea of books, their pages like waves. Sometimes he thought he would drown in words, all those words.

Wolf set the envelope on the bed and went to boil water for tea on the hotplate. The room had a gas heater operated by coins. He inserted money into the device, willing it to work. The room was cold and when he exhaled a fog rose from his mouth like a shroud. When the tea was ready he carried it with him and sat hunched on the bed as close as he could to the radiator. His leg ached dully. He sipped his tea. His eyes were still irritated by the smoke from the club. The money from the Jewish woman was still in his pocket. He kept his coat on. He set the tea on the windowsill and reached for his letter opener. Inside the envelope was a card printed on expensive paper. *Sir Oswald and Lady Mosley request the pleasure of your company*. The address was the Mosleys's house in Belgravia. The date was for two days hence: a Friday. Wolf fingered the worn hem of his coat. He could not afford to hire a suit, and his clothes sat uneasily on him.

He turned the card over. On the back, in the same rich black ink and impeccable handwriting, Diana had written: *My dear Wolf, it has been so long since we had the pleasure of your company. Oswald will be so happy to see you as, of course, will I.* She had signed it with her name, and Xs and Os. Underneath, a P.S.: *Unity may also be in attendance.*

Wolf slid the invitation card back into its envelope. He drank his tea. He rose and washed the cup in the sink thoroughly and left it to dry. He hung up his coat. He sat on the bed and then stretched out on his back, staring up at the ceiling. The past was re-emerging, threatening to catch up to him. He had not seen Oswald and Diana since their wedding, in '36. He had been their guest, but no longer an honoured one. Things were different, after the Fall.

What did it mean, to be invited, now? What did Oswald want with him? Wolf was under no illusions. Oswald wanted something. They were the same in many ways; though he, Wolf, was strong and Oswald was weak. Had always been the weaker man.

Briefly, he thought about Unity. He lay on his back and stared at the darkness beyond the window and listened to the voices of the night until he fell asleep.

Wolf's Diary, 2nd November 1939

In my dream I was back in the trenches in Neuve Chapelle, in the dugout we called Löwenbräu, after the brewery. In my dream it was night time, some days after the battle that had raged over the 9th and 10th of May 1915. The battle was not significant enough to be named, though I suppose it was significant enough for the dead.

In my dream I stood half-crouched in the trench during inspection. In the night beyond, mortar fire bloomed and in the no-man's-land the cries of the dying could be heard. Hundreds of dead British soldiers littered the barren ground and the stench of their death filled the night. When we had first arrived at the front the land had been filled with orchards and fields and the hum of bees could be heard. Now it was a wasteland. The British soldiers lay rotting in the sun during the day. At night their bloated corpses lay ripening as flies laid their eggs on the entry points of the bullets that killed them. Beetles crawled inside them, feeding, and the stench of the rotting corpses filled the warm spring air. Worse yet were the ones still, miraculously, alive; the ones who took so long to die. Their moans were unholy sounds. We wished them dead so we would be spared their horror.

In my dream Ziegler, the commander of the Tenth company, was walking down the line of inspection, slapping the soldiers he deemed slovenly or disrespectful. As he approached me I saw him as a being of great shadow, his face invisible behind a pool of darkness, the shadows lengthening behind him in the light of the moon like the wings of a great beast. When he reached me he stopped, and I could smell the rank odour of alcohol on his breath. He leaned towards me, into the light, and I saw his face, but it was not Ziegler's face but my father's, Alois. I cowered from him, his small eyes set in a fleshy face, the smell of wine on him. I saw him smile with unholy joy as he raised his fist and swung and hit me. The impact threw me back against the sandbags and then he was on me, kicking and cursing my name.

It is my habit to read a book a day. When I woke it was early and the sun had not yet risen. I washed my face in the sink, and the cold stung where my father had hit me in my dream. I made myself an infusion of camomile tea and set it on the windowsill. Soho at this hour is as close to silent as it ever gets. Even the whores were asleep. From down below came the smell of freshly baked bread. I picked up a book, Harold Laski's *The Grammar of Politics*, published some years back by Allen & Unwin. I spent the next two hours thus quietly occupied. Then I rose, donned my coat and my hat and went into my office.

The morning passed uneventfully. I paid bills, caught up on paperwork. I have always loved working at my desk. From behind a desk, a man can force an order on things. From behind a desk, I once believed, I could rule the world. Now other men sat behind other desks, in offices grander than mine, and told the people what to do and how to think. In the afternoon my telephone rang.

'Wolf Investigations, this is Wolf.'

'This is Isabella Rubinstein speaking.'

'Miss Rubinstein.'

Her voice sounded brisk on the phone. 'Have you made any progress yet?' she demanded. I pictured her in a vast London residence in Mayfair or Belgravia, somewhere anyway where they let Jews move in. Talking to me on the phone while her father's chauffeur washed the Rolls and her father's gardener pruned the rose bushes and her father's chef prepared their Jewish meal in a kitchen with two separate sinks in it. 'You only came to see me yesterday,' I said.

'I expect results, Herr Wolf,' she said.

I held on to the phone for a long moment, watching how the blood drained from the tips of my fingers where I was gripping the receiver.

'Hello?'

'Yes, Miss Rubinstein.'

'Well?'

'I have met with one of my . . . old associates. He has given me the address of a club. I shall be visiting it tonight.'

'What sort of club?'

'The sort nice society girls shouldn't go to,' I said, and she laughed, a little breathlessly.

'You'd be surprised what nice society girls do,' she said. 'When they have the mind to do it.'

I let that go. 'If that would be all, Miss Rubinstein . . .'. I said.

'No,' she said.

'No?'

'I want to come with you.'

'That is entirely out of the question.' I think I was shouting down the line. She got me that way, did Isabella Rubinstein.

'Where is this club?' she said. I could hear steel sheathed in her voice.

'Miss Rubinstein, you hired me to do my job. So let me do my job.'

'I hired you for who you once were,' she said. The intensity of her voice changed. I pictured her on the other end of the line, lying on her bed, the window open, a warm breeze wafting into the room (it is always spring, for the rich). Was she playing with the cord? Running her long slim fingers up and down the shaft of the receiver? 'They used to scare us with your name. Did you know that? My mother told me if I misbehaved the big bad wolf would come and get me. I would lie in my bed at night in the dark and picture you, creeping into the house, climbing up the stairs, softly pushing the door to my room . . .'

'Yes?' I said. My mouth was dry.

'You'd stand over my bed and I'd know you were there but pretend that you weren't,' she said. 'You'd reach down at last and lay your claws on my bare shoulder and slowly push the strap of my nightie down, peeling it off, but gently. We all hated you. Your voice was everywhere, on the wireless. I used to hear it as I fell asleep.'

'Yes?'

'Like now,' she said, and she suddenly laughed, gaily. 'And now you work for me,' she said. There was unholy glee in her voice, and something else, syrupy and sickly-sweet.

'Yes . . .' I said.

'You will do what I tell you, won't you, Wolf?' she said.

I shifted uncomfortably in my seat. How dare she presume to order me about! I hated her and wanted to punish her and yet I wanted to be punished, too. Something to do with violence a long way back, no doubt, or so some hack like that Jew, Freud, would tell you.

I pictured her on the four-poster bed with the gardener outside watering the damned roses. Pictured her slowly lifting up her dress, her fingers trailing along the smooth whiteness of her leg. 'No,' I said, almost moaned. 'No.' I waited for her to say something, but all I could hear was her heavy breathing down the line and then abruptly she hung up and the line went dead. I swore and shifted in my seat. How I hated all Jews! They were a parasitic race, preying upon the honest portion of mankind.

Power. It all came down to power. To control. I thought of Geli. I missed her every day. At seventeen she was such a beautiful creature, vivacious and alive. With Geli I had found what I had sought. All women have a will. With Geli I had thought I could control that will, mould it to my needs. We had lived together, uncle and niece, I took her to the opera, to the picture houses in Munich. I had loved her and she had betrayed me with my own gun.

When I stood up the pressure had eased but a dark wet patch stained the front of my trousers. Men should never excuse their needs but subordinate them to a greater cause. But my cause was gone, shot down in flames when I was betrayed by the people, and now Ernst Thälmann presided over Germany, the fat loathsome prick. And so I went and got changed before setting out.

Wolf had decided to walk, though the day was cold and occasional lashings of rain stung his face. He drew his fedora low over his head, hunching his shoulders as he pressed against the wind. Outside the British Museum he saw a group of Gurkhas, each wearing a curved kukri knife. They passed close by, their faces alien to him. They marched in a unit. Wolf remembered them on the battlefield, the black devils they used to call them, these Nepalese soldiers serving the British king. In the trenches during that war he had been a dispatch runner, serving with the Bavarian List Regiment. As the warm spring turned to bitter winter, the rains flooded the trenches and the men lived in eternal damp.

Liquid mud covered their faces and ran down their eyes, its taste was in their mouths. It was cold and their blankets were as wet as they were: they could not get warm. The walls collapsed, their bread was wet and inedible. Wolf remembered men who shot themselves in order to escape the front. Remembered one man who, on capturing a British prisoner of war, calmly cut the man's throat with his knife. When challenged, the man had said, 'I just felt like it.' As was the practice, the PoW was reported as having died of heatstroke.

He remembered the winter of 1914 and the Christmas Truce. Night time, Christmas Eve, and a sky shining with cold stars like frost. Across the no-man's-land the English troops of the Devonshire regiment began to sing carols and from the German side rose hymns in response. A soldier from RIR 17 stepped out of the trench and shouted in English, 'You no shoot, we no shoot! It is your Christmas. We want peace. You want peace.'

The next day was cold and bright and the men from both sides met in the middle, shaking hands, exchanging hastily written Christmas cards, even dancing. Dancing! The others were over-joyed but how he had resented them! He had been enraged by the men, by their betrayal. Wolf did not participate in the truce and on the 27th the rains returned and with them the mud, and lightning flashed in the sky, etching indelible scars in the skin of night.

Wolf walked past the company of Gurkhas. As a young soldier he had admired them in battle. Later, as a leader of men, he had often wished he had a company of such men in his service.

Right now, as a down-at-the-heels private eye, Wolf just couldn't give a damn.

He walked down Museum Street past the offices of Allen & Unwin and turned left on High Holborn. Already it was growing dark and the streets were filled with Londoners of all stripes. London reminded him sometimes of the Vienna of his youth, a godless city of sin and corruption. Here there were lawyers striding about in their robes, clerks hurrying at their sides; insurance men and bobbies on the beat; labourers grimy with dust; housewives returning late from market and society wives from their shopping; orthodox Jews arguing the Torah and the rising price of gold; newspapermen with cigarettes in their mouths congregating outside the Cittie of York pub; churchmen and pickpockets and here and there an early-rising prostitute; and the businessmen not in their offices yet.

When he reached Leather Lane, night had fallen and the air was fetid, rank with the smell of cooking and waste dumped openly into the street. Wolf began to hear German spoken, and saw in the people the lost gaze of the eternal refugee. These were his people, mostly: Austrians and Germans displaced by the Fall, rejected by the nations of Europe until they had made their way, in one secret form or another, across the Channel into England. They were people without papers, without hope. Their clothes were shabby and their habits frugal, and the women did not walk alone in the night and the men congregated in small furtive groups on the steps of their tenements, smoking thin cigars and drinking home-made schnapps that was little better than rotgut, but it was all they had.

They were a sign to him of how far he had fallen.

Running adjacent to Leather Lane was Hatton Garden, and here there were still Jews. Shuttered shops held behind them jewellery of gold and diamond, silver and sapphire and rubies, yet here too rubbish collected in the street; the fronts of the buildings were dirty and the brickwork exposed. Wolf walked slowly, his hat pulled down low. He walked the city and the darkness welcomed him as its own. Down Hatton Garden to the noisy thoroughfare of the Clerkenwell Road, where Wolf saw signs in the language of his birth and rowdy bars lit with electric lights that yet reminded him of Vienna and Berlin. The smell of bratwurst and sauerkraut wafted in the air from covered stalls and men, already drunk at this hour, walked with arms linked together singing of the glories of the Fatherland. Wolf averted his gaze and walked in the shadows, west along Clerkenwell and back down Leather Lane. Receding in the distance he could hear the Horst Wessel Song.

Wessel had been an SA-Sturmführer in Berlin, only 22 when he was murdered by a communist assassin, shot in the face when he answered a knock on the door. It was gimp-leg Goebbels's idea to turn the young idiot into a hero, his song into an anthem for the Party. Wessel had lived with a young prostitute, Erna, and had probably acted as her pimp. It was just as likely that he died over her affections as for not paying the rent. Strange, though, how the song had caught on, that men were singing it even now, years after the Fall.

In Munich in '31 he never would have imagined the coming of the Fall. He was living with Geli then, the daughter of his older half-sister Angela. He was so taken with the child; she was like a bright butterfly. Wolf liked his women cute, cuddly and naïve, or so he liked to say at his more expansive moments back in Munich: he liked little things who were tender, sweet and stupid.

Geli was all that and more, she was young and she was powerless and she was malleable. He could be like a god to her, he could fashion her in the image he desired. Geli had depended on him, wholly and utterly.

And yet she had tried to rebel. When he found out about her affair with Emil, the chauffeur, Wolf was incensed. But he had loved her, too. Had loved her perhaps more than any other woman in his life, more than Eva, who he was also seeing at the time, lovely Eva who was such a simple creature, as comfortable as slippers.

Then came that fateful night. Strangely it was Hess who had rung him. Wolf had gone to Nuremberg for a meeting. Geli had used his own pistol against him, perhaps that was what had hurt most of all. His trusty .22-calibre, the No. 709 made by Messrs. Smith & Wesson of America. The pistol he had left in the apartment, loaded, in the middle drawer of the nightstand. He pictured Geli's small hot hand enveloping the inlaid metal of the handle, her index finger with its manicured nail hesitating on the trigger. It was the ultimate betrayal. Frau Winter, his housekeeper, had found her. Geli had missed her heart and punctured her lung. It must have taken her hours to die, alone in the room. He imagined the sounds she made, the hoarse breathing, the whistle of air, the grunts and whimpers like a slaughtered pig.

Frau Winter had called Hess, and Hess had called Wolf. By the time he arrived in the apartment, the police had already been and gone.

Wolf took a breath of night air. He had failed so many times since Geli; and each failure was worse than the last.

Before him was a plain door set into a thick brick wall. It was the right place. He knocked on the door, three times.

A metal shutter he hadn't noticed slid open at head height, revealing an iron grille. Glittery black eyes regarded him through it. 'Yes?'

Wolf pushed the card Hess had given him through the iron grille. 'Herr Wolf,' he said. 'Herr Hess sent me.'

The shutter slid shut. After a moment the door opened noiselessly. Beyond it he could hear a piano playing and the sound of laughter and conversation. The man in the doorway looked vaguely familiar but Wolf couldn't place him. He had a boxer's round face and a scar on his left cheek and his hair was cut short. 'Have we met before?'

The man shook his head, unsmiling. 'No, but I have seen you.'

Wolf shrugged.

The man said, 'I am Kramer, sir. Josef Kramer.'

'You work for Hess?'

At that the man did smile. 'Not Hess,' he said. 'Though Herr Hess has a share in this club. Please, welcome.'

'Thank you.'

Wolf stepped through into the hallway and Kramer shut the door behind him. It was a thick oak door on oiled hinges. It allowed no sound to escape.

'Please, follow me.'

Wolf listened for sounds. Muted conversation. Faint music. The hallway was thickly carpeted.

'I joined the Party in '31,' Kramer said. 'The SS in '32, sir.'

'Good for you.'

If he was offended Kramer didn't show it. 'Through here,' he said, leading Wolf into a large sitting room. Wolf stopped in the doorway. A man in a tuxedo sat at a grand piano, playing Beethoven. All around him were comfortable sofas and chaise longues, and men with ties loosened sat with drinks in their hands. Along one wall ran a walnut-coloured bar and behind it a barman was polishing glasses. 'Can I get you a drink?' Kramer said.

'I don't drink,' Wolf said.

The air was thick with the smell of expensive cigars. Wolf recognised several of the faces in the room. He had thought some of them dead. Around the men, shimmering through the room in their too-short sequinned dresses, were the girls.

They were an upscale version of the streetwalkers of Soho, Wolf thought. They were dressed like brazen flappers, in costumes that revealed more than they hid. He noted their diversity. He saw Slavic features and Aryan faces and a black girl who reminded him of Dominique. He eyed the girls and they eyed him back, but there was a vacancy in their eyes. He had seen such an expression before, in the eyes of a doped-up horse before a race. He saw the men look up at his entrance. He kept his face blank and watched them turn away.

'Please, Herr . . . Wolf,' Kramer said. His hand swept around the room. 'You may have your choice of the girls. It is on the house, sir,' he added.

'I am looking for this girl,' Wolf said. He drew the little sister's picture from his breast pocket. Isabella had given it to him before she had departed his office. Now he and the man Kramer studied it together. The girl was thin-faced and mousy, her features almost mannish. 'A Jew?' Kramer said.

'Do you stock any Jews?'

A slow, unpleasant smile broke across Kramer's crater-moon face. 'Yes, sir,' he said. 'This is just the antechamber.' He nodded his head as if some things had become clear to him. 'Please,' he said. 'Follow me.'

Wolf followed him, leaving the men behind to the attentions

of their whores. He half-expected Kramer to lead him upstairs, to the rooms that no doubt waited there, beds and mirrors and perfumes and lace, a wardrobe for a gentleman to hang his coat in, a washbasin for when his sordid business was done. Instead Kramer led him through a second door and locked it behind him. They were in a corridor in marked contrast to the pleasant sitting room they had vacated. Here bare light bulbs hung from the ceiling and the walls were plain cold stone and so was the floor. There were scuff marks on the stone. He could hear faint sounds, cries and a scream cut short. Kramer led Wolf down a stone staircase, down below ground. Wolf's fingers itched, and for one irrational moment he wished he still had a gun. But he no longer carried one.

It was cold in the basement, and the air was scented with a familiar tang: a mixture of blood and semen and shit. It was the smell of the camp they had kept him in, before he escaped, the smell of captivity and hopelessness and fear.

They stood in a wide corridor and to either side of the corridor were the metal doors to locked cells. Pinned to the wall like billiard cues were black leather whips. 'Come,' Kramer said. He reached for a whip, lashed it through the air. The sound was like a gunshot. Each door had a sliding metal shutter. Kramer slid the first one open and Wolf looked through. In the cell beyond a white girl no older than fifteen lay naked on a mattress, a worn one-eyed teddy bear held in her arms. Her ankle was chained to the wall. The room was bare but for a hook on the wall for a gentleman's hat and, in the corner, an old-fashioned chamberpot to piss in. The girl was asleep.

'No?' If Kramer seemed disappointed he didn't show it. He slid the shutter back. Wolf took a deep breath.

In the next room two lithe women lay back to back on the same mattress. 'Identical twins,' Kramer said, with some pride. 'Prime specimens. The Marshall always makes sure to keep the cellars well stocked.'

'The Marshall?' Wolf said.

'Göring, sir?'

Wolf nodded as some things became clear. 'The fat oaf always did like to give himself a grand title,' he said.

Kramer shrugged. In the next cell Wolf saw an elderly man hunched over a dwarf woman, his pale quivering buttocks rising and falling steadily. Wolf shook his head. Kramer shut the window. 'This one's occupied,' he said, unnecessarily.

'All Jews?'

'What?'

'Are they all Jews?'

'Yes. Of course.'

'You said Göring sends them over from Germany?'

'The Marshall? Yes. There's good money in people smuggling, these days,' Kramer said.

'And these ones?'

Kramer shrugged. 'Jews,' he said, as if that explained everything. 'Who will miss a Jew?'

'This girl,' Wolf said. He brandished the photograph again. 'Where is she?'

'I've not seen her,' Kramer said. He seemed hurt. 'I thought—'

'You thought,' Wolf said.

'I thought your tastes ran into more . . . I mean, when you said Herr Hess sent you . . . Herr Wolf, I did not—'

Wolf grabbed the whip out of the man's unresisting hand. He felt the familiar rage rise inside of him. 'You dare?' he said. He lashed the whip. It caught Kramer on the cheek and left an angry red welt. Kramer screamed. 'You cavort with filthy animals, you, an Aryan, you deal in the flesh of Jews? What perversion is this?' He was screaming, spittle was coming out of his mouth in long strings that hung from his lips. He was lashing Kramer with the whip, behind the cell doors the drugged specimens were whimpering and the copulating man could be heard banging on the metal door demanding to know what all the God damned ruckus was about, he was trying to finish his business.

'Herr Wolf, enough!' Kramer had half-risen and grabbed Wolf's wrist in a painful grip. His coarse peasant face rose over Wolf. 'I beg you.'

They stared at each other, motionless. Wolf saw Kramer's eyes open wide at something behind Wolf's back. His mouth opened, his lips beginning to form words. 'Please, don't—'

Wolf didn't have time to turn. He felt something cold and sharp sting his neck. It penetrated his skin. His fingers opened. The whip dropped to the floor. His neck felt numb. The numbness spread, fast. His vision blurred and the last thing he saw was Kramer's face blooming in a silent explosion of blood and bone.

★   ★   ★

In another time and place Shomer lies dreaming. In his blessed half-sleep he can pretend if only to himself that he does not hear the other men sleeping below him and the ones pressed against him so that when one wants to turn they must all turn. In sleep Shomer is not aware of Yenkl beside him shitting himself and the liquid shit dribbling down from their bunk onto the sleepers down below, and he can also pretend that it is not at all freezing cold, that it is in fact a lovely warm day and that this isn't Auschwitz but some tropical beach, perhaps some South Seas paradise and that his belly is full and when he smiles his grin is a dazzling white and full still of all his teeth.

In his half-dream which he had begun some time ago on the train on the way here and continued through the selection process and the cleaving of his family, in that murky half-world which was once his novelist's mind, there is a detective and a damsel in distress; there always are. He shifts and murmurs, instinctively trying to pull away from Yenkl. He feels lice crawling inside his striped prisoner's pyjamas but he pretends that he does not. It becomes easier by the day.

Instead Shomer, this once upon a time purveyor of Yiddish *shund*, that is of cheap literature or, not to put too fine a point on it, of trash, dreams of a dark city and of dark deeds, and of a watcher in the dark: for in the camp there is always someone watching.

★   ★   ★

On Berwick Street Edith could feel the watcher, the way his gaze lingered on her body, and paid particular attention to her breasts, and then down to her inguen, where it lingered further. She had grown used to the attentions of men, wanted and unwanted both, since the moment she and her family had fled from Bregenz into Switzerland and the border official who had helped them claimed her for himself as part of the overall price. He had been her first and she remembered how he had buckled his belt afterwards, not his face but only for some reason his buckle; it was shaped like an iron eagle. They had made it to England at last, smuggling themselves across the Channel in a fishing boat, on a moonless night, with no lanterns or lamps. It was a miracle they hadn't drowned. By then she had grown accustomed to her body being her currency. The fishermen each took their turn to fuck her, as her mother and baby sister sat huddled at the bow. Her mother never mentioned it. Perhaps she had no words with which to speak. Maybe there was nothing to say. It was just one of those things you did to survive.

But she could feel him out there, though no doubt he thought he was invisible, the watcher. He was back a second night in a row. None of the other girls saw him but Edith did. She knew he was there and she knew he was watching her.

At first she thought he was just shy, that he was watching in an effort to gather his courage and approach her. Many men were like that, requiring drink or darkness for their base natures to emerge, their desire to be made manifest. But after a while she did not think this was the case. The watcher disturbed her, though she could not say why. He wore the darkness too comfortably, as though he never intended to emerge from the shadows. A watcher – a *voyeur*, as the French girls said. Sometimes they got men like that, sad pathetic things with one hand twiddling away in their pocket, masturbating as they watched the whores. But the watcher was not like that, either. He got his thrills another way, she was sure.

She was busy that night, going first with a sailor off a Royal Navy ship docked in Greenwich, then with a proper gentleman whose English was as sharp as cut glass, like the King's or the BBC man on the wireless. Lastly with a young Jew, a yeshiva boy with curly peyos, dressed all in heavy black, who thrust against her quickly but enthusiastically, against the wall of the alleyway they used as combined brothel and latrine. Now she was smoking a cigarette with quick inexpert jerks, stamping her feet against the cold, when the watcher came to her.

She saw him emerge across the road. It was late, and the other girls were all either working or had gone home and she was alone. She smiled at him. Her mother had always told her to smile.

There was nothing much very remarkable about him. His suit hung on him a little uncomfortably. It looked like a hand-me-down. He had good teeth, and the smile he gave her back was surprisingly charming. 'You want to fuck?' she said.

His hand was in his coat pocket. He didn't take it out. He looked nervous and excited. 'Where can we go?' he said.

'It's ten shillings,' she said. He agreed with a nervous jerk of his head. 'In there,' she said. The alleyway was empty, a fresh pile of shit against the wall where that fat pig Bertha had taken her evening constitutional. They wouldn't be disturbed.

'The money first,' she said.

He took his hand out of his pocket, and she felt strangely relieved. He was holding a note. He passed it to her and she took it and tucked it in her brassiere. She took him by the hand. It was warm and dry. 'Come on,' she said.

He followed her meekly into the dark alleyway.

3

Wolf's Diary, 3rd November 1939

I woke up in pain. I was not lying down and yet I couldn't move. I tried to shift my hand but it was held fast. It was dark but I was still in the club, I could tell; the smell of fear and shit was the same and there was blood and fragments of bone and brain on the front of my suit, which would cost me a fortune to clean. My vision swam in and out of focus. It was a warm room and a flame came alive as a dark figure lit a match and applied it to a large wax candle, and then another candle and another. In the light I could see the chains that were holding me upright. I was secured to the wall, arms and legs spread. The figure turned to face me. It was a woman. She was not an attractive woman. She had a peasant's wide face and a petulant expression as if life had never failed to disappoint her. She wore black leather with the SS insignia on her armband, for all that there was no more SS. She wore thigh-high boots and black leather gloves and in one hand she held a horse whip.

'I am so sorry, Herr Wolf,' she said. 'For the unpleasantness.'

'I'm afraid you have me at a disadvantage, Fräulein . . .?'

'Koch, sir. I am Ilse Koch.' She gave a simpering little curtsey. She had a Dresdener's accent.

'What happened to Kramer?' I said.

'Josef?' she shrugged. 'He was remiss in his duties. He shall be replaced.'

'And I?'

A small, cruel smile briefly illuminated her ugly face. I felt a sudden rising panic. Ilse Koch tested the whip. The crack it made filled the small hot room. I looked around, seeking escape. Instead, what I saw in that room were implements of torture.

Her gaze followed mine. 'Yes . . .' she said. Her smile again, like a deformed butterfly. She lashed the whip with a flick of her wrist, missing my face by inches. She came and stood close to me. I could feel the warmth of her body, the press of her soft heavy breasts against me. She reached out a gloved hand and ripped my shirt open, buttons popping. Her hand grabbed my jaw, her fingers digging into flesh. Her face was close and hot on mine, her breath sour with drink. 'I know what it is you want, Herr Wolf,' she said. Her other hand reached down and grabbed me painfully. Her smirk etched itself into my face. 'You are a hard man, Herr Wolf.'

'Let me go, you filthy whore!'

She slapped me. The sound rang through the room. My cheek burned. My eyes narrowed and my mouth opened and I licked my lips, tasting blood. Her hand was down below grasping me and moving with a certain rhythm.

'I can stop whenever you want,' she said. 'Just say the word.' Her smirk told me she understood. She reached beyond my vision and returned with a vulcanised rubber ball on a studded leather strap. She fitted the strap on my head but left my mouth free. 'Well?' she said.

'Don't stop,' I whispered.

Ilse shoved the ball in my mouth then yanked a lever and suddenly my body was jerked from the wall and I hung suspended in the air before her. She pulled roughly at my trousers until they dangled around my ankles. I dangled there like a mounted butterfly, bare to her. She swung me round. I faced the wall. I felt her behind me, looming. My breath came short and sharp and I was stiff as a boy. I felt her gloved hands on my bare behind. She stroked my cheeks, first one and then the other, before she slapped me, hard, and I cried out. Her hand on my back, rubbing softly . . . 'I will please you, mein herr,' she whispered. I felt the weight of her against my back. Her lips against my ear. She pushed her finger deep inside me. Her other hand came round and took hold of me and stroked as she kept up a rhythm. A second finger joined the first, violating me. I shuddered with pleasure, hating her and all women, and thinking of Geli and the things I had taught her to do.

When Wolf re-emerged onto Leather Lane it was early morning and the market was already being set up with vegetables and fruit and bright materials and cloths. He made a sorry sight, and he wrapped his coat tightly around him and hunched his shoulders and drew the hat low over his face. In the old days he had Emil to chauffeur him around, men to do his bidding, a comfortable apartment to return to and his library and, after Geli, there was Eva, sweet good-natured Eva of the blonde hair and pleasant disposition and soft white flesh.

Now he had to trudge through early morning mist, on foot, in order to return to a cold unfriendly room rented out to him by a Jew.

'It's on the house,' Ilse Koch had told him, before he left, refusing his offer of payment.

'Is it Hess?' he asked her, the same question he had asked Kramer before her. She shook her head. 'Who is it?' he had said and she shook her head with finality and said, 'It is better if you do not come back here again, Herr Wolf.'

But Kramer had been indiscreet, that much was clear. The Marshall, he had said. Wolf remembered Göring, a fat ruthless man with a great many appetites, who had built the storm troopers from a ragtag collection of misfits into an efficient paramilitary organisation in the '20s. A decorated air-force pilot, a flying ace in the Great War. Wolf did not trust pilots; they changed course with the wind. Last he heard, Göring had survived the Fall and even thrived, changing allegiances once again. Now he was Comrade Göring, working for the communists he once despised, and trading in human flesh on the side. The hero of the skies had become a simple pimp.

The Jew girl, this Judith Rubinstein, could have been smuggled out of Germany by this same network. Her father, the banker, would have paid dearly to take his only daughter out of the communists' grasp and bring her to the relative safety of London. But then, why would she disappear? The women in the cells were disposable; no one would be looking for them. But the Rubinstein girl would be valuable cargo. Unless there was someone willing to bid even more for her . . .

He was deep in thought, calculating possibilities and avenues of inquiry, and wincing slightly as he walked. So when, at last, he approached Berwick Street he did not at first notice the presence of policemen all about until they stopped him. They crowded Walker's Court holding sausage rolls and steaming mugs of tea, as if they were at a picnic.

'You can't go through here, sir.'

'What happened?' Wolf said.

'Police matter, sir.' The policeman took in Wolf's rough appearance, paused with a bacon roll halfway to his mouth. There was brown sauce on the ring of his lips. 'Is that blood on your shirt, sir?' he said.

Wolf was aware of the other policemen's attention all turning to him. He began to back away. 'This is a misunderstanding,' he said. 'I live here.'

'Would you mind coming with me, sir?' the fat policeman said. The tea and roll disappeared from his hands to be replaced by a nightstick. Wolf looked around. He was surrounded by the policemen. His shoulders slumped.

'This is all a misunderstanding,' he said.

'I am sure it is, sir,' the policeman said. 'I am sure it is.'

A second policeman grabbed Wolf; he did not resist. The first one placed handcuffs over Wolf's wrists and called out, 'Inspector! I have something for you.'

A man in a worn suit appeared. He had a thick moustache and short thinning hair and there was a light scattering of dandruff covering his shoulders. He took one look at Wolf and shook his head. His eyes were brown, soft and mournful, as if he had already seen all of the evil that men can do to each other. 'Not here,' he said. 'Take him to the station.'

'Hear that, precious?' the fat policeman said. 'You're nicked, my son.'

'Go to hell,' Wolf said. The policeman just smiled. He led Wolf to a waiting car, and then they took him away.

* * *

In another time and place Shomer is no longer sleeping.

The guards raise them for roll-call with their usual charm and rubber truncheons. Yenkl won't move and the guard roars until Shomer and another prisoner carry his inert form outside and leave it in the snow, where he lies as fat and peaceful as a snowman, with his eyes closed and his hands like twigs. At roll-call they stand in the cold in their wooden clogs and striped pyjamas as the guards entertain themselves until such time as an SS officer arrives to take count of the living and the dead. At last the ordeal is over and the boys of the Sonderkommando take Yenkl away, and Shomer is assigned to a work unit: today they are digging graves. 'Lovely weather we are having,' he remarks to Yenkl. Yenkl is beside him now, smiling and looking at ease. 'Fresh air and physical labour,' Yenkl says and rubs his hands together, 'what's not to like, eh, Shomer, old friend?'

Shomer nods enthusiastically. 'Just what the doctor ordered,' he agrees. Shomer and the other prisoners are given shovels and dig in the hard ground while Yenkl walks around quite at leisure, his hands behind his back as he pontificates.

'What is a man!' he says. 'What is a man but mended cloth, hastily worn and discarded?'

But it is a rhetorical question. He does not expect an answer. 'What makes a man?' he ponders. 'What makes a hero, Shomer? Is it simply to live when there is nothing left to live for, when all you knew and loved is gone? Is it, simply, to survive? For like

the threads of an intricate shawl, we have been pulled at and
torn, Shomer. We have been unravelled.'

A great barren sky, in which the sun is distant, spreads above
Shomer's head. And he closes his eyes against the glare.

'Invigorating!' Yenkl says, and rubs his hands again. And to
Shomer he seems suddenly transparent, and through his friend's
outline he sees the chimneys belching soot, black soot and ash,
flakes of black snow falling.

'For what is a man,' says Yenkl, 'if not ash? And did not Rabbi
Akiva say—'

But Shomer doesn't hear what Rabbi Akiva, God rest his soul,
ever said, for the overseer at that moment shoves his boot in
Shomer's ass and Shomer falls flat on his face on the hard ground
the better to amuse the SS guards. And so Shomer returns to
the twilight world which is the writer's mind and in which, though
he has no pen or paper, he is nevertheless concocting another
shund, a cheap little tale for amusement and a little elucidation,
for did not Rabbi Akiva say—

But the guard is screaming, 'Get on with work, you filthy little
Jew!' and Shomer digs, he digs for all the dead: those that are
and those who are yet to come.

Wolf's Diary, 3rd November 1939 – *contd.*

They brought me down to Charing Cross nick and took
my blood-soiled clothes and gave me woollen slacks and
shirt instead and left me in a cell and locked the fucking
door.

My head throbbed and my mouth tasted of vulcanised
rubber. I lay back on the bed and stared at the ceiling. I had
been incarcerated before, in Bavaria in the '20s. Hess had
been with me then, he was as close to a friend as I had ever
come to having beside Gustl.

Did they think they could intimidate me by incarcerating
me in a prison? Childhood is a cell. The happiest day of my
young life was the 3rd of January 1903: my father on his last

morning visit to the Gasthaus Wiesinger for his last glass of wine. I was not there; later, I could only imagine it, his face turning red, the breath growing faint in his throat. Did he gurgle? Did his hands reach to his neck in incomprehension? Did he feel his last breath departing from his lungs with none to follow, ever again?

His last breath; a key to my freedom. Do not threaten me with jail cells. And I held my mother that day the way a man, not a child, would. I held her, my mother's delicate loving flesh that no young boy could protect, as she cried, the way she had held me when he came home and the drink was upon him and he took to the belt and the boot. My mother looked after the household and lovingly devoted herself to the care of her children. I respected my father, but I loved my mother.

I will give him this, though: the old man looked after his books.

But I did not wish to think just then of my poor dead mother, nor of other cells in other times. What were they holding me for? That was what had me worried. I had done nothing wrong.

I must have dozed off for when I came to, the cell door was open and the same fat policeman was standing there, smiling his greasy smile. He said, 'Detective Inspector Morhaim will see you now.'

I followed him without comment. Down a corridor busy with the cries of drunks and the thud of policemen's boots and into a small interview room with a large desk and the plain clothes policeman I had last seen on my approach to Berwick Street. He gestured to me civilly. 'Please. Sit down.'

From somewhere he brought forth a meerschaum pipe and became busily engaged in the ritual of such men with such things, stuffing it with foul tobacco. At long last when all was to his satisfaction he lit a match and applied it to the pipe's bowl. 'Sit!'

The fat policeman pushed me into the chair. I sat with my back ramrod straight. 'Tea? Coffee?'

'I drink neither.'

'That must be satisfying.'

He motioned to the fat policeman, who withdrew and shut the door behind him. We were alone. 'Morhaim,' I said. 'Isn't that a Jew name?'

'It can be. In this case, it is. Does that bother you?'

'Many things bother me,' I said, and he laughed. 'Tell me,' he said. 'Where were you last night? You were not at your flat.'

'Is that a crime?'

'Not yet,' he said. He puffed on his pipe. The smell of it filled the room. 'You are an alien here, Mr Wolf.'

'I have been granted asylum.'

'From Germany.'

'Yes.'

'All such asylums are by their nature temporary.'

I said nothing and he nodded, to himself. 'I see that after the Fall you were kept for some time in a communist konzentrationslager.'

'Concentration camp, yes,' I said, enunciating it clearly for him in English. He smiled. 'You escaped?'

'Eventually.'

'You are a lucky man, Mr Wolf.'

'What is this about?'

'First things first, Mr Wolf. Where were you last night?'

'I work as a private investigator,' I said. 'I was out. On a job for a client. Surely you can appreciate the need for discretion in my line of work.'

'That's a curious line of work for a man such as yourself.'

'It requires an orderly mind and a keen sense of justice.'

He was biting the stem of the pipe, blowing smoke rings into the air from the side of his mouth. A hard trick to master, I would have thought. Also, without use. 'Your old associates seem to prosper. You don't.'

'So you know who I am.'

'I know who you were.'

That one hurt, but I let it go. 'What is this about?'

'Do you have an alibi for last night, Mr Wolf?'

'Do I need one?'

He sighed and sat back in the chair. 'Why did you kill her?'

'Who?' I almost shouted in frustration. My fist hit the desk. 'What is the meaning of this? I am an innocent man! I demand to be released!'

'You used to have a moustache,' he said suddenly. 'A funny little moustache. We used to see a lot of you on the newsreels, but this was all a while back, wasn't it?'

'I do not see why we need to discuss one's choice of facial hair, surely.'

He shrugged. 'Perhaps it was merely the interest of one man with a moustache in another.'

I knew their tactics. Did he think I had never been interrogated before? He would give me nothing, and he would take his time in trying to break me.

'I would like a solicitor,' I said.

His pipe seemed to have gone out. He fiddled with it distractedly. 'Do you have one?'

'No.'

'We can certainly appoint one for you. You haven't been charged yet, Mr Wolf. Would it make you feel better to confess?'

'Confess to what?'

'To the murder, of course.'

I stared at him, no longer willing to talk. Perhaps he saw it in my stance, for he put down the pipe and reached into a drawer and returned with an envelope, which he opened carefully. He slid out a set of photographs and laid them neatly in front of me.

I stared at the photographs.

The watcher in the dark truly *was* invisible. Wasn't he? He felt so calm now, so different from the way he'd felt the night before. Then he had been eager, almost frenzied with desire. She didn't understand, no one understood. It wasn't lust, it wasn't *sexual*, he was not a monster.

It was *ideological*.

How trustingly she had taken his hand and led him into the dark! He shifted uncomfortably in his hard chair, wetting his lips in concentration. He had so much work to do, paperwork to get through, but no one paid him any attention: no one ever did. The office he worked in was grey like the light outside. Had he made mistakes? He had planned so carefully, had thought about it for so long and then it just happened. It felt so natural, the way they always said it should. He had not wanted to hurt her. On the contrary. He had wanted to set her free.

Wolf's Diary, 3rd November 1939 – *contd.*

I stared at the photographs. They were stark black-and-white. The Austrian girl I had spoken to, Edith, was lying on the ground. The photographs were from different angles. In one I could see a pile of human shit against the brick wall, not far from Edith's blonde hair, which was made near-white by the photograph. Edith was situated in rest, on her back, her arms carefully crossed over her abdomen. Blood matted her hair. Her shirt had been ripped open and her breasts, full and wholesome, lay exposed. Carved into her chest was a swastika. Her face had been battered and her eyes were bruised and open to the sky. Beside her head stood a little toy figure. I leaned forward and drew one of the pictures close and studied it.

It was a little wind-up toy.

A tin drummer.

'Who did this?'

Inspector Morhaim studied me levelly. 'Did you know her?'

'I live on Berwick Street, Inspector. It is hard not to see the whores.'

'So you did know her.'

'I spoke to her, last night. Briefly. She propositioned me. I do not like whores.'

'Is that why you killed her?'

'I did not kill her!'

'Do you recognise that symbol?'

'It's a swastika.'

'Why would anyone carve a swastika into a woman's chest before killing her?' He saw my look. 'Yes, she was alive when he did it, though probably unconscious.'

'I hope you find this man and hang him,' I said.

'But what if we *have* found him?'

I sat straight in the chair. One did not see the swastika much, any more. In Germany it had been banned by the new communist regime. In England it was irrelevant. One saw Mosley's lightning bolt enclosed within a circle in its place, instead. Mosley, who had tried to copy Göring. It was the fat man's initial idea to adopt the swastika as a symbol.

They used to call you the drummer . . .

Did Morhaim just say that? Was it my imagination?

I raised my head and looked the Jew straight in the eyes. 'I did not kill her,' I said.

'Your coat was covered in blood.'

'It wasn't hers.'

'Then whose?'

'I am being set up.'

At that Morhaim laughed. 'Set up?' he said. 'Why? You're nothing but a washed-out dick. You're nobody, a nothing. I don't like you, Wolf. You have the face of a cockroach. Is that why you killed her? To reassert yourself, what you once were?'

'I did not kill her!'

'Then where were you?' he said. The door opened and the fat policeman came in carrying a tray with tea and biscuits on it. He set it down before Morhaim.

'Thank you, Constable Keech,' Morhaim said. He picked a sugar cube with small silver tongs and dropped it into his tea. 'No, Constable. Stay, please.'

'Sir.'

I knew what was coming. It didn't hurt any less.

Morhaim pinched a second sugar cube and held it aloft above the tea. I felt Keech move behind me. Morhaim looked at me sadly. 'A confession would go such a long way in your favour,' he said.

'Fuck you, Jew.'

'Such a long way.' Morhaim dropped the cube into the tea. Keech's fat pig's hand slammed into the side of my head, sending me sprawling to the floor. Then he was on me, a sadistic smile on his face, his fists and his boots speaking volumes. I curled up into a ball as best I could, covering my head with my arms. His boots caught me in the ribs, the side of the head, the back of the legs; his huge hands slapped me, his fists rained on my body. Through all this, Morhaim sat behind his desk and stirred his tea and took delicate little sips and looked down on me sadly.

'Stop,' he said, after a while. Keech lifted me up, one-handed. 'For what it's worth, Wolf, I do not think you did it. Only a fool would return to the scene of the crime when it is riddled with policemen, and I do not think you are a fool.'

'That's the nicest thing anyone's said to me all day.'

'I think you're a despicable rat of a human being, a shit I would wipe off my shoe on the pavement, an anti-Semitic bully and leech who should have been left to rot in a communist konzentrationslager. I think you're a murderer and a psychopath.'

'You're too kind,' I said. I spat blood on the floor, hoping to catch the fat copper's shoe, but I missed.

'You're all that, Wolf,' Morhaim said. 'But I don't think you killed Edith Griesser. And while I would have no problem having you thrown in jail for the rest of your unnatural life, it occurs to me that, if you are not the killer, the real killer will still be out there, and that he may well kill again. And I do not want that on my conscience.'

'How admirable,' I said. 'For a Jew.'

Keech grunted above me and slapped me on the side of the head, hard. I blinked back tears of rage. Morhaim looked at me with those sad brown eyes.

'I will ask you one last time,' he said. 'Where were you last night?'

I hung loosely from Keech's enormous hand. Stared into the unsettling brown eyes of Inspector Morhaim. Lowered mine.

And told him.

4

In the dream he was standing on a high podium in a town square in Nuremberg. It was a beautiful day and the sky was bright and blue and before him, below him, were thousands of people, men and women and children, their faces raised to him, their lips slightly open, adoration in their eyes. He spoke, and it was like an angel speaking down from Heaven, and the festivities below ceased, little boys with yellow and red balloons and women in their Sunday dresses and good German men who worked hard and went to church and paid their taxes, and the sausage sellers and the candyfloss sellers and the beer sellers and the SA men in their uniforms like a guard of honour and all for him. He spoke, with passion and intensity, raising his fist in the air, slamming it on the stand, shouting, spittle coming out of his mouth, but easing them in, at first, then rising, rising, rising until they were all a-frenzy – shaking, some of them were. He pictured the women wet under their dresses; it was said the power of his voice alone could bring them to a shuddering climax. The men with their fists raised, ready to follow him, the boys and girls watching wide-eyed as history was made. Higher and higher until women fainted and men grew berserk, ready to march now and fight and fulfil his orders, for it was the future he promised them: a glorious one.

Higher and then lower and gently until they rose blinking as if they had been sleeping and were now awake and looking all about them in wonder and awe, at a world remade anew. They had called him the Drummer, then: and it was said that all of Germany marched to his tune.

★　　★　　★

In another time and place Shomer rises blinking. Shomer rises energised and refreshed from the bunk he shares with nine other men and he makes the bed exactly to specification and puts his feet into the wooden clogs with illicit paper padding them and the sores on his feet rubbing and pussing. With the others he shuffles to roll-call, with the others he stands in rows as they wait, and Yenkl stands beside him, puffing on his pipe.

They wait for two hours in the cold before the SS officer arrives to take their numbers and tally the figures of the living and the dead. Shomer's *kommando* once again marches to the same frozen piece of ground to continue the digging of the graves. The routine does not vary, and the graves do not end. At last Shomer is allowed to go to the latrines and Mischek, the scheiss-begleiter – that is, the toilet companion or timekeeper – comes with. The latrines are cesspits divided into partitions for the Jews and the non-Jews: the common criminals and the politicals and the prisoners of war. Shomer goes into the Jews' latrine and Mischek, the dirty little Russian Jew, keeps time.

'Have you read my latest review?' Shomer says to Yenkl, sitting beside him on the shared latrine and opening up the latest broadsheet from Berlin. He lets out a loud fart and laughs. 'I must stop eating such heavy meals,' he says, patting his stomach.

'Soup!' Yenkl says. 'What is more wholesome than soup, with a slice of bread, to keep a man's spirit up?'

Shomer's stomach rumbles but he pretends to ignore it. A ration of bread and margarine with a ladle of watery soup must serve: the bread is currency, with bread one may buy and sell and trade, but not in futures. There are no futures here.

'I was mistaken for Freud, once, you know,' he tells Yenkl.

'Do tell?'

Shomer shrugs. 'It was at a literary party, I forget who for.'

'Which means you remember exactly but resented their success?'

Shomer laughs. 'I had been to the washroom and stood pissing next to a young boy not long out of cheder, a young poet who blushed when he saw me and addressed me as Herr Freud. Of course I set the little blighter straight. Did he not know who I was?'

'Did he not?'

'Do you think yeshiva boys do not read shund?'

Yenkl laughed. 'I imagine they do, in secret.'

'He apologised profusely when I told him who I was. Would have asked me to sign something if his pisser wasn't in his hand. I told him to watch where he aimed and washed my hands and returned to the party. Half an hour later, I ran into Freud. 'Hello!' I said, civilly. 'Someone just thought I was you, which is really stretching credibility to the limit!"

'You said that?'

'Sure I did.'

'And what did Freud say?'

'He said, "He managed to insult both of us in the same sentence"!'

Yenkl laughed. The Russian, Mischek, popped his head in and told Shomer in broken Yiddish to hurry the fuck up or the kapos will punish both of them.

'Did I tell you about the time I was mistaken for Freud?' Shomer asks Mischek, but Mischek shakes his head miserably and says, 'Freud? Who is this Freud.'

'Some people can't take a joke, can they,' Shomer says to Yenkl but Yenkl is no longer there and the other prisoners look away from him as though he is mad: do they not know who he is?

He gets up and contemplates washing his hands in the foul water and at last does so, his belongings held tight between his thighs, rubbing his hands together to wash off, at least, the worst of the shit. Then back he goes across the camp with Mischek at his side, back to digging graves – 'And what after all should we be digging for?' he says to Yenkl, 'turnips?' and Yenkl laughs and so, with renewed spirit, Shomer returns to work, while his mind conjures up a different kind of cell and a different prisoner; one who, unlike Shomer, does not have a blue number tattooed on his arm.

*   *   *

Wolf woke from a deep dark sleep, and dreams in which he fled from booted Jewish hordes, ugly and screaming, with hooked noses and yellow stars, and looking like a caricature from Julius Streicher's *Der Stürmer*. He, Wolf, was running, but run as he might the Jews like the living-dead were relentless, and they pursued him across a map of Europe, like in the pictures from America in which a dotted line grows across a map to symbolise flight. He sat up on the cot in the cell as the cell door swung open.

The fat policeman, Keech, was standing there, no longer grinning. 'Rise and shine. The Inspector wants to see you.'

'It's about time.'

Wolf stood up. Outside it was growing dark. Once again he trod the corridor to the Inspector's office. Morhaim was inside sitting behind his desk. 'Sit down, Wolf.'

'I prefer to stand.'

'Keech?'

The big policeman grinned. Wolf sat down.

'Did you find it?' he said.

'Find what?'

'The club. The body in the basement.'

Morhaim rubbed his eyes. He looked tired, and mean. 'My men and I have indeed visited the address you mentioned in Leather Lane,' he said.

'Full of them filthy foreigners,' Keech said.

'Quite,' Morhaim said.

'Them German refugees and whatnot.'

'Indeed. Keech?'

'Sorry, sir.'

'So?' Wolf said – demanded. 'You know I was telling the truth!'

'We found nothing.'

'What did you say?'

Morhaim shrugged. 'We found an empty house. There were scuffmarks on the floors, as if furniture was hastily removed. A door opened onto a cellar like the one you described. However, there was no one there, and the cell doors were open and empty.'

'They moved them . . .'

'Who are *they*, Mr Wolf?'

'I don't know.'

'You're lying,' Morhaim said, and smiled a small, bitter smile. 'But it does not matter. On the cellar floor we found marks, stains. Possibly something has happened down there, but what?'

'I told you. She shot the man, Kramer. For . . . for taking me down there.'

'A man named Josef Kramer is indeed on our list of alien residents,' Morhaim said. 'His occupation is listed as market porter. His whereabouts are unknown.'

'No body,' Keech said, and grinned. 'No body, no crime. No crime, no nothing, shamus.'

'But that's—' the reality of his situation sunk home for Wolf. They had cleaned up, and in a hurry. Moved the white slaves, the furniture, the still-cooling corpse. He couldn't help it: he felt just a touch of pride. His people had always been efficient.

But that meant he could not prove his innocence. He looked at Morhaim. 'Are you going to charge me?' he said.

He saw the fat policeman look to the Inspector; look away. Morhaim was jittery, distracted. The silence lengthened in the room.

'No.'

'No?'

'Mr Wolf,' Morhaim said. 'You are free to go.'

'I am?'

'Get this piece of shit out of here,' Morhaim said. Keech said, 'Yes, sir,' and picked Wolf up. 'Get your hands off me, you fat pig.'

The copper's ugly face froze in a snarl. 'You want more of what I've got?' he said.

'Leave him be, Keech.'

'But Inspector—!'

'We'll be keeping an eye on you, Wolf.'

'You do that,' Wolf said. He half-turned and smiled. Touched the bruise on the side of his face. He felt like a piece of meat chewed by a giant angry dog. He leaned close to the fat policeman. 'I'll get you back for this, precious,' he whispered. 'That's a promise.'

Keech beamed at him. 'I'd like that,' he said. 'I'd like to see you try.'

'I said get him out of here!'

'Yes, sir!'

Keech pushed Wolf out of the door. Back into the corridor. Shut the door behind them, gently, as on a sickroom. 'Tetchy, isn't he?' Wolf said.

'He's in mourning.'

'For what?'

'For you walking the streets free and all.'

'You know I didn't kill her.'

'You're guilty of something, Wolf. People like you always are.'

'What are you, a Jew lover?'

'No. Just someone who knows the difference between right and wrong.'

'Are you sure you're in the right line of work?'

'Enough wisecracks, shamus. Get dressed.' They were back in the cell. The door was open. Wolf's blood-spattered clothes lay on the bed, neatly folded.

'Can you turn round? I'm shy.'

'Just do it already, will you, Wolf? You have guests and we don't want to keep them waiting.'

Wolf did as he was told. He folded the clothes they had given him, neatly, and put on his suit and his coat and his hat.

He assumed they'd gone through his clothes: it was just a shame no one had bothered to clean them after.

Lastly he put on his shoes; they were good English shoes.

He followed Keech out and Keech opened a door and though they merely transitioned from one room to another room it was a transition from captivity into freedom; and he felt the need for air and drew it in, in a big shuddering inhalation. Somehow the air tasted different this side of the door: more sweet and more pure.

Behind the reception desk a bored policeman was reading *Black Mask*, an American pulp Wolf himself was fond of. The lurid cover showed a woman lying in a pool of blood, a faceless assassin standing over her with a knife. Wolf scanned the people waiting patiently, eternally, on the benches beyond the desk. They were lined with whores and drunks and thieves: the people he now lived amongst.

One who stood out was unfamiliar to him. It was a man decked out all in black leather with black boots and black gloves and a black peaked cap. He marched up to Wolf and gave a Prussian click of the heels.

'Herr Wolf?'

'Ja?'

'I am your chauffeur.'

'My chauffeur.'

'Yes, sir.'

'But I do not have a chauffeur.'

The man almost smiled, but not quite. 'Please, sir. You are tired. I have been instructed to take you to your flat, where you will no doubt wish to wash and change. Do you have the invitation?'

'The invitation?'

'To tonight's soiree, sir.' The chauffeur sounded almost reproachful.

'Mosley's soiree?'

'*Sir* Oswald would be delighted to see you, mein herr,' the chauffeur said. 'As will Lady Mosley. It promises to be quite the night, sir.'

'Did . . . did *Oswald* have me released?'

'I am sure it is not my place to comment, sir.'

Wolf kept a calm expression. You had to, when dealing with the help.

'Let's go,' he said.

'Sir.'

Wolf followed the chauffeur out of the police station and into the night.

Wolf's Diary, 3rd November 1939 – *contd.*

I was furious, though I tried not to show it. The chauffeur drove me the short distance to my apartment. Outside, the whores were at trade as usual. It would take more than a murder or two to stop them.

How I hated whores!

I well remembered, as a young man, the prostitutes of Vienna, walking one night with Gustl along their Sink of Iniquity, after the opera. How I loved the opera!

And yet worse was the time we had been approached in the street by an older man, on the corner of Mariahilferstrasse-Neubaugasse. Well-dressed and prosperous-looking. He spoke to us pleasantly, asked us about ourselves. When he learned that we were students he invited us to dinner. I was studying architecture at the time, while Gustl studied music. Sometimes I missed Gustl. He had been my only friend.

The man took us to the Hotel Kummer. I was very poor at the time and he let us order whatever we desired. I must confess I had at the time a predilection for pastries and tarts and I had sated myself at the man's expense. He was a manufacturer from Vöcklabruck, in town on business. Over dinner he told us of his indifference to women. He wanted nothing to do with them, for they were all gold-diggers. He and Gustl discussed music. Towards the end of the meal, as Gustl was stuffing his face obliviously, the man slipped me a *carte de visite*. At the end of the meal we thanked him and then left. Gustl was entranced, the infantile. Charmed by the man. 'Did you like him?' I said, as we were walking home.

'Very much,' Gustl said. 'A very cultured man, with pronounced artistic leanings.'

'And nothing else?'

'What else should there be?'

I took out the *carte de visite* and showed it to him. 'That man,' I said, calmly, 'was a homosexual.'

Poor Gustl! He had never even heard the word. I had had to explain it to him, in some detail. His poor little eyes opened up in horror. The idea of two naked, sweaty men engaging in unnatural copulation, grappling with each other, muscles straining, their hard bodies rubbing against each other, fingers and tongues working over buttocks and nipples, a hard thrust and I . . .

It disgusted me. The card went into the fires of our oven.

If it were left up to me all homosexuals, along with communists and Jews, would be sent to specially built camps for their kind.

But the world I had once envisioned was not to be. The future I had envisioned had been robbed from me.

I washed, wincing with each movement as my bruises began to turn dark. I dressed carefully, in my one remaining suit.

There was this, too, about Gustl: he was a compulsive masturbator. At any given opportunity, in his bed, in his wash, behind his piano, sometimes at his desk in class or even on the corner of the street, his hand in his pocket, Gustl would relieve himself the way I had denied myself. He was a sweet, innocent boy; I wondered how he fared under communism.

Germany was lost to me. I put on my tie and my hat. Touched my face. My eye was swollen. I was angry. Not at Keech. He was a mindless thug, and mindless thugs I understood. Not even at Morhaim, the Jew. He only did what was his nature, as the personification of the devil, the symbol of all evil, assumes the living shape of the Jew. No – I was angry at being obliged to Mosley. I refused to be in anyone's debt, and least of all an inferior man's.

I took a last look in the mirror. An old, broken man stared back at me. I took a deep breath and felt the hatred fill me, animating me. I would not be broken that easily. I raised my hand, fingers outstretched, in the old salute. I straightened my shoulders. Then I went downstairs to the waiting car.

It was a black Rolls-Royce and it fair glided through the London streets, heading for Belgravia.

Wolf sat at the back and schemed, thinking furiously. He had not given the girl's murder enough consideration. The location of the attack, the swastika carved into flesh, and the final insult: that damned wind-up toy.

The little tin drummer.

How *dare* he!

Somewhere out there, beyond the car's window, out there in the dark city, there was a man not unlike himself. Wolf did not want to admit it but it was true. And Wolf was a man who seldom deluded himself. He knew who he was; he was always true to himself.

He felt hatred, yes. But it was hatred in service of a greater power: of destiny. Wolf had been shaped into a weapon by the circumstances of life. But a weapon did not kill indiscriminately. It was used, for a purpose.

What, then, was the killer's *purpose*?

He was talking, Wolf realised. He was *communicating*, but his communication was not meant for the police.

No. It was meant directly for Wolf himself.

They were driving through St James's Park. Wolf rested his head on the glass and looked out of the window at the dark trees as they passed. He had made little progress with the missing Jewish girl, though it was early days yet. Did his former associates hold her? And which of them owned the club he had visited? He determined to have another little chat with Rudolf Hess. He tried not to think of that woman, Ilse, and her cellar. He winced and shifted in his seat and his thoughts were as dark as the night.

The drive went smoothly. The driver spoke little; Wolf appreciated that. At last the chauffeur indicated and pulled onto Ebury Street. Wolf had been there once before, shortly after his arrival, a landless, penniless refugee on this cold and foreign island. Then, Sir Oswald and Lady Mosley had owned a flat in the building. Now, Wolf saw as they approached, they must have owned the entire bloody thing.

Torches were burning outside. Wolf wound down the window. The air smelled warm and scented as though he had crossed some invisible meridian line by coming here and was now in another country entirely, some tropical land divorced from both space and time. The flames of the torches reflected in the neighbours' windows across the road. In their light Wolf saw Blackshirt foot soldiers standing to attention like an honour guard, and the flags of the lightning bolt that was the symbol of the British Union of Fascists waved in the breeze to either side of the grand entrance with its faux-Doric columns. The driver stilled the engine. Spilling from the house Wolf heard music, laughter, the tinkling of glass and the hum of conversation. The Mosleys's party, it seemed, had been going on for a while.

The chauffeur came round and opened the door for Wolf and Wolf stepped out. He straightened his tie, brushed his hair to one side of his forehead.

'Thank you,' he said.

'You're welcome, sir.'

Wolf nodded. Then he took the invitation out of his breast pocket and marched to the entrance of the house.

'Help you, sir?'

They were fresh-faced boys, really. They wore the Union's futuristic uniform – high-waisted black trousers and black tight-fitting tunic tops that showed off their pectorals, and the whole thing set off by a wide black belt with a large square silver buckle. They looked like they belonged on a rocket ship from one of the American pulps. Most of them sported a pencil moustache, aping their leader. They looked like bulls: well-fed and aggressive. On the left breast of their tunic tops was the jagged lightning bolt of the BU.

'My invitation.'

'Of course, sir.'

The boy scanned the card and stepped aside. Wolf nodded to him civilly enough and went in.

Inside, a pungent cloud welcomed him: eau de toilette, eau de cologne, eau de parfum. Full-bodied cigars and slim ladies' ciga-rettes and lawyers' fragrant pipe-tobacco: it made his eyes water.

'Wolf!' It was almost a shriek. He turned and there, descending the grand staircase, was Lady Mosley in a fetching Parisian dress. Jewels sparkled on her wrists, at her neck. She came down to his level and hugged him.

'Diana,' he said.

'It is *so* good to *see* you!' Diana Mosley said.

'Thank you for inviting me.'

'But of *course*! My dear *Wolf* – it *is* Wolf, still, isn't it?'

'It is, yes.'

'Wolf. How *romantic*.'

'I'm sure.'

'It's been so *long*!'

Wolf nodded his head in silent acquiescence.

That night in '34 he had been welcomed to their apartment like an exiled prince – valued, sympathised with, even admired – yet one whose power had waned, whose time had come and gone. He had come like a beggar, limping with the wound in his leg that he had sustained in the concentration camp, and they had spoken of what had passed and what was to come, but it was obvious to all of them, by then, that Germany was lost.

He had left. He would not take charity. Since then he never went back. Mosley then was a minor figure in British politics, almost a figure of ridicule. In the intervening years, with the dark shadow of communism growing ever longer across the Channel, he too had grown, in both power and status. And Wolf had not been invited back; there was that, too, to consider.

Until now.

'You poor *dear*!' Diana continued on, in that prattle British society women were so well-practised in. Wolf knew better than to underestimate her. None of the Mitford sisters were entirely stupid, though one of them, Jessica, *was* a devoted communist. Diana touched Wolf's cheek, lightly. 'What happened to your poor *face*?'

'I fell.'

'Did the police do this? How utterly *dreadful*. Things like this will never happen when Oswald is in power.'

When, Wolf noted. Not *if*.

'I'm sure it was just a misunderstanding.' Still, he was angry: the anger was never far from the surface. 'There was a Jew inspector—'

'A Jew! How *ghastly*!'

'Well, it is of little significance.'

She squeezed his arm. 'Oswald is just *dying* to see you,' she said. 'But he can wait. Come. Let's get you something to drink.'

She led him into a large room with high windows. Guests milled about and he saw familiar faces, politicians and film stars, the usual assortment of trash one could find at any such gathering. A buffet ran from one wall to the other, every manner of beast and fowl represented, and Wolf realised just how hungry he was. Diana Mosley, *née* Mitford, brought him a tall glass. He took it from her. 'Fresh orange and strawberries,' she whispered, smiling. 'We have them shipped over, darling. I made sure we'd have something waiting especially for you. Come. You must be *ravenous*!'

One buffet table, Wolf saw, was covered in vegetarian dishes, from an Indian-style curry to Italian lasagne and British shepherd's pie. Diana took a plate and began to heap food onto it. 'Here you are.'

He took it from her. Put his drink down on the table. Picked up a fork. Delicately sampled the curry. Diana watched him like a wife. 'Eat!' she said.

Wolf ate. The assortment of foods all blended together. He barely tasted any of it, the hunger was so strong. He ate with quick strong strokes, like a swimmer – like that good Aryan boy Johnny Weissmuller, who played Tarzan in the pictures.

When he was done he put the plate down and in seconds a waiter whisked it away. Wolf picked up his drink and took a sip. 'You look well,' he said.

'I feel well,' Diana said, and laughed. She touched his arm. 'It really *is* so good to see you, Wolf. You have always been *such* an inspiration, to both of us, you know. Oswald values you highly.'

'Is he here?'

'He's around. He would be delighted to see you.'

'And I, him,' Wolf said, politely.

'Good!' She clapped her hands. 'But do let me show you around first, Wolf! It's not often we get such distinguished company.'

'You're too kind, really.'

Wolf found himself dragged along in her wake. Her hand on his arm was surprisingly strong. She had always liked him more than she should have, he thought. The way her sister had. Now he was her prize, for one night. She was determined to show him off, the way she did her jewels. But unlike gold, Wolf's value had not gone up in the intervening years.

'Ah, Lady Mosley. What a delightful party.'

'Thank you *so* much! Wolf, this is Mr Fleming. He's a stockbroker.'

The man was handsome, with the bearing of a military man. 'Call me Ian, please.' He had a strong grip when they shook hands.

'Mr Fleming almost bought our old flat from us, do you know!' Diana said. 'In the end we bought the whole place and did it up instead.'

'A great gain for all of us,' Fleming said, smiling. He looked at Wolf. That same look he always got. 'You remind me of someone.'

Wolf shook his head. 'I get that a lot,' he said.

'You are German!'

'Austrian, actually.'

'I studied in Austria. Kitzbühel.'

'Did you,' Wolf said. It was not exactly a question.

'I'm sure you look like someone.'

'Believe me, I am no one.'

Fleming peered at him closely. 'Have you been in a fight?' he said.

'Really, Mr Fleming!' Diana turned to Wolf, apologetic. 'Mr Fleming was a journalist, you see. He was in Moscow, in fact, in '33. At the time of the . . .' she hesitated.

'The Fall?'

Wolf noticed that the Fleming fellow had lost his smile. His eyes took on a cold aspect. Wolf knew that look, too.

Recognition.

'Excuse me,' Fleming said. He turned rather abruptly and went to join a group of City men by the half-open windows.

'How rude!' Diana said. 'I am so sorry, Wolf.'

'I take it he is not a supporter of the BU, either?'

Diana shrugged. 'This is a private party, not a political one.'

'I see that is Lord Rothermere of the *Daily Mail* there, talking to the writer – Williamson?'

'Henry Williamson, yes. Wonderful writer. *Wonderful*. Have you read *A Chronicle of Ancient Sunlight*? No, well, anyway, of course yes, both of *them* are supporters, naturally.' She looked at him steadily. 'Was that your point?'

'I was just curious.'

'Do you know,' Diana said, whispering mischievously, 'It is rumoured Mr Fleming is sleeping with Baron O'Neill's wife? While not knowing meanwhile that she, at the same time, is also having an affair with Lord Rothermere's heir?'

'A busy lady.'

'Busy *indeed*!' And Diana burst into laughter. 'Poor Fleming,' she said. 'But he's young.'

Wolf was rescued at that moment with the arrival of a young man as grey and unremarkable as his suit. Clearly, not a guest, but an employee. The man – a boy, really – whispered in Diana's ear.

'Yes, thank you, Alderman,' she said. She turned to Wolf, apologetically. 'Oswald is in his study, upstairs. He wishes to see you. Would you . . .?' She gestured with her palm.

'Of course.'

'Just follow Alderman. It is *so* lovely to see you, Wolf.'

'You too, Lady Mosley.'

'Diana, *please*!'

Wolf took her hand and kissed it, gallantly. 'Diana,' he said.

'Oh, Wolf!'

She fanned herself and laughed. Wolf took his leave, following the taciturn Alderman.

Up the stairs through more festive people, the men in suits and the women in dresses, and all expensive and expansive and all laughing gaily, and drinking and smoking, and chattering and parting before Wolf, like the Red Sea at the approach of Moses and the Israelites.

'Please, sir,' the boy said.

'Yes, yes? What is it?' Wolf said, impatiently.

'I'm a big admirer of yours, sir.'

'I see,' Wolf said, who didn't. 'What of it?'

The boy reached into the breast pocket of his suit and brought out a small rectangular object and began to say, 'Could you perhaps sign this—' but Wolf wasn't paying attention. 'Mosley?' he said, crossly, if only to the air. 'Mosley, are you there? Blasted man.'

'Here, sir,' the young man said, with some obvious regret. Whatever it was he wanted to show Wolf had disappeared. They had reached the top floor. Oswald Mosley's private office was in what had once been an attic. Alderman knocked, waited and pushed the oak door open. Beyond was a small, comfortable-looking room, with bookshelves and an antique desk and bronze lamps. It was warm and well lit. Behind the desk sat Oswald Mosley, perusing papers.

'Mr Wolf to see you, sir.'

Mosley raised his head. He was a good-looking man, with thick black hair slicked back and a pencil moustache that made him look a little like a screen villain. He was dressed in a Savile Row suit rather than the BU uniform he had himself designed. The smile he gave Wolf was genuine, and beaming.

'Sir Oswald,' Wolf said.

'Wolf!' Mosley rose, his arms outstretched. 'You may leave us, Alderman.'

'Sir.'

Mosley advanced on Wolf as the door closed with a soft snick, leaving them alone in the room. Wolf bore the hug stoically. Before the Fall, no one would have dared greet him so informally.

'It is so good to see you, my friend.'

'And you.' He was relieved when Mosley released him. He looked around the room. 'You have come up in the world.'

Mosley shrugged. 'I worked hard for it. There is much work before us. You of all people know—'

'You are running for prime minister,' Wolf said. He looked more closely at Mosley's face, searching for those telltale signs of age since the last time they'd met. But it was strange. In recent months he had grown used to Mosley's face, wherever he turned, looking down on him from billboards and posters glued to the city's walls. At first no one had taken the British Union of Fascists seriously; now, the Blackshirts were everywhere and Mosley's image, larger than life, haunted the dark city.

'Yes,' Mosley said. Shrugged with his palms open, disarmingly. 'I am.'

'Can you really afford to go to war with Germany?'

It was the question people were asking. Mosley ran on a platform opposing Marxism. He claimed a coming war was inevitable.

Mosley said, 'Can we afford not to?'

'A war with Germany is a war with Russia,' Wolf said. 'With Stalin and all his power.'

'Marxism must be destroyed,' Mosley said. 'It is the poisoned ideology of the Jewish race.'

Wolf rubbed the bridge of his nose, feeling a headache coming on. To see Mosley, that clown, with such power! It filled him with irrational rage. Even the man's words were second-hand.

'But I am sorry to go on,' Mosley said. 'Please, sit down, my friend. Can I get you anything?'

'Thank you, no. Your wife has been most kind.'

'Diana is a loyal woman.' Mosley re-seated himself behind his desk. Wolf had heard of the man's little indiscretions. When Oswald was married to his first wife, Cynthia, he was also having an affair with her younger sister Alexandra, *and* with their stepmother. Sometimes Wolf wondered how the man ever found the time to be a Fascist. But then didn't Mussolini carry on as if he were single-handedly responsible for repopulating the entire Earth after a holocaust?

Whatever the case, he knew they were weak men, where he was strong. And yet their hearts were in the right place for all that, as the English said.

'So,' Wolf said. He watched Mosley, who sat back in the chair and folded his hands in his lap.

'So,' Mosley said.

They regarded each other across the desk.

At last Mosley sighed. 'Unfortunate business with that young prostitute,' he said.

'Nothing to do with me,' Wolf said.

'Of course. Of course. Nevertheless . . .'

'Yes?'

'It's bad publicity, Wolf. I am fighting for my political life here! For the very future of this country, if not the world! I cannot afford even a whiff of scandal. Not now.'

'What are you suggesting, exactly?'

Mosley raised his hands. 'I am not suggesting you are embroiled in all this,' he said. 'This . . . murder and what have you. But the signs are all too clear. The swastika most of all. Not many would understand the clue of the tin drummer. Not any more.'

It was a stark reminder of how far Wolf had fallen.

'Yes.'

'I cannot afford to be linked to these murders.'

'You invited me to your home.'

'Diana did that.'

'I see.'

'I had asked the driver to bring you directly to me. Perhaps he misunderstood.'

Wolf thought of the chauffeur and his Munich accent and his veteran's poise. A loyal man, he thought. But not to Mosley.

'What is it you want?'

Mosley lowered his hands. He looked tired suddenly, older than his years. 'I want to hire you,' he said.

'*Hire* me?' Wolf had not expected that. 'To do what? To disappear?'

'No, no.' Mosley shrugged. 'Look, I apologise. The murderer will be caught. So far I have managed to keep the details out of the newspapers. It is a problem, but it is a matter for the police. As for that Jew, Morhaim, I shall make sure he is dealt with. We do not want Jews in our police force, do we? But these are critical times, and I cannot be seen to interfere directly. Not yet.'

'So you would do nothing.'

A hurt look entered Mosley's eyes. Then he smiled.

'You were always the most astute of us all,' he said.

I was always your superior, Wolf thought, but didn't say.

'Thank you for getting me out,' he said.

'It was the least I could do.'

'Something is troubling you.' He adopted his detective's voice. The voice of a confidant. 'Tell me what it is.'

'Someone is trying to kill me.'

'Oh?'

'Three nights ago an assassin opened fire on my car as I was driving to a rally in Derby,' Mosley said. 'I lived. The assassin escaped. We had kept the news from the papers.'

'You must have been shaken.'

'I was certainly bothered, yes,' Mosley said. Wolf thought, You pompous coward. I bet you all but pissed yourself.

'You were very brave.'

'I serve a greater purpose,' Mosley said.

Yes, your prick, Wolf thought.

'Sorry? Did you say something?'

'Oh, nothing.'

'And two weeks ago there was an attempt on my life as I stepped out of a soiree in Kensington. My men found a suspicious package taped to the undercarriage of the car. It turned out to be a bomb. Only by luck it did not go off.'

'So you are suggesting an orchestrated campaign?'

'I am afraid, Wolf. I am afraid that next time they will succeed. I am afraid not for myself, but for the world I shall leave bereft of my leadership.'

Wolf would have been happy at that point to kill Mosley himself. But he brought himself under control. He always did.

'Do you know who they are?' he said, calmly.

'Who do you think?'

'Jews?'

'Who else? They call themselves the Palestinian Liberation Front. The PLO.'

Wolf said: 'Palestine?' The word left an unpleasant taste in his mouth.

'They want it for themselves. A land for the Jews. They demand Parliament cede it to them. Just imagine! Next thing you know the Indians will be demanding independence, or the blacks in—' he waved his hand vaguely, 'Bongo Bongo Land. Can you imagine, Wolf?'

'It is a way of, in the first instance, removing the Jews from Europe,' Wolf said. Such a plan had been put forward before, by Himmler, Göring, even Julius Streicher. 'Surely that should be the main objective?'

'Our problem in Britain has never been a large population of Jews,' Mosley said. 'Until recently, at any rate. The Fall and the influx of immigrants is rallying the country round to my way of thinking, at long last.'

'But they are blaming all immigrants, not just the Jews.'

As an alien in Britain he had experienced his share of hostility, but he was not going to mention that to Mosley. He had his pride.

'The Jews are behind it. They are behind everything. And is communism not just a Jewish ploy? But this is getting us nowhere, Wolf. The point is that the Jews have formed in recent years – no doubt emboldened by the rise of their kind in the communist East – several covert military groups even as they engage in illegal immigration to Palestine – very much *against* British Mandate law, I should add. They buy ships! They purchase false papers! And Palestine is a lawless land, a Wild West – we can hardly spend the resources to administer it properly.'

Wolf sighed inwardly. No doubt Mosley saw conspiracies under the bed – that is, if he was not himself hiding under it, having been surprised by the unexpected arrival of a lady friend's husband.

'I assume they have communicated with you.'

Mosley laughed, a short bitter sound. 'Do you know the number of threats I have received over the past few years?' he said. 'They are all after me, Wolf!'

'The cost of power,' Wolf said, coolly.

Mosley subsided. Reluctantly, he smiled. 'You are right. I am letting their tactics of terror affect me – but the danger *is* real, Wolf. I want you to work for me.'

Wolf clenched his fists, his short nails digging into his palms. How much he resented those words.

'I want you to find them. Money is not an issue.'

'What about your own MI5?'

'They're working on it.' He lowered his voice. 'To tell you the truth, sometimes I think the intelligence services don't take me quite as seriously as they should.'

Wolf suppressed a rare smile. 'Is that so.'

'Please, Wolf! You I can trust, implicitly.'

Wolf said nothing. Mosley opened a drawer with some force and took out a cheque book. He tore out a cheque and wrote down a number and handed it to Wolf. Wolf looked at the cheque.

'Well?'

Wolf was still looking at the cheque. Then he folded it, neatly, and tucked it away in his pocket.

He nodded, tight-lipped.

Some offers you just couldn't refuse.

5

Herr Wolf—

Did you like her? She was so pretty. When we
went into the alleyway her hand was warm in mine.
It reminded me of going to Spitalfields with my
mother shopping for vegetables, cabbages and peas.
She was taken by God when I was very young. We
have so much in common, you and I. Your mother,
too was taken. But we are soldiers, we soldier
on. Be brave, my mother said, she held my hand
and it was moist and warm, she was lying in bed
and she was running a fever. I don't know what
she died of; a doctor never came. Be brave, he
needs you. I thought she was talking about my
father but now I know the truth of it, and she
must have known one day I would meet you. I took
the whore into the alleyway and my knife came out
all slick and sharp and she tried to cry, but I
put my hand over her mouth and pressed my body
against hers, against the wall, and put my lips
close to her ear and said, Shut up you whore, or
I will kill you. I put the knife to her throat.
How she trembled! Her neck was so white and I
could feel her heartbeat, I could cup it in my
hand like a flame from a match. I kissed her.

It was so romantic. I remember the sky spread
out above us, and the stars and the smell of
pines - for some reason I could smell pines, and
freshly cut grass, and her cheap perfume. I

remember the taste of her lips, and the heat of
her body against mine, and the sky all above, and
thinking what lay beyond it, beyond air and the
sun: did they have other worlds up there, like
ours and yet unlike, where lovers met in secret
in the strange byways of an alien city?

I stuck the knife in her. She dropped in my
arms and I held her, tenderly, and looked deep
into her eyes and saw the suffering ease and at
last she was at peace, like my mother was at
peace. I laid her down on the ground. The blood
gushed out of her. I had the irrational desire
to taste it. I stroked her hair. She was so
blonde and so pretty. The front of me was wet. I
knelt over her like a priest at prayer. I gave
her benediction. Can't you see that? The knife
was in my hand and I delicately etched the sign
on her. I had to make it deep. I was so excited
that my hands shook. I arranged her properly. I
made her beautiful again. Innocent. She wasn't a
whore now; she was like a new bride. I folded
her arms on her belly, and finally I reached into
my coat and took out the little toy. The little
drummer. I was going to wind it up. I wanted to
see it march across the ground of that alleyway,
march along her body, march like I would have
marched for you. But I heard voices and I was
suddenly afraid. I left it by her head. I
touched her one last time. I was shaking when I
stood up. I wore a raincoat for the blood. The
voices came closer, and so I went the other way
and no one saw me.

The problem, Wolf reflected, was Balfour. Arthur James Balfour
and all the other Jew-lovers in His Majesty's government. Long
dead now, the old fool — but promises hastily made are

nonetheless remembered, especially ones made by the Foreign Secretary of the greatest empire in the world.

Wolf was only a young soldier then, serving with the First Company of the List Regiment in the Bavarian army, but he could still remember his outrage when news of Lord Balfour's promise reached the front. Back then, of course, Jews were still a part of German and Austrian society. Jewish officers served in the war against the British, just as on the British side Jews fought against the Kaiser.

But already the Jews were agitating for *emancipation*. An insidious form of nationalism took hold of the Jewish people, a desire for a *homeland*. They had called their movement Zionism, and they had been spurred on by the vision of one Theodor Herzl, an Austro-Hungarian journalist Jew.

In 1917, Lord Balfour wrote a letter to Baron Rothschild, in which he asserted British support for the establishment of a Jewish homeland in Palestine (then still in the possession of the Ottoman Empire, though it fell to British forces shortly after). Of course, Wolf thought, no one had *actually* intended to commit to such a disastrous course of action, but the Jews persisted, and were becoming increasingly more militant in their nationalist aspirations.

But it was absurd, Wolf thought. Try as he might he could not take the threat to Mosley seriously. The Fall had changed things. Communism was a Jewish sickness and Austro-Germany had become a Jewish paradise in which their thinkers and their scientists flourished – did not Freud found and radically expand his very own Sigmund Freud Institute in Vienna, with branches in Berlin and even Moscow itself? Was not that clown Albert Einstein now Chair of the Max Planck Institute in Berlin? It seemed nearly every day his famous image, with that wild unruly hair and smirking face, stared out at Wolf from the dailies or in the newsreels, an icon used by the communists as a threat of terrible weapons to come, should war ever be declared.

Marx, Freud and Einstein: the three corners of the evil that was international Jewry, Wolf thought.

If only *he* had been in power . . .

But then reality, of course, sank in. He was not in power. He was a nobody, a grey man in a cheap grey suit, and his only reason for being at Mosley's party was that they wanted to hire him. As the *help*.

Scheisse!

He left Mosley's office and started down the stairs clutching a large brown envelope containing – or so Mosley said – all of the communications he had received from the Palestinian terrorists. He intended to dump the file as soon as was convenient. There would be nothing useful in the anonymously mailed threats.

'They have influence, still,' Mosley told him. 'The Jews. They've worked themselves into British public life, insidiously, and with money. The Rothschilds have been funding Jewish immigration to Palestine for decades. Don't underestimate them, Wolf.'

Implicit in the words: *Like you have before.*

Now he went down the stairs and all he wanted to do was get away. He was beat-up and tired and old. In his pocket, Mosley's cheque was a reminder of everything he had once been and would never be again.

Not looking, he bumped into something soft and full that smelled of expensive perfume. A squeal of delight followed and a familiar female voice said, 'Wolfy!'

He raised his head and found himself staring directly into the adoring eyes of Unity Mitford.

'Valkyrie?' he said. He had always used her middle name.

'Don't you recognise me?' she said, laughing.

Wolf winced. He found he could not draw away from her, his eyes kept searching that sweet, smooth face, the full red lips, the mischievous eyes. She had not changed. Her delicate perfume tickled his nostrils. 'You haven't aged a day,' he said.

'Always so gallant,' she said, laughing. 'Did my sister not say I would be here? I've been looking for you *everywhere*.'

Wolf took her hand in his. 'It is very good to see you again, Valkyrie,' he said.

'And you, too. So, so much.' She slipped her arm through his.

In her other hand she was holding champagne. 'Oh, Wolf!' She looked up at him with those adorable, adoring eyes, a sad look just like the one Wolf remembered, so fondly, from his German Shepherd, Blonda. Leaving his dog behind had been one of the hardest things he'd ever done. 'Oh, Wolf, where did we go wrong?'

'You were too beautiful,' Wolf said, 'and I was a penniless prospect. A cat may look at a king.'

'But you hate cats!'

He grinned, a wolf's grin, and didn't speak again.

'Come,' she said. 'Let's get some air.'

'I should get back.'

'Not yet you don't.' She led him and he followed. Down the stairs and out to the garden in the back. It was a beautiful night. The rich never live in winter; only the poor.

Music was playing, Glenn Miller's big band tunes, and couples were dancing in the garden. Tall torches set into the ground cast shadows from their flickering flames, like snakes shedding their skin. Unity took Wolf's hand in hers. 'Do you still think of me?'

'Always.'

'You lie.'

'In every great lie there must be a kernel of truth,' Wolf said.

'Always the cynic.' She sighed and leaned against him. 'Do you remember?' she said.

Wolf said he did.

There are all kinds of truths and most of them are uncomfortable.

1933: the last of the Nuremberg Rallies.

Wolf, bitter in defeat. But not yet defeated.

It was an unofficial war and it had raged over the Roaring Twenties and early thirties, across Germany and in particular Berlin. Brownshirts and communists, SA men and KPD comrades fighting for control. That poor dumb fuck Horst Wessel was an SA-Sturmführer when a communist assassin shot him in the kisser. People were predicting civil war, though there was nothing civil about it. Germany was a powder keg, as the saying goes.

Wolf was the match. Then came the elections and the communists, the KPD, came to power, shocking everyone but especially Wolf.

1933 and he still thought he could win. The commies were still consolidating their unexpected authority. It was time for a last, desperate push.

The Reichstag burned.

And Wolf marched in Nuremberg. Not in victory but in defeat, but he marched all the same. It was then that Valkyrie and her sister Diana came to see him. He had been taken with Valkyrie. She was only nineteen. In a way, she reminded him of Geli.

He was keeping Eva at the time. She was a pretty, uncomplicated little creature. At twenty-one years old she was two years older than Valkyrie but less mature. He had first met her at the photographer's where she worked as a model and assistant. She had been seventeen, then.

He often wondered what had happened to Eva, after the Fall. Did she die in the camps? Or did she, a simple creature not much given to politics, get by? Did she find herself a handsome young commissar to marry and did she bear him children? Wolf supposed he could have tried to find out, but he never did.

Valkyrie came into his life when his life was all but over. She was a precious thing, and she doted on him. Those puppy eyes, just like Blonda's. He took her to balls and rallies while Eva was left behind in the apartment he had bought her. Valkyrie looked good on Wolf's arm.

It was the last ever of the Nuremberg rallies. He remembered the flags waving in the wind, the people standing down below looking up at him with heavy, veiled eyes. Remembered the heat, the sweat, the feel of the woollen suit against his skin, chafing. The smell of defeat was the smell of a homeless soldier back from the war, the smell of gangrene and sour alcohol.

'Do you remember?'

Two months later the KPD thugs came and arrested him. The organisation had been broken, mass arrests were made, and Wolf was sent to the camps. Some of the others fled: Hess, the coward, took a private plane across Europe and into Britain. Göring joined the communists. Julius Streicher was killed in a shoot-out in Nuremberg. Even Wolf didn't mourn his passing. The man was a menace, a rapist and a drunk, but he had been effective. Streicher's newspaper, *Der Stürmer*, was shut down.

National Socialism was dead.

'I remember,' Wolf said. His teeth were clenched. All around them ghostly couples danced in the light of the burning torches. Valkyrie was close against him, her warmth like a promise, her perfume an invitation. Her lips by his ear. 'Remember when we were alone. I could do those things for you again, that you like.'

He pushed her away, but not roughly, more with a sense of loss and regret. And tried not to think of the monstrous woman, that Ilse Koch as she had called herself, and her torture chamber under that now-abandoned club on Leather Lane.

'I am no longer that man.'

'Oh, Wolf.' There was so much sadness in her voice it made him ill. 'People don't change. You are still who you were! A leader, a visionary. You are what poor deluded Oswald could never be.'

'You're young,' he said. 'And I am not. And time comes upon all of us, like a thief in the night.'

'Oh, how I hate the Jews who did this to you!'

'You were always steadfast in your hatred of them, Valkyrie.'

'No one says my name like you do.'

One memorable night in Nuremberg, he and the two Mitford sisters . . . but no. He would not think of that.

'Diana still worships you as I do,' Valkyrie said.

Wolf smiled. 'No one does it like you do,' he said.

'Come with me. Back to my flat.'

There was such naked need in her voice. Wolf shook his head. The past had a habit of catching up with you. 'I had better go,' he said. 'I think Oswald would have preferred me to use the servants' exit.'

'The man is a buffoon.'

'He *is* your brother-in-law.'

Valkyrie shrugged. 'Let Diana warm his bed for him,' she said. 'He might be the next prime minister.'

'Is that what this is?' Valkyrie said. 'Is it about *power*, Wolf?'

'It is *always* about power,' Wolf said.

'Do you think I love you less for having lost your power?'

An ugly word: *love*.

Perhaps sensing she had made a mistake Valkyrie, too, withdrew. 'I'm sorry. I didn't mean—'

'Did you not?' Wolf said, darkly.

'Please, Wolf.' As if she couldn't but move closer to him, a moth to his banished flame. Whispering in his ear, 'I will fuck you the way you like it.'

He pushed her away, roughly this time. 'Whore,' he said.

'I will be your whore, if you'd only let me!'

People were looking at them now. 'Lower your voice,' Wolf said, and his own voice was distant and cold.

The woman was close to tears, he saw. Wolf touched his fingers to the brim of his hat. '*Auf wiedersehen*, Valkyrie.'

'Wolf, no!'

But already he was going, walking away, and the English people parted before him, as though they could sense the lethal mood he was in. Unity didn't follow. She remained standing there, alone, with people staring and then looking away and murmuring amongst themselves. 'Damn you, Wolf!' she shouted. 'And damn you too, you nosy bastards—' pointing a finger at the assembled guests, who studiously avoided eye contact.

'Come on, pet.' It was that young broker, Fleming.

'Oh, Ian,' Unity said. She let him lead her away. She leaned her head on his shoulder. 'It's all so very *beastly*,' she said, miserably.

Wolf's Diary, 3rd November 1939 – *contd.*

That stupid bitch Valkyrie had made a miserable ending to a miserable day and I suspected it was not yet over. I did not like women trying to assert an authority over me. The Mitford girl was too unpredictable, too *independent*. I liked my women the way I liked my dogs, obedient and devoted, like Catholics suddenly confronted with their maker.

I did not make a good Catholic. My father hated the clerics and I had hated both the clerics and my father. My mother was devout, and I remembered as a boy going to church and waiting on my knees, as God in the form of a priest stuck his flesh and dribbled his blood in my mouth. My mother had so much love to give, to her Lord and to me. Even to my father. And I remember, too, as a young boy, hearing the sounds coming from their bedroom, at night, my father's grunting, my mother's soft sobs and sighs. Perhaps it was as early as that that my dislike of my father began, with the sounds of his nightly assault.

But though I loved them, women always betrayed me. First and worst, Geli, of course. How dare she escape me, and using my own gun as the key to her freedom! But she was only the first of them.

I met Eva when I came to visit Herr Hoffmann's studio in Munich. It was a place I frequented regularly. The first time I saw her she was climbing a ladder in the shop and I saw her pretty ankles and the rising hemline of her dress and I was smitten, I will admit that I was smitten. She was a model of Aryan womanhood and at seventeen she glowed with good health, her eyes were innocent and clear and yet unspoiled. Whenever I came in to see Hoffmann I would take her hand and kiss it with decorum and call her my lovely siren from Hoffmann's. I would make her blush. She knew me as Herr Wolf, which was the nom de guerre I was using at the time. No doubt she thought of me as that politician what was in prison. Her language was plain. There was no guile about her. Later I would take her on holiday to Berchtesgaden where she would sun herself in the clear air, as naked as the day she was born. She was Eve before the fall. We would go rowing on the lake together. Such a simple, delightful creature she was.

In Munich I would take her out to the opera or to my favourite restaurant, the Osteria Bavaria. I would buy her

presents – the first thing I ever gave her was a yellow orchid.
It was the first flower a man had ever given her. I had given
the whore everything! And yet she, too, tried to escape me.

I had found her diary, the pages of which I had not
destroyed but kept, as proof of her guilt. She was a silly girl!
All she could speak of was of my taking her away from the
shop, of perhaps giving her a little house of her own. At first
she was jolly but as the days went by her distress grew. One
Sunday, for instance, I had promised to see her. She had
phoned the Osteria, left a message with Werlin to say she was
waiting to hear from me. I was not there, of course. I had
gone to Feldafing, and when Hoffmann invited me to coffee
and dinner I told him where to stuff it. The silly girl waited for
me all through the night. The Hoffmanns had even given her a
ticket for the Venetian Night that evening, but she didn't go.

Her diary became increasingly confused. I am utterly
miserable, she wrote, the little slut, as if she could know true
misery! *I* had been on the Front. Eva threatened to buy more
sleeping powders.

He only needs me for certain purposes, she wrote.

Later I invited her to dinner at the Four Seasons. At the
end of it, I gave her an envelope with some money.

A few days later the stupid whore Frau Hoffmann told Eva
I had found a replacement for her, called Valkyrie.

On 28th May she took thirty-five sleeping pills and tried to
kill herself but she failed.

The stupid whore! She could not even kill herself
successfully.

The whole thing was a pathetic ploy, a cry for my attention. Well, I suppose she did get it, after all. I have always
had a soft spot for a plump bit of dumpling and no mistake.

*   *   *

In another time and place Shomer lies dreaming and tries to forget.
In memory there's no escape.
He remembers them fleetingly, in jumbled fragments. Avrom's

dark curls gleaming in candlelight, Bina's laughter as he made faces at her and she snorted like a certain treife animal; their smell when they were babies, in those sleepless days when he sat by his typewriter morning and night churning out tales of Yiddishe gangsters and chaste girls with a wild heart hidden within, of bloodied murders and anti-Semite conspiracies and of detectives who walked the cold streets in search of a justice they knew to be an illusion – in those early days when the babies cried and Fanya feeding and the shouts of merchants outside silenced by snow, and a fire burning, and his fingers on the warm hard keys, and the smell of milk, of babies, everywhere in the house, and in everything he touched, and in his clothes – those were the happiest days of his life, he realised, and you only learn that too late, when they are vanished like smoke.

Those are the moments he wishes to burn like the pages of a manuscript. To see them consumed by flame so he would never have to see them or remember them or how they were, their smell eradicated for ever. He resents Fanya when she appears to him, unexpectedly, in unguarded moments; he resents her for leaving him. He wants her gone from his mind the way she had left this world, so abruptly: one moment they were together a family, and the next the man severed them with his horsewhip, they to go one way and he the other. They to the ovens, he to the work units. And he didn't know, they didn't know, Fanya held Avrom and Bina's hands and looked back at him as they parted, and her lips tried to form a smile. 'You will see each other again, they are only going to the showers, to be washed,' a soldier said, a voice lacking in emotion, and an old man masticating toothless gums said mournfully, 'Auschwitz, Auschwitz, what is this Auschwitz?'

He is angry at them not for leaving him but for coming back. They come from a world that no longer exists and has no right to intrude upon his present. Auschwitz, Auschwitz: there is only Auschwitz.

'Do you remember?' is a sentence never spoken, it is *verboten*, a transgression against the now. There is only now, no past, no future, there is only Auschwitz, an island floating on the Polish ground. The dead rise in black ash into the sky, day and night the ovens burn, day and night the trains come laden. And Shomer's mind retreats into itself, the way it had when he was still a man. For he had been a writer of *shund*, of pulp, for *Haynt* and other publishers. He had made his living with his hands, at his desk, writing lies for money.

He had had some success. He was read by yeshiva boys in secret, passing his books from hand to hand; by young Zionists filled with ideological fervour, who would have denied it stoutly were they challenged; by the rabbis who confiscated the books from their wards, by the women who picked them up for a few kopeks along with a bag of onions in the shop, by intellectuals who railed against this prostituting of literature, by wealthy merchants and farmers and cobblers and clockmakers, carpenters and engineers: they all knew the name Shomer, which means guardian, or watchman, and was his nom de plume, for it was not respectable for a man to be writing *shund*.

For it was hopeless. His life had been erased like his books, set alight, reduced to ash and scattered. It no longer existed. But then, all lives were ultimately extinguished, and in their passing nothing remained of the person who'd been – their dreams, their thoughts, who they loved, what they hated – from Neanderthals and Cro-Magnon and down the ages to Jews.

And yet Shomer lives still.

He'd met Fanya at an open-air showing of a film about Palestine and the work of the pioneers there. She wore white. He was in his best suit, he had only recently begun to write: stories about detectives and dames, with no redeeming literary value. He'd sported a thin moustache at the time (Fanya made him shave it off before the wedding). In the film, men and women no older than he were tilling stony fields and sleeping in tents and picking oranges. They looked like Biblical peasants reborn in distant Palestine; he couldn't imagine why anyone would want to live in this way. But he only half-saw them, anyway. All he really saw was Fanya, more real than anything the screen had to offer, like a woman out of the pages of one of his stories.

Of course, in hindsight, he realised that she wasn't. She was not cut out of cardboard like the dames in the stories. She had an internal life he would never see (and now never could), irrational likes and dislikes, moods he could not interpret, times she was happy for no reason he could tell and times she was sad and he could do nothing to change it. But she loved him, he loved her, and they were happy for a while. Even in the ghetto they could still make each other happy, even on the train here he was still telling her and the children stories.

Stories, stories, he is sick to death of stories!

Yet they are all he has.

Wolf's Diary, 3rd November 1939 – *contd.*

I was in a foul mood when I left the Mosleys' party. The taciturn driver waited outside. He hailed me but I refused his offer of a ride, foolishly perhaps. I walked away, though I walked with a slight limp from my old injury. The night was dark and quiet but I was not fooled, for it is in the night that one comes most alive. To know the light you must understand shadows. I walked through Belgravia though I had the feeling I was being watched, and often I turned abruptly but there was no one there. Nevertheless the feeling of being watched persisted.

In this manner – that is to say, furtively – I traversed the city in an easterly direction. My mind was busy like a rat's.

Vicious, dirty creatures, rats. Julius Streicher's genius with *Der Stürmer* was, firstly, the graphic caricatures he ran: the long-nosed rat-like Jew, always lusting after German maidenhood. It was a magazine appealing to the lowest common denominator, glorying in gruesome tales of sex crimes and murders, all naturally blamed on the Jews. He was rat-like himself, was Julius Streicher, vicious and dirty and oh so effective. His magazine was all but pornographic; it put the English *Daily Mail* to shame. I didn't know why I was thinking about him again after all those years. The past was threatening to catch up with me.

My mind returned to the symbol carved on the dead woman's chest. I had thought the swastika forgotten. A red star rose over Germany now. In my preoccupation, I was tired and footsore, and perhaps not as cautious as I should have been. I had failed to pick up the signs of danger.

The approach through Walker's Court in Soho was quiet. Too quiet. I did not see the whores. Of the murder scene there was no sign, but then again it was only the death of a whore, and the police had other matters to engage themselves with. My footsteps echoed lonely in the abandoned street. I took off my hat momentarily and passed my hand over my damp hair and replaced the hat over my head. I took out my keys and opened the door and went up to my room. It was dark but the stairs were familiar. I had traversed them up and down so often I sometimes thought that I knew them better than I knew myself. I opened the door to my office. I seldom bothered to lock it. I had nothing to steal. Nevertheless, I was sure I had locked it on my departure. I was too slow, too tired. I was not yet alarmed.

I stepped through and switched on the light and saw the damage.

The desk was lying with its legs in the air like a corpse, its drawers open, their contents tossed out at random. The painting was torn off the wall. The books were scattered across the floor like the pearls off a broken necklace. Someone had taken a shit on the floor and used Ernst Jünger's *Fire and Blood* as toilet paper. The two visitor chairs were broken into pieces. For some reason my own chair was left standing, as though someone had calmly sat watching while the destruction was being wreaked. The phone was pulled off the wall and the typewriter lay on its back like a drunk.

I won't mention what they did with the hat rack.

I heard footsteps behind me but by then, of course, it was too late. They must have waited in the next room, my room, waiting for me to return. I began to turn but all I could see were shadows and then something smacked into the side of my head, near breaking my jaw, and I fell, the pain searing through me hot and bright. I tried to crawl away and for a moment they let me, just watching. My face was against the floor and the smell of piss was overwhelming. They had urinated on my effects and I would have killed them if I could.

A voice said, 'That's enough. Pick him up, boychiks.'

I tried to get away from them but they reached for me, two big men, one on either side, and lifted me up, as easily as if I were a doll. I dangled uselessly between them. 'Stay away from my daughter, you fucking anti-Semite.'

He wore an expensive black wool coat and a black fedora and his shoes were polished to within an inch of their lives. He had big hands and hairy knuckles and a single item of jewellery, a plain silver wedding ring. He was older than me and heavier and he was unshaved, not out of worry but because he didn't give a damn.

'Put him in the fucking chair.'

'Yes, Mr Rubinstein.'

They dropped me into my desk chair, not gently. My head was throbbing and blood was gushing from the wound they had inflicted on me. One of them held a blackjack and it was stained with my blood.

'Who the fuck let you in?' I gasped.

'Watch your language. Moishe?'

The big brute on the left raised the blackjack and tapped me on the knee and I thought I would die from the pain.

'Yes, Mr Rubinstein.'

'Ready to be civil, now, Mr Wolf?'

'I'm sorry?' I said. 'I don't speak Yiddish.'

He sighed, now. 'Moishe . . .'

'Yes, Mr Rubinstein.'

This time I thought I was ready for the pain but I wasn't. He boxed me on the ear, nearly tearing it off. His hand came back covered in blood and he wiped it on my coat distastefully.

'You're Julius Rubinstein,' I said. 'The banker.' I spoke with
difficulty. My lips found it hard to form words and my tongue
felt sluggish

'I'll say it again, shamus. Stay the fuck away from my
daughter.'

'Which . . . one?'

'Dovele?'

'Yes, Mr Rubinstein.' The brute on the right picked me up,
one-handed. Then he tossed me against the wall. I fell down
on the pile of books, my cheek coming to rest on the big
brown heap of shit they'd left for me there. It stung my eye.
'You . . . filthy animals,' I said. It came out as a moan.

'Pick him up.'

'Sir, he's got shit all over him.'

'I said pick him *up*!'

'Yes, Mr Rubinstein.'

They picked me up, grimacing, and deposited me back in
the chair. I tried to wipe the excrement off my face but only
managed to smear it around.

Rubinstein paced before me, his hands behind his back, as
though delivering a lesson of the Torah to an errant yeshiva
boy.

'My daughter,' he said, 'can be headstrong.' He turned to
me abruptly, studied me with his pale eyes, then continued
pacing restlessly. 'It is not easy having daughters. You never
married, did you, Wolf?'

'No.'

'Wise, perhaps. You never had children?'

'No.'

He sighed. It was a long-suffering sigh. 'Daughters,' he
said. 'They'll break your heart and laugh as they do it. Boys I
can understand, boys know where their duties lie. But God
never saw fit to give me boys.'

I kept my mouth shut. I had nothing to gain by antagonising
him further. 'What did she want?' he said.

'Who?'

'My daughter.'

'Isabella.'

'Don't use her name, you piece of shit. You're not worthy of speaking her name.'

'She told me your other daughter went missing. She wanted me to find her.'

'Judith?'

'You have another one?'

'Moishe, please!'

'Yes, Mr Rubinstein.'

This time he slammed my head into the wall. I think I blacked out. When I opened my eyes again he was still there, silhouetted against the open door. I blinked, tasted blood. 'Don't give me lip,' Rubinstein said. It seemed redundant to reply so I didn't.

'Did she say why?'

'She told me . . .' I licked my lips. Moved my mouth but no sound came. 'Dovele, give him a drink.'

'Yes, Mr Rubinstein.'

Dovele pulled out a hip flask and unscrewed it and put it to my lips. He forced my head back and forced me to drink. The alcohol hit me like an uppercut from Max Schmeling.

'*Scheisse!*' I said, when I could speak again.

'It's the good stuff,' Dovele said.

'I don't drink.'

'You do now.'

'Go to hell.'

Rubinstein smiled. 'This *is* hell,' he said. 'But this is your hell, not mine.'

'Where is your daughter?' I said.

'Which one?'

'The one I was hired to find.'

'That is not your concern. And Isabella should never have approached you. You will not see her again. I very much recommend that you don't try to either.'

None of it made much sense to me but then at that point I could barely make sense of my own face if I had a mirror. 'Did you pay to smuggle her out of Germany?'

'That is not your business.'

And yet he did not cease pacing, nor did he stop answering my questions. If I had to venture a guess at that point, I may have said I was looking at a very worried man.

And worried men are often angry.

'You don't know where she is, do you,' I said.

'Listen to me, *Wolf*, or whatever you call yourself these days – do you think I don't *know* you? You are nothing, you are less than nothing; you are the shit beneath my shoe.'

'Göring,' I said – throwing it out to him.

He stopped and stood stock-still. That was enough for me. 'You paid him to get her out of Germany, didn't you,' I said. 'But she never made it out the other end and now you're panicking.'

For a moment he looked murderous, then abruptly he subsided and shrugged. 'So you still have some contacts with your old comrades,' he said. 'You think they value you? One thing that can be said for Nazis, Wolf, they make shitty sentimentalists.'

'One thing that can be said for Jews,' I said, 'is that . . . no, I've got nothing.'

Unexpectedly he laughed. 'You used to have plenty to say.'

'I can help you find her. If you let me go.'

'You?' He gestured at the room, the broken furniture, my broken face. 'You can't even help yourself, you schmuck.'

I had a moment of clarity, then. Perhaps it was the whiskey. 'You don't think they did it, do you? You don't think they did it because you work with them.'

Again he went still. This time, I had the feeling I was on thin ice. He was a man always in control, but it must have cost him, and inside he was coiled tight. The wrong pressure could set him off and then there'd be no telling what he'd do. 'How can you, a Jew, work with—'

'Nazis?' He laughed. 'Cock-sucking opportunists,' he said. 'That's all they are. Rats growing fat having jumped a drowning ship.'

He kept mixing his metaphors or perhaps it was the whiskey and what it was doing to me. I felt so drowsy, drowsy and warm. 'How much did you pay Göring?'

'Comrade Göring is a good communist now.'

It was hard to believe that fat Göring had once been a decorated flying ace: he often boasted of having shot down twenty-two Allied airplanes during the Great War. He had even been awarded an Iron Cross, First Class: but then I had one myself.

'You stay away from my daughter,' Rubinstein said again. He sounded less sure of himself, somehow.

'Whatever you say.' I was too tired to argue, and I sensed he didn't know any more than what he'd told me. It must have driven him mad, not knowing where his daughter was, what had happened to her. Did she lie dead even now in some Alpine fissure, or worse, was she even now being made to pleasure some rich old man in barbarous Egypt or Hindustan, another slave amongst many? Whatever he said I knew he didn't truly believe in Göring's innocence. You lie down with dogs and you're liable to get up with fleas, as my mother used to say.

Though I loved dogs.

'What did he say?'

'He mumbled something about dogs,' Dovele said.

'Huh.'

Rubinstein stopped pacing. He leaned towards me, putting his face close to mine. I could smell his expensive cologne. His voice was quiet and lethal like a stiletto. 'I want you to remember what I told you.'

I nodded, or at least my head fell on my chest. 'I'll remember . . .'

'You will,' he said. And then he smiled, and it was a smile that brought me suddenly wide awake. It was the coldest and meanest expression I had ever seen on a human being. 'Hold him, boychiks.'

'Yes, Mr. Rubinstein.'

'Let's do this.'

'Do what?' I said, but they ignored me. I tried to struggle against them but I was too weak. 'Take his trousers off.'

'What? Stop!'

I fought them. Panic gave me strength I thought lost. They knocked me about and then they pulled down my trousers and my underpants and I was lying there with my trousers round my ankles and my private parts exposed.

'Cold, Wolf?'

His men obediently laughed. 'Pick him up, pick him up! We haven't got all day.'

They picked me up and righted the chair and sat me down again.

'Dovele, you hold him still. Moishe, spread his legs.'

'You fucking animals, you dirty fucking Jews—!'

'Put a sock in it.'

'Yes, Mr Rubinstein,' Moishe said, though it had been addressed to me. He took off my left shoe and peeled off my sock and scrunched it up into a ball and shoved it into my mouth. My teeth bit down on cheap cotton soaked in sweat and I gagged and almost choked. Dovele held my body secure while Moishe took hold of my legs.

'Don't fucking struggle,' he said. He sounded almost compassionate.

'Tie his legs to the chair.'

'With what?'

'God damn it,' Rubinstein said. 'Just hold him still, will you?'

Moishe slammed his fist into my face. I felt my legs go limp.

'Don't knock him out!'

They had me the way they wanted me. I was too weak to struggle, and the men were too strong. My legs were spread wide, my private parts exposed to Rubinstein's scrutiny. He leaned in, studied them dispassionately, like a scientist examining an insect. 'Thought you'd have a bigger dick,' he said, conversationally. 'Saw you in Munich, once, you know.' He mimed, his hand waving between his legs, near dragging on the floor. 'Thought you'd be swinging like a bloody elephant, almost, the way you carried on,' he said, and his men laughed.

I couldn't speak. I could barely breathe. I was hyperventilating, flooded with fear. He didn't rush, Rubinstein. He savoured the moment. Outside the window I thought I saw the first rays of dawn, but I could have been imagining it. It was so very quiet.

In the silence the flick of his knife was as loud as the strike of a clock.

In another time and place Shomer lies dreaming. He tosses and turns on the upper bunk he shares with two other men, an emaciated ginger-haired Jew from Slovenia and a short once-fat Transylvanian trader whose folds of skin flap like loose sails in the wind. All around him are the groans and snores and murmured cries of the other inmates, hundreds of men crammed into this block.

Shomer dreams of women. Big busty Austrian girls with breasts as white as cream, nipples like dark chocolate truffles, girls who smile with saucy eyes and press close against him, murmuring filthy words, enticing him to touch, to feel, to experience their inherent goodness. Shomer dreams of small dark Jewish girls with bright clear eyes, whose modest dresses hide their lithe bodies and wanton desire.

Shomer dreams of gypsy girls moving in the light of torches, sweat glistening on their skin, a dancing bear sitting forlornly with its back to a tree, chewing on bark. The girls dance and clash their cymbals and their dresses rise and give him a flash of ankle, even of thigh. Shomer dreams of Viennese housewives waiting for the milkman all alone with their husbands and children out of the house, dressed in nothing but a shift they wait by the door, touching themselves through the thin material. He dreams of posh English girls and society ladies, slowly unlacing their elaborate dresses to reveal sheer nakedness underneath. He dreams of the women held prisoner in the Joy Division, the camp's brothel explicitly prohibited to Jews, where the spoils of war wait every night for the other prisoners to come and rut with them like the animals they are. And out of nowhere comes the image of his wife Fanya, her small serious face and her dark eyes that could nevertheless twinkle so mischievously, and the smell of cholla bread fresh out of the oven and the sweet taste of kiddush wine and the candles burning on the windowsill and Avrom and Bina his children looking up to him as he breaks the bread and dips it in salt and passes it to them, on a Friday night dinner not that long ago. And he tosses and turns, fighting off the dream for he does not want to see their faces, does not want to hear the sound of their voices or their laugh, their baby smell, their love, and moreover and most of all he does not want to think of the day they had arrived here, in Auschwitz, and at the gates were parted, he to go one way, they the other, never to be seen again.

And all around him the men toss and turn and cry in their sleep ten to a row, dreaming of loved ones, and their dreams turn to ash in their mouths and they turn and they dream of food, masticating in their sleep, hollowly, that endless sound of hundreds of men all chewing food they would never chew again.

And Shomer is awake, his bladder pressing painfully, and so he climbs down cautiously from the bunk pushing and fighting his way and down to the ground and makes his way in the darkness of the block to the bucket, this big monstrous iron bucket full of piss, and he pulls down his prisoner's pyjamas and holds his penis in his hand and stares down at it in wonder, this alien appendage, unfamiliar and awful strange. He urinates painfully, and the piss slops off the rim of the bucket and he knows he has lost tonight's lottery, it is his lot to carry the bucket outside to be emptied, but something inside him almost welcomes the humiliation and pain. For a long moment more he stands there, listening to the camp and the sound of nightmares made literal and given voice. He shakes his penis sadly, with resignation, and folds it back into the uniform pants. At last he picks up the bucket and carries it with careful pained precision into the cold outside but the piss still slops onto his feet and soaks the bottom of his pants but at least he's no longer thinking of Fanya and the children and the night so full of ghosts; there is that at least.

* * *

'Hold him still, damn it!'

Wolf was struggling in the chair, his eyes bulging, the veins standing out on his forehead, pulsing with blood. He made strange, animal-like sounds.

Rubinstein knelt between Wolf's legs with his knife in his hand. Wolf's penis dangled uselessly, his stomach was knotted with revulsion and fear. Rubinstein grabbed Wolf's penis in his hand. Dovele looked on, impassive, as Moishe turned his head away, in disgust or sympathy it was impossible to tell. Wolf was screaming, screaming through the sock stuffed in his mouth, the sound muffled but no less terrified for all that. Rubinstein, almost gently, pulled on Wolf's cock, drawing forth Wolf's foreskin until it protruded beyond the tip like a monk's cowl. He pinched the foreskin, pulling it still, with Wolf shaking and shaking above him and the two men holding him down.

'Filthy thing,' Rubinstein said, dispassionately. He pulled, sharply, then with almost the same smooth easy movement, almost as though he had had plenty of practice, he brought the knife up to the penis and sliced neatly through the foreskin.

Wolf screamed.

On his knees before Wolf, Julius Rubinstein regarded the slice of human skin he held between his fingers.

'Huh,' he said.

'Mazel tov!' Dovele said. 'It's a boy!'

Still, for a long moment Rubinstein remained where he was, an almost puzzled expression, it seemed, clouding his face. He stared at Wolf's foreskin like a scientist confronted with evidence; but evidence of what, he didn't seem able to say. Slowly he raised his eyes, regarded Wolf's withdrawn and shrunken penis. At last, with an almost contemptuous gesture, he tossed the shred of foreskin to the floor and stood up. 'Who's the fucking Jew now,' he said.

He made a gesture with his head. His two men released their hold on Wolf and stepped aside. That head movement again, so slight as to be almost missed. Moishe kicked the legs of Wolf's chair as Dovele back-handed Wolf across the face. The chair collapsed and Wolf was sent sprawling on his back, his pants down, his newly-circumcised penis flopping sadly.

Rubinstein took two steps that brought him directly over Wolf. He looked down on him, like Moses looking down on the people from the heights of Mount Sinai.

'Stay the fuck away from my daughter,' he said. He pulled at his belt buckle. Untied himself. His member loomed above Wolf, dark and foreboding. Rubinstein was built like an ape.

'No, no,' Wolf tried to say. It came out muffled. Rubinstein grunted. A stream of hot piss burst forth from his member, hitting Wolf. It was in Wolf's hair, on his face, in his mouth soaking the gag until Wolf thought he would choke to death. Wolf moaned and tried to crawl away. No one said a word. It was silent in the room but for the hiss of urine. It seemed to go on and on. Wolf closed his eyes. For a moment it seemed to him it was his father standing above him, that this was just a repeat of the nightly ritual of childhood. Then Rubinstein grunted again and the stream trickled to a halt and Rubinstein buckled his belt. He bent down and, almost gently, pulled the sodden sock out of Wolf's mouth. 'Sweet dreams, sunshine,' he said – whispered. Then he kicked Wolf viciously in the ribs. Wolf screamed and this time the scream was not muffled.

'Let's go, boychiks.'

In moments, like silent shadows, they were gone; like they had never been. Wolf lay on the floor for a long time. The only sound in the room was the sound of his sobbing.

6

Wolf's Diary, 4th November 1939

. . .

Wolf's Diary, 5th November 1939

. . .

Wolf's Diary, 6th November 1939

. . .

Herr Wolf—

In my dream I was alone in the house upstairs.
It is a big old house, and when I was a boy I
believed there were ghosts living in it. My mother
said ghosts are mean old people who don't go away
even after they die, and that is all there is to
it. My father said, he served in the Great War
and he'd seen no ghosts, but he had seen plenty
of the dead. Like my father, I do not believe in
ghosts.

In my dream I was alone in the house upstairs,
and I could hear the floorboards creaking. It is
an old house and it breathes as if it were alive,
grunting and farting, but it is only the water in
the pipes or the rats in the attic or the floorboards contracting and expanding with the weather.
That's all there is to it.

In my dream I felt a great dark presence in the
house. It stalked from room to room, but quietly,
like a parent, and I hid in my room. It was coming
close to my door and still I knew there was no one
else in the house, and that I was truly alone. I
called out, Father, Father, but he was not there.
When I was born he had touched me with his
calloused fingers and traced my face, so he could
see me: God took his eyes in the Great War with
gas. Let me look at you, let me look at you. I
cried, No, and the presence at the door huffed and
it puffed and I became so frightened that I cowered
in the corner of my room with my hands over my
head, and the floorboards creaked and creaked.

No one can see me, but it saw. In my dream I
looked through my pockets but the knife was not
there, and it is my only friend. At last I became
too frightened to cower and I went to open the
door and see the face of my tormentor, but there
was no one there, and the house was silent; there
was no one there at all.

On the Tuesday the telephone rang and this time Wolf picked it
up. The voice on the other end was cool and collected. 'Well?'
she demanded.

'Miss Rubinstein.'

'Have you made progress?'

'I met your father.'

That gave her pause.

'Oh?'

'He is a violent man.'

Her voice changed, became soft and concerned and rushed.
'Did Daddy hurt you? What did he do to you?'

Wolf didn't answer.

'Stay right there. I will come over.'

'I do not think that is a very good idea.'

The line went dead. Wolf stared at the receiver before placing it back.

Het set to tidying the office. It would all have to go. After the assault he had at long last dragged himself upright and tottered to his bedsit. The room was relatively undisturbed but in the middle of the small bed there lay a human shit. On Sunday Wolf's landlord, the baker Edelmann, came and knocked on his door, but Wolf called him vile names and the baker withdrew.

The phone rang twice on Saturday and three times on Sunday and had begun to ring at half-hourly intervals on Tuesday until Wolf finally picked up.

After the call he dragged himself to the communal bathroom on the landing. He shared it with an ageing prostitute named Martha, a corpulent old crone who now made ends meet by selling seeds to feed the pigeons in Trafalgar Square. She had once confessed to Wolf that the seeds were poisoned. In her own small way Martha was a mass murderer, working in secret and without need for fame or acknowledgement of her deeds. She sold the seeds, the visitors to the capital fed the birds, and she watched them die with a sense of quiet achievement. 'One day,' she said to Wolf, 'there will be no more pigeons in London, then the world. Then at last we will all be free.' Wolf never knew what she had against the pigeons, which she seemed to view with the same hostility and suspicion as she did people who lived south of the river, immigrants, sailors, stone angels, moss and Wolf himself. He tended to avoid her after that.

He stared at his gaunt face in the mirror. Some of the bruises were fading. Others had turned a nasty shade of black and green. He shaved, though his hand shook from hunger and fatigue. Grey and black hairs stuck to the surface of the washbasin. He rinsed them off.

He washed himself. Scrubbed himself with soap. The water was lukewarm to begin with, then cold. He emerged shivering, dried himself and dressed awkwardly. He was still aching all over, and his cock burned. Wolf gritted his teeth and carried on. He went back to the room and put on his coat and his hat and then he went out.

Wolf's Diary, 7th November 1939

Just a short hop to Gerrard Street. Down the stairs to the Hofgarten. The same dark atmosphere, the same brutish barman. Emil, I remembered Hess calling him.

'Herr Wolf.'

I ignored him. I saw Hess at a corner table. He was beginning to rise as I came to him. Without stopping I slammed my fist into his jaw. He fell back against the wall, surprise and blood mixing on his face. His bodyguards were rising, coming for me. I saw the flash of gunmetal.

'Wait.'

He shook his head and coughed. 'I would not do that again, Wolf, if I were you.'

'You set me up.'

'How?' He looked tired. He sat down again. 'Please, Wolf. Sit.'

'Who owns the club you sent me to?'

'Does it matter?' He shrugged.

'Who controls the trafficking?'

'Why do you care?' His anger surprised me. He looked at me wanly. 'Why do you care,' he said again. 'You're not involved. You didn't want to be. You could have led us.'

'To be like common criminals?' I barked a laugh.

'For the cause. For Germany.'

'Germany is lost, and you are a fool, Hess. Do not lie. Not to me.'

Old pain in his voice. 'Wolf . . .'

'You cheapen yourself and your race,' I said.

'Wolf! Enough!'

His open palm slammed on the table. Abruptly I sat down, opposite him. 'No more lies,' I said. 'Who works the trafficking network this end?'

'I tried to warn you,' he said. 'You didn't want to listen.'

'I heard you loud and clear.'

Thinking of that nameless club, the man Kramer with his face blown off, Ilse and her whip. 'Give me a name.'

'You should leave, now.'

Movement behind me. I stayed sitting down, looking straight. 'You sold yourself for thirty pieces of silver,' I said. 'Oh, Rudolf . . .'

'We are no longer your disciples!'

I stared into his eyes and saw nothing but craven greed there. Who was he so afraid of?

'Where do they operate? Give me a name!'

He sighed. 'Try Petticoat Lane,' he said. 'Ask for Barbie.'

I nodded. There was that movement again behind me. Hess's agonised face stared at me. 'Don't come back here again, Wolf,' he said. 'You put me in danger as well as yourself.'

'The Jew,' I said, in hatred. 'Rubinstein. You work with Jews now, Hess?'

'This is out of my hands, Wolf. I've given you all I can.'

'How much did he pay you to bring his daughter out of Germany?'

'Wolf!' He rubbed a weary hand over his face. 'This is bigger than me, bigger than all of us. Don't go poking your nose into business that doesn't concern you.'

'But it does concern me, Hess. It concerns me very much,' I said. My groin burned with a pain I could barely keep under control. 'What happened to her?' I said. 'What happened to the daughter?'

'I am sure I don't know what you're talking about,' he said. 'Now go. We shall not see each other again.'

He motioned with his head and the big barman, Emil, loomed behind me. I nodded, ceding his warning – or perhaps it was a premonition.

I stood up. 'I'll leave on my own,' I said. Emil's ugly mug of a face stared at me without expression.

'Very good, Herr Wolf,' he said.

*

Wolf left the Hofgarten, his shoulder blades tense, half-expecting a cosh to the back of the head, a knife between the ribs. Nothing happened. Hess had always been a follower, not a leader.

So who was he trying to protect?

Or perhaps more cynically he was wringing his hands and protesting, all the while steering Wolf in the direction he wanted him to go. You could trust Hess to be untrustworthy, Wolf thought. You always knew where you were with an ex-Nazi.

He had no intention of staying off the case; not for Hess's warnings, not for that murderous Jew gangster Julius Rubinstein and his assault. For did not the Jewish Bible itself say, 'a man who inflicts an injury upon his fellow man, so shall be done to him: fracture for fracture, eye for eye, tooth for tooth. Just as he inflicted an injury upon a person, so shall it be inflicted upon him.'

His thoughts were murderous as he hopped on a bus going to the East End. The advert running along the side of the bus proudly proclaimed that Swan Vestas Were The Smoker's Match. Wolf sat towards the back, sandwiched between the window and an elderly woman carrying a woven basket filled with something that stank: rotten fish or something even more vile. She was talking all the time, mumbling with a soft, emaciated mouth. 'Bloody foreigners, coming over here, taking our jobs, taking our homes, pissing in the streets don't they, the filthy buggers, selling their women cheap, the dirty whores, and their thieving children, a woman isn't safe any more, not anywhere—' She clutched the basket to her chest as if afraid Wolf was going to steal it. 'Nasty buggers the lot of them, things like this would never have gone on in my grand- mother's time, we had proper law and order then didn't we, not let any Tom, Dick and Kraut into the country, if it was up to me I'd gas the lot of them I would, put them in camps and gas them or chuck them in the sea.'

'Jews?' Wolf said, interested despite himself.

'Germans,' the woman said, and gave him a nasty, beaming toothless grin.

'Disgusting old witch.'

'Witch! Did you hear what he called me!' the woman shouted. Heads turned, then turned away. No one wanted to be too close to that smell. 'Witch! You people make me sick, you do! That Mosley fellow has the right idea, you just wait, coming over here, taking our jobs, pissing everywhere, bums! Bums!' and off she went again, in a repeating cycle, while Wolf stared out of the window and breathed through his mouth and tried to ignore her.

Was that what Mosley was doing? he thought, uneasy. Mosley was right. He could not shift blame to the Jews in England, not easily. But was he really cultivating European immigrants as a whole to take the brunt of the British's hatred? There were Jews amongst the refugees from the Fall of Germany, but there were also honest, respectable men and women, good Germans!

He was relieved to escape the bus at last, when it stopped outside Liverpool Street Station. The fresh air revived him, and it was raining in a thin drizzle that stung his face but brought with it relief for his bruises, if not for the fire in his groin where the bastard Jew had circumcised him. He went past bagel shops and pickle vats taller than a man, past black-clad children playing with stones and chalk, and yeshiva boys congregating in murmured conversations, past women with their shopping bags laden with food, apron-clad butchers with naked turkey birds displayed in their windows, fish-mongers calling out in Polish and Yiddish, shoemakers and cloth merchants and fences and thieves, and amidst this population of Jewish Londoners the new arrivals, gentiles like Wolf, the refugees of Germany and Austria and of a once-bright dream that had burned to cinder and ashes. He made his way through the narrow crammed streets and pulled his hat low against his forehead.

He'd first met Jews in large numbers while living in Vienna. In his first few, heady weeks in the city he hardly noticed them. The Jews were a minority, after all, and at the time Vienna was, to the young Wolf, the very centre of the world. There amidst the politicians and artists, rabble-rousers and architects and opera-goers and poor young students not unlike himself, Wolf barely cared about Jews. One day walking down the street he saw one of their number in the black Hasidic garb and he was plain bemused: was this a Jew?

And yet the longer he resided in that city the more he saw them; wherever he turned, like an alien entity forever embedded in the Germanic population; and more than that he thought them dirty; their very odour made him sick.

Besides all of which, the Jews were everywhere; manipulating all behind the scenes; and no doubt they were the reason he had been rejected from the Academy of Fine Arts, to boot – was it a wonder that he hated them?

He had begun to perceive the great conspiracy behind all things; perhaps even then, so early, he knew it was his destiny to fight it; and yet in the final tally, he had lost. The Fall had made a mockery of Wolf. Imagine only if he had succeeded; if Germany was his, its military and its citizens, to wield as he saw fit: what would have happened to the Jewish people then?

But Wolf had given up what-ifs long ago. And so he made his way amongst the throng of Jews in this alien city, the way he had once walked through the Jewish ghettos of Vienna; and the same hostile alien faces stared back at him. He came to a fish-monger and stopped and said, 'I am looking for a man named Barbie.'

The man pursed his lips and shook his head and Wolf moved on. He came to Petticoat Lane where all the Jewish cloth merchants congregated at one end. It tapered slowly towards vegetables and fruit, fish, crockery and badly made toys, and various and sundry merchandise which had happened to fall off the back of carts only to wind up here.

'Barbie. I am looking for Barbie.'

More heads shaking, lips pursing, Jews cursing: the name resonated but no one wanted to talk. He was almost on the Whitechapel Road where the market became more unruly and the wares more decrepit and less legitimate and for a moment he stopped and admired a gold watch.

'Palestine for the Jews!' The man was wild-haired and wild-eyed, swarthy and thin, and he was holding an armful of pamphlets and offering them like a priest offering the flesh and blood of Christ. 'Palestine for the Jews, comrade! Take one!'

Without having time to reply the man shoved a grubby pamphlet into Wolf's hands and moved on. 'Respect the Balfour Declaration! A homeland for the Jews!'

Wolf stared after him thoughtfully, his eyes cold. He looked at the pamphlet. The cover showed healthy-looking men and women, the men in khaki work clothes, the women in white dresses, against the background of a clear blue sea and distant mountains. Orange trees grew around them and a group of laughing, happy children stood in a circle, holding hands. Some sort of electric train, brightly coloured, vanished into the distance and high overhead, above the blue-chalked mountains in the distance, there hovered a bad artist's impression of an airship. *The Old-New Land*, the cover said, *by Theodor Herzl.*

Wolf crumpled the pamphlet into a ball and dropped it on the ground.

'You a Jew?'

Wolf turned again. The gold watch he had been admiring lay on a none-too-clean blanket on which sat various items pilfered who knew where. There were watches and rings, bracelets and necklaces, silver- and gold- and pearl-handled letter-openers and their like. The man was squatting behind his wares, on the ground. The look he gave Wolf was neither hostile nor friendly; it just was.

'Do I look like a fucking Jew,' Wolf said.

'Can't say as I could tell, mate.'

The man was speaking German. He spat on the ground. 'Jews,' he said. 'Don't mind them, myself. Sure got a lot of them around, though.'

Wolf nodded.

'Live and let live,' the man said. 'I come from Dortmund, myself. Got in trouble with the commies, had to make a run for it, didn't I.'

'Political?'

'Nah. Got caught with some things what didn't belong to me. You?'

Wolf shrugged, vaguely. 'You know how it is.'

The man nodded. 'Times are hard for everyone,' he said. 'You want to buy that watch?'

'I'm looking for a man. Name of Barbie?'

'Oh, you mean Santa Claus?' the man said.

'Excuse me?'

The man grinned, a little sheepishly. 'It's what they call him, around here, the English. The Jews don't like him much.'

Understanding dawned. 'His name is Klaus?'

'*Ja*, Klaus. You can find him down that end.' He gestured towards where the market met the Whitechapel Road. Kept his voice low. 'Deals in this and that, if you know what I mean.'

Wolf threw the man a shilling. The man caught it deftly and made it disappear. 'Cocky looking devil, if you know what I mean,' the man said. 'You can find him in the bicycle shop down there. Can't miss it.'

'Thanks.'

'Go in peace, my friend. By the way—' the man jerked his head sideways, 'did you know you're being followed?'

Wolf didn't turn to look. 'How many?' he said.

'Two.'

Wolf nodded. 'Black suits?'

'Sure. Friends of yours?'

Wolf shrugged. 'Who isn't,' he said. The man smiled back but he didn't look convinced. Wolf walked on.

The bicycle shop was indeed there. The window was dark and dusty and the bikes seemed to have been sitting there for at least twenty years. A faded poster on the wall showed a young black boy riding a bike while being chased by a lion. *Raleigh: The All-Steel Bicycle*, the poster proclaimed. Wolf pushed the door open and went inside. It was dark and dusty and smelled of aniseed. There was a wireless on the counter, tuned to Radio Luxembourg, playing the *Horlicks Tea Time Hour*, which changed into a spirited advert for Brown and Polson's custard powder as the door clanged shut.

'Waiting for the racing news, see.' Two men stood in the gloomy interior leaning against the counter. One was tall; one was short.

Both had pencil stubs behind their ears. Both turned as Wolf came in. They regarded him with puzzled curiosity. 'Who's your money on?' the tall one said.

Wolf said, 'Me.'

The tall one laughed, dutifully. The short one scowled. 'Everyone's a clown,' he said.

'Maybe he's a copper.'

The short one scratched his head. 'You a copper?' he said.

'No.'

'Didn't think so, mate. Didn't think so.'

'Well what does he want?'

'Yeah, what do you want?'

'Is this a betting shop?' Wolf said.

'Is this a betting shop, he says,' complained the tall one. 'Well, what does this look like to you, friend?'

'Maybe he's in the wrong place,' said the short one. 'Are you in the wrong place, mate?'

'I'm always in the wrong place,' Wolf said.

'He's a smartarse isn't he,' the tall one said.

'German, isn't he.'

'Austrian,' Wolf said, stiffly.

The tall one waved a hand vaguely. 'All the same,' he said. On the radio a woman was trying to convince them of the benefits of Lifebuoy Soap – *More than a Good Soap, it's a Good Habit!*

'I only got bad habits, me,' the short one said. 'So what do you want, kraut?'

'I'm looking for a man called Barbie. Klaus Barbie.'

'Oh, *him*.'

'Santa Claus, eh?'

'You know him?'

'Sure we know him. But does he know you?'

Wolf saw a shadow move on the other side of the counter. And he was ready when the short man pulled out a nasty looking shiv and made a lunge at Wolf. Wolf grabbed his hand and twisted, breaking the small bones of the fingers with vicious pleasure. The man screamed. The knife clattered to the floor.

Wolf kneed him between the legs and kicked him when he was down. He felt much better now. The tall man watched them mournfully. 'Everyone's a clown,' he said. 'Come on.' He knelt and tugged at his friend, who cried with a soft whistling sound. Wolf came round and helped him drag the man outside. At the door he stood and watched them both, the tall one and the short. The tall one pulled out a note from his pocket. 'Put a tenner on Bogskar for us, will you?' he said.

Wolf took the money and they walked off, the one tall, the other limping and hunched. On the corner of Petticoat Lane and Whitechapel, Wolf saw a man in a black suit he thought he recognised. The man raised his hand and smiled in apparent greeting. He had very even, white teeth; like an American's. Wolf went back inside and shut the door.

'You Barbie?'

The man was good-looking with sharp Aryan features and a cruel sensuous mouth. He leaned on the counter. His sleeves were rolled up. He said, 'You're not good for business.'

'You know who I am?'

'I know who you were.'

Wolf had to hand it to him: the man was cool. He said, 'I hear you can get things.'

'What sort of things.'

'Girls,' Wolf said. Barbie shrugged. 'Sure,' he said. 'Plenty of girls all about.'

'Young girls.'

Barbie looked at Wolf. His eyes were clear and he didn't blink much. 'Never had you pegged for one of those.'

'What did you have me pegged for?'

Barbie shrugged. 'What do I know,' he said.

'Sell many bicycles?'

That made him smile. 'Sometimes,' he said. 'You'd be surprised.'

'Who owns the betting book?'

'A man.'

'Has he got a name?'

'Sure,' Barbie said. 'Everybody's gotta name.'

'Do I know his name?'

'If you did, you wouldn't be asking, now, would you?'

Wolf didn't like the man's attitude. 'So what can you get me?'

'It depends. You got money?'

Wolf took out a roll of notes. 'I don't suppose you'd take a cheque.'

Again the man smiled. 'I don't suppose you're wrong, at that,' he said.

'I'm looking for a Jewish girl.'

'Jews,' Barbie said. 'The world's got too many damn Jews in it.'

'And Jewish girls?'

'Sure. Girls, boys . . . whatever you like.'

'This one would have been out of Germany a few weeks ago,' Wolf said. 'Family paid to have her delivered safely. She never made it.'

'All families pay,' Barbie said, and shrugged. 'Who cares if a Jew goes missing.'

'I care.'

'You want to fuck her? I can get you a Jew girl to fuck six ways from Sunday.'

'I want this girl.' Wolf took out the photograph Isabella had given him. Laid it flat on the countertop. 'Know her?'

Barbie was still looking at Wolf. 'Don't seem familiar,' he said.

'You're not looking.'

'I've seen all I need to see.'

'Look at her,' Wolf said. The man was staring at him. 'I said, *look at her.*'

Barbie looked down. Wolf grabbed Barbie's head and slammed it against the countertop. There was the *crunch* of breaking bone. Wolf lifted Barbie's head and slammed it down again, and again, until the man's face was a mess of blood and snot and the photo of the girl was unrecognisable with blood. At last Wolf released him and Barbie slid slowly down to the floor. Wolf went and opened the hatch in the counter and passed to the other side. He pulled up a chair and sat down.

'You're just a fucking follower,' he said, though Barbie couldn't hear him. Wolf looked through the man's clothes. He found a set of keys and a little black book. He opened the book. It was full of lists, numbers in an ascending serial order and amounts next to each one. 'You supply them,' Wolf said. 'Clubs like the one on Leather Lane, or men who come to you wanting something special, little girls, little boys. But you're still only a middleman. You're a nobody.' He straightened up and then kicked Barbie hard in the ribs. There was something thoroughly satisfying about the sound of breaking bones. Barbie didn't make a sound. Wolf rather expected that he would choke on the blood. Eventually. He kicked him in the head just for good measure and then went to the back of the store. There was a safe and one of the keys opened it. Inside was a fat brown envelope. Wolf took it out and put it in his coat pocket and closed and locked the safe again. There was a door and it too was locked. He tried the keys until one worked. He opened the door and saw steps leading down to a basement. He had a sense of déjà vu. He switched the light on and went downstairs.

There were no cells this time, no mattresses, nothing of the luxury afforded the slaves at the club. There, consideration was made for the clients. Here it was just the holding pens.

It must have been a warehouse, once. The door was securely locked but there was a grille and he could look through it. Inside the large room there were some sixty to a hundred women. They wore nothing but undergarments. They were crammed into the space. The place smelled: of unwashed bodies and piss and shit. The women stared up at him with eyes as dull as cattle. The light was dim inside. He saw that they had been tattooed, a blue number, a serial corresponding, he assumed, to the numbers in Barbie's little black book.

'Hey, you,' he said. Some of them turned to look at him. 'I am looking for Judith Rubinstein. Is there a Judith Rubinstein here?'

A slim black-haired girl roused herself from a pallet. 'I'm

Judith,' she said. She approached him cautiously, like a wounded animal. Wolf squinted at her. Could it be that easy? He tried to compare her to the photograph. The girl in the photograph had been healthy, happy. This one was just a number. He didn't know.

'Come closer,' he said. 'Let me take a look at you.'

The girl shook her head, this way and that. She looked unsure of where she was, now that she had spoken.

A blonde girl stood up. 'I'm Judith,' she said.

'I'm Judith—' from an old grandmother.

'Take me, mister, I'll be your Judith!'

'Does she fuck you like I would? Does she take it in the ass?'

One of them was yelling curses in Yiddish. Another tried to shush her, fearfully. Wolf rapped on the bars. Immediately all the girls fell silent.

'You,' he said, pointing at the first one. 'Come here.'

'I didn't do nothing, mister.'

'Come here.'

The girl was shaking. 'Don't make me, don't make me,' she said.

'I said come here!'

The other girls were pushing her. 'You have to go, otherwise he will come back—' Wolf assumed they were talking about Barbie. He could imagine how Barbie liked to amuse himself, when business upstairs was quiet. He said, 'I won't hurt you. I just want to ask you a question.'

The girl stumbled forward, pushed from behind. Her face was pressed to the bars of her prison. Her hair was dirty and lank, Wolf saw, her face pale and drawn. She had a dark bruise under one eye. He said, 'Did you know Judith Rubinstein?'

'She's not here, mister. Honest.'

'Do you know where she is?'

The girl lowered her voice. 'If you let me out, my father is a rich man, he could pay you, whatever you asked. Just let me go.'

'Who is your father?'

The girl said a name. Wolf shrugged. The affairs of Jews did not interest him. 'Tell me about Judith.'

'We went to school together in Berlin.'

'Before the Fall?'

'Before, during.' The girl shrugged. 'Her daddy wanted to leave. So did my daddy but he couldn't get us out. And the Party confiscated everything he had. We were poor.'

At least she was being honest now, Wolf thought. 'And Judith?'

'She wouldn't leave. She wanted to be a revolutionary.' The girl laughed. It was a terrible sound, in that room. 'The stupid cow,' she said.

'But you were still friends.'

'Sure. And she still had money. Her daddy kept her safe. He had contacts, people high up. I joined the Party too. We all did. We had to, after the Fall. I remember once our Youth Group was sent to Unter den Linden, some squat hellhole in a crumbling old building that used to be a nice hotel. It was full of Brownshirts, you know, ex-Nazi boys. They'd formed into gangs after the Fall, ran wild, robbed and killed to stay alive. We went to school with some of them.' There was a bitter sort of wonder in the girl's voice. 'They had a man on watch but he was only one and the rest of them were asleep. Judith was scout. She went up to the watchman as quiet as a *fledermaus*. He never saw a thing. Didn't even see her when she pulled out her knife and cut his throat. We went inside then and killed them. Every single one of them boys lying there asleep. We shot them, just went through twenty, thirty boys it must have been, a bullet in the head, in the chest, some of them woke up and tried to flee but how do you outrun a bullet?' She stared at Wolf through the bars and her eyes – he didn't want to look into her eyes. 'Yes, Judith was dedicated,' she said. 'The rest of us just went along with it but she did it for herself. I never wanted to kill nobody.'

Wolf was aware of the pressure of time, but it was so quiet down there, and all the girls were silent, listening. Perhaps they all had the same story. 'What happened to Judith?' Wolf said.

'She fell in love.' The girl laughed again. This time her laughter rose and threatened to escalate out of control. Wolf tapped the bars again and she stopped, as abruptly as she'd started. 'She fell in love with a nice Jewish boy.'

'A Zionist?'

'I don't even think that he was, that's the funny thing. He was a good comrade, even. Worked at the Ministry of Public Enlightenment.'

'So what happened?'

The girl shrugged. 'He got shot. Everyone said it was Brownshirts who did it, but how many were left by then? Judith was convinced it was an execution. Someone at the Ministry, or a different branch of the Party. She said that even the communists hated Jews. She started talking about Palestine, as if anyone would ever want to go to Palestine. I heard there's nothing there but camels and desert. I wouldn't want to go there. I wanted to go to America. I wanted to be a movie star.'

All the girls were quiet. Wolf waited. The girl said, 'She got her daddy to pay a smuggler to take her out of the country. She told me and I begged her to let me come. She couldn't get the money from her daddy, he said he wasn't a charity. But she took me anyway. Everyone knows the smugglers are Brownshirts, what's left of them. Ex-Nazis. The organisation is still there, only instead of killing people for politics they do it for money. On the border the man who took us made me go on my knees and he put his cock in my mouth. Judith was asleep in the next room, she didn't even know. He said I'd have to work off the debt. When we crossed the border they took all of our papers and drove us in a closed truck with a lot of other people. I thought we would die; we had no air. We drove for hours and hours. Then we were on a boat. We only stopped once, when we came off the boat. I remember smelling the ocean. I think we were in England by then but I can't be sure. A man came and we all got out and lined up in rows and he went and checked each of us against a list. Some of us went away. Some of us went back in the truck. I went in the truck. Judith went away. The truck drove for another long time and then we came here.'

'You don't know where she went?'

'She went to her daddy.'

'I don't think she did.'

'Then I'm sure I don't know.'

Wolf stared at the girl. The case was becoming bewildering – if Judith had been paid for and delivered, then where was she? And if she had been added to the tally of the lost, then why wasn't she here? Had she already been resold? He said, 'That will be all.'

'Don't you want to know my name? My name!' She was close to tears. 'This is my number,' she said. She raised her arm. He could see a number tattooed on her wrist. 'They did that here. He did that here. Do you want to know my name?'

'No,' Wolf said. 'But you can have the God damned keys.'

He tossed them to her, through the bars, and turned away. There was silence behind him. He climbed up the stairs again and stood looking down at the girls' jailer. The man groaned and tried to crawl away. Wolf smiled. He didn't care what happened to the girls but he liked the thought of them coming up the stairs and finding themselves face to face with Klaus Barbie. What was left of his face, anyway.

'Have fun, sweetheart,' he said. He went back through the hatch and closed it neatly behind him and then he left the shop and closed the door softly, so as not to disturb the neighbours.

Wolf's Diary, 7th November 1939 – *contd.*

When I stepped outside the air was cold and the sun was gone. Barbie was a lapdog, a man of no consequence. I left him the way I had as a message to his unseen employer. I rather thought that would get his attention. Somebody ruthless and meticulously organised was behind the trafficking ring, someone I could not help but feel a touch of admiration for. I admired efficiency. And I wondered which of my old comrades it could be.

I began to walk down Whitechapel Road. Soon I had the

feeling of being followed again. I stopped. It seemed to me two shadows moved in the distance but it was hard to tell with the bad illumination of the streetlights. I had had enough of shadows, then. My anger and hatred were all the illumination I needed. I faced up to the dark, defiantly. I raised my arms, daring them to come. 'I'm here!' I screamed. 'Come and get it if you think you're tough enough!'

The darkness did not reply and after a moment I dropped my arms and continued walking, feeling deflated. They were out there, nearby, and they were watching, but that was all. Well, let them watch.

I was walking aimlessly. The brown envelope I had taken from Barbie's safe was heavy in my coat pocket. When I came to London Wall I stood there for a moment admiring the ancient Roman architecture. Had I still been painting I would have wanted an easel and brush at that moment. The dying light cast a gloom over the ancient stones and I thought of all that had come before, and of the Greek and Roman emperors I had so admired. Sometimes it occurred to me I had been born into the wrong era. I was Alexander, without a world to conquer.

I was sunk in melancholy thought. Architecture affects me that way. Too late I heard the soft purr of a car behind me. I turned. It was a black Mercedes-Benz without headlights. It was a marvel of German engineering.

Behind the car came dark shadows: my two men in black.

They came and stood before me. I recognised one as the man from the Charing Cross Road, the one who had claimed to be an American tourist.

'Mr Wolf.'

'Do I know you,' I said.

The American smiled, a little embarrassed, with those even white teeth. 'We ran into each other the other day.'

'That's right,' I said. 'Were you trying to make sure that I saw you, or were you just being sloppy?'

'He was being sloppy. He's since been disciplined.'

The voice that spoke was older, graver. I turned. A rear
window had been rolled down. For a moment a stray beam of
light caught the speaker's face. He had a well-maintained
beard, black woven with a tapestry of white and silver. His
eyes were clear and strangely innocent, like a child's. He had
a hook nose and a scar under one eye that trailed down like a
long tear and finally disappeared under his beard.

'Who the hell are you?' I said.

'You can call me Virgil,' he said.

'Like the poet?'

'If you like.'

'I don't think that I do.'

'Mr Wolf, I mean you no harm.'

'Then why are you following me?'

'Because I have a great interest in the well-being of
Germany, Mr Wolf. Please. Let me give you a ride.'

'I'd rather walk.'

The two men took a step forward each. I stood my ground.

'Who do you work for?' I said.

Virgil said, 'The President of the United States of America,'
and I laughed. 'America is a racial cesspit,' I said. 'It is a land
fit only for dogs and Jews.'

One of the men in black made to move towards me then
but his companion grabbed him by the arm. 'Stand back, Pitt.'

I glanced again at the man in the car, this Virgil. 'I can
smell spooks a mile off,' I said. 'You give off a special smell,
the stench of rats.'

He laughed. He had a rich, deep laugh, the sort a man
makes when he thinks how easy it would be to kill you. 'Get in
the car, Wolf.' He moved down the seat, his face disappearing
from view. 'Pitt, open the door for Mr Wolf.'

'Sir, yes, sir.'

The one called Pitt went and opened the door like a
servant. There was resentment in his eyes. I went up to the
car. I put my hand on Pitt's shoulder, gently. My other hand
reached down and grabbed his balls and squeezed. 'Next time

I see you, sunshine,' I said, 'it won't be just your balls you'd need to worry about.'

His companion laughed and made no move to help him. I released Pitt and watched him sink to the ground, his hands covering his testicles. There were tears in his eyes but he never made a sound. It made me feel I may have been wrong about him.

I got into the car. Waited with the door open until the second man came over and closed it. I smiled at him through the rolled-down window. 'Look after your girlfriend for me,' I said.

'Let's go,' Virgil said, beside me. The driver in the front of the car was a shadow in a black peaked cap. He pressed on the accelerator and the car pushed forward as soft as a thief in the night. He was a big man, Virgil, spread out against the seat. He looked like an old tomcat, one who was brought up in the streets and took his punches, but seldom lost a fight.

'Mr Wolf.'

'Virgil.'

He smiled. We were heading south. I could smell the river. The old Roman wall was left behind. The Tower of London lay ahead, with its lame ravens. They reminded me of the soldiers who had returned home broken from the Great War.

'I'd like your opinion of the current situation in Austro-Germany,' Virgil said.

I looked out of the window. 'And what is the American interest in the region?' I said, politely.

'Do you always answer a question with a question?' he laughed. 'You answer questions like a Jew,' he said.

'Are you trying to insult me?'

'Just making conversation.'

'You didn't answer my question,' I said.

He sighed. 'Mr Wolf,' he said. 'My government is *acutely* concerned over the rise of communism in Germany and its neighbours. The German government may pretend it is

independent, but you and I both know the decisions come
from Moscow.'

'Yes.'

'What is your take on it?'

'I believe war is coming,' I said. He was silent beside me. I
knew that I had his attention, then. 'I believe Russia is building
up to drastically alter the map of Europe, and beyond. Its
neighbours are already under threat. The purpose of communism is nothing less than world domination. A global revolution.
They will not sit on their laurels having won the German election. Once communism takes hold it never relinquishes power.'

'A world war,' Virgil said.

'Yes.'

'That is something my government is acutely concerned
about.'

'So you said.'

'How would one go about . . . *counteracting* the communists
in Germany?' he said.

I turned and looked at him. That coarse face, his hands
folded in his lap. He had enormous hands. 'Who, *exactly*, do
you work for?' I said, softly.

He chuckled, not in the least put out. 'Just a group of
concerned citizens,' he said.

'Intelligence? Sig Int? MI-8? The Treasury Department?'

He chuckled again. 'Your sources are outdated,' he said.
'Let us say concern over a possible second war with
Germany has suggested to us some form of consolidation
of departments was in order. I work for the Office of
Strategic Services. The OSS. Our main concern lies in the
former German Republic. A second war in Europe could
be disastrous for all concerned. But we cannot allow
international Bolshevism to raise its ugly head! No, sir!' His
enormous fist punched his enormous palm. 'Mr Wolf,' he
said, turning his head and looking into my eyes, 'how
would you like to work for *us*?'

We were driving along the river, now. I saw the Tower

sinking behind us, and I wondered where we were going. East along the river, east to – where? The docks?

'Am I being kidnapped?'

'Mr. Wolf! Please! We are not *communists*.'

'Then where are we going?'

'I wish to show you something,' he said. 'You are free to leave at any moment. Just say the word.'

'Then stop the car.'

'Bernie, stop the car.'

The car slowed, then stopped. We were somewhere past Tower Bridge. It was dark and quiet. 'Bernie, open Mr Wolf's door, please.'

The driver, still only a featureless shadow, slid out of his seat and came round the car and held the door open for me. The cool air rushed inside and I could hear the cry of seagulls in the distance.

'Well, Mr Wolf?'

I stared out at the quiet street. Turned back and looked at Virgil. He smiled at me. His teeth were large and square like an ogre's.

I gave a tiny nod of assent.

'Start the car, Bernie,' Virgil said. 'We haven't got all night, now, have we.'

The driver shut my door softly and went back to his seat and started the car up again.

'Work for you,' I said, 'work for the United States of *America*?'

'It's the greatest country in the whole God damned world,' Virgil said, complacently.

* * *

In another time and place Shomer stands naked in the snow, clutching his bleeding leg. It was all Mischek's fault, Mischek the dirty little Russian Jew, the commissar of the latrines. He has an in with the Salonician Jews, those hardened gangsters of the camp: three years those bastards are inside and still alive, their blue tattooed numbers like badges of honour, the low numbers that shame all the others, the latecomers. But it wasn't the Greeks' fault, those black market traders in bread rations and spoons and gold teeth. It was Mischek's, or it was Shomer's own, who was digging in the hard ground, digging when he stumbled and fell and Mischek's spade came down and an ugly bleeding gash opened in Shomer's leg, and the overseer barked an order and work was halted, momentarily; and the others, he knew, were grateful for the respite: whether Shomer lived or died he had bought them a few moments' rest.

Shomer was clutching his wounded leg and biting his lip to keep from uttering curses and for a moment Yenkl's figure, always beside him, grew faded, like clouds or ash, as if he weren't there. And Shomer waited as the overseer studied him, assessing the severity of the wound, assessing this skeletal human shape with its loose skin and sunken eyes, receding hair, receding gums, sores on the feet and lice everywhere else. Assessing him to decide if he is worth conserving, or whether it is cheaper and easier to dispose of him now.

'Go to the infirmary,' the overseer said, at last.

So simple, those words! And yet Shomer gets to live another day. Now he stands naked in the snow, for his old clothes are not allowed in the infirmary block, and only his feet are still crammed into the ill-fitting wooden clogs, until the very last moment he keeps them on, and the queue moves, so slowly, one by one they disappear into the lighted door. He shivers and holds his wound, triumphant. The infirmary! It is like Heaven, spoken of in hushed voices, a place of rest and heavenly comfort, like reclining on clouds. And Yenkl is beside him, how has he ever doubted his friend, Yenkl, who says, 'You call this a wound? When I was a kid, we had *wounds*.' And Yenkl is in full flight and the queue shuffles slowly and the snow starts to fall and Shomer hugs his bony naked arms around his hollow chest and shudders and so Yenkl tells him a joke.

'This one time in Poland,' Yenkl says, 'the people of the shtetl discovered that a Christian girl had been found murdered nearby. Murdered, Shomer! How afraid they were. Oh what will we *do*? they said. Oh what will the goyishe Poles *think*? Surely soon they will come for our blood, oy but we are doomed, surely a pogrom is coming and we will all die!'

Shomer nods and shuffles forward, staring at the square of light, the pearly gates into the infirmary of Heaven.

'The Jews,' says Yenkl, 'have gathered as is their wont in the shtetl's main synagogue, with much wringing of hands and gnashing of teeth. "What shall we do? What shall we do?" Suddenly, the president of the synagogue bursts in through the doors. "I have wonderful news!" he cries. All talk ceases. All eyes turn on him.

"The murdered girl, she's *Jewish*!" the president says.'

Shomer laughs, dutifully. He shuffles forward and at last enters the hut, leaving his clogs behind, standing there as naked as the day God had made him, though far less fat, it must be said. Inside the queue continues, to see the doctor, but it is also warmer, and there is only one bored Polish guard, and so Shomer's mind wanders yet again, and it is drawn inexorably to murder most foul, that hoary old staple of the pulps and of *shund*.

7

The watcher in the dark watched; only watched. He had seen the detective leave his building for the first time in days but he elected not to follow him. The detective wasn't going anywhere. The watcher eyed the girls and it was as if his cloak of invisibility was somewhat worn for he thought they seemed more nervous now, more brightly brittle, casting their eyes into the shadows as though searching for the mystery man there. But still they could not see him; no one ever could. He eyed the half-caste, Dominique. Those long brown legs bare in the cold, that saucy smile, the eyes that promised much, the muscled arms . . . . she was not like the other girls, she was more dominant somehow, and the men who came for her were different, more affluent and when she went with them she took a small bag of her accessories and, once, the bag had opened and the watcher saw the contents inside, though he could barely comprehend their meaning, a coiled whip and a black thick object, long and rubbery, which the watcher thought must be a *godemiche*, that is to say, a dildo. And there were other things there, but he had caught only a fleeting glimpse and then she had shut the case and climbed into the john's car; and was gone. But the memory of it kept the watcher awake at night and when he slept he dreamed of a woman perfumed like a whore who lashed him with a whip, lashed him until he shuddered and came.

In the mornings before going to work he made his father breakfast and hung the bib round the old man's neck and fed him, and listened to the old man tell him stories of the War. The old man listened to the wireless for hours, and cursed Mosley for a weakling and a fool, and spoke of the bravery of the German soldiers he had had to fight in the Great War. After the watcher cleaned up he left the old man listening to the BBC and went to work, which was soothing to him and involved paperwork. It was only when his work was done for the day and darkness descended, and before he had to return to make supper and help the old man wash, that he went to visit the whores, and dream, and plan; and the knife was in his pocket always, and whispering to him, curses and promises, and the watcher knew that he had promises to keep.

★   ★   ★

'National Socialism,' Virgil said, 'is a pile of steaming bullshit on the roadside of history, friend.'

Wolf said: 'I beg your pardon?' The car, German made and German engineered, drove smoothly along the poor English road. On their right the Thames expanded as it flowed onwards to the distant sea.

Virgil laughed. 'Don't get me wrong,' he said. 'It was a great con. A *great* con. *Deutschland über alles*! Eh, Wolf? Promise them the world and blame all their ills on the Jews. That's like blaming it on the weather. Do you know, I was stationed in Berlin in the twenties. Naval intelligence liaison.' He patted his stomach. 'I was slimmer then. Berlin! It was full of whores. The clubs, the jazz, the girls – they called it the filthiest city on Earth and I can't say that they were wrong. Killed a man for the first time in Unter den Linden. Got laid every other day. It was good to be young in Berlin.'

'I don't think you were ever young,' Wolf said. Virgil laughed again. He laughed easily and, Wolf thought, with no more sincerity than a whore. 'OSS,' Wolf said, as though tasting the letters, the shape of them in his mouth. The idea of the Americans involving themselves in the affairs of Germany again was abhorrent to him. It was American intervention in the Great War in 1917 that had finally ended the conflict.

And Wolf ended up blind, in a nerve hospital for those deemed deserters or insane . . .

'The communist threat *must* be contained,' Virgil said. 'America cannot easily afford another war, but we cannot and *will* not tolerate further Russian expansion.'

'So what do you want from me?'

Virgil half turned in his seat. His eyes were bright. His voice was soft. The car was approaching the docks of Limehouse. Here lights burned in secretive little pubs and wharf-side establishments, and furtive Chinamen walked the streets. 'You could go back to Germany,' Virgil said, his voice as slow and treacly as honey. 'You could lead again.'

'Lead?'

'Lead Germany. Resurrect National Socialism!'

'You're mad,' Wolf said.

'The remnants of the organisation are still there. The men retain their loyalty or, if not, are at the very least practical. Nazism has always attracted ruthless, practical men. Listen to me, Wolf. Listen to me!' He grasped Wolf's thigh in his meaty hand, crushing it, and Wolf winced: the American's fingers would leave their mark. 'You could do it. We'll parachute you back, in due course. We have agents in place. Working for us. When everything is ready you'll go in, you'll claim back what was rightfully yours!'

'A *putsch*,' Wolf said.

'An assisted regime change,' Virgil said.

'You can do that?'

'You bet your sweet ass we can! At least,' Virgil amended, with a feral grin, 'we can try.'

'Get your filthy hand off me, American.'

Virgil's squeeze grew even stronger. Then he abruptly released Wolf. The car turned a dark corner into a quayside alley lined with looming warehouses. 'Stop the car, Bernie.'

'Yes, sir.'

'Come, Wolf.' Virgil did not wait for his driver but opened the door himself and clambered out, as big and ungainly as a bear. Wolf remained seated, for just a moment staring ahead. Unseeing.

Could it be true?

It could not possibly be true. To even imagine such a thing was to open himself to the worst agony he had ever suffered.

The agony of defeat.

To offer him the impossible was not a gift but a hideous curse, and he did not trust Virgil, did not trust any American.

Wolf had never trusted anyone: it was why he was still alive.

Wolf thought but only fleetingly of the nerve hospital in Pasewalk and what had transpired there.

Six hundred miles by train from the front to the small hospital near the Polish border. Blind – he had been blinded! As a boy he feared the dark, in the darkness was the ogre reeking of drink, the ogre and his belt whistling through the air, as a boy he sometimes cried, but silently, sometimes like all boys he wet his bed. Then his mother would comfort him, hold him close, and he would breathe in the softness of her, the smell of fresh laundry and apfelstrudel, and all would be better once again.

And then she was gone, and Wolf was on a train, in absolute dark, and he was terrified. Remembering the attack, the whistle of mortar, the gas – the gas! Quick, boys, and fumbling with the straps of the mask, too late, and the light thick as green honey. His comrades fell beside him. 'My eyes! My eyes!' he screamed. The mud welcomed him and he rolled in it but still he could not see, and the pain burned and when they came and carried him away he was still like that, screaming and sobbing and blind, blind, and he thought he would be blind for ever.

He was stoic before the doctor, one Karl Kroner, a Jew.

Sometimes Wolf thought of his life as having two distinct phases: the one before his blindness and the one that came after. Before, he had been a boy, an artist, a soldier. After, there came a man.

He did not understand what the doctor said, whispering to the nurses, the sound of his pencil tap-tapping on the clipboard. 'Hysterical,' Wolf heard. 'Pasewalk,' he heard, and, 'Dr Forster.' Whoever he might be.

Then his orders, which he could not see, invalided out when all he wanted to do was continue fighting, and what did the doctor mean, *hysterical*?

And those long interminable hours on the slow train away

from the front and the groaning of the wheels and the murmur of soldiers and the taste of hot strong tea which he never drank but was given anyway, his shaking hands all but spilling the drink, and turning his head, this way and that, helplessly: where was the *window*?

In that slow procession of the train Wolf died and was reborn and died again. Could this really be the end of him? To be just another casualty of the war, another disabled soldier, blinded, lame: never to hold a brush and paint again, never to know the sun setting over a field, the colour of fire or blood, and to become – what? A beggar in the streets of Vienna or Berlin, coins rattling in a tin cup, Spare some change, spare some change for an ex-soldier?

He put his hand against the window, feeling the cold outside. He could not see; and yet could see so clearly.

The future lay ahead like a broken road. He would kill himself, he thought with sudden savagery. Put the gun in his mouth and pull the trigger, no time for thought, a quick ending denied him by the war. No more would he be Wolf, he would be nothing, dust as all men must become dust. And was that so terrible? Was that so wrong?

He must have dozed off, eventually. He was woken to the silence that follows the breaking of a train, the lull between stop and renewed motion. Outside, the other soldiers were gathering their kitbags, calling to each other, doors were opening and slamming, boots on snow, and Lance-Corporal Wolf roused himself to follow, into the cold and the unknown.

Although he did not know it, the future lay ahead for him still . . .

'Mr Wolf?'

Wolf roused himself. 'Yes, yes,' he said, almost spitting out the English word. That sibilant sound. He ran his tongue around his mouth. It tasted sour. He stepped out of the car. 'Yes, what is it?' he said testily.

'Come, Mr. Wolf,' Virgil said grandly. He nodded and, as if

responding to his command, the wharf was suddenly bathed in bright electric light. Wolf was momentarily blinded. He blinked back tears. When he opened his eyes again the wharf was transformed and he took a step back unwittingly.

The warship floating down the river was enormous. Its grey hull shone wet and above it rose an armoured citadel, topped by the rising conning tower, with gun-slits like malevolent eyes. It was a marvel of engineering, lying low in the water yet carrying enough firepower, Wolf saw at a glance, to lay waste to a small coastal town. Wolf was immediately in love.

'What *is* she?' he said, awed.

'She's an amphibious HST Destroyer,' Virgil said, with obvious pride. He was like a cowboy out of one of Karl May's Western novels, speaking of his prized cow.

'High Speed Transport?' Wolf said.

'Indeed, Mr Wolf. American born and bred, our USS *Valkyrie*.'

Wolf turned his head sharply, but Virgil seemed not to notice.

'The Chooser of the Slain . . .'

'Indeed, Mr Wolf. You have a knowledge of the classics.' Virgil barked an order and the doors of the warehouses opened as one, and Wolf saw men streaming out. They wore civvies but they were military men all the same, American soldiers in civilians' clothes. Beyond the open doors he saw the warehouses were in fact giant hangars. There were planes inside, crates of ammunition and arms, camouflage netting, an arsenal for a small and private war.

Wolf said, 'Does the British government . . . *know* of your presence here?'

Virgil waved his hand dismissively. 'We are not officially here, Mr Wolf.'

'And unofficially?'

Virgil shrugged. 'Everyone wants to see the Red Menace removed,' he said.

Wolf surveyed the dock, which only moments before had appeared abandoned. The warship floated serenely in the Thames. 'What if I say no?' Wolf said; he spoke low; the words were loath to depart his larynx.

Virgil seemed amused. 'You would refuse?' he said. 'We would make you great again, Mr Wolf. We would put men at your service, arms at your disposal. The offer of the might of the entire United States of America behind you, Mr Wolf, is not something to refuse lightly.'

Probabilities swam in Wolf's mind, futures diverging like roads in a yellow wood. His mouth felt dry. He nodded his head, slowly, uncertainly. 'No, it isn't,' he agreed.

'Good man!' Virgil clapped him on the back, as if all were decided, nearly sending Wolf sprawling. 'Come. Let me show you our little base.' He walked with great purpose, his giant hands swinging loosely by his side. He looked like a great ape then, and yet he walked as though he owned the very earth he stepped on. Wolf followed him with trepidation, and yet with wonder, too. Like a sleepwalker he was dragged in Virgil's wake through the bright unreal glare of floodlights high overhead, and when he moved his hand before his face it was as though bio-luminescence had clung to his skin and trailed a ghostly band of colour through the air. Inside the first warehouse he saw men with a military bearing and civilian clothes sitting tensely around a radio receiver; maps of Europe on the wall, dotted with coloured pins; unmarked heavy wooden crates piled in one corner; camou-flage nettings in another; an upturned rubber dinghy, a mechanic working patiently with a boat engine between his knees; more crates, one open, showing Wolf the armaments inside, guns oiled until they shone. Then through to the second warehouse where two Cessna light aircraft were sitting at rest, a group of men in overalls sitting playing cards on upturned empty crates. Then last to the water where the destroyer, *Valkyrie*, sat in all her glory, with her silent power, and the men climbing on board her like worshippers at temple, for all that they seemed as small as ants. And more warehouses, on the other side, filled with ammo and guns, tinned food, parachutes, rockets, grenades, bayonets and handguns, an Aladdin's Cave of lethal wonders, not to mention the explosives. Round and round in the empty space before the jetty Wolf turned and turned like a bride whose face was raised to the high sun, round and round he turned as though he'd been dancing.

'All laid at your service, Mr Wolf, and in the service of your country, your Fatherland, to be liberated, made whole, replenished and resplendent once again.'

As in a dream: 'And if I say no?'

'But you won't, Mr Wolf. Why would you?' A paternal chuckle, perhaps that is who Virgil reminded him of: his old man the ogre, dead and buried these many years. 'How could you refuse?'

And, still in that dreaming state: 'But think it over. And Bernie will drop you off wherever you like.'

★   ★   ★

Half-asleep in the infirmary, Shomer listens to the sounds of Jews gossiping.

'I heard he can't get it up.'

Laughter.

The same speaker: 'Not in the . . . usual way.'

'What does that mean.'

'*I* heard . . .' the man lowers his voice. '*I* heard he likes to be . . . whipped.'

A shocked indrawn breath. 'Whipped?'

'Spanked. Like a child.'

'Feh!'

'*I* heard he only has one ball.'

'One ball! Can you imagine such a thing?'

Shomer stirs. Around him there is temporary merriment. In the infirmary no one has to work, there is nothing to do, and nothing to wield but words.

And he thinks of *him*. And pictures him humiliated, gagged, dominated, abused.

'I heard he has a thing for young *shikses*. The blonde, zaftig ones. Good Aryan types.'

'What I wouldn't give to shtup one.'

Laughter.

'*I* heard he's fucking that film director.'
'Who, Fritz Lang?'
Laughter.
'No, Leni Riefenstahl.'
'Her? I heard they're thick as thieves.'
'I'd slip her the sausage!'
'What sausage? You mean your toothpick?'
'Screw you!'
'I thought she was good in *The Blue Light*,' someone says.
'She's a Nazi!'
'So *nu*? They're all Nazis.'

A lull. Shomer turns, blinks. Thinks of *him*, in bed: does he ever think of them, in the camp? Does he imagine what they feel, what they miss, how they die? Does he know them at all, beyond the numbers on their arms? And he pictures a book of accounts, filled with rows and rows of endless numbers, a book as large as a world.

'I heard he likes them to . . .'
'To what?'
'No, no.'
'What?'
'No, no . . .'
'Go on!'
'I heard he likes them to, to *piss* on him!'
'*Feh!*'
'Are you *meshuggeh*? Who does such a thing?'
'A wilde *chaye*, a wild beast!'
'I have a bucket here for him, a bucket of piss!'
Laughter.

Then silence, as each man withdraws into his own private cell of the mind. Shomer tosses and turns, restless. From below: 'And what do *you* think, *luftmensch*?'

Shomer almost smiles. It's what they'd taken to calling him: a dreamer, a man with his head in the clouds.

'What I think, boychiks?' he says. He pauses to consider. Says, 'I think what I think doesn't mean a God damn.'

'Putz!'

'After the war I'm only going to buy German-made pens,' someone says. Waits expectantly.

'Why?'

'The ink won't come off!'

Groans all around, then a silence.

'May he die a thousand deaths,' someone says, but quietly.

Wolf's Diary, 7th November 1939 – *contd.*

It was a glorious dream. 'Bernie will take you wherever you want,' Virgil had said. The car moved soft and smooth like a young woman; the whole city glittered that night, its lights burned clean and clear; the very air was warm, enchanted. To be old and in love with an impossible dream is the bitterest thing.

'Where to, sir?'

'Just drive.'

As the docks receded behind us, the dream lost tangibility, the air became colder and thinner, and I felt as though I were waking up.

A dream. It was just a dream.

And I was cursed with greatness, or had been once. I knew when I was being sold a falsehood. Shit wrapped in roses smells no less like shit.

Oh, I had no doubt this man who called himself Virgil was, in his own mercenary way, sincere. And for a moment I had let myself be dazzled by the promise: the grand warship, the airplanes, the guns, the men. For a moment longer I was seduced by the American dream.

Then reality set in.

One ship, two rickety airplanes and a handful of men with guns.

Did Virgil propose to take over Germany with *that*? It would have been laughable if it weren't so heartbreakingly sad. Once I had held all of Germany in the palm of my hand. I had men beyond count, the army on my side. What

Virgil was offering me was a group of mercenaries who
would not get farther than a Hamburg suburb before they
were slaughtered and fed to the local farmers' pigs. What was
I saying – that bunch of American cowboys wouldn't have
made it as far as fucking *Glückstadt*.

'God damn you!' I said, with feeling. '*Scheisse!*'

'Excuse me, sir?'

'Just drive!'

He must have been told to humour me, for he obliged
without a murmur.

Which led me back to my first question, the one I had
asked Virgil, and then again: the one he would not answer.

What if I turned down his offer?

Virgil wanted a regime change in Germany. What he
needed was a symbol, a figurehead to reunite the remnants of
Nazism into a resistance force.

I knew better. The communists had put what was left of the
Party in prisons and camps, and brutally oppressed any and all
dissent. National Socialism was done, finished, its practitioners
dead or scattered. My old comrades who had managed to
escape were now homeless émigrés, and small-time gangsters in
all but name . . .

But the Americans were mad enough to try. Maybe. Not
too mad as to provide more than a handful of mercenaries,
though. Working without official sanction, maintaining
deniability.

If not me, I thought: then *who*?

And somehow answering that was important: more
important than I could say.

Who could replace *me*?

Göring was a good comrade, now. He was fat but he was
smart: he would sell his own mother if it benefited him and
he would have sold the Yanks down the river without a blink.
But Göring had gone over to the communists, was no doubt
flourishing in the new Germany.

So Göring was out.

Hess? But Hess was in London and comfortable with his émigré club and his principles lost. Hess could have been second only to me, but he had always been weaker, softer: and he corrupted.

Not Hess.

Then who? Goebbels? Himmler?

Whereabouts unknown.

Streicher? Dead.

Bormann? He had been Hess's deputy but I could not underestimate him. He liked to work behind the scenes.

Last seen in a communist concentration camp, though.

Alfred Rosenberg? My ideologue, a man who knew his higher and lower races, and his conversation on the World Ice Theory, the *Welteislehre*, has always been fascinating and erudite.

Dead by firing squad, though.

Albert Speer? A gifted architect. Escaped to South America, or so I had last heard.

Reinhard Heydrich? Wonderful musician, fine Olympic-class fencer, a dedicated Jew-hater. Ruthless. He would be a good choice. I did not know what had happened to him after the Fall. Suspected he survived. He was the sort to survive.

But that same list of – and what were they, suddenly? Suspects? That same list could lead me to the man behind the white slavery ring. The man who controlled Hess, the one who was perhaps behind Judith Rubinstein's disappearance, too. One of my former comrades, my associates, my . . .

The men who had once served under my absolute command.

'Sir? Charing Cross Station, sir.'

'Did I ask you?'

'No, sir.'

'Then shut the fuck up, Bernie.'

'Yes, sir.'

'Drive up Charing Cross Road.'

'Yes, sir.'

'I want to buy a book.'

'Yes, sir.'

I made the young American drop me off outside
Marks & Co.

'Goodnight, sir.'

'You take care of that car, young man. That's German
engineering you're handling, not one of your Buicks or
Fords.'

'You a fan of automobiles, sir?'

'I admire workmanship.'

'You should come visit us, sir. In the States, I mean, sir. I
think you will like the cars.'

I felt old just talking to him.

'Where are you from, soldier?'

'Los Angeles, sir. It's a beautiful country. All the sun and
sea in the world.'

'And the movies, eh?' I said.

'Sir?'

'Have you heard of Leni Riefenstahl?'

'Who?'

'A great actress and a personal friend of mine,' I said.

'I'm sorry, sir. We don't get much German cinema back
home. You know how it is.'

'Yes,' I said. 'Yes, I suppose I do.'

'Goodnight, sir.'

'Drive carefully, soldier.'

The night sky was clearing as I watched him drive away.
Moonlight came down through an opening in the clouds and
for a moment the world was tinged silver. I went inside the
shop. Marks & Co. was a wonderful shop for all that it was
owned by Jews.

I was able to spend a pleasant thirty minutes or so just
browsing indoors. In the back of the shop, in a section
devoted to bargain books, I found a small octavo of Thea
von Harbou's *Metropolis*. It was the English edition,

showing a sort of mechanical woman against the background of a Bauhaus city. A Jewish form of architecture, and I loathed it both as an artist and as a man.

'The book sensation of Europe', said the front jacket.

'The great romance of the century,' said the back jacket.

'Prune-faced bitch,' I said out loud. 'And a talentless hack.' I held the book in my hand. The future of Germany stared back at me from its cover, a nightmare land of automaton workers and their Jewish masters. I was not in a good mood. I wondered how much von Harbou had made from the sale of her English-language rights. I had been paid £350 from my British publisher, Hurst & Blackett, but I was in the concentration camp by then. I needed to talk to my literary agent. I had been working on a sequel to *My Struggle* on and off since before my exile, but my creative juices refused to flow. Nevertheless, I determined to get in touch with them, at least to demand a royalty statement.

I replaced the book on the shelf and eventually found a copy of *Max und Moritz*. What charming illustrations! What beautiful rhyme. I found myself laughing quietly as the two fell into a vat of dough while trying to steal pretzels from the baker. How they rolled in the dough! Then the baker came back and baked them in his oven. I was laughing so hard my ribs were hurting.

'Sir? Sir? Are you all right?'

But I couldn't stop laughing. Everything hurt and I couldn't stop, and I stood there, holding the book, helplessly, laughing and laughing and trying to stop until they helped me out of the shop and closed the door on me, softly, with a final clang of the bell.

In another time and place Shomer lies sleeping; and he is neither too hungry nor too cold; and in the large block of the infirmary there is a relative quiet: nothing to do but lie there and try to sleep amongst the other sick or dying men; and try not to think in all that quiet, try not to think at all, of what has been, and what there is no more.

*　★　　★　　★*

By the time Wolf reached Berwick Street the hysterical laughter had drained out of him and left in its stead a cold burning fury. It was never buried deep, never too far beneath the surface; it motivated him, it drove him on; anger and hate were the beats of a great primitive drum, of the sort the Germanic tribes had played before marching into battle; they were the beats of the drum to which he, too, marched; always.

There was a car parked outside the Jew's bakery, a white Crossley Sports Saloon with no one inside. Wolf unlocked the side door by the bakery and climbed up the stairs and when he reached the corridor he saw that the door to his office was open.

He went cautiously; he was afraid, perhaps, of another attack.

She was standing in the middle of the room surveying its destruction. Her dress hugged her figure. A slit down the side exposed a flash of long white leg. She was biting her lower lip.

'Did Daddy do this?' she said.

'Get out.'

'He can be so *mean.*'

'I said, get out!'

'It's those two boys of his,' she said, not paying him any heed. 'They do indulge him so. He always wanted a boy, you know.' She turned to Wolf and gave him a quizzical smile. 'After Judith I guess he gave up trying. Instead he tried to make her into the boy he never had but she did what boys always do and left him.'

'Get—'

'Out, I know.' She sighed. 'I have *just* the decorator in mind. You'd *love* him. Sydney. He's a *genius.*' She walked up to Wolf. She was a little taller than he. She touched his cheek with the back of her hand and he flinched. 'Your face,' she said.

'My face? My *face?*' For the first time Wolf's face twisted in open fury. The anger and hate had been building up inside, the fury that in the past drove men to madness and murder. Once he had commanded men not unlike those Jew thugs of her father's, men who obeyed orders without question, who beat and maimed and tortured and killed at his command. 'My *face*?' He pushed her roughly against the wall. She bumped against it gracefully and stayed there regarding him with that same quizzical smile. Wolf fumbled with his belt buckle. The sound of the belt slithering out of its hooks whistled through the air and Isabella Rubinstein bit her lower lip again. The belt hit the floor. Wolf unbuttoned his trousers and with the same hurried gesture pulled his mutilated penis free. It was half erect, and painful. 'My fucking *face*?' He advanced on her, his penis in his hand.

'He did this to you?' If she was afraid she didn't show it.

'You fucking *whore*!' He was screaming, up in her face, strings of spittle falling from his lips. His cock was pressed against her now, this Jewish woman, the source of his humiliation, his pain.

She slapped him.

The sound resounded in the room. For a moment he couldn't believe it. His cheek stung. She had slapped him with force; there was heft in her action. 'Listen to me, you fucking little *worm*,' she said. Her hand reached down and grasped his penis, painfully hard, and he almost screamed. It was the second time in a week that a Rubinstein was holding Wolf by the balls. So to speak.

Isabella leaned close until her face was almost touching Wolf's. 'You think I don't know what you are? Who you are?' She gave his cock a painful squeeze, making him yelp in pain. 'You think I don't know what you *want*?'

'Let me go, you *bitch*—'

She slapped him again. Released his cock and pushed him with both hands splayed open against his chest. He staggered and fell back. He couldn't believe this was happening to him, nor did he know why he felt so weak at that moment. His penis was fully erect now, the unhealed wound burning.

Isabella advanced on him. She knelt, for just a moment, and rose with Wolf's belt in her hand. 'I used to watch you,' she said. 'Watch you on the newsreel when I was a girl. It was only a few years ago to you, a lifetime to me. How we all hated you! Hated and feared you.' Her free hand came down her body, as if it had its own will. She stroked her flat stomach, slowly, and came down lower, at last, to the triangle between her legs. It was pronounced, now. Her fingers grasped, pushing against the material, in between her thighs, as she touched herself. A small moan escaped from her lips, the sound suspended like ice crystals in the cold air of the room. 'You're a monster,' she said, whispered, 'or you were, once. You're a nobody now.'

'Yes,' Wolf said. Isabella whipped the belt through the air. It made a whistling sound and hit Wolf on the chest, the metal buckle nicking his skin. 'Yes. Yes.'

Isabella stared at Wolf's erect penis as though hypnotised. Her eyes were feverishly bright. 'Lie down.'

'What are you—'

She whipped him again. 'Lie *down*! On your back.'

He fell back. Lay down, his eyes on the ceiling, his head on a pile of books about the superiority of the Aryan race. His penis stood erect, at attention like an SS-Sturmführer. Isabella stood and watched him, her chest rising and falling with her breath. Slowly, making sure he watched, she began to lift up her dress.

'I used to sit in the cinema and watch you,' she said, dreamily. Wolf's eyes were fixed on the slowly rising dress. 'Giving speeches, your fist raised in the air. You had that funny little moustache, like Charlie Chaplin.' She laughed. Her thighs were bare. Her dark triangle of pubic hair was wet. 'We all used to hate you so.'

Holding the dress above her waist, she approached him and stood over him. He looked up, staring at her. 'I know men,' Isabella Rubinstein said, softly. She stood over him, one leg on either side of Wolf, affording him a view straight up her engorged commodity.

Slowly, she lowered herself down. She squatted over him until the lips of her cunny were inches away from Wolf's face. He could smell her, could inspect every fold of this most intimate aspect of hers. It had been this way with Geli. Slowly Isabella Rubinstein rocked back and forth on Wolf's face, rubbing herself against him. She rubbed against his nose, his lips, his reluctant tongue, lowering herself, positioning herself at last so that her anus was over Wolf's nose, her vagina over his mouth. The smell and warmth of her threatened to suffocate him. He tried to struggle but she reached and took hold of his manhood and held him still. Pain shot up his body, but he liked it. She tugged on his newly circumcised penis, not harshly, this time, but not gently either. '*Deutschland über alles,*' she murmured, rocking back and forth, back and forth, forcing herself on him. '*Deutschland über alles!*'

Then, quickly, she shuddered over his face and cried out, a high, keening single note. Wolf choked, his mouth filled with the product of her orgasm. She relaxed, sinking lower, crushing his face. Her hand was on his penis like on the rudder of an aircraft.

Then the pressure eased. She pushed herself up and stood squatting over him. Her lips twitched and then a trickle of urine came out, stopped, and then began again with more force. It fell down on Wolf's face and some of it ran down the inside of Isabella's thighs and some of it soaked Wolf's hair and his shirt. Wolf shuddered uncontrollably and shot semen into the air and onto his belly. He bit his lips to stop from crying out from the pain of his orgasm; he bit them until they bled. Isabella finished her toilet and shook the last drops into Wolf's mouth and stepped over him and pulled down her dress. Wolf lay there. Then he too stood up and pulled up his pants and tidied his shirt. He looked at her. She was standing by the window, in profile. She flicked her gold lighter alive and lit a cigarette. She blew a cloud of smoke at the sky and turned and looked at Wolf dreamily. 'We *really* must do something about that ghastly wallpaper,' she said.

8

Wolf's Diary, 8th November 1939

In the morning the bitch was gone and I tidied my office as best I could. I had slept fitfully. I was woken in the night by terrible dreams in which I was a Jew incarcerated in some sort of work camp. My leg was sore and tender with pus forming over a bloodied wound. In my dream I was a writer but all my readers were dead.

My bruises hurt and the little wolf, too, was sore. I woke early with the sounds of the bakery down below and the smell of the ovens. My mouth tasted of ash. I washed and dressed and grabbed a bite to eat at a cafe down the road and then returned to my office. I cleaned and tidied up but the smell of urine and my own excitement still filled the air and I cursed all Jews as I worked. My painting was ruined. It hurt unreasonably. It was another link to my past that had been severed.

When the office was more presentable I sat myself down behind my desk. I took out the fat brown envelope I had taken from Barbie's shop on Petticoat Lane. I slit it open with my letter opener, etched with the image of twin lightning bolts of the old, defunct SS. I took out the papers, carefully, and spread them out across the desk.

Interesting.

They were identity documents. The girl in the cellar, Judith's former schoolmate, had told me they were taken off them once they crossed the border out of Germany. There were all manner of papers, German identity cards, passports from a variety of nations, visas, onward tickets to Palestine or

America, a whole plethora of identities, a life in papers. Most were women, but not all, and I found myself staring in fascination at the passport of one Moshe Wolfson.

This Jew was about my age, that is to say, fifty. He had been born in Vienna and worked as a furrier. In his photograph he wore the black clothes of Hasidic Jews. He looked older than me.

Perhaps it was the similarity of the name that gave me the idea. Though I no longer painted, I could still use my skill as an artist. I went out and returned later in the day having visited a photographer and an arts supply shop near Covent Garden. One curious thing happened while I was out: as I walked past the Seven Dials I saw the fat policeman again, Keech. He was just loitering about, and when he saw me his eyes lit up and he approached me, twirling his nightstick like a performing monkey in the circus. 'So, Mr Wolf!' he said. He poked his nightstick at me and I dodged it, restraining the anger that was threatening to make me lose self-control.

'Constable,' I said, coldly.

'Spend time with any whores lately?'

'Not since I climbed off your mother last night.'

At that his fat face lost its fat smile. 'I'd tread carefully if I were you,' he said.

'It's a free country, last I checked.'

'Not for long, sweetheart. Not if your boyfriend Mosley has anything to do with it.'

'Scared, constable?'

That brought the big fat smile back to his face. 'Fucking immigrants,' he said, poking the nightstick at me again, half-heartedly. 'You should all go back where you come from.'

'What about your boss, Morhaim?'

'Morhaim's as British as anyone.'

'I'm not sure Mosley sees it that way.'

'What is your problem, Wolf?' he said. For a moment he seemed almost sincere. 'What is it with you and Jews? Why do you hate them so much?'

I stared into his big fat face in silence. After a moment he laughed. 'On your way,' he said. 'Don't do anything stupid. If that's at all possible.' And, as I began to silently walk away – 'We'll be watching you, Wolf.'

I was more disturbed by the encounter than I let on. Was it coincidence? Were the Metropolitan Police watching me, following me? I needed to go about my business without the pursuit of shadows. But that afternoon I gave no one cause for concern. From the photographer I obtained several self-portraits of myself, cut to size, and from the arts supply shop I purchased scalpel and ink, glue and a selection of rubber stamps. So equipped, I returned to the office, where Herr Moshe Wolfson's pitiful face stared up at me from his passport. I wondered where he was, and whether he was dead or alive – dead, I assumed, smuggled out of Germany only for his body to be dumped somewhere in the Alps, his possessions stolen: there was much to be admired in the efficiency of such a system, I thought. And again I wondered, futilely, which man was behind it all; I was sure that I would know him; would I not?

And so I spent a pleasurable hour at my desk, with scalpel and ink and stamps. I began by gently removing Wolfson's photograph from his passport. I set it on fire and watched it burn to ashes and then returned to the document. The passport, I saw, had been used several times in the years before the Fall, with trips to France, Switzerland and Belgium. More intriguingly, it contained a brand-new, genuine Palestinian visa, granted by the British High Commission only a few months earlier. Such visas, I knew, were rare, and I wondered how much he had paid, and to whom, in order to gain one. Next I set about ageing my own photograph and, while it was drying, I put the other papers of the dead or enslaved Jews back into the envelope and into a drawer: I had no further use for them.

I inserted the photograph bearing my own face into Wolfson's document and set about reproducing the official stamp over it. It had been a long time since I worked in such a trade and my concentration was complete. At last I had finished and with a sense of achievement sat there. For a long moment I stared at my new passport. 'Moshe Wolfson,' I said, trying out the name. 'Moshe Wolfson, *ja*. It is a pleasure to meet you, *mein herr*.'

My face stared back at me, severe and mute, from the photograph. It was the face of a Jew.

Wolf's Diary, 9th November 1939

Were I ever asked to offer my professional observations on the art of detection, I would merely note that it is a truth universally acknowledged, that once a detective acquires two concurrent cases, the two must be in some way related.

I call it Wolf's Law.

It is a point of contention with me that I had never, in fact, been asked to offer my professional observations on the art of detection. That big fat oaf Gil Chesterton once said that the criminal is the artist, the detective only the critic. He was a Catholic and a prude and was never shy of a meal or an opinion. In this, as in all things, he was wrong. I *was* an artist, for it is an artist's purpose to make order out of chaos. A criminal defaces; a detective restores. Had I been asked to proffer my observations, I dare say they would have made for a gripping and elucidating read. I had, in fact, been working, on and off, on a sequel to my first, and so far only, book, and in this *Zweite Buch*, or *Second Book* – for I did not yet have a title for it – I intended to set aside a chapter, at the very least, in order to discuss my methods and views on crime, which I believed would make a significant contribution to mankind's understanding of the criminal mind.

Yet the manuscript eluded me; and I did not have a publisher.

My enquiry had led me to combine my twin investigations: these being Judith Rubenstein's disappearance and the question of Mosley's Palestinian assassins. The root of all crime, of course, is the Jew; and so it was only natural that it was in that direction that I next turned my attentions. I needed to understand the Jewish angle.

Jews always had an angle.

The headquarters of the Jewish Territorialist Organisation were in the basement of an office block off the Strand, towards the Fleet Street end. They were dark and dim and did not look busy. It was the sort of place rented in a hurry and abandoned even faster. It was exactly the sort of place I was looking for.

It was Thursday; and I was on the job.

Eric Goodman looked like a con man who'd seen better days. He was in his mid-30s, with receding black hair and watery blue eyes that were magnified by his too-large glasses. The collar of his shirt was open and his nails were bitten down to the quick and I didn't like his eyes. They were those of a man who trusted no one and nothing and least of all me. Behind him in the office was a receptionist as old as Napoleon and as attractive, and she was bent over a cumbersome typing machine, pecking desultorily at the keys.

'Moshe Wolfson,' I said, trying out the name. 'It is a pleasure to meet you.'

'Funny,' the man from the ITO said. 'You don't look Jewish.'

'You want funny?' I said. 'Let me tell you a joke. A goy comes to a Jew acquaintance of his. "You Jews," he says, "everyone knows you're smart with money. Teach me how to be smart like a Jew."

'"Well," the Jew says. "It's simple. Go to the market and look for my cousin's fish stall and buy his pickled herring. Once you eat the pickled herring, you'll become smarter in no time."

'The goy, delighted, goes away. The next day, he shows up again, fuming with anger. "You cheated me!" he cries. "I bought your cousin's pickled herring like you told me, then this morning I was at the market and I saw the same fish being sold on another stall – for a third of the price!"

'"You see?" says the Jew, delighted. "You're *already* smarter!"'

I beamed at him expectantly. Goodman looked at me sour-faced. 'You're a regular comedian,' he said. 'You'd be packing them in at the Hackney Empire in no time.'

'How do you get to the Hackney Empire?' I asked him.

'You can take the bus,' he said, and I stopped him in frustration before he could give me directions and said, 'No, no . . . practice!'

He gave an involuntary shudder.

'What exactly did you want again, Mr Wolfson?'

I stared into his ugly mug of a face and considered my response.

'I am interested in the activities of our brothers and sisters in Palestine,' I said at last, with what I hoped was an ingratiating smile.

'Well, then I'm afraid that you came to the wrong place, Mr Wolfson.'

'I'm not sure that I understand.'

He was of the English Jewry, like Morhaim, the prick from the Met. Thinking himself at home on this island and arrogant with it. But earlier, when I had gone down the Strand, the Blackshirts were marching and little old ladies were throwing them flowers and little boys ran about waving the Union flag; and as I passed Charing Cross Station I saw a Hasidic Jew, dressed all in black, propped up against a brick wall as young men took turns beating him about the face and body, until his thick white beard was matted with red blood. His heavy felt hat lay crumpled on the road beside him, as though he were asking for alms. The policemen who were set to patrol the march did nothing but watch. It was not becoming any easier for Jews in this country. But then it never does, for the Jews.

'Mr Wolfson, the Jewish Territorialist Organisation was founded in 1903 by the author Israel Zangwill and the journalist Lucien Wolf—'

An author, and a journalist, I thought. Jews! They were good with nothing but words.

'Following the offer, from then-Colonial Secretary Joseph Chamberlain, of a Jewish settlement in British East Africa.'

A sensible offer, I thought, but didn't say. Stick them as far away from civilisation as possible. 'I take it that did not carry through, in practical terms?' I said, politely.

'The Zionist Congress sent an expedition to British East Africa—'

'You mean Uganda?'

He looked pained. 'That was the name the *common person* on the street referred to it by.'

'I see.'

I would see his face smashed into the naked glass, if I had my way.

'Unfortunately the expedition did not return a favourable report.'

'Too hot?' I said.

'The heat, hostile tribes . . .' He waved his hand airily. 'Details to be overcome, in our opinion. But the Congress voted the offer down.'

'How . . . short-sighted.'

For the first time he expressed real emotion. 'Indeed! Quite right! And so the ITO—'

Why they called it the ITO and not the JTO was beyond me.

'—was established and continued to explore alternative propositions for Jewish settlement beyond Palestine, believing, as we do, not in the need for a return to a Biblical land, but rather for a practical solution to the question of a national homeland for the Jewish people, for—'

'Quite, quite,' I said, cutting him off hurriedly. 'Indeed.'

He sighed. 'Anyway,' he said, 'the Balfour Declaration in 1917 did rather take the wind out of that particular sail. For a while, at least. As you are probably aware, the inherent anti-Semitism of the British, like elsewhere in Europe, has prevented commitment to *any* particular national homeland for the Jews for many years now.'

'So you are considering other possibilities? Besides Palestine, I mean?'

'Of course. Uganda still.' He glared at me. 'I mean British East Africa, of course.'

'Of course.' I grinned at him charmingly. The little *scheisskopf*. 'Where else? I inquired.

'Argentina, for instance. El Arish, in Egypt. Albania. British Guiana. There are many possibilities.'

'But Palestine amongst them, surely.'

'Well, yes. I'm sorry, I think I forgot your name.'

'It's Wolfson,' I said. Pictured him on the ground being kicked by hobnailed boots. But said, 'That's quite all right, young man. You cannot be expected to remember every visitor's name, surely!'

'So you do understand. Yes, yes, we are quite busy here, I can assure you. *Quite* busy!'

His was the third office I had tried, after the Palestine Jewish Colonisation Association (too legit, engaged in arranging visas and work for Jews in Palestine) and the Council of British Zionists, or CBZ (who seemed to spend most of their time arranging black-tie fundraisers). The ITO was different. I liked the look of this con man in his too-large glasses. I liked the cut, as they say, of Eric Goodman's jib. I liked the furtiveness of his glances and the disused air of the office and the comatose receptionist. I knew deceit like a lover and here, I thought, was somebody giving out all the right signals for a quick and dirty lying fuck.

'So if there is nothing else I can help you with . . .'

'It's only, you see,' I said, 'that I have recently come into

some money and, of course, the Palestinian cause is close to
my heart, as it is to the heart of all Jews . . .'

'Is that so?' His demeanour became instantly sympathetic
when I mentioned money. He all but beamed at me, like a cat
smelling his favourite tinned fish. I hated cats. Cats and Jews.
What kind of a name was 'Eric' for a Jew? It was typical of
the Jews, to give themselves seemingly Anglo-Saxon names,
the better to try and fool the unwary man or woman. No
doubt he was a pervert, too, a sexual deviant of some kind.

'If you would like to make a donation . . .'

'Let me think about it.'

He lowered his voice. 'Palestine is not out of the question,'
he said. 'In fact . . .' then he shook his head and smiled. 'But I
get carried away.'

'No, do go on.'

He looked at me with returning suspicion. 'You're not a
policeman, are you?' he said.

'Do I look like a copper to you?'

'I don't know. There is something about you, Mr Wolfson,
that doesn't feel quite right to me,' he murmured, raising his
head and removing his glasses. I stared into his pale blue eyes.
He stared back at me, unblinking.

'I do not need to stand for this kind of treatment!' I said.
'And as for a donation, young man, you can forget about *that*!'

He did not try to stop me. In fact I didn't think he would.
I marched out of there and closed the door and walked back
down to the Strand and round the corner, never once looking
back, not doubting that he'd be following, if only for a little
while. If only to make sure that I was gone.

Yes, I liked Mr Eric Goodman, for my purposes. I liked
him very much indeed.

It was surprisingly uncomfortable for Wolfson the Jew to walk
the streets of London that day. Wolf realised that for all of his
recent association with Mosley, he had simply not paid enough
attention to the forthcoming elections. The signs for Mosley's

campaign were everywhere, his aristocratic face staring down from billboards and posters glued to the ancient walls, and his men, the Blackshirts stood and glared at passers-by like truant schoolboys.

'Enough is Enough!' screamed their signs. 'Fight, Fight, and Fight Again!' – 'Stop the Open Door Policy!' – 'Say No to Mass Immigration!' – 'Vote BU: Putting Britain First' – 'Mosely for Prime Minister' – and so on and so forth.

Wolf's strawmen had been the Jews; for Mosley, it was the European refugees from now-communist Germany who must serve – and that included Wolf himself.

It was an uncomfortable realisation.

Equipped with a Thermos of hot herbal tea, and cheese-and-tomato sandwiches, and his raincoat and fedora, he returned two hours later, near closing time, to the little narrow lane off the Strand; and there found himself a sheltered space in a doorway and there he stood, unobtrusively, and sipped his tea, and ate his sandwiches, and watched the door of the Jewish Territorialist Organisation.

At 5.30 in the afternoon the comatose secretary emerged, wrapped up like a large ham, and made her way down to the bus stop. It was already very dark and it had been raining inter-mittently and dark wet patches covered the pavements.

At 6.30 on the dot the door of the ITO offices opened and Eric Goodman emerged, huddled in a coat, and shut and locked the door. He looked from side to side but apart from a handful of theatregoers lost on the way to the Strand there was no one on the lane. Wolf's Thermos was still half-full but so was his bladder and he needed to pee. His leg ached from the old wound. Goodman turned right and Wolf followed him. Goodman went through Covent Garden and Wolf hobbled after.

They passed the Royal Opera House and came finally to Dryden Street, where Goodman entered a small cafe of the sort reactionaries and penniless artists frequented; that is to say, it was a dive. Wolf waited some moments, adjusted his hat and entered. The place was crowded and noisy, the clientele boisterous and young. Goodman was sitting in a corner with his back to the door. He was not alone. Wolf went into the small water closet to urinate and stared in horror at his circumcised penis before tucking it away again. He went back into the cafe and got himself a fruit juice, and sat two tables away from Goodman. He tried to listen to their conversation but they spoke in low voices. The other man was Goodman's age but there was something hard about him, in his eyes and the shape of his mouth, in the way he held himself. He sat with his back to the wall. Wolf had the impression he was not the kind of man to ever leave his back exposed.

The conversations swelled around Wolf.

'The situation in Europe – my brother says—'

'Those damned Fascists!'

'Revolution by peaceful means. The British people are too sensible to give in to a charlatan like Mosley—'

'—understudy for *Hamlet* at the Theatre Royal, the bastard—'

'Yes, do you like it? A wonderful artist, utterly *wonderful*—'

'Only a matter of time before war is declared, the Americans—'

'I blame the French, myself.'

'Utterly *divine* cakes—'

'Playing Rosenkrantz – well, a job's a job, you know what they say—'

'I didn't like the look of him, is what I'm saying, Bitker.'

'Listen to me, Goodman! You're supposed to keep a clean front—'

Wolf, ears perked, trying to isolate snatches of conversation.

'A shamus, a shamus or a copper is what he seemed to me, Bitker—'

'You simply *must* see *Gaslight* at the—'

'The revolution—'

'Wolfson? But his papers were kosher?'

'Kosher like a bagel.'

'You let me know if he comes again, Goodman. Do you understand—'

'My publisher? Stanley Unwin and C—'

'Nothing can interrupt the plans, Goodman, do you understand!'

Wolf was hunched low but he saw the other man, the one he thought Goodman had called Bitker, shove his chair back, leap to his feet and leave the cafe. He was a big man, this Bitker. Wolf got up and followed.

The man strode across Long Acre. He was wary of a tail: twice Wolf saw him check reflections in shop windows, but Wolf was an anonymous face amongst others and the man did not see him. He hopped on a bus and Wolf climbed aboard too. The bus went down Holborn and Newgate and past St Paul's. The man Bitker got off there and Wolf did too. It had begun to rain again. Somewhere in the distance he could hear a wireless playing Judy Garland's 'Over the Rainbow'. Wolf had seen the film but, had he been the one swept up to the magical land of Oz, he would have raised an army of flying monkeys, stuck the witches in a concentration camp, razed the Emerald City to the ground and executed the wizard for communist sympathies, being a Jew, a homosexual, intellectually retarded, or all of the above.

He did like the tune, though.

He followed Bitker in the dark through the City, abandoned to the night at this hour. The streets were taken up by the homeless and the criminal, and police presence was light. Outside the Bank of England Wolf saw a group of protesters, their faces obscured by scarves, setting alight a vast straw figure dressed in the Blackshirts' uniform. Policemen did arrive then, and the protesters threw bottles and stones and the policemen cursed and advanced on them with their clubs and Wolf walked on, following the elusive Bitker.

The night made Wolf uncomfortable. It was filled with grotesque human shapes, shambling through the narrow streets, their feet bare in the cold or wrapped in hastily torn bandages: some were missing limbs, others had scars from torture or acid, others still carried sharp implements the better to remove a man's valuables or life. All were beggars, the lowest of men, the lost, those who had despaired; refugees, unwanted, undesired, holding on to life tenaciously, hungrily, like beasts. They frightened Wolf, he saw himself bared, ugly in the mirror of their suffering.

Yet Bitker navigated these selfsame streets with ease and Wolf in his wake was left unharmed. They came shortly to Threadneedle Street and descended a flight of stairs to the door of a basement flat. After looking from side to side but missing Wolf again, Bitker knocked three times and waited. Presently the door was opened and light spilled out, illuminating a plain-faced Jewess in a flower-patterned dress. Bitker disappeared inside and the door closed and Wolf was left outside in the darkness. He crouched on the stairs and peered through the lace curtains.

*   *   *

The watcher in the dark, too, was watching, but this time he could no longer control the eagerness. He was watching the whores and had missed the detective's whereabouts and only knew that the detective wasn't there. Earlier he had fiddled with the cheap lock on the door and opened it and gone up the stairs and into the detective's office and he sat behind Wolf's desk. It felt so good to be sitting there. It felt so right.

The detective was so *stubborn*, he thought. It was because the man had lost a part of himself after the Fall, and was unable to get it back. It was pitiful, watching him hobble along, this once-great man, this *leader* of men, now like a decommissioned soldier, blinded by gas, a beggarman, a sleepwalker almost. The watcher in the dark wanted to grab him by the shoulders and shake him, shake him so hard and shout, *Wake up! Wake up, you daft old fool! We need you!* but no sound emerged and the detective wasn't there and hadn't been listening so far, but by God the watcher was going to get his attention. You did not just abandon a *destiny*.

Tonight. Soon. He could feel the need and the desire and he knew he could not put it off any longer, he needed . . . he shuddered in the chair and got up, moved softly around the room, not touching anything, just . . . *feeling* it. Was this what it was like to have been in his presence, before? In his office with men always coming and going and the sound of hobnailed boots on hard floors, the rustle of stiff leather, the whisper of flags like silk, the smell and taste of *power* so strong it suffused the very air and changed all who came into contact with it?

He left the office regretfully, softly, and picked Wolf's bedsit's lock. Once the door was open he closed his eyes for a long moment and stood there, and when he opened them again it was as though the room was transformed and for just a moment he was standing in Wolf's old bedroom, in the Berlin residence, and the swastika flags were moving in the breeze, and outside the chauffeur was polishing the official car. For a moment he pictured a young blonde woman in the bed . . . she opened her eyes and smiled sleepily, her eyes filled with slowly fading dreams. Her long blonde hair was the colour of the sun and her skin was white as snow, but hot, so hot . . . the watcher was so erect just standing there and he moved with a great effort, looking at Wolf's books, Wolf's *toilette*, his meagre possessions: his razor, his soap, his threadbare blanket and the books, all those books everywhere. The watcher stood over the sink, imagining Wolf brushing his teeth, shaving his cheeks, washing his hands. The watcher looked in the mirror but it was only his own ordinary face staring back at him and that broke the spell. He left and locked the door behind him and went back down to Berwick Street. He had work to do, so much work.

Wolf's Diary, 9th November 1939 – *contd.*

It was an ordinary basement flat, sparsely furnished with heavy Victorian high-backed chairs and two tables joined together in the middle of the room, for all that their heights didn't entirely match. A flower-patterned cloth covered the tables. Sitting in the chairs were five men and, entering the room, was the plain-faced Jewess. Bitker trailed behind her.

I'd not seen such an assembly of reprobates since the camp. They were a shifty lot, swarthy and hairy like the *untermenschen* Jews that they were. They sat with no decorum, in their white undershirts, and hairy arms on the table, all but one, and all but one smoking. The ashtrays were filled to overflowing with what the English call 'fags'. I was glad I was outside in the cold clean air. The beasts had not even opened a window. It must have been like an oven in there. Of the five men one was a skinny lad with smooth cheeks and a face like a hooked fish and he wore an oversized shirt with sleeves that covered his wrists. He reminded me of someone but I couldn't think of whom.

The men were talking animatedly but stopped abruptly when Bitker entered. They all stood up and shook his hand and one or two of them slapped him on the back

I heard his name, Bitker, once or twice but could not hear the discussion, which took place in low voices. The Jewess disappeared and reappeared later with a large tray of tea things. I became convinced this was, indeed, a Palestinian terror group, but could they be the ones behind the assassination attempts on Mosley? I pressed closer to the window, trying to hear, when I felt more than saw a dark shape drop down from the windowsill of the flat above. It meowed at me and, startled, I banged my head against the window.

The voices inside ceased at once. A moment later the lights went out. I pushed the cat away and it hissed at me. I kicked it, feeling a savage satisfaction even as I could hear running feet and the door to the conspirators' flat crashing open.

I ran.

They moved like professionals. They didn't shout, didn't curse as they chased me. They ran quietly and swiftly and with violent determination. My lungs burned and my leg throbbed with old pain and I fled for my life, down narrow alleyways, trying to lose them, my traitor leg hurting and my chest heaving until I thought I would be sick, and as I ran I caught sight of a sign and realised I was on Old Jewry. For a moment I thought I'd lost them.

The God damned cat tripped me up.

It came out of nowhere, streaked between my feet like a spirit of animal vengeance, screeching hideously. I tripped and fell, hard, catching myself with the palms of my hands. I felt skin tear and my knee crack, sending a shudder of fresh pain up my body and I cried out: I could not help it.

In moments they were on me and I could smell the bloodlust on their unwashed bodies. I curled into a ball, trying to protect my head and my genitals as they kicked me.

I think they were shouting questions at me, and the foreigner, Bitker, was ordering them to stop but they had lost discipline. I almost prayed, remembering the old words, my mother's and the priest's. To die like this! Ignobly in the Old Jewry at the hands of the selfsame Jews who once before were evicted out of England. It was too much to bear.

The sound of a whistle cut through the night and my pain. The kicking, miraculously, stopped. I heard running feet and saw the bouncing light of several torch beams. 'Jews! They're Jews!' came the cry.

I opened my eyes. I saw a group of young Blackshirts rushing towards the Palestinian terrorists. 'Fascist pigs!' someone yelled. I saw the blade of a knife gleam but who held it I wasn't, afterwards, sure. In the uncertain light of the torches I saw the face of the smooth-cheeked youth in profile and for a moment I almost laughed, for it was no man at all, it was a woman!

'Hello, Judith,' I whispered, softly.

Then all hell, as they say, broke loose. The two groups, the Jews and the Blackshirts, went at each other. I heard punching, grunting, saw a Jew raise a brick and smash it into a Blackshirt's head, caving in his skull. I saw a Blackshirt choking a Jew by the throat, his thumbs driving into the other man's windpipe. I saw the God damned cat standing a foot to

my left, looking at me with a smirk on its dumb animal face. I
crawled away, though every movement hurt. In moments they
were behind me. In the darkness and the fight no one saw me
go but the cat.

I straightened up, eventually. I stood and then walked, away
from that awful place. I caught a bus and sat on the upper
deck. On my swollen lips, I tasted blood.

'Why are you all on your own, a good-looking boy like you?'

The fat whore leered at him. She was rouged with cheap
make-up over a too-pale face. Her jowls shook with her smile.
Her teeth were small and uneven. Her tongue was red and she
stuck it out at the watcher in the dark. 'You want to fuck old
Gerta?' she said. 'You want old Gerta to suck your baby cock?'

Her bosoms were immense. She grabbed her breasts from
below and shook them at him, and the pale white flesh wobbled
like waves on a sea. The other whores were busy. The street was
quiet. The watcher in the dark was ready. His hand closed on
the hilt of the knife, the shiny, shiny knife. 'Come here,' Gerta
said. She pulled him by the hand and forced his head between
the twin mounds of her breasts. 'Give Aunty a kiss!'

She was strong; stronger than he had guessed. She released
him and he could breathe again. Her hand tested him down
below and she leered again, knowingly. 'Let's go,' she said.

She did not lead him to the alleyway where he had done
the other. The girls did not use it any more. She led him
somewhere else, past the dirty bookstore and a florist and a
haberdashery and a cafe run by émigré Italians, all shut now,
and pushed him against the wall near the rubbish bins where
no one could see them. His heart beat fast and wild. She raised
up her voluminous skirts, revealing pink fleshy thighs and a
dark unruly bush of pubic hair. 'No, what are you doing,' he
tried to say, 'no, not like that,' and he tried to struggle with
her, then, but she was having none of it, she held his neck in
a hug that was all but a chokehold, and with her other hand
she pulled down his pants and took his stiff cock in her

hand and before he even knew what was happening she had guided him inside her, squeezing his buttocks roughly as she pulled him in.

She seemed oblivious to him then. Her eyes were half closed and her lips parted and she made strange animalistic sounds, grinding him against her, over and over. The watcher had never done it before and he felt sick, sick being inside of this grotesque old creature, and only the thought of the knife kept him going until at last Gerta gave a shuddering little laugh and abruptly released him, pushing him off her. She looked down at his now-flaccid member, flopping there in the dark, and gave a little laugh again, contemptuously.

He pulled up his trousers quickly. She was still looking at him but then her eyes changed: when she saw the knife.

'What the hell do you think you're doing—' she said, or began to. He lashed out at her with the knife but she raised her arm and the knife grazed her but he had obviously missed his target. 'You little fuck hole!' she said. She sounded outraged more than scared.

'You disgusting whore!' He stabbed with the knife, again. They were so close to each other, it was as if they were making love, still. She grabbed him, pulled him close and then the knife was sticking out of the right side of her chest and she stared at him in surprise, or shock, clutching him to her, her blood staining the front of the watcher's shirt.

'Just *die!*' the watcher pleaded.

Instead, Gerta kneed him in the balls.

The watcher collapsed. He was still holding the knife. It pulled out of Gerta's chest and it emerged with a sickening, *sucking* sound. Gerta gasped, clutching her hands to the wound. There was very little blood.

'You little *worm!*' Gerta said.

The watcher had never felt such agony before; his body seemed on fire. He backed away from her. Gerta advanced on him like a figment of the watcher's nightmares, gigantic and terrifying. 'You little . . .'

At that moment he could hear footsteps coming rapidly down the street and a voice say, in foreign accented English, 'What is going on here, please?'

*   *   *

'What is going on here, damn it,' Wolf repeated. He had been nearly at his door when he heard the sounds of a scuffle. He did not want to get involved. Only fools got involved.

He saw, by the rubbish bins, the fat whore Gerta and a man, but he only knew Gerta from her profile, and he did not know the man. The man turned and ran. Wolf didn't give chase. He went to Gerta. Her face resolved when he came closer. It looked like a ghastly clown's mask. 'Wolfie,' she said. 'Is it really you, dear boy?'

'What happened, Gerta? Gerta?'

She had pulled down her dress and her pale bosoms swung free, and there was a knife wound on the right side of her chest. It was frothing weirdly.

'I'll call a doctor,' Wolf said, alarmed. He didn't want to get involved. He was repulsed by the prostitute's appearance. 'He looked so . . . harmless,' Gerta said. She was breathing heavily. 'It's always . . . the quiet ones.' She tried to leer at Wolf, but just looked pained, and old, and beaten.

Wolf shouted, 'Help! Help!' He was too tired to run any more. Too tired to walk. He just kept shouting until the other prostitutes showed up and, after them, the police. He was sitting next to Gerta by then, both of them coated in blood, their backs to the rubbish bins. He only just remembered to stash the forged Jewish identity document in a crack between the stones before the policemen finally came and arrested him.

*   *   *

The watcher was panicked, his breath caught in his throat. He tasted bile. Police whistles tore up the night. In Soho Square he found the bag he had hidden earlier that day. Quickly he stripped off his blood-soaked clothes and changed, the air freezing on his exposed skin. He shoved the clothes into the same bag and continued at a slower pace. On Oxford Street he caught a bus home.

How could it have happened? How could he fail? His mission was a holy one. He *could not* fail. At home Father was asleep in his armchair by the unlit fire. The wireless was on, playing a Chopin étude. The watcher stroked his father's thinning white hair, gently, and the old man shifted but did not wake. The watcher went up to his room and stripped again. His penis throbbed as though it was infected. Naked, he walked into the bathroom and washed. The water was lukewarm and he was shivering. He scrubbed himself and scrubbed himself, scrubbed at the whore's smell on him, her cunny juice on his penis. As much as he scrubbed he couldn't get it off. He sat in the bath and hugged himself, rocking in the dirty water. The blood coloured the water pink.

She . . . she raped him.

The taste of bile was in his mouth still. He couldn't afford to fail again. He had been sloppy. Next time there would be no mistakes. No more mistakes! He got out at last, shivering, and wrapped a towel around himself and brushed his teeth, over and over, until his gums bled and his spit was red. Later he lay in the cold bed and shivered and that smell clung to him still, that disease-ridden old hag's awful smell. Everything had gone so wrong. What if he had caught something? Whores were nasty creatures, they had crabs and the clap and God alone knew what other terrible diseases. He held his penis in his hand, like a child, trying to comfort himself. He was so cold. The knife was in the bedside drawer. The knife was whispering to him, calling him names. He'd cleaned the knife from the whore's diseased blood, he'd cleaned and cleaned and cleaned until it shone. When they'd beat him as a boy he would hide under the covers, later, clutching his penis. Why are childhoods so awful, the watcher wondered, and he remembered suddenly and with aching clarity Mr Woodford, the neighbour, a jolly chap always

popular with the ladies of the neighbourhood, he was friends
with Father, too, always nice to the kids: and he took him in,
once, after a beating, and offered him candy and then took out
a gross fleshy thing and asked the watcher to touch it. It was
warm and it changed shape as the boy touched it, and Mr
Woodford made strange sounds and spurted a milky viscous
liquid that covered the boy's hand. But he always gave him
sweets, after. Sweets and affection.

For a long time, the watcher blamed himself. It was their secret,
his and Mr Woodford's. And you don't tell secrets. You never tell.
Mr Woodford had fought in the war; he was a hero. The watcher
closed his eyes but in the darkness he could still hear the footsteps
approaching, and the rank hot breath of the prostitute, strangely
similar to Mr Woodford's.

He couldn't sleep. He took the knife out from the drawer and
ran the tip of his finger down the blade, drawing blood. There
was comfort in that, a way of asserting control. He cut himself
slowly, with great deliberation, running the blade down his ribs,
littered with old scars. The blood stained the bedsheets. At last
he could sleep.

* * *

In another time and place Shomer lies restlessly awake. There is
nothing to do in the infirmary, no work, nothing to do but think
of all that had been and is no more. Outside, the camp goes on
its inexorable daily routine, and to the place where the tracks
terminate the trains keep coming, carrying Jews. Every day more
come to this Auschwitz-Birkenau complex, so vital for the interests
of the war, from all across Europe they come, Poles and Czechs,
Slovaks and Greeks, Italians and Hungarians, but all Jews, marked
with the yellow star, all bound to be processed, quickly and effi-
ciently, children and women and men, and the black smoke rises
from the ovens, day and night the black smoke of Jews rises, so
many Jews: who would have thought there were so many Jews
still left in the world?

Prisoner 174517 is a recent arrival, an Italian, Levi by name. 'And how can we write this rent in the world,' he says, waving his hands animatedly while his voice remains soft. Like Shomer he has suffered a leg wound. 'Only by science, by using a language as accurate and dispassionate as possible can we describe the atrocities, for it is a scientific genocide we are subject to, with gas they are killing us, with charts and lists they record us, and in Mengele's lab they dissect us like animals. And this must be recorded, for future generations, to never forget, and for that the novelist must employ a language as clear and precise as possible, a language without ornament.'

He is not speaking to Shomer but to a veteran of the camp, a Polish Jew with soft sad eyes and curly black hair, skeletal like the rest of them. When asked his name, he says, 'I have no name. They took my name and now I am Ka-Tzetnik 135633, and no more—' *Ka-Tzetnik*, that is to say, 'inmate'. And Ka-Tzetnik says:

'But there you are wrong, for this is no longer the world you knew, the world any of us knew. That world is dead, everything is divided, Before-Auschwitz and the Now, for there is only now, even to think of a life beyond is to indulge in fantasy. But to answer your question, to write of this Holocaust is to shout and scream, to tear and spit, let words fall like bloodied rain on the page; not with cold detachment but with fire and pain, in the language of *shund*, the language of shit and piss and puke, of pulp, a language of torrid covers and lurid emotions, of fantasy: this is an alien planet, Levi. This is Planet Auschwitz.'

And Ka-Tzetnik says:

'We have no names. We have no parents and we have no children. We do not dress the way they dress on Earth. We were not born here and we do not give birth. We breathe by different rules of nature. We do not live by the laws of Earth and neither do we die by them. Our name is a number.'

And at those words the world makes sudden sense to Shomer, for here he is, an astronaut on an alien and hostile world – and isn't everything trying to kill him? 'Death and sex,' Ka-Tzetnik says, but mournfully, 'death and sex,' and he and Levi begin to argue, and Levi says, 'But that is kitsch, and bordering on pornography,' and so they go on until another inmate tells them to shut the fuck up about literature and they lapse into a heavy silence.

'Well, that's another fine mess you got us into,' Yenkl says, cheerfully, dangling his legs from an upper bunk bed, contentedly puffing on his pipe. And Shomer's mind shies from the glare, conjures up a safe haven, a world of mean streets and buxom dames and flat-footed detectives, as if, if only he could open up a secret door, he could be transported there; and be free.

9

Wolf's Diary, 10th November 1939

'Well, well, shamus. Here we are again,' Keech, the fat policeman, said.

'Fuck you, pig,' I said. I wasn't in a good mood. I seldom was, these days. 'What are you holding me for this time? Last I checked fucking your mother wasn't a crime.'

His face darkened and he said, 'You're a right old funnyman, aren't you, Wolf.'

'What do you want, Keech? I'm trying to sleep here.'

They put me in a cell again in Charing Cross nick. This time I rather welcomed it. A doctor had looked me over but had better things to do. I got soup and bread and I fell asleep until the morning without being disturbed. I was aching all over but I would live. I was getting used to being beat up. It was all on a par for this line of work.

'How is the whore?' I said.

'She'll live,' Keech said.

'Is she talking?'

'Do you mean, does she confirm your story?' He laughed, a short ugly laugh. 'She don't remember much.'

'What the hell do you mean?'

'I *mean* that all Gerta remembers is being assaulted by a man, and that the last face she saw was yours. So why did you do it, shamus? You have a thing for whores?'

'I didn't do it!'

He leered at me, this fat fuck of a pig.

'God damn it, I didn't *do* it, Keech!'

'Scared, Wolf? You should be.'

'But this is absurd! I came to her rescue. Keech, you have to believe me!'

'I don't have to believe shit, shamus. This isn't the church. It's the law.'

'You have no proof!'

He shook his jowled face. 'You won't get off again this easily,' he said. Then he went and shut the cell door on me and turned the key in the lock.

Wolf's Diary, 11th November 1939

'Enjoying your time with us?'

'Are you going to charge me, or let me go?'

'We'll never let you go, kraut.'

I sighed. 'You're walking a dangerous line, Keech,' I said.

'Are you threatening me?'

I stared at him and he laughed, but there was no humour in his eyes. 'Inspector wants to see you.'

'Tell him to go to hell,' I said.

'Oh, play nice, Wolf,' Keech said. 'You look worse than a beat-up old whore, you know. You could do with a friend.'

'Are you going to be my friend, Keech? We could go fishing together up the Thames.'

'How are you feeling?' He was being solicitous and that had me worried.

'I've been worse.'

'Then come along. We don't want to keep the inspector waiting, do we.'

I followed him, stretching. I was beginning to like the cell. Maybe I could finally write that sequel to my book, if they kept me in there long enough. Once again down the corridor and to Inspector Morhaim's small office. He sat behind his desk as if he hadn't moved since the last time I saw him. 'Mr Wolf. Do sit down.'

I took a chair. I saw no reason not to.

'You know Mr Freisler?'

We were not alone in the room. I nodded, politely. 'Hello, Roland.'

He had a long mournful lawyer's face and a lawyer's fidgety manners. The bald dome of his head was bookended by black hair like a wig. He was an anti-Semite and an early Party member and I had met him in Berlin a few times. I hadn't realised he had escaped Germany after the Fall, or that he was still alive. To be honest, I had given the man no thought at all. In the early days he had helped defend members of the SA when they inevitably got into trouble with the law. How he came to be here, now, I had no idea.

'Herr Wolf.'

'What are you doing here, Roland?'

'If it pleases you, sir, I am here as your representative.'

'Are you,' I said. I looked at Morhaim. I could see he had to hold down his temper. He did not like Freisler's being there. 'And who, if you don't mind me asking, sent you?'

'My employer would rather remain anonymous,' the lawyer said.

'I don't doubt that,' I said. He nodded, briefly. 'It is good to see you again, sir,' he said.

'I wish I could say the same. You are not needed, Freisler. You are dismissed.'

'But sir!'

Morhaim sighed. 'Mr Wolf,' he said, 'do you know why you are here?'

'I am unjustly accused of a crime I did not commit,' I said.

'Yes, yes. But since I am sure there are many crimes which you did commit, and of which you have never been accused, don't you think that rather cancels out?'

'I object,' Freisler said.

Morhaim turned mild eyes on him. 'To what?'

'My client is not guilty of any crime.'

'And I am not accusing him of any . . . yet.'

'Is this about the whore?' I said. 'I told your man Keech, I had nothing to do with it.'

'How do you explain being covered in blood? Again?'

'I cut myself shaving.'

Morhaim almost cracked a smile. 'Gerta will live,' he said. 'Though she won't be whoring for a while, I'm afraid. A brave woman, and very spirited.'

'Good old Gerta,' I said, with feeling.

'How do you explain your close proximity to both murders?' Morhaim said.

'I object,' Freisler said again. We both ignored him. 'They were committed right outside my office,' I said. 'You can hardly blame me . . .'

'Yes . . .' Morhaim said. 'It is strangely suggestive, though, don't you think, Mr Wolf?'

'Someone is trying to frame me.'

'No doubt, no doubt. You must have many enemies.'

I had no answer to that. It was true I'd not exactly been making friends, of late. Genius is often lonely.

'I'd like to show you something,' Morhaim said.

'You could show me the door.'

'Very witty, Mr Wolf.' He looked pained. 'Mr Freisler?'

'Yes?'

'You will remain behind?'

'I must represent my client—'

There was something unspoken in the air and I didn't like it. The lawyer subsided. 'He goes free?'

'Do we have a choice?'

'Very well. Mr Wolf.' He nodded to me again and departed abruptly, a dark bird taking flight. I wondered what had spooked him.

'I'm free?'

'I want to show you something.'

'Will it take long?'

'Do you have other plans?'

'Who hired the lawyer?' I said.

Morhaim stood. 'Please. Follow me.'

Once more I was led back to my cell, once more my own clothes were returned to me. I followed Morhaim out of the police station. A wan day, the sun struggling behind grey clouds. Morhaim's car was a beat-up Trojan Tourer, at least a decade old. 'You have treated this vehicle abominably,' I said, unable to help myself. He shrugged, almost in apology.

'Please,' he said, gesturing. I entered the passenger side.

He drove badly. The car's suspension was all but non-existent. I suffered in silence though my bruises had stiffened in my two nights of captivity and the journey was agony. 'Where are we going?'

We were headed west. The cityscape changed, buildings became grander, the make of cars better, the streets cleaner. We came to Hyde Park and Morhaim parked the car. I was just grateful, at that moment, that we'd stopped.

He led me through the park gate, still not speaking. He seemed lost in thought.

'Are we going to feed the ducks?' I said.

He turned to me abruptly. There was something like real agony in his eyes. 'Why do you hate the Jews so much?' he said. 'What have Jews ever done to you, Mr Wolf?'

I felt embarrassed for him. I didn't reply. After a moment he turned away and continued walking. I followed.

We were walking through pleasant green grass, Kensington Palace to our left, a low rising hill ahead. People were out walking their dogs. I missed Prinz and Muckl very much at that moment.

'Where are we going?' I said again. Then we crested the low rise and I saw the duck ponds ahead of us. I saw a police van and men in uniform idling by and I prepared myself for what I'd find there.

'Another dead whore?' I said.

'In a manner of speaking.'

He led me, not hurrying. As we approached I saw a body

had been dredged out of the pond. It was a man, lying face down in the mud. A rather majestic swan was preening nearby, calling to a mate.

We stood over the corpse. Morhaim nodded wordlessly and a policeman in thick boots rolled the body onto its back. But even before he did I knew who it was. I stared down at Rudolf Hess's bloodless face. His head was twisted at an unnatural angle, the grass framing it almost gently, like a crown. He was as dead as anyone I ever saw.

It was Saturday. As Wolf stared down at his one-time companion the church bells began to ring from across the park, from Kensington and from Bayswater. Beyond their huddled group, people went about their lives, strolling in the park, admiring the trees and the autumn colours, enjoying the brisk chill air. People were on their way to church or to market. Life went on everywhere at once: the ducks stared disinterestedly and the swans preened on the calm surface of the water.

'Who did this?' Wolf said. His voice was low.

'I understand you saw him recently?' Morhaim said. 'There is a club he frequented. Owned, in fact. The Hofgarten on Gerrard Street. I understand it is popular with German émigrés . . . of a certain bent, anyway.'

'I . . . was there, yes.'

'I understand that you had a fight.'

'Please!' Wolf was agitated. 'This is persecution! First the whores, now this?'

'Can you identify the victim?'

'What for? It is quite obvious that you know who it is.'

'Who is it?'

'Hess. Rudolf Hess. He is . . . he was a businessman.'

The young policeman with the thick boots snorted. Morhaim silenced him with a gesture. 'You knew each other before? In Germany?'

'You know that we did.'

'In fact you were in prison together, were you not, Mr Wolf?'

'This is irrelevant!'

'Can you tell me what you talked about? When you last saw him?' Morhaim consulted a notebook. 'November 7th?' he said. 'It was a Tuesday.'

'It was last Tuesday.'

'Indeed?'

Wolf said, 'You are well informed.' He stared down at Hess's lifeless face. 'He was a good man,' he said.

'What did you talk about?'

Wolf waved a hand. 'Old times,' he said.

'Were you close in recent years?'

'We did not see each other often.'

'And yet you saw each other twice in the space of a week? Following which Mr Hess' – Morhaim gestured at the corpse – 'was found earlier this morning in a fatal condition.'

'I did not murder Rudolf!'

'Then who did, Mr Wolf?'

'I don't know.'

Morhaim nodded. 'Thank you.'

'Excuse me?'

'I said, thank you, Mr Wolf.' He waited a beat. 'You can go.'

'Is that *all*?'

'I'm afraid we *are* rather busy . . . was there anything else you wanted to add?'

'No.'

'Then goodbye, Mr Wolf. I'm sure we'll meet again.' He gave a faint half-smile. There was nothing warm in it, nothing at all. 'Who knows what we'll find floating in the duck ponds next, eh?'

Wolf stood there, glaring. He wanted to wipe the smirk off the inspector's face. But the man would not look away and, at last, Wolf about-turned and stalked off.

Wolf's Diary, 12th November 1939

On Sundays, London becomes almost bearable. I did my laundry. I saw Martha, the woman who lived down the hall.

The corpulent old bitch came and stood in the doorway of the washroom and regarded me with her arms crossed as I washed my clothes in the bathtub. 'You wash like a woman,' she said.

'Don't you have any pigeons to poison?' I asked. She chuckled. 'Soon, ducky,' she said. 'It's a bit early in the day.'

I thought of the families who came to Trafalgar Square to look at the pigeons. At this old woman smiling at the children like a lost aunt, and selling their parents a small bag of seeds; the children scattering the feed in an arc, the grey birds descending. Pigeons were like Jews: as many as you killed there were always more to take their place.

I scrubbed bloodstains out of my clothes. The tub filled with pink swirling shapes. 'Been in a spot of trouble, have you, ducky?'

'None of your God damned business.'

'Heard you was out on the street, night someone took a knife to old Gerta,' she said.

'I didn't do it.'

'No one saying that you did, ducky.'

'A friend of mine died yesterday,' I told her. I don't know why I told her that.

'I'm sorry to hear it.'

I shrugged. Lathered up soap. 'He was weak. The weak die.'

'And the strong survive,' she said. There was a sad note in her voice I couldn't interpret. 'You and me,' she said. 'The pigeons and the whores.'

'He was so loyal,' I said. 'To his last breath, he was loyal. I value loyalty.'

'Heaven knows there's little enough of it to go around,' Martha said.

'Someone killed him. Drowned him in the ponds in Hyde Park.'

'That's nice.' She gave a shuddering, dramatic sigh. 'It's so peaceful there. I went once, with one of my old johns. He liked to do it in nature, you see. He was French.' She shrugged, as if that was explanation enough for everything. 'It must be a nice place to die.'

'I hadn't thought of it that way.'

'Do you ever think how you will die, Wolf?' she said. The conversation was turning morbid but somehow I didn't mind. My mind had been occupied with death, of late.

'I always thought I'd die in the course of my duty,' I said. 'Serving the Fatherland. It hasn't worked out that way.' I thought of the Americans' offer. I wondered if they were still shadowing me. No doubt they could make life difficult for me, if they so chose. To return to Germany . . . it was a dream, a sweet dream, but nothing more. And if, by some insane miracle, their *coup d'état* succeeded . . . what then?

I would become their puppet.

'I would have liked to die peacefully,' I said, 'in my sleep. With a book on my chest and a woman beside me and my dogs at my feet.'

'How . . . pleasant.' There was a rude loud sound and a look of surprise momentarily suffused Martha's face, followed by a bellowing laugh.

'God damn it, Martha, that stinks!'

'I knew I should have laid off them Brussels sprouts,' she said, fanning the air. 'Well, I better go. When is your friend's funeral?'

'I don't know. The police haven't released the body yet.'

'Will you go?'

'I don't know.'

'Goodbye, Wolf.'

'See you later, Martha.'

She left me alone with her stink still in the air. I scrubbed blood off my clothes and watched the soapsuds form in the bathtub, pink and red, pink and red.

Wolf's Diary, 13th November 1939

On Monday I went back to the Jewish Territorialist Organisation
but the lights weren't on. There was no sign of Goodman or the
typist and a notice on the door simply said 'Closed'.

I made an anonymous phone call to the police and
watched the flat on Threadneedle Street. I ate a sandwich
and drank lemonade. The police arrived promptly enough
but, as I suspected, the flat was empty and seemed to have
been that way for a couple of days. I crumpled the paper I
had used to wrap the sandwich and put it and the empty
bottle of lemonade back in my bag, to dispose of later. I
loathed litter.

I had come so close! That mannish Jew bitch had been all
but in my grasp and I let her slip away. It seemed obvious to
me now that Judith Rubinstein's escape had been facilitated
by her Palestinian comrades. Either they had struck a deal
with my former associates or they had known to hijack the
shipment of illegals before it was delivered into that loathsome
Barbie's hands. Either way I now had no idea where she was,
and I had lost both her and the terrorists threatening Mosley.

I had hit a temporary dead end. It was in the nature of such
work, and yet I felt angry. I wanted those Jew conspirators
caught. I could only hope that the Blackshirts who had
unwittingly come to my rescue the night I trailed Bitker had
put some of them into hospital.

Hospital!

I returned to my office and set to work. For the next hour
I dialled the local hospitals. No luck! Wherever my Palestinian
terrorists went, it was not to a public hospital.

'*Himmel, Arsch, und Zwirn!*' I said, with feeling.

Wolf's Diary, 14th November 1939

'What do you mean Mosley is not there?' I said.

'*Sir Oswald* is not here.'

'Sir Oswald, yes, fine. Where is he?'

'I'm afraid Sir Oswald is unavailable at the moment, sir. Would you care to leave a message?'

'No, I do not *care* to leave a message! Who is this?'

'Thomas Alderman, sir.'

'Alderman? Who the hell are you?'

'I'm Sir Oswald's assistant, sir. One of his assistants.' An embarrassed hesitation on the line. 'We met, briefly? At Sir Oswald's soirée?'

'Did we? Well, Alderman, is Lady Mosley there?'

'No, sir. I'm afraid no one is available. It is the elections, you see. The final push and all that? Sir Oswald is speaking to supporters around the country all week.'

'And Lady Mosley?'

'She is with Sir Oswald, sir.'

'I don't like your tone, Alderman.'

'Sir?'

'Tell him I called. Tell him I expect to hear from him!'

'Of course, Mr . . . Wolf?'

'You know bloody well who it is,' I said, slamming down the receiver.

The sheer arrogance of it all!

Wolf's Diary, 15th November 1939

'Hello?'

She had the kind of breathless voice that promises sin, that teases you with it. I hated her and wanted her and I didn't lie to myself about it. I never lie to myself. It is the core of my strength.

'Miss Rubinstein.'

'Wolf!' Her voice changed, became a delighted tinkle. I pictured her urinating on herself, surrounded by silk sheets. 'Is there progress on my sister's case?'

'It has become somewhat more complex than I at first anticipated.'

'What does that mean?'

It means a terrorist conspiracy, I thought, but didn't say.

And a dead man in a pond. I was trapped in a maze, beset
on all sides by those with evil intentions. I alone was pure
of thought and deed. Were I ever asked to offer my
observations on the art of detection – for which I am
uniquely qualified – I would say that a good detective is
but a soldier in the universal chaoskampf, the cosmic battle
with anarchy. Murder is a frustration not just of the
individual: it is a frustration of the race. Indeed, I had
written several times to the *Private Investigator's Gazetteer*,
of Boston, Massachusetts, offering to share my views on
detection – on condition, naturally, of receipt of a modest
author's fee – but had yet to receive a reply. The impudence
of those Americans!

For murder is a simple art – if it can be said to be any art
at all – and it seems to me it is merely a question of *scale*. I
believe it was that French scientist, Rostand, who wrote that if
you kill one man, you are a murderer, yet if you kill millions,
you are a conqueror. I would have been a conqueror!

Chaos, all my life I have battled chaos!

Was I the only completely sane man still left in the world?

'Wolf!'

'Yes,' I said, coming back to myself with a start.

'You were saying?'

'I may need your help,' I said, hating myself for it.

'Oh?'

'I am working on a case that may be related. I need access
to . . . . a part of the Jewish community.'

I heard her laugh. 'You want me to work with you? Solving
. . . crime? Like Nick and Nora Charles!'

'Very amusing, yes. But no.'

'Really!' I could hear rustling sounds on the other end of
the line. Imagined her rubbing her naked thighs against the
sheets. Bit my lip, trying to concentrate. 'You can't manage
on your own, Wolf?'

'Let's just say my previous attempt has not been a
complete success.'

'I can't imagine why!'

'Listen you horrid little bitch, don't you—'

'I love it when you talk dirty,' she said. 'And I'd be delighted to help – in fact, we may be able to help each other.'

'Oh?'

'I'd like you to come with me to a party.'

'I beg your pardon?'

'It's the event of the season!' she said. 'I'll pick you up, tomorrow, at six thirty sharp. Dress nicely, Wolf.'

'What sort of party? Wait—' but she had already hung up.

I sat there staring at the phone and cursing all Jews.

Wolf's Diary, 16th November 1939

'You look so dashing,' she said. She was standing in my office smoking a cigarette through a silver holder. Her white dress shimmered as she moved around the room.

'*Must* you smoke?' I said.

'Does it antagonise you?' She grinned at me with her lovely white teeth and shimmied to me. Her hand reached down and grabbed me by the crotch, hard. She had no shame; no shame at all. She leaned her head into the crook of my neck, licked upwards. Her teeth nibbled my earlobe. 'Why do I like bad boys so . . .' she murmured.

'You're a harlot,' I said. 'A slut.'

She pulled away from me and slapped me, hard. 'Fuck you, Wolf!' Her eyes flashed. 'Get on your knees,' she said.

'Get away from me, you whore.'

She laughed, a cruel high-pitched sound. 'Get down on your *knees*,' she said. She kicked me, suddenly, sweeping my legs from under me. I fell, painfully. 'That's better.'

I whispered, 'Whore . . .' My mouth was dry. She lifted up the hem of her dress. She wore nothing underneath. She grabbed me by the back of the head and forced my face between her thighs. My mouth was on her engorged lips as they rubbed against my face again. She made strange animal sounds; her intensity was building up too quickly, but then she stopped. She stepped away from me, holding the hem of the dress carefully so as not to stain it. 'Turn over,' she said. 'I said turn over!'

Then she was kicking me, calling me names, terrible names, tearing at my trousers, pulling them down. My behind was exposed to the air and she slapped it, again and again, leaving angry red marks on the white flesh, and she was moaning: the room was a cacophony of animal sounds. I held myself in my hand, I felt her finger slide, coated in her discharge, suddenly and painfully into my anus. I screamed and came, spurting seed over my hands, but careful, careful not to stain the rented suit. She stood over me, breathing heavily.

'We'll be late,' she said.

I stood up carefully, pulled up my trousers one-handed. Isabella wiped herself clean with a monogrammed handkerchief, quite unselfconsciously. I left her there and went to the bathroom down the hall and stared at my face, shining with her wetness, in the mirror. I washed my hand, watching my seed wash down the sinkhole. I washed my face. When I left I saw Martha at the end of the corridor. She watched me without expression until I turned away.

In my office Isabella Rubinstein was a model of decorum. Her cigarette holder was set between her teeth again. She blew out a cloud of smoke contentedly and smiled at me. 'We don't want to be late, do we,' she said.

I followed her down the stairs when I remembered I had stashed the Jewish identity document behind the bins, after the fat prostitute's attempted murder. 'Excuse me,' I said. I went back down the road and retrieved it: it was still there, in a crack in the wall. Dried blood was still splattered, in dull patches, on the stone. I returned to Isabella. Her white Crossley Sports Saloon was parked outside the dirty bookstore, magnificent and shining like a beacon of wealth. Isabella drove. I sat beside her. The car was filled with the smell of her expensive tobacco and the musk of our hurried sex.

She drove with easy abandon, the way she did everything else. She was young, so much younger than me, yet something inside her was rotten and corrupt, and it withered her from within.

We drove with the windows open and a cold breeze wafting past and the smell of London, of salt and tar from the Thames and urine from the sewers and roasting chestnuts and exhaust fumes and dung from horse-drawn carriages. In what seemed like moments we were by the British Museum. Greek columns rose into the air and a thin drizzle of rain began to fall as Isabella parked the car. A glow of festive light came from behind the windows of Number 40, Museum Street.

I clenched my fists.

These were, after all, the premises of Allen & Unwin, the publishers.

People were spilling out of the open doors of the publishing house. They stood in clumps in the rain, smoking and drinking and laughing, an unruly crowd of artists, writers and painters and their hangers-on. 'Oh, how *exciting*!' Isabella said, weaving her arm through mine. We strolled up to the party; I felt conspicuous in my suit and hat amongst the mob of scruffy bohemians. And yet I was once one of them; I, too, was once a penniless artist, in Vienna, painting bright water-colours of the city's architecture and scenes, selling them to the tourists for a handful of coins. It had felt to me then an honest way of making a living. But that had been before the war, before the blindness and the hospital, before my fate had been shaped to follow a different path: to lead, to rule!

At last, to Fall.

'Managed to insult both of us in the same sentence!' someone said.

'Wolf? Are you with us?' Isabella said.

'Yes, yes, of course,' I said. 'Is that Evelyn Waugh talking to Cecil Forester?'

Isabella shrugged. 'Are they painters?'

'Writers,' I said. Isabella went ahead of me, her arm slipping out of mine. She nodded and smiled, greeting people she knew. 'Who is the Chinese-looking man?' I said.

'That? That's Leslie Charteris!' she sighed as though in ecstasy. 'Don't you just love *The Saint*?'

'Charteris?' I said. 'I thought he was working in Hollywood.'

'He is. There's a company of them arrived in town for filming. But no one's going to miss this party.'

We went inside.

'Wolf!'

I turned to see, without much surprise, the big American, Virgil, bearing down on me, a glass of wine in each hand. He handed me one without asking. I held it without sipping. I abhor drink, always have. To me, a man must always be in supreme command of himself.

'Virgil,' I said; for a moment I felt like a gunslinger in one of Karl May's westerns, facing a showdown. The feeling persisted.

He smiled at me but his eyes were hooded. 'Have you thought further of my proposition?' he said.

'I have.'

He waited, but I said nothing more. He nodded, slowly and inexorably, the way a mountain moves in an earthquake. 'Don't think for too long,' he said, softly. 'Everyone can be replaced, Wolf. Even you.'

'I have never liked Americans,' I said, and he laughed. He had the coldest, hardest eyes of any man I'd ever seen. 'Cheers,' he said, clinking his glass against mine.

'Are your people still following me?' I said.

He sipped from his drink and shrugged. 'Do they need to?' he said.

'Is that a yes?'

He shrugged again. One had the sense of contained

physical threat in every gesture he made. 'I hear you're having troubles,' he said, 'with some prostitute murders.'

'*One* prostitute murder,' I said, 'and I didn't do it.'

'You're not a killer,' he said, sympathetically. 'You're a soldier, like I was, like many of us will be again once war breaks out.'

'You believe war will break out?'

'It's only a matter of time,' he said. His glass was already empty. He looked at mine. 'Do you mind?'

'Not at all.' He took it from me and drank as though he had been deprived of drink for months. 'Yes,' he said, after draining my glass. 'War with Germany will come – war with Russia, I should say, and its proxy, Germany. A European war. Perhaps even another world war.' He put his hand on my shoulder, squeezing. His rank breath blasted into my face, coarse with the fumes of cheap red wine. 'You can help stop that,' he said. 'Do you want to see your country ravaged by war, destroyed by bombs? International socialism *must* be stopped, Wolf. Stopped before it is too late!'

The words sent a chill down my spine. Or perhaps it was the draught from the open door. 'At what price?' I said. 'You want me to serve Germany by turning her into a whore, spreading her legs wide for America?'

He laughed. 'Everyone needs must be a whore sometimes,' he said. 'Would you rather be fucked by the Russians, or us?'

'I would rather my country slit its own throat than prostitute itself,' I said.

'Listen to me, Wolf.' He was standing close, now, his hand on my shoulder reaching for my neck, almost choking me. 'You do not say no to me. No one does. I am America, and America does not take no for an answer. Refuse us, and we will bomb the shit out of your country, kill your women and rape your dogs and burn your houses and piss on the embers. Do you understand me? I said, do you understand me!'

'I understand you perfectly,' I said. I gathered up phlegm

and spat in his face. My aim was perfect. The mucus hit him in the eye and ran down his cheek. His face turned red in fury; his grip on my neck slackened. 'And the answer is no. *Nein*. Never!'

'You will regret this, you little shit stain,' he said.

'Get your fucking hands off me!'

'Wolf? Who is this man?'

I felt rather than saw Virgil's hand leave my neck. He wiped his face with a handkerchief. When he turned back his face wore a semblance of charm. 'Just an old friend,' he said. 'I apologise if I was monopolising his time at your expense, Miss . . .?'

'Rubinstein. *Excuse* me.' She led me away, to a corner of the room. I felt Virgil's glowering presence receding behind us. 'Who *was* that ghastly man?' Isabella said.

'I . . . am not sure,' I said. I had a bad feeling about Virgil: about the possible fallout from my refusal. Could the Americans be better allies than the Russians, in the long run? Could I still somehow use them to my advantage? And his mention of the prostitute murder – if they were following me, could they have inadvertently come across the real killer's identity?

But I had no time to dwell, for at that moment I saw a figure I recognised, and all thoughts of such things fled from my mind. 'Albert!' I yelled. 'Albert! It's Wolf!'

I abandoned Isabella to her own devices and hared across the room. He turned slowly, with a smile of polite inquiry on his face, which disappeared when he saw me. 'Ah, Wolf,' he said, awkwardly.

Albert Curtis Brown was my literary agent. He was originally an American journalist who had then settled and made his home in Britain. He was in his seventies, but still wiry and strong. 'I wanted to discuss with you a sequel to *My Struggle*,' I said.

'Quite, quite. Mr Wolf. A sequel.' Was it my imagination or did a fleeting look of distaste pass across his face like a cloud?

But I did not care for Mr Curtis Brown's approval; I cared for what remained of my literary career. 'I have written to you repeatedly,' I said, '*repeatedly*, in the past few months, regarding the manuscript I am in the process of preparing—'

'Let me stop you there, Mr Wolf,' he said. 'I am no longer actively involved with the agency. My son is taking care of all outstanding contracts and the like. Now, if you'll excuse me—'

'Wait!' I said. 'Mr Curtis Brown, I really must insist that the agency treat me with more respect. I have never even received payment of royalties due to me!'

'Mr Wolf, there *are* no royalties.' He sighed, looking suddenly old. 'The manuscript was taken on, from the German publishers, in the good faith that it would be of general interest to contemporary readers as a view of the situation in Germany.'

'Yes? Yes?'

'Well, Mr Wolf, the belief was that National Socialism would win the elections of 1933, therefore catapulting Nazism into the international spotlight. This has failed to happen, and interest in the manuscript, accordingly, waned. I'm afraid there's little to add, really. Interest currently is in material by or about Stalin, or Ernst Thälmann, the current German Chancellor. Your advance never earned out, Mr Wolf. In fact, I believe unsold copies of *My Struggle* will soon be pulped, and the title allowed to go out of print.'

'Out of print!' I said; deeply shocked.

He nodded sadly. 'I'm afraid so,' he said.

'But that is an *outrage*! You must do something!'

'I'm afraid there is little I can do, Mr Wolf.' He patted me on the shoulder, awkwardly. 'History has passed you by, old chap,' he said. 'But look on the bright side. You're only – what? Fifty or so? – you're young enough to start again. Write something new. Not another diatribe against the Jews. That stuff is out of fashion now. Of specialist interest, certainly, but not of a mass market appeal. Why not try

your hand at a proper novel, Mr Wolf?' He regarded me
thoughtfully. 'Do you know,' he said, 'detective tales are
always popular.'

'*Detective* tales?' I said. I was so dumbfounded I could
only echo him. 'A work of *fiction*? Mr Curtis Brown, my
book is a treatise on politics, on race; it draws from the most
distinguished sources, not to mention my own autobiography
– do you have any *idea* how many copies it has sold in
Germany *alone*?'

'Like I said, I am no longer involved in the day to day
running of the agency,' Curtis Brown said. 'I wish you all the
best, Mr Wolf. But a word of advice – don't give up your day
job just yet.' And with that, and chuckling to himself, he
walked off abruptly, joining a circle in which I could only
identify Alan Milne, the author of a popular children's book
about a talking bear.

The outrage! The provocation!

For a few moments, I must confess, I wandered the party in
a daze, seeing faces familiar to me only from their dustjackets'
photograph, yet paying them no attention. My book was to be
pulped? My *book*? *My* book?

It was inconceivable!

Across the large room a makeshift bar had been set over
cartons of books, and there I saw Isabella chatting to Lord
Rothermere, the owner of the *Daily Mail*.

I needed fresh air.

Instead, as I turned, I caught a hint of perfume, the flash of
gold, a breathy voice saying my name, over and over. I turned
and there she was, the most real woman I had ever seen, as
bright as the star that she was.

'Leni?' I said, in total disbelief. 'Leni, is that *you*?'

The watcher in the dark was aware of the other watchers in the
dark. There were so many eyes in the night. London was a city
of watchers, all watching each other watching each other. It made
him giddy just to think about it.

He knew so many secrets! He knew, for instance, that the detective was seeing the Jewish woman, and the shame of it was almost more than the watcher could bear. The detective, with a Jewess! The horror and the disgust it evoked in him were visceral, physical; he almost retched. He thought more and more of the woman, these days. She was a whore, as all Jewesses were. He thought of the knife, safe and hidden in his pocket, and how it might sing as it touched her flesh. He'd seen them, earlier, in her white car, together as they left. The whores on Berwick Street were more careful now. Some had moved away entirely, but not all. Business had to continue and this dark street was a foil for desire and a shelter for the men who frequented such creatures. Evil creatures, succubae. In ridding the world of them he was only easing their pain. And yet he could not lie, not to himself. He was not easing their pain. He was using them, if for a noble cause – using them to try and awaken the detective. Still: the whores were merely a means to an end.

The night was full of eyes and they made the watcher in the dark apprehensive. There were the American shadows, for instance. They were good; he had missed them entirely at first, and he suspected they may have seen him, the way shadows can see the other shadows in the night. He was worried about that. No one should have been able to see him. He watched one now, young but hard-faced, the way he melted into the night; the way he, too, was watching the detective's office. Earlier the watcher saw him break in, with far more ease than the watcher himself had mustered. The American had slipped in as easily as a ghost. Now that he knew they were there the watcher found it easy enough to avoid them, but he had the feeling they had been there when . . . at the time of that unfortunate incident with the fat whore, and when he ran. He was reasonably sure he had shaken off any pursuers, overt or covert, by the time he changed his clothes in Soho Square, but he couldn't be positive. They might still come for him. Or maybe they didn't care. Or they even thought they could use him, now or later; but in that they were sorely wrong.

The detective was away with his Jew whore but sooner or later he would return and when he did the watcher would be ready. But not tonight. Tonight he only watched, and touched the knife, and he thought, suddenly and inexplicably, of the Alps, in winter, which he had never seen; and of the snow, falling and falling down on the slopes, until the whole world was white and pure.

*   *   *

In another time and place Shomer lies on the bunk bed as the snow falls outside; it falls and falls, as if, by its mere presence, it could silence the world. There is no work to be done in the infirmary, no hard labour, only time. And time is dangerous. It is a space in which to think. All is silent, until the doctor comes, walking past each patient, marking in his little black book. The doctor is a tall skeleton, with no face. He is dressed in a long black leather coat that rustles by his ankles as he walks. His pen is black and he examines each man with a cursory glance, checking each man against his number, in his little black book. A cross, a cross. And the men with the crosses rise without a murmur, without a murmur they walk to the gas chambers. The doctor like Death walks the rows of beds until at last he finds Shomer, and he gives him with a cursory glance and his diagnosis, what of his diagnosis? And he nods, once, and says, 'You're fit to leave,' and so with these words Shomer is once again saved; for a little while longer he's saved.

10

'Wolf!' She leaned in to the shorter man, kissing him on both cheeks. She smelled intoxicating to him. 'Darling, where have you *been*? Have you simply dropped off the face of the *Earth*?'

'Leni? Leni Riefenstahl? My God!' Wolf said. He could not take his eyes off her, she was radiant, a star. 'I thought you had been caught behind, in the Fall!'

'You silly man,' she said, laughing, 'do you not read *Photoplay*? I'm in Hollywood now!'

'Leni, but that is incredible! Let me look at you!'

He held her at arm's length, admiring her cool Germanic glamour; she was the most perfectly Aryan woman he had ever known.

'I remember seeing you speak in '32,' Riefenstahl said. 'You were incredible, amazing. The most magnetic man I'd ever met.'

'You're too kind.'

'And *My Struggle*! The book made a *tremendous* impression on me, Wolf.'

'You were always faithful to me, Leni. To the cause. Remember Nuremberg?'

'But of course.' Her face clouded. 'But what a terrible time it's been. I was all set up, mein kleiner Wolf. Ready to film the glorious victory of National Socialism, its inexorable rise to power!' For a moment she almost looked like she would cry. 'I would have called my documentary film *Sieg des Glaubens*, the Victory of Faith. But it was *der Verlust des Glaubens*, the loss of faith, instead. How could Germany do this, Wolf? How could history turn out so different than it should have?'

Wolf shook his head. 'Let us not speak of these things, *meine liebe.* I had thought many things impossible, yet here you are, and here I am—'

'Isn't London wonderful?' Riefenstahl said. Wolf said, 'I would not say it is wonderful, exactly.'

'But Wolf, what do you do here?'

'I'm a private investigator, Leni.'

For a moment she looked stunned; then she exploded in laughter. 'A private eye? A shamus? A *dick*? You, Wolf?'

'I believe in law, in order. There must always be order, Leni. There must always be an account.'

'Then you may as well become an accountant,' she said, dismissively. 'Oh, Wolf! You were meant for better things. You were meant to shape the future in your hands, to mould it like clay! You break my heart.'

She was crying. Wolf put his arms round her. People looked their way, then looked away. 'Come, *meine liebe*, come. Tell me of yourself. Tell me of Hollywood!'

'Oh, Wolf.' She pulled away, dried her tears with the tips of her fingers, began to tentatively smile. 'I went to America shortly before immigration out of Germany became impossible. I had friends, a director who wanted to work with me. I'd been offered a job with the studios in the past, but had turned them down. This time I accepted. I work for the Warner brothers now, in California.'

'Warner?' Wolf said.

'Jews,' Leni said. She shrugged apologetically. 'It is an industry dominated by Jews, Wolf. But it is what I do. We must all make a living.'

Wolf briefly thought of Isabella, on the other side of the room; pushed her out of his mind. 'I do not blame you, Leni,' he said. 'It is as you said: we must all make a living.'

'Oh, Wolf.' Her eyes filled with tears again. 'You don't know how much it means to me, to hear you say that.'

'Please! No more tears.' He put his arm round her waist. 'Let us go outside,' he suggested.

She acquiesced. Outside the rain was still falling, but softly, a

London drizzle. The poet Stephen Spender was arguing loudly with Christopher Isherwood. Isherwood ceased abruptly and was violently sick on the pavement. Spender held his head gently, encouraging him to 'Let it all out!' to loud cheers from the assembled smokers and drinkers. 'Artists,' Leni said, as though that explained it all.

They had shared a powerful attraction, though it was never more than that; there was never talk of Wolf leaving Eva, for instance. They were two strong and charismatic people and their auras intertwined, for a while, and what they did behind closed doors was nobody's damn business.

'But what are you doing here?' Wolf said. 'In London?'

'You really don't read the film magazines,' she said. 'I don't know why that should surprise me – why should you? It's just that, in Hollywood, everyone knows your business in advance, before even you do. It's a city of hustlers, Wolf. Hustlers with big dreams.'

A small smile played on Wolf's lips. Leni always brought out his softer side. 'One could say the same of me.'

Leni laughed. 'It's a city of dogs,' she said. 'And you're a wolf.'

Wolf was touched. 'But you didn't answer my question,' he said. 'What are you doing in London?'

'We're filming!' Leni said. She saw the surprise on Wolf's face and laughed again. 'It's a wonderful picture,' she said. 'It really is. It's about Germany, in a way, you see. About the war. Everyone in America is convinced there is going to be a war, and soon.'

'Yes,' Wolf said, thinking of Virgil. 'But I hate the idea of my Germany at war, even a Germany fouled and abused by communism.'

'A war for the liberation of Germany,' Leni said. 'Surely that would be a good thing? Communism is an international threat.'

Wolf shook his head. 'I don't know,' he said, slowly. 'But I do not trust the Americans.'

Leni shrugged. She lit a cigarette, blew smoke as blue as a bruise into the cold humid air. 'But tell me about your film,' Wolf said. 'Your . . . your *picture*.'

Like all actresses, she was essentially shallow and self-involved, with the attention span of a child, he thought. She liked bright things and dominant men and an easy life. But she was charming, enchanting, with that ill-defined quality of the movie star about her: as if she could only ever truly exist on the silver screen, beyond the reach of mere mortals. There was something of the *waldelfen*, of the fey, about the screen folk like Leni, something ethereal and strange.

'Do you know the writer, F. Scott Fitzgerald?' Leni said.

'Not personally,' Wolf said.

Leni smiled tolerantly. 'Well,' she said, 'Scott was on contract to Metro-Goldwyn-Mayer, but Jack Warner stole him from them, and to be honest I think they were glad to be rid of him. He drinks, you see. And his health is quite poor as a consequence.'

'A wonderful writer,' Wolf said. '*The Great Gatsby*?'

'Yes,' Leni said. 'Well, it is about Gatsby, you see. Jack – Mr Warner – he's been after Scott for years, for a sequel.'

'But Gatsby dies!' Wolf said, shocked.

'Yes, yes,' Leni said; a little impatiently. 'But it's Hollywood.'

'So then, what does Warner want? You say it's a . . . a sequel?'

'In a way. You see, he's offered Scott rather a lot of money for an original screenplay. Scott originally called it *Everybody Comes to Gatsby's*. He was rather inspired by visiting Europe with his wife, Zelda – a lovely woman – and seeing the plight of the refugees fleeing the communist regime. In the screenplay, Gatsby survives his gun wound from the first book, and after several years travelling the world, working as a gun runner and revolutionary, ends up a jaded, cynical bar owner in Morocco. War breaks out but Gatsby maintains his solitary existence even as desperate refugees come to Morocco en route to Free Europe. He spends his time drinking and smoking and playing complex chess problems against himself. Until one day Daisy Buchanan walks through his door, and everything changes.'

'Daisy? The woman he was so desperately in love with? But she left him, without a moment's thought!'

'Who knows the heart of a woman, Wolf,' Leni said. 'In any

case, Jack didn't like the title. He felt it was too long. So the picture is named after the town Gatsby's is in. Tangier. We're shooting some of it here in London. I'm in it, you see, Wolf. I'm the star!'

Wolf stared at her, for once open mouthed. '*You're* Daisy Buchanan?' he said.

'And Humphrey Bogart is Gatsby,' Leni said.

'Who?'

'He's a great actor. Anyway, we've run into some problems with the production, so everyone's a little tense right now. You know how it is in motion pictures. Nothing is ever certain.'

'Like politics,' Wolf said, darkly.

'Yes. I suppose. It's all politics, isn't it, Wolf? Oh, Wolf, I wish things had been different!' She clung to him, fiercely. 'We'll always have Nuremberg, won't we, Wolf? We'll always have that, at least?'

'Leni,' Wolf said, and then, in a different tone of voice, 'Leni, who is that man?'

'What man, Wolf?'

'There is a man coming towards us, Leni. He seems to want your attention.'

Leni turned her head. A man was indeed coming towards them, yet he did not approach, but waited in the drizzle, his fedora cocked to one side, a cigarette dangling from his lips. He was young and not unattractive, with dark wavy hair. Wolf knew his face immediately; but he did not think the man would have caught sight of his, before.

'Oh, it's only Robert!' Leni said, laughing. 'For a moment there you seemed so intense, I was almost scared!'

'Robert?'

'Robert Bitker. He's with the production crew. A Jew from Poland, but he's in with that Warner lot. Why, do you know him, Wolf?'

'I would like to know him better,' Wolf said, but quietly.

'I could introduce you!'

'Better not. Can you tell me where he's based?'

'Where we all are. The Grosvenor Hotel, by Victoria Station. Why, what's the matter, Wolf?'

'It's nothing, Leni. Leni, he seems to be trying to get your attention.'

'It must be a message from Hal. Hal Wallis? He's our producer. I think we're expected elsewhere. Oh, Wolf! Can I see you again?'

'I hope so. I would like that.'

'Come see me at the Grosvenor!' Leni said. 'We're here for another week. We were supposed to be shooting already but there'd been a problem with the studio, so we're just doing publicity and the like. Party, party, party, Wolf.'

'You seem to hang out with plenty of Jews, these days.'

'Oh, Wolf! Don't be like that. I don't like it any more than you do. It's just Hollywood.'

'Yes,' Wolf said. 'Well, you better go, Leni. I will come for you, soon.'

'Please do.' She kissed him on both cheeks, held him again at arm's length, marvelling. 'You look *tough*, Wolf. You should have been an actor!'

Wolf laughed, the sound startled from his throat. He couldn't remember the last time he'd laughed. He was not a man much given to frivolity, but Leni had a way with her. She was not like other girls. And she had taken his little predilections as something entirely natural, not even worthy of comment. She had been very accommodating in that way. He kissed her on both cheeks and off she went, to that man Bitker. Wolf watched them together. Bitker touched the brim of his hat, briefly, in acknowledgement, then turned his back on Wolf. Could he have recognised him?

But Wolf didn't think so. So the man he had been seeking and thought lost was there all along! A movie man, of all things. It made sense. Hollywood was full of Jews, Bitker must have been their appointed go-between, their bagman to the London cells: the American Jews sponsoring terror attacks on the Fascist leader carried out by their brethren in Britain.

But now Wolf knew where Bitker was. And he would not lose him a second time. And Bitker, in turn, would lead him to Judith. He was sure of it.

He went back inside. The party was picking up volume as drunken authors, poets, artists and their various editors, agents, copy editors and sales reps were polishing off Allen & Unwin's discretionary wine supply. 'Wolf?' It was Isabella, her cheeks flushed, her eyes shining with a mixture of alcohol and excitement. 'I have just met the most fascinating man, a professor of Anglo-Saxon at Oxford. John Tolkien? Apparently he has a novel with Allen & Unwin. Have you heard of him?'

'I've read his book,' Wolf said, grudgingly, though he had enjoyed it awfully. 'It is a trifle, a fantasy for toddlers, as all fantasy literature is inherently for children.'

'You're in a bad mood,' Isabella said, and there was a flash in her eyes, something dangerous and promising at the same time. She pressed close to him; her fingers closed hard on his crotch. 'Do you need to be punished?' she whispered, close in his ear. Her breath smelled of wine.

'Get away from me, you whore!'

Conversation quietened abruptly. People turned, watching them. A trim, energetic-looking gentleman in his fifties approached them. 'Is there a problem?' he said.

Isabella was pale. 'How dare you,' she said. 'How *dare* you!'

'Stay out of this,' Wolf said to the man. Isabella's hand rose to slap Wolf. He grabbed her wrist, his face burning in fury, his words coming out in spittle that hit her face. 'Whore! Foul, disgusting *whore*!'

Suddenly and terribly, Isabella laughed. 'And you like it!' she shouted. She pulled back her hand. Her smile was cruel. She pulled out a wad of notes from her handbag and tossed the money in Wolf's face. The money fluttered in the air, falling down gently around Wolf, settling between their feet. 'Who is the whore now, Mr Wolf?' Isabella said. Her beautiful young face was split by an ugly leer. 'You know where to find me, when you need more.'

She turned and stalked off.

'What do you want?' Wolf screamed, into the dapper gentle-man's startled face.

The face hardened. 'I'm afraid I'm going to have to ask you to leave,' he said.

'And who the hell are you!'

'I am Stanley Unwin, sir. I am the owner of this office, and the host of this party. And . . . I don't believe that you were invited?'

'You're Stanley Unwin?' Wolf said. '*You're* Unwin?'

'I don't believe I've had the pleasure?'

'You rejected my *book*!' Wolf said. The man looked blank. 'I did? We receive so many books here at Allen & Unwin, it really is quite impossible for us to publish them all—'

'*My* book! *My Struggle*! I wrote it in *prison*! Do you know what I had to go through, the years of suffering, Vienna, the War, *imprisonment*, and you, you . . . you uppity God damned *Englishman*, you had the *gall* to *reject* it?'

'Like I said, it really is impossible to—'

'It wasn't even a *personal* rejection!'

'Sir, I must insist that you – *sir*! I must ask you to leave the premises immediately.'

'You damned Jew-lover! Don't you know who I am? And him' – Wolf was pointing wildly at the awkward, genial pipe smoker standing by the makeshift bar – 'you publish *him*? This . . . this *Tolkien*? With tales of . . . of *hobbits*? I would have changed the world! My book *mattered*!'

'Sir!'

Two of the more burly authors present had materialised beside Unwin and were moving on Wolf, who backed away, his face red with anger, spittle dribbling from his lips in his passion. 'Damn you, Unwin! No one rejects *my* manuscript!'

'Get *out*!'

He wasn't, afterwards, sure who the men who threw him out were: Leslie Charteris and Evelyn Waugh, perhaps, as unlikely as that pairing may have seemed. They dragged him, still screaming and cursing, outside. They didn't let go until they reached the end of Museum Street and there they threw him bodily to the ground. Wolf landed in a puddle, cold rain soaking his coat. The two men stood panting above him, and one of them lit a cigarette while coughing. 'Forget it, man,' he said. 'It's just a God damned party.'

'Everybody gets rejected, sometimes,' the other said. They stood there breathing heavily and watched him; until Wolf picked himself up and dusted himself down, and without another word walked away.

Wolf's Diary, 16th November 1939 – *contd.*

When I had arrived at the hospital in Pasewalk, in 1918, I was scared – terrified. I won't deny it, won't lie. I was a ghost of the man I had been, a shadow. I moved in the dark, in a place into which no light was allowed to penetrate. I was frantic with fear.

The hospital was cool and calm and the nurses abrupt but not unkind. I remember being led down a corridor, trying to picture my environment using my other senses – smell and touch and sound. It was terrifying, the noises I could hear from the rooms we passed, the screams and the groans and the mutters of the inmates. I had been plucked off the battlefield and placed in an insane asylum. But I was not mad!

I was the sanest man I ever knew.

That first day, and the smell of disinfectant, of cabbage boiled too long, of the nurses' uniforms, that smell of clean washing. The nurse helped me to my room, to the narrow bed beneath a window out of which I could not see. I was blind! For hours I lay on my back, staring into absolute dark. I was clean, washed, scrubbed. There was no mud, no sound of shells whistling overhead, no cries of the dying, of my people, my people. Germany suffered, and I suffered with her. At that time, perhaps, though it is hazy to me now, I still believed I would be an artist. But how could an artist work who could not see the canvas? I was no longer one thing, but not yet another. I was myself an empty canvas, waiting to be filled with light.

It was only the next day that I met him. The nurse led me to his office and helped me sit down. Before me was his desk; I felt its edges, holding the thick board of wood between thumb and fingers, as though to reassure myself of its reality. I knew him only as a voice then. It was his voice that haunted my sleep, his voice that shaped me.

He said, 'My name is Dr Forster.'

I gave him my name and my rank. He began to question me, noting down my answers with a scratch of his pen on the paper. His voice was gruff, his manners equally so. I felt he was quizzing me, pushing me. He was challenging me, calling me a deserter from the front, a coward, telling me I was shirking my duty! I protested, spoke of my desire to go back to the front, to fight for the Fatherland. I felt him become puzzled as the time went by. I got the impression, never spoken aloud, that many of the inmates at this hospital were just of the nature he accused me of being: faking injuries and mental states to escape the trenches and the war. But I was not like that! And my injury was real: I had been blinded by the gas!

'You must help me!' I said. 'Is there nothing you can do?' and then, when he said nothing, 'Why was I brought here? These people are crazy! Do you say my blindness is not real? That I too am faking it?' My voice rose in pitch and fever. 'You must help me, doctor! I must see again!'

His silence lengthened. At last he promised to speak with me again, later, but I could sense that he was puzzled. I was not what he had expected. I was led back to my room and once again stretched out on the bed. I whiled away hours in this manner, thinking furiously, blaming God though I did not believe in him, blaming my father, blaming the British and even my own leaders, for failing to secure us a victory.

I was then but a boy, a child. I had seen death and

destruction of the most terrible kind, but I did not yet appreciate the larger shape of the war, of the world. I cried, I blamed others.

But Dr Forster cured me.

The next day I was called in to his office. We sat in silence. At last he began to speak. His voice was low, gentle, hypnotising. He was a neuropsychologist, I learned later; a decorated, veteran medical officer, and a German patriot. He spoke of his other patients: malingerers, hysterics. The day before he had examined my eyes. Now he told me the worst: what I had suspected was true. I was blind, my eyes irreparably damaged by the gas. I would never see again!

Perhaps I burst out crying. I am no longer sure. His voice kept speaking to me, gently, authoritatively. 'You are not like the others, Lance-Corporal,' he told me. 'You are special. In you I see something of the past glory of Germany. A Siegfried, an Attila, a Wotan!'

'I am blind!' I wailed. 'I am nothing, I am dirt.'

He slapped me. My cheek burned. My pity was replaced with rage. I rose, I swore at him, I kicked away the chair. I stumbled blind and cursing in the dark. 'Yes, yes!' he said. 'You are angry! Passionate! Do not whine like a dog who has been hit! There is a chance yet, Lance-Corporal. Yes! I must tell you, there is one chance.'

His words penetrated my agonised consciousness. 'A chance?' I said, quietly.

'Yes,' he said, 'for you see, you are exceptional, Lance-Corporal; you are nothing short of an *Übermensch*! I believe in you, Lance-Corporal.' I heard him move about the room. Heard a match being struck. He said, 'I have lit a candle. All else is in darkness. Can you see the flame?'

'No,' I said. 'No!'

'Yet I believe that you *can* see it!' he cried. 'Use the power of your mind, Lance-Corporal! Believe yourself great, greater than any who had ever stepped upon this earth. With the

power of your mind alone, you can achieve anything! Do it
for Germany, do it for the Fatherland, now under threat from
its many enemies. Can you do it?'

'No,' I said, 'no, I can't!'

It was lunacy, surely! I had been blinded, physically
blinded. How could I heal myself through the power of
thought alone? But his voice kept at me, urging me, like a
conductor facing an orchestra. 'Prove yourself!' he said. 'If
you can see the flame, then you are indeed a great man, an
Over-Man. If you can see the light, then you could lead all of
Germany, lead our nation to victory! Show me,' he said, 'the
triumph of the will!'

I was roused by his speech, by his words. I had always
thought myself special, not like the others. I always knew
better. Secretly, I believed him. His words made me see the
truth at last. I had tried to pass for normal when I was
nothing of the sort! And as I thought this, as his words kept
running through my mind, my eyes became acutely sensitive.
I began to discern a dull flickering light.

Perhaps he could tell as much from the movements of
my eyes. 'You are doing it!' he cried. I concentrated – could
I really heal myself? Cause organic damage to be replaced
by healthy tissue? Slowly, slowly the image resolved, grew in
depth and detail. It was a flame! A bright flame in the dark
room. I could see the candle now, the wax running down
the shaft, its grooves and irregularities. Slowly, the room
came into focus, shelves of books, the grand desk. The
flame threw shadows on the walls. And there he was, too.
Dr Forster.

He had a bespectacled, round face with receding dark hair.
He had an intense expression. His eyes shone with fervour, or
so it seemed to me in my state then. 'You did it!' he said. 'You
can see!'

'I can see, doctor!' I said, overwhelmed. But I was not
overwhelmed for long. So many things had suddenly
become clear to me then. The truth of who and what I was,

and the destiny that lay before me. The boy I had been was dead, gone. A man – an *Übermensch* – had emerged in his place.

I don't know why I recalled my sessions with Dr Forster as I walked back through the rain. I was in a fog of rage. For a moment I imagined myself an Übermensch again, leaping into the sky, soaring over the city as I sought out my enemies with my powerful vision. But events have proven me wrong. The Fall had crushed my dreams. Forster had restored my sight, but he had done so by trickery, by sleight of hand.

For I had seen the details of my file from that time: 'A hysteric', he had written. In those notes he claimed there had been nothing wrong with my sight. That I had merely suffered a nervous reaction, believing myself blind; but that there was no organic, no physical damage to the eyes.

The foul man had tricked me!

And in the process he had made me into an instrument of righteousness. The man who would lead Germany. Or so I thought, until the Fall; until I lost everything I had once believed in and became, once again, nothing but a man.

How I hated them all!

I was so wrapped up in my thoughts that I did not notice the black car driving past me, slowly, too slowly, until it was too late. I heard the doors open and heavy footsteps and turned and saw the face of an old friend, Emil, the big barman from the Hofgarten. 'I'm sorry, Mr Wolf,' he said. He held a lead pipe in one enormous hand. I was too slow in trying to avoid it. It connected with the back of my head with a dull echoing crack and a burst of blazing pain and then, mercifully, darkness.

'Martini?'

She was a simpering old bitch and always had been, Wolf thought. She lusted after power the way other women lusted after movie stars or the milkman. He grimaced. His head felt raw in a terrible way. 'No, thank you, Magda.'

They were in a drawing room having tea. He thought they were somewhere west of the city, Kensington perhaps. It seemed to make sense. His head hurt. He had woken up halfway there, in the back seat of the car, Emil on one side and another man he didn't recognise on the other side of him. They drove without speaking, through the quiet night, arriving at this quiet residential house on a quiet residential street. Briefly Wolf imagined the whole place blown up, airplanes swooping low, dropping down bombs, air-raid sirens wailing, residents running for shelter, but all was quiet and peaceful and clear. Emil helped him out. 'I'm really very sorry for hitting you, Herr Wolf,' he said. 'I was just following orders. You understand.'

They walked in through the gate and the lights in the house came on and the door opened and a shadow stood in the doorway. A neat but rat-like man came forward with a limp, his arms extended, his face plastered with a smile Wolf knew only too well.

'Joseph?' he said. 'Joseph *Goebbels*?'

'Wolf! Wolf, Wolf, *Wolf*!'

They stopped and stood facing each other. Goebbels was small, skinny, lame and dangerous. He had been their propaganda man, before the Fall. His smile turned into concern. 'Are you hurt?' he said. 'What did they do to you! Emil?'

'I'm sorry, Herr Goebbels,' the large barman muttered. He shifted on his feet as though afraid of the much smaller man. 'You said to—'

'I know what I said! Nincompoop! My dear Wolf, I am so, so sorry. Please, come in, come in! It is so good to see you again!'

'You live here?' Wolf said.

'This old place?' Goebbels said, shrugging, as if to say it was nothing, really it was nothing at all.

'You've lived here all this time? In England?'

'I wanted to seek you out,' Goebbels said. 'But Hess told me you no longer wanted to associate with your old friends . . . I did not wish to intrude.'

'I thought the communists had got you!'

Goebbels shrugged again. He led Wolf into the house. The wallpaper was ghastly. 'I survived,' Goebbels said. 'You know how it is, Wolf. The things we do to survive.'

Wolf stopped. He felt the back of his head. His hair was matted with blood. He was tired and hurting. Slowly, he said, 'You cut yourself a deal.'

Goebbels was silent. Outside, Wolf heard nothing. Even the birds were asleep. He felt cold inside. 'You cut a deal with the communists, in exchange for your release. What did you do, Joseph? What did you *give* them?'

'It was all gone, Wolf. We lost. We had to be practical. I only gave them that which they would have already got, sooner or later. Some names, some details. What does it matter, now? Some S.A. beer boys? Streicher?'

'You gave them *Julius Streicher*?'

'His usefulness had come to an end. And the man was a pig, a veritable pig, Wolf!'

'He was,' Wolf said. He began to laugh. 'Joseph, you haven't changed one bit.'

'Wolf.' The gimp-legged man turned to him, and Wolf could have sworn there were genuine tears in his eyes. 'I have missed you. So much have I missed you.'

'It's good to see you, too, Joseph. But you could have just sent a card.'

'I did not mean for them to harm you! Emil, come here.'

'Sir?'

'Close the door behind you, Emil.'

'Yes, Herr Goebbels.'

'Good.'

Goebbels took out a gun from his pocket. He waved it carelessly in the air. 'American made,' he said. 'Do you like it?'

'It's wonderful. You have been talking to the Americans?'

'We have cause to do business together, sometimes. Why not? It is good to have friends. Again, I am terribly sorry, Wolf.' He raised the gun levelly at the puzzled Emil and pulled the trigger.

The sound was deafening in the small hallway. From upstairs there came a woman's shriek. Emil collapsed to the floor, half his head now smeared on the wall behind him. His blood soaked into the carpet. Wolf stared down at the corpse.

'I liked Emil,' he said.

'So did I,' Goebbels said. 'But discipline has to be maintained.'

'Are you just going to leave him there?'

'Franz will clean it up. Come. Magda is just *dying* to see you.'

Wolf's ears were ringing. He followed Wolf to the drawing room.

'Magda? Where the hell are you, woman?'

Wolf heard footsteps come down the stairs and halt for a moment. Then a long beat as she stepped over Emil's corpse, before resuming her progress towards the drawing room. She wore a black evening dress and a veil and gloves and high-heeled shoes. 'Wolf!' She ran to him, hugged him. Her hand squeezed his buttock covertly. 'It is so good to see you again,' she whispered, her breath soft in his ear. He pushed her away, but gently. She had always been like a minx in heat around him. 'It is good to see you too, Magda.'

'How long has it *been*?'

'Too long,' Wolf said. But he felt tired, depressed. This was not a social call. The balance of power between them had changed. He no longer commanded the Goebbelses. They had grown apart from him, had changed. He was cautious.

'I will make drinks! Martini?'

'No, thank you,' Wolf said, politely. He turned to Goebbels. 'Where are your children?' he said. The Goebbelses had bred like rabbits, as though almost single-handedly they could populate the Earth with their Aryan offspring. Goebbels had been loyal; a gifted orator; an ardent Jew-hater; and, though he didn't like people to know it, a failed novelist.

'Upstairs,' Goebbels said.

'Asleep,' Magda said.

Wolf thought of the gunshot. They must be some children to sleep through the sound of a shot in their own hallway. But then, for all Wolf knew, such things were not so uncommon in the Goebbels household. He said, 'Speaking of Hess.'

'Were we speaking of Hess?'

But he saw Goebbels and Magda exchange glances, and Magda got up. On her way to the kitchen she looked back. 'Chocolate cake?' she said.

'That sounds lovely, Magda, dearest,' Goebbels said. She disappeared through the door and the two men were left alone.

'Hess is dead,' Wolf said, without preamble. 'I saw him floating face-down in the duck pond in Hyde Park.'

'What a way to go, eh?' Goebbels said. It wasn't exactly a smile. It wasn't exactly a smirk. But it was unpleasant and oily and rat-like all the same.

'Did you kill him, Joseph?'

'Me?' Goebbels said, looking shocked. 'Of course not, Wolf!'

'So who did?'

'Must we speak of Hess?' Goebbels said.

'That's why I'm here, isn't it?' Wolf said.

'You wound me. Is this what you think?'

'I know you, Joseph. All of you. You were mine. You were children I had let run wild. And when the Fall came you ran, and some of you came here, and now you do – what? Pimp out girls? Run numbers? You've become nothing, Joseph. Nothing but common criminals.'

'Some would say that is all we ever were,' Goebbels said, still with that faint, mocking smile. 'You lost your power, Wolf. You lost!'

'I was betrayed!'

They stared at each other. Goebbels was no longer smiling. 'I love you, Wolf,' he said. 'But you have not wanted to get involved. You prefer to play at being a private eye like some grotesquery out of a Fritz Lang movie. Hess was a good man, but he was weak. Weak, and he talked too much. In this business, it's not healthy to talk too much.'

Wolf regarded him without expression. The silence sat between the two men, the threat still hanging in the air. 'Hess talked to *me*,' Wolf said, softly.

It was Goebbels's turn not to reply.

'Who is behind it, Joseph?' Wolf said. 'Behind the smuggling, the whores, the white slavery? It's not you. You're not smart enough, Joseph. You're not ruthless enough. You talk a good talk, and I have to admit you impressed me just now with the gun and that little show of yours, and poor Emil. But it was a waste. It's not – it can't be – you. Then who?'

'Wolf,' Goebbles said. And his eyes were filled with sorrow.

'Yes,' Wolf said.

'It's not good to ask too many questions,' Goebbles said, softly. 'Do you understand?'

And Wolf did. Truly, he did. He knew better than anyone, for had he not written the rules of this dangerous game himself? And he began to say yes; to nod; to say that he did understand. He saw Magda come in through the door with a chocolate cake on a silver tray in her hands. And he saw Goebbels's eyes flicker upwards, to a point behind Wolf's head. And Wolf remembered the second man, the one who was going to clean up the dead Emil; Franz, he thought Goebbels had called him.

Wolf half-parted his lips, began to form a syllable, noticed the look, began to turn his head. Again he was too late. There was a bright explosion of pain in the back of his already tender head and, for a moment, Wolf saw spiral galaxies and interstellar clouds, suns and planets and moons, all drifting past at inexorable speed, growing brighter, converging to become the faces of departed comrades: of Hess and Streicher and Göring and Goebbels, Himmler and Bormann and Speer. And he knew that one of them was behind it all; one of them pulled the strings behind the scenes. The galactic vista sped all about him until his field of vision became the bright light of a supernova, of a dying star, and it suffused him, incinerating every cell and atom in his body, and he was once more swallowed up by the cool and blessed darkness of deep space, of a place entirely outside of time.

Wolf's Diary, 16th November 1939 – *contd.*

In my dream I was in a cold, bright place and it was snowing. The earth was hard, frosted over. Men, skeletal men, shuffled all around me. They wore striped pyjamas, and wooden clogs on their feet. I had never seen such men before. They were grotesque, caricatures of men. There were watchtowers and fences holding us in. Blocks of housing squatted on the frozen ground. I saw a bird soar overhead. It was shot by a sniper in one of the towers and dropped to earth, its wings clipped, feathers flying. It plummeted to hit the ground with a splat of blood and tiny breaking bones. I saw one of the men hurry to it, scoop it up and attempt to hide it under his tattered coat. The gun barked again and the man dropped to the snow and lay there. No one came to him. The bird had fallen from out of the shelter of his coat and lay there beside him, a single drop of red blood decorating its tiny crushed head.

Though I knew it was cold I did not feel it. I walked through the throng of inmates like a spirit. They did not see me and I could not interact with them. The light was very strong. The skies were blue and clear. The sun shone in the sky but it was small and a long way away. It was a cold brightness, it provided only stark illumination. It eradicated shadows. I don't know how long I spent in that place. I lost track of time. The sun never seemed to set. The snow hung suspended in the air. The men were frozen in their places, in the act of lifting a weary leg or bending down to dig, bony fingers wrapped round the handle of a shovel.

I thought it must be a model village, populated by waxwork figures. The snow wasn't real at all; it was paper, thousands and thousands of tiny balls of paper all suspended by strings. The sky was painted over canvas, the sun was a splash of yellow paint. I walked through the exhibits marvelling at it all, the amount of detail that must have been required to create all that was staggering. I saw black smoke in the distance. I realised I had been breathing it all along. It rose from a set of chimneys in the distance and suffused the air. It got into my eyes and my nose and my ears. It coated the inside of my lungs. The black smoke was everywhere, rank and yet strangely sweet, but it never left, it clung to me, to my clothes, my skin, my hair. I ran my tongue around my mouth and my gums were raw and painful. I felt a loose tooth. I prodded it with my tongue and it came away entirely and I spat it out. I was suddenly frightened and I didn't know why. I knew it was only a bad dream but even so, I couldn't wake up. When I looked at the back of my hands I did not recognise them. They were like an old man's hands and the skin hung loose, in folds. My clothes felt heavy on me, and I was terribly weary, they pressed me down, they didn't fit me any more. Then I realised I wasn't even wearing them. I was wearing dirty striped pyjamas and wooden clogs that opened the sores on my feet. A band struck a rousing martial tune. I heard a shrill whistle. A man in uniform came to me, shouting. He asked me where I thought I was going. I tried to explain to him it was all just a terrible mistake, that I didn't belong here, but he just laughed. I was so hungry. He began to lead me towards the source of the black smoke. There had been a mistake, I kept saying. There had been a mistake. I didn't want to go. I kept saying no, no, I don't want to go there. We walked and walked, into the black smoke. There had been a mistake, I kept saying. There had been a mistake. It became very dark. I need to open the blinds, I told him, desperately. But he wasn't even there.

11

I woke up and proceeded to retch violently, the rancid contents of my stomach burning my lips and tongue, leaving a disgusting puddle on the floor. Light was seeping in through the windows. The blinds were drawn. The room was clean and impersonal. It smelled of disinfectant and my puke. A voice above me said, 'Settle down, now.'

Hands pressed me back down onto the bed. 'You've had a nasty accident.' I blinked as a face came into view, hovering over me like a vision. Her blonde hair framed her pale face. 'I didn't have an accident,' I said, petulantly. 'I was beaten up.'

'I know.' She plumped my pillows. 'I'm so sorry, Mr Wolfson.'

'Wolfson?'

'We found your identity card in your pocket,' she said.

'Wolfson!' I said. 'Of course. I am . . .' what in all hell was it? 'Moshe Wolfson,' I said.

'Do you know who hit you?' she said.

'No.'

'They were probably Blackshirts,' she said. 'We've been treating so many of your people recently, Mr Wolfson. It's best that you rest now.' I saw her reaching for a syringe.

'Wait!' I said.

'Yes?'

'Where am I?'

'Guy's Hospital.'

'Guy's?' That meant I was on the south side of the river, by London Bridge. 'How did I get here?'

She shrugged. 'You need to rest now, Mr Wolfson.' She primed the syringe and I saw the tiny bubble of liquid at the needle's end. 'Wait! My name isn't Wolfson, it's—'

The needle penetrated my skin. A sense of great relief and of peace washed over me, and I sank into the mattress and in seconds I was asleep again.

Wolf's Diary, 18th November 1939

'We're being overrun with the damn Jews,' a male voice said. I could smell pipe-tobacco in the room. 'I keep telling them, we need more staff, we can't cope, they should rein in the bloody Mosley boys until after the elections, at least.'

I opened my eyes. He was about my age, with ample facial hair, round glasses. He left his pipe smoking by the window and approached me. 'Let's have a look at you,' he said. His hand went to the back of my head and I nearly screamed. 'Yes, yes,' he said. 'That's a nasty wound you've got there, Mr . . .?'

'Wolfson,' the nurse said. It was a different nurse.

'A nasty wound. It's a good thing you came to us,' the doctor said. At last he released my head. 'We need to keep you for a few days. Is there anyone you wish to call?'

'No,' I said. Then, 'Yes.'

'A wife, a friend?'

'Call Oswald Mosley,' I said, and he laughed.

'Call Oswald! Tell him it's Wolf.'

The doctor sighed. 'Why do they do this,' he said. Again it wasn't clear who the 'they' referred to. 'Keep him sedated for the time being. He needs time to recover.'

'Wait, listen to me! You don't understand!'

But the doctor had moved on to the next bed. I looked up at the nurse. My head hurt terribly. 'Please, call him. Tell him it's Wolf.'

'I thought your name was Wolfson,' she said. She primed the syringe. 'Don't do that,' I said, 'don't—'

Again, the cold touch of the needle. Again, that near-immediate relief. I smiled up at her goofily. 'Call him, tell him I'm—'

'Sleep well,' she said.

Wolf's Diary, 19th November 1939

'Mr Wolf?'

It was dark. In the beds beside mine men were snoring and crying and farting in their sleep. My visitor perched on a chair beside me, an unremarkable young man in an unremarkable grey suit. His face was pleasant, plump, and shiny with a thin film of sweat. 'Who the hell are you?' I said.

'I'm Alderman, sir? Thomas Alderman? We met at Sir Oswald's . . . party? And we spoke on the phone, more recently.'

'Alderman? Who the hell are you, Alderman? Where is Oswald?'

'*Sir* Oswald is on the campaign trail, sir. As the Americans say. He is unavailable but he of course sends his best regards. There seems to have been a mishap, if you don't mind me saying, sir, but you appear to be registered here as a Jew named Wolfson.'

'Don't you worry about that. What was that about the Americans? Did they get to him? Is he cutting a deal? I demand to know!'

'Sir Oswald is of course speaking to many different factions—'

'I knew it! The dirty worm has cut a deal! The man has no moral fibre, he has the spine of a snail!'

'Snails . . . don't have spines, sir.'

'That's what I said!'

The young man looked pained. 'I hate to see you like this, Mr Wolf.'

'Like this? Like how!'

'All frail, like.'

'Frail! How dare you! What did you say your name was?'

'Alderman, sir. Thomas Alderman? We met at Sir Oswald's party—'

'I know who you are! Do you think I have no eyes? Do you think I'm crazy? You tell that slimy Englishman this is Wolf, Wolf he's talking to! Where is Oswald?'

'He's . . . electioneering, sir.'

'Why is he not here? Who the hell are you?'

'I think I should call a nurse, sir. You seem agitated.'

'Agitated? *Agitated*? I could have ruled the world, you know!'

'I know, sir. Let me just say, Mr Wolf, I have the utmost admiration for you. I . . .'

I stared at him, dumbfounded. The young man reached into the breast pocket of his suit and brought out a tattered little book and presented it to me. 'I know this is hardly the right time, but . . . would you sign this for me?'

It was my book.

My Struggle.

I took it from him; held it in my hands. It was the British first – and, if I were being honest, only – edition, published by Hurst & Blackett, useless asses that they were. It was in a plain yellow dustjacket, like the books published by that Jew, Victor Gollancz.

'I'm . . . touched,' I said. I blinked; my vision had become blurry. A single drop fell on the open title page. 'Do you have a pen?'

'Here,' he said. I accepted it from him.

'What was your name again?'

'Alderman, sir. Thomas Alderman.'

'A good name. You're a good man, Alderman. A good man. We need more like you in this world.'

'Thank you, sir. That means a lot.'

To Thomas Alderman, I wrote. My hand was shaky. *Best wishes* – and I added my signature with a weak flourish.

'Here,' I said, thrusting the book back into his hands. 'Thank you, young man.'

'Thank you, sir. Thank you so much.'

'This is a time of war, Alderman,' I said, sinking back into the sheets. I felt so weary. 'And we're all soldiers, whether we know it yet or not.'

'Yes, sir.'

'Come and see me some time.'

'I'd like that, sir.'

'You tell that Oswald Mosley . . .' I said. But I was too tired. My eyes closed. I felt almost weepy. Like a woman – like a weak woman! 'You tell him . . .'

From a long way away I heard him get up, the scrape of the chair legs on the floor. 'Sleep now, sir.

'You tell him . . .'

Wolf's Diary, 20th November 1939

On her sickbed in Urfahr my mother lay dying.

I was eighteen. My sister, Paula, was eleven years old. I had been residing in Vienna at that time, attempting to enrol in the Academy of Fine Arts. I had hurried back home when I received the news from her physician. I returned in October. Dr Bloch, her doctor, was a Jew. I remember him sitting us down, Paula and I. 'Your mother's condition is hopeless,' he said. Paula cried. I myself cried. I am not ashamed to admit it. I only cried like this again when I thought I had lost my sight, in the war. I remember most strongly the smell in her room. Death has a special smell, that slow wasting of a human body. It is a sickly, sweet smell, a special odour that comes off the sick body, a rotting from within. That and, mixed with bodily waste, the smell of constant cleaning, of old carpets, of my mother's perfume which she insisted on wearing to her last day. I slept beside her, in a cot in the corner of the room. The windows were kept closed, as my mother was always cold. The air in the room was stifling. I had to hold her naked body in my arms, washing her, washing her and trying not to cry. The cancer was in her breasts and it had spread: there was no cure. Her hospital stay at the start of the year had cost one hundred Kronen.

Leaving her – going to Vienna – was the hardest thing I had ever done. Returning, I could do nothing but watch her die slowly. For two more months she lingered, becoming light as air; time seemed suspended, each particle and mote of dust froze in the everlasting air; in my mother's eyes I saw past and future meet.

She had become unchained from time. In lucid moments she spoke haltingly in alien tongues. Her eyes were open windows allowing me a glimpse into strange other worlds: in one the very moon was carved with an image of my face, while in another the Earth lay in ruins and corpses filled the seas from shore to shore and the foam bursting on the rocks ran red with blood. My mother's blood was black ichor. Her tears were purest crystal, like those found only on virgin sands. In the night she cried in broken syllables, but more and more she faded, with every passing day there was less of her.

My mother died that December.

Never will there be another woman like my mother.

Wolf's Diary, 21st November 1939

'Damn you all to hell, this food is *scheisse*!' I said. 'Bring me vegetables! *Vegetables*, I said! No, don't tell me to be quiet. Get your hands off of me! I said get your dirty hands off of m— no, don't you dare reach for that syringe! I said don't you dare—'

Wolf's Diary, 22nd November 1939

'Enough!' I yelled. My headache was gone, I was hungry, I needed to urinate, and I was sick and tired of being sick and tired. 'I want to be discharged immediately.'

'You have suffered serious trauma,' the nurse said. It was a different nurse again. I was getting sick of nurses, and needles, and what passed for hospital food.

'Then bandage me up and give me some pills,' I said.

'It might not be safe for you out there,' the nurse said. 'It's ugly outside, there are mobs, everything is tense – it's the elections today, isn't it.'

'*Today*? How long have I been in here!'

'A few days. And I really do think you should—'

'Don't you worry about me, *bubeleh*,' I said. Was I really using Yiddish? What was happening to me? 'I have friends,' I added, darkly. 'I have friends in high places.'

'I'm sure that you do. And we could use the bed. But the doctor—'

'I don't need a doctor! I healed my own blindness with the power of my *mind*!'

'I . . . see.'

'Look,' I said, calmer now. Trying to reason with her was like trying to teach National Socialism to a goat. It was an enterprise doomed to failure and bound to disappoint both parties. 'I'm leaving. I want my clothes.'

'This is highly irregular—'

'I'm *leaving*! Don't you know who I *am*?'

'I have no idea who you are.'

'How dare you!'

'Sir, please!'

But I was already standing, tottering on the hard floor. I regained my balance, smiled at her contemptuously. 'It was a minor setback,' I said. 'It's only a matter of time until I'm on top of things again.'

'Sir—'

'Get out of my way!'

I barged past her to the cheering of the other patients, found my clothes folded tidily and carried them to the bathroom where I changed. When I emerged I felt like a new man. I was myself again. 'Goodbye!' I said. I tapped my finger on the brim of my hat and walked away.

She didn't follow.

Wolf emerged into a cold November day. A pale sun hid behind clouds. It was raining again, a thin, constant drizzle. The railway arches rose ahead of Wolf, obscuring the river. Men in suits flowed down Southwark Street.

It was Wednesday.

His head no longer hurt. He was rested, he was irritable and he was still on the case, whether anyone wanted him to be or not.

It was time to act.

Wolf hailed a black cab. Settled himself into the back seat. 'Where to, mate?' the driver said.

'The Grosvenor Hotel, Victoria. And step on it!'

The driver chuckled as though Wolf had said something funny. On the other side of the window, grey clouds gathered on the horizon.

The city flowed past outside the windows of the cab. The streets deepened and the sky darkened overhead and the clouds seemed like giant ships doing battle, raising the black flags of pirates and privateers. The water of the Thames churned and Wolf imagined vast spirits underwater, entwined in a battle reflecting the heavens above, great amorphous translucent creatures of some primordial ooze, ancient beyond all imagining, things that were beyond good and evil but merely *were*, from even before the world was formed.

It was possible he was still somewhat under the influence of the hospital drugs.

The Grosvenor Hotel rose before them then like a castle. The driver stopped the cab. Wolf paid the fare.

'Sooner or later,' he thought groggily, 'everyone pays the fare.'

'Pardon?'

'Nothing,' Wolf said. He exited the car. Went up the steps to the hotel entrance where liveried doormen stood like toy soldiers. He went inside and marched up to the reception desk. 'Leni Riefenstahl,' he said. 'Tell her it is Wolf.'

The hotel clerk behind the desk was severe in a beige and cream suit. His face had the faintly disapproving air of a maiden aunt. He said, 'I'm afraid Miss Riefenstahl is no longer staying with us, sir.'

Wolf took a step back from the desk. He hovered there uncertainly for a moment, looking one way and then the other,
helplessly. The hotel clerk said, 'Are you unwell, sir?'

But Wolf recovered.

Wolf always recovered.

'Where did Miss Riefenstahl go?' he said.

'The film crew left two days ago,' the clerk said. 'I believe they
went back to America. There were issues with the production of
their film that necessitated their decampment.'

His eloquence irritated Wolf. 'She is not here?' he said, shortly.

'No, sir. Are you sure you are all right?'

'I'm fine. I'm fine!' Wolf turned from him. How could it be?
He had counted on Leni. She stood for everything he had once
believed in, she was Aryan womanhood incarnate. She was loving
– uncomplicated – sexually compliant – she was his! And yet
even she was gone now, had gone back to Hollywood, leaving
him with an aching emptiness, a dull pain. He was hollow inside,
and the hollowness was spreading, beginning as a tiny seed,
undetectable, and growing through him over the years, replacing
healthy cells and blood vessels, bone marrow and muscles and
nerves, until he was entirely hollow, until he was lighter than air.
He felt as though he were floating, untethered. He no longer
knew who he was.

Then movement caught his eye. A man, with a face he had
seen before, emerging from the lifts. For a moment Wolf stared,
disbelieving, though he didn't quite know why. He had assumed
they'd all left with Leni, yet here he was.

It was the Jew, Bitker.

Wolf turned away before Bitker could see him. He observed
him through the mirrors fixed above the hotel's plush entrance.
Bitker went right past Wolf, heading outside. Indecisive, Wolf
stared after him, then broke into a run. 'Herr Bitker!' he said.
'Herr Bitker!'

The Jew turned. A look of polite bemusement filled his face.
'Yes . . .?' he said.

Wolf stopped, disbelieving again. 'We've met,' he said.

'Have we? I'm afraid I do not recollect, Mr . . .?'

'Wolfson,' Wolf said, thinking quickly. 'We have not been introduced. Unwin's party? You are working with Leni?'

'I am part of the film crew,' Bitker said. 'How do you know Miss Riefenstahl?'

'We . . . I am, was, an artist. I did scenery work on one of her Berlin films,' Wolf said.

'I see. Well, she has gone back to California, I'm afraid,' Bitker said.

'So I understand.'

'I am sorry I can't be of more help,' Bitker said, politely.

'Herr Bitker!' Wolf's voice was desperate; hungry. He put his hand on Bitker's arm. 'Please.'

'What is it, Mr Wolfson?'

'I want to help!'

'Help? Help with the film? The production is halted. I myself only stayed behind for, well, for some other business. I shall be returning to California tonight.'

'No, Herr Bitker!' Wolf lowered his voice, leaned in closer to the Jew. 'I want to help. With the cause.'

'The cause?' For the first time Bitker looked alarmed. 'What cause?'

'Herr Bitker, please! Do not play games with me!'

'This is not the time or place—!'

'I want to help. I am ready to do whatever it takes. Life is intolerable, here, for us Jews!'

'I don't disagree. But I don't see what you think I can do—'

'I want to do what has to be done. I want to join. I know things, Herr Bitker.'

'I can see that. Come with me.' Bitker grabbed Wolf roughly by the arm, half-dragged him into the empty hotel bar. 'Who are you and what do you want?'

'I told you, I'm Wolfson. Moshe Wolfson. Here.' Wolf fished out his forged passport. 'Take it!'

Bitker took it from his hands, leafed through it. He stared at

Wolf and his expression turned puzzled. 'Have we met before?' he said. 'Not at Unwin's party.'

Wolf thought of following Bitker to Threadneedle Street, of being discovered, chased and beaten. 'No,' he said.

Suddenly a small smile materialised on Bitker's face. He laughed. The sound was unexpected, startling. 'Do you know—!' he said. 'If you grew a moustache, you would almost be the spitting image of—'

'Please, Herr Bitker! Do not joke of such things!'

'No, of course not. My apologies.' Still, some of the man's good humour seemed to return, as if Wolf's superficial similarity to that long-vanished leader had put him at ease. He put a hand on Wolf's shoulder. 'Listen to me, Wolfson. There is nothing here for you. Nothing remains. The election will not go our way. England will become a hell for the Jews. The Americans are closing their borders to our people. Europe remains hostile to us. There is only one place remaining, Wolfson.' He stared into Wolf's eyes with a deep and dark intensity. 'There is only Palestine, now.'

'We must kill Mosley,' Wolf blurted.

'Don't worry about Mosley! That scum will be taken care of.'

'How?' Wolf said. His hands were shaking with excitement.

'I have said too much. Listen to me, Wolfson. There will be a ship, leaving tomorrow morning before dawn. If things go wrong for us here. Greenwich docks. The *SS Exodus*. Now go! You're putting us both in danger.'

'But Herr Bitker! Wait!' Wolf tried to halt the other man but Bitker shook his head.

'Good luck,' he said, softly. He shook Wolf's hand and then, with quick, hurrying steps, disappeared into the grey daylight outside the hotel. Wolf stood staring after him. His brain was awhirl. What had Bitker meant about Mosley? He had successfully caught the Jew off-guard, had extracted valuable information from him. It was obvious there was a threat to Mosley's life, planned sometime soon, planned, perhaps, for that very evening. He had to warn Mosley.

Wolf left the hotel and saw Bitker enter an Austin Tourer. It

was an ugly two-seater car with an open top. Bitker sat behind
the wheel while, beside him, Wolf could make out a face he knew
and loathed.

It was the little sister, Judith Rubinstein.

She was dressed inexplicably in a domestic servant's uniform.

'Wait!' Wolf shouted, but neither heard him. The car's engine
came to life with a hacking cough and the Tourer slid away into
the traffic. 'Judith!' Wolf cried. 'Judith!'

He ran after the car but the road was clear and the car disappeared. Wolf's lungs burned and his leg throbbed with the old
wound.

He stood there with his hands on his knees, breathing hard.

He should warn Mosley, he thought dully. A weak sun momentarily shone from a break in the grey clouds. Wolf felt himself
filled by the light, once again seemingly detached of space and
time: he felt as if he could just float away, into the clouds, for
ever; but the feeling passed and he was himself again, and after
a moment he straightened up.

He found a red phone box and went in and shut the door.
Reached for coins and gave the operator the number to call. The
ringing seemed to fill the air, becoming a flock of dark birds
against the cloudy sky.

'Mosley residence.'

'This is Wolf.'

'Mr Wolf! It's Alderman.'

'Who?'

'Thomas Alderman, sir. I came to visit you at the hospital.'
There was a note of reproach in the voice.

Wolf conjured up with some difficulty the image of a serious,
pale-faced young man, sitting beside the bed in a high-backed
chair, asking him to sign a book. Had that really happened? He
thought he had dreamed the episode up – they *had* given him
rather a lot of drugs at the time.

'I must speak with Mosley. It is of the utmost urgency!'

'I am sure. Sir . . .'

Wolf did not like the boy's tone. 'What is it?' he demanded.

'Sir, I'm most awfully sorry.'

Was he too late? Was Mosley even now lying dead or dying by the side of the road or in some beer hall somewhere, or wounded from an assassin's bullet or mutilated by an explosive device? 'What is it?' Wolf said. The dread rose in bubbles above his head, his speech encapsulated inside.

'I'm afraid—' he could hear the boy swallowing, over the phone. 'Sir Oswald has found it necessary to terminate your employment.'

'I . . . what? I beg your pardon?'

'Your services are no longer necessary. I'm so sorry, I really am, Mr Wolf.'

'My . . . my *services*? What are you – who do you think – how *dare* you! How *dare you*!' Wolf was screaming at the receiver, his lips trembling in rage, his spit flying onto the mouthpiece of the telephone. 'I have important *news*, urgent news for this . . . little . . . fucking no-good wannabe Fascist *imitator*!'

'I truly am very sorry.'

'Sorry? You will be sorry! You will all be sorry!'

The boy, Alderman, said something, 'Can I see you?' perhaps, which would have been an odd thing to say, but anyway Wolf was no longer listening. He bashed the receiver against the phone box, over and over, splintering the casing, wantonly destroying the property of His Majesty's General Post Office. Having done this, at last, and panting heavily, he exited the red phone box like an *Übermensch* awakened and transformed.

* * *

In a place beyond space and time Shomer stands, his back bent, working. Released from the infirmary he has wandered with a child's gaze back into the camp. Everything about him has been replaced anew: his wooden clogs, his fetching striped pyjamas, his plate, his spoon. All those he knew are gone and he has been placed into a different block with different company, a new capo to command him, two new bunkmates on either side of him, one tall and skeletal and French, one short and skeletal and Polish. Also in the block is a rabbi, or in fact several rabbis, or perhaps only one rabbi and several yeshiva students (it is hard to tell), who in the rare moments of rest at the end of the day after the soup and before fitful sleep sit together and debate issues of the Torah and the Talmud, and did not Rabbi Akiva say—

'Just as the house is proof of the builder,' Rabbi Akiva said, 'and the cloth is proof of the weaver, so is the world proof of its creator, so does the world proclaim the existence of God.'

And it is certainly something to think about, is it not, Yenkl says, cheerfully. They have given Shomer a new job, too: no longer digging graves but working in a factory, a job as though from very Heaven, where it is warmer than outside, though the breath of the men frosts in the air before them as they work on the assembly line.

They make doors.

What the doors are for Shomer doesn't know. There are hundreds of doors every day going round and round, with men to sand the wood and men to polish it and men to attach the hinges and men to carry the doors to the trucks. Large doors and small doors and toy doors and great big thick doors that would stop a bullet, and it is Shomer's job to attach the handles, for without a handle, how can a door be opened, and therefore what good is a door? And for each door there is a lock but never not once does he see a key. And every day for hours at a time he stands there with his back bent and his feet throbbing with their new sores and his muscles straining and he attaches handles and every single nail must be accounted for. He sees men die on the assembly line, of accidents and carelessness or for trying to steal from the factory, men shot on the spot and the numbers on their arms carefully recorded. How many numbers, how many names, how many men have died to build this house, to weave this cloth?

One day he sees a plane fly overhead and it is not a German plane. The guards in their guard towers shoot it but it flies past unscathed. And on the secret wireless, the rumour goes around the camp, it says an army is advancing across the winter land, that it is coming closer. And yet the trains still come, the black smoke rises, the gold teeth of dead men collect in ever-growing piles, extracted by those unfortunate few, the *Sonderkommando*. All those corpses, all that gold and the hair harvested and every few weeks a new squad to shave and harvest the corpses of their predecessors on the job – their first assignment.

But Shomer works indoors; how this miracle happened he does not know. And Yenkl keeps him company.

*   *   *

In his office the watcher tidied his desk and the papers on his desk and aligned the telephone just so and the pens and the ledgers and he looked around the empty room and he was happy. And then he left and closed the door and locked it and went out in the night, into a darkness whispering promises of blood and murder.

12

I was dressed in my beat-up old raincoat, a suit that's seen better days, scuffed shoes and a fedora that didn't quite fit me. I was shaved but awkwardly. I had a bruise the size of a hen's egg on the back of my head, where I had been knocked out twice in the space of an hour several days back, and I was sober but for the drugs they had given me at the hospital. When I took a piss I held a Jew's cock in my hands. I didn't know how much Rubenstein's house was worth but my guess was plenty. I was calling on Jewish money.

The Rubinstein residence was a three-storey mansion off Sloane Square. It had a white stucco front and a driver in black leather and a black peaked cap washing a black Rolls-Royce parked in front of the house. I did not see Isabella Rubinstein's white Crossley. It was a quiet street in a quiet neighbourhood and the air smelled fresh and clear, as though it had been laundered with money. I went up the steps and rang the bell and waited. A maid in a starched apron opened the door and stood there looking at me. 'Yes?' she said.

'I'm here to see Miss Rubinstein,' I said.

'Miss Rubinstein is not in.' She made to shut the door in my face. I stuck my foot between the door and the frame, prohibiting her from doing so. 'I know she's in there,' I told her. 'I can smell the whore's wet snatch all the way from out here.'

The maid blanched white as a hard-boiled egg. 'I'm going to call the butler!' she said in a rising voice.

'I wish that you would,' I said.

'You repulsive man!'

I watched her disappearing back, pushed the door open the rest of the way and stepped inside. It was a cool antechamber with dark panelled oak and the kind of boiseries to give Syrie Maugham heart palpitations.

I heard hurried footsteps and in a moment a large pink butler in a tight black suit appeared with the maid in his wake. 'Who the hell are you?' he said, in a New York accent. He looked like a goon gone to seed and stuffed like a goose into a suit two sizes too small for him.

'Wolf,' I said. He sneered. 'The gumshoe? You have a lot of nerve coming in here.'

'Where is Isabella?'

'Miss Rubinstein is not accepting visitors,' he said. 'Now scram.'

I tried to push past him but he was having none of it. I heard the maid hurry behind the butler's back. For a long moment we stood facing each other, the butler and I. I had never liked butlers.

'Get out,' he said.

I reached down and grabbed him by the testicles and squeezed, hard. His face turned red and a low slow moan emerged from his blubbery lips. I leaned in close and whispered endearments in his ear. He nodded, once, to signal that he understood. I put my other hand flat against his chest and pushed, and in this ungainly way we progressed into the house, my one hand on his precious jewels, the other navigating him: it was just like driving a car.

We came into a large sitting room and I saw portmanteaus, black travelling bags and suitcases piled against one wall. They seemed hurriedly packed. One suitcase was still part open and I could see feminine toiletries and items of underclothing inside. 'Going someplace?' I said.

'Let me . . . go . . .'

I heard the same hurried footsteps again and the maid

A Man Lies Dreaming   217

reappeared, looking agitated. 'Let him go!' she screamed. She
came at me like a demented pheasant, flapping her hands.
She was surprisingly strong and I had to release the butler to
protect my face from her. He leaned against the wall, taking
deep breaths. There was no fight left in him.

'Enough!'

For a moment I couldn't tell where the voice had come
from. Then I noticed an odd instrument, like an ear trumpet,
placed high in one corner of the room, close to the ceiling. I
knew the voice. The maid stopped abruptly and stood very
still, breathing heavily.

'Show him into the conservatory,' the voice said.

The maid glared at me. The butler slid to the floor and
remained there clutching his testicles and moaning faintly to
himself. He was as red as a cockerel's hood.

'Would sir please follow me,' the maid said. I grinned at
her and, when she turned, I pinched her rear and heard her
squeal, then swear in a very unmatronly way. I followed
her through a corridor and a turn and to a door that she
opened. Warm humid air wafted from within and it was dark.
The maid said nothing. The whole house was silent, pregnant
with anticipation. I suddenly did not want to go in. It seemed
to me, irrationally, to be like the entrance Dante had
described into the circles of Hell. My palms were sweating. It
was too warm in there, too quiet. The maid stared at me with
hate-filled eyes, her lips curling into a cruel mocking grin, but
still she said nothing. The air smelled of death. I clenched my
fingers into fists. I imagined fires, the sweet cloying smell of
burning bodies, the hiss of gas. The maid was as still as a
statue. I stared into the dark hot room, paralysed with
indecision.

Dominique, too, was staring at the darkness. She had never got
used to the dark. One of her strongest memories, the one she
carried deep inside of her, wrapped and carefully hidden, was of
a summer when her mother and her father were still together,

and they had gone to visit her mother's old home in Abidjan on the Ivory Coast. Dominique remembered her mother in her summer dress, purchased on the Champs Élysées, her father's cool linen suit, made for the tropics. They had been so happy. In the memory, her father held her small hand in his, and they walked on the sands, on the banks of the _lagoon n'doupé_, and the air was so still, the water shimmered like a mirror, reflecting an immensity of sky.

It had been a good time.

Then came her mother's illness, her father's bursts of anger, the alcohol which took hold of him like a serpent and squeezed, squeezed until one day his heart had burst. She was a nothing after that, a girl of mixed blood abandoned at her father's final posting, somewhere in the Lebanon. Her father's relatives disowned her, her mother's were in faraway Abidjan or scattered. She was alone.

She had never got used to the darkness, not truly. Not on the ship taking her to Paris, not in the dark hold, with the grunting men, nor on the streets of the city nor later, following a handsome cavalry officer to London, more fool her.

There were times when she didn't have sex with clients. There was more money in specialising, and she had learned during her time in Paris: the art of the _dominatrice_. There were men who liked to be controlled, humiliated, abused, in a mockery of giving away power while still controlling her with their money. She had her kit, whips and chains and dildos, but there had been so many girls who came to London after the Fall, so many refugees, and competition was fierce and so she found herself once again on the streets, once again turning _triques_.

Now she watched the darkness, with an anxiety she hid well. Gerta was still in hospital; her whoring days were over. The young German girl, Edith, was dead. There was a devil out there, out to kill and mutilate. She did not understand such hatred. That strange symbol carved into Edith's chest – she had seen it before, the swastika. But why anyone would want to cut it into a woman's flesh she couldn't comprehend. She hugged herself against the

cold. Would the killer come tonight? The night after that? She
did not like this cold, this city. Footsteps in the dark, unhurried,
almost awkward, shy. She put on her professional face. Would it
be him this time? There were so many watchers in the dark,
eyeing the girls with a terrible beastly hunger. Her fingers closed
on the knife in her handbag. A face came into view as he crossed
under the streetlight and she sighed with relief. He seemed so
harmless, almost earnest, really. A clerk from a nearby office,
perhaps, at last tempted by the girls he must have observed,
covertly, so often. She smiled, revealing even, sharp white teeth.
She knew the effect her smile had on the men. The other girls
catcalled to the boy – the man – but he had eyes only for
Dominique.

She knew his type. Her smile widened. She'd once been told
there was a predatory quality to her smile, by an old French-
Lebanese orange trader who had kept her for a time, when she
was sixteen. She hadn't known what he meant, exactly. There
was something about her that men found both frightening and
exciting. And this man – he was really not so much more than
a boy. And so nervous!

'Good evening,' he said. His face was pale, his eyes wide.
Dominique let him look her over. The boy's gaze was drawn to
her brassiere. He licked his lips, unconsciously.

'Shouldn't you be at school?' Dominique said. The other whores
crowed with laughter.

'Can we talk somewhere more private?' the boy said.

'About what?' Dominique said. She stepped closer to him. He
seemed to radiate such heat. She leaned her cheek against his.
'What do you want to talk about, *boy*?'

Her hand went down to his front. He was so hard, his whole
body shivered when she touched him. 'I know what you like,'
Dominique said. 'Don't I.'

'Yes, yes,' the boy said.

'The other girls, they don't understand,' she said.

'No . . .'

'You have money?'

The boy reached into his pocket. Brought out a handful of notes. It was more money than Dominique had seen in a long time. The notes were crumpled, in disarray. She took them from him quickly, before the other girls could see. She put the money in her handbag, feeling inside for her instruments. Her hand closed on her favourite *godemiché*. She could bugger him with it, bugger him until he cried for mercy and came in the dirt. He would be quick, they always were, the eager ones.

The boy reached for her with clumsy hands. She pushed him away, laughing. 'Not here, love,' she said. She could tell he loved her accent. His eyes were so feverish-bright. She shivered.

'Where?'

'There's a hotel not far from here,' Dominique said. The boy shook his head. 'No. I have a place.' He took her by the hand, almost gently, and pulled her away. The other girls were no longer interested; they had new marks to entice, burly men who had spilled out onto the street from some nearby pub – dock workers or labourers.

'It's my friend's place,' he said. He was so tense. His whole body seemed to vibrate, like a single note, a single string holding mad music inside. The door was right there.

'I don't know,' Dominique said, doubtfully. The boy stood there and looked at her. She thought of all the money he'd given her. He opened the door. She stared into the darkness beyond.

★   ★   ★

How Wolf made the transition, how he had crossed the threshold, entered from the lit world of the house into the dark one of the conservatory, he didn't, afterwards, know. He remembered no conscious step, no movement. One moment he was standing before the door; in the next, the door was behind him. It shut noiselessly. He stood still and breathed in the rank odour of the air. It was very hot, very humid. The conservatory had once been the back garden of this London townhouse. It had since been roofed over with glass and now provided a tropical atmosphere. Dim red lights provided the only illumination. Wolf heard the drip-drip-drip of water and the buzzing of insects and the thrum of a water pump. He felt nauseated from the smell of the flowers.

'Orchids,' a voice said. Wolf started; he had half-fallen asleep on his feet. 'Did you know there are thousands of different orchid species? They're beautiful, don't you think?'

'They smell disgusting,' Wolf said, and the other chuckled.

'I didn't have you pegged as a gardening enthusiast,' Wolf said. There was movement ahead and then he saw him, approaching: Julius Rubinstein, banker, gangster, loving father. Hatred swamped Wolf. He blinked sweat from his eyes. It was on his lips. It tasted of salt and blood.

'You have a lot of nerve coming into my house,' Julius Rubinstein said. He spoke without haste or seeming anger. It was more of an observation. His body was open, his arms at his side, his face exhibiting nothing but a sort of puzzled curiosity. It was this that offended Wolf's sensibilities most of all, perhaps. The man had not even taken notice of him, had mutilated him and then dismissed him as though he were of no consequence at all.

It was a cold ruthlessness Wolf could almost admire.

'I have unfinished business with your daughter.'

'You have *no* business with my daughter!' With this, the genial look disappeared from Rubinstein's eyes. For a moment he seemed grotesque, demonic, a great shadow towering over Wolf. Then the impression subsided and Wolf saw him more clearly: a man no longer young, and for all his presence small, almost slight, with greying hair and tired eyes. 'What will it take?' Rubinstein asked. 'What will it take to make you leave my daughter alone?'

He turned his back on Wolf and walked deeper into the dark jungle of the conservatory. Wolf followed him, unbidden. Though the distance between them was small it seemed huge to Wolf; it seemed to him that he walked miles and yet the shadow before

him never grew closer or farther away but always remained at
the same distance, never turning, and that he could dawdle or
hurry but the shadow would always be there, awaiting him; and
that sooner or later it would consume him.

But really it was merely a few steps. And Wolf saw that, in the
middle of the conservatory, Rubinstein had built himself a makeshift office. He had a wide oak desk and a comfortable chair and
a makeshift bar. He reached for a bottle of scotch and two glasses
and put them on the desk and then poured. Wolf said, 'I don't
drink.'

'You'll drink.'

He handed Wolf the glass and Wolf accepted it. He didn't know
why the Jew had this power over him. He put his lips to the glass.
The rank smell of the alcohol nearly choked him.

'I said drink!'

Wolf sipped. The alcohol burned his lips, his throat. He coughed
and Rubinstein smiled. Wolf said, 'I am still on the case.'

'The case!' Rubinstein laughed, an angry or bemused bark.
'Who do you think you are?' he said. His hand fluttered up and
down, taking in Wolf from his beat-up old fedora down to his
scuffed shoes. 'What *is* this? At least I knew what you were before.
I have no idea what you are now.'

Wolf's composure abandoned him; packed up its suitcases and
left. 'I'm a private detective!' he shouted. 'A shamus, a gumshoe,
a flatfoot, a peeper, a snoop, a sleuth, a, a . . .' words abandoned
him momentarily. 'A dick!' He waved his finger threateningly in
Rubinstein's face. 'This is all I have *left*!'

The silence left was like a vacuum; it demanded to be filled.
Rubinstein laughed again. He laughed and laughed, holding
his belly in, his entire body convulsing, shaking. 'You . . . you
. . .!' he couldn't speak. Wolf watched him, hatred burning. He
smashed the glass with the scotch against the desk. It broke
into pieces and the rank stench of the alcohol filled the air,
worse than the orchids. Wolf attacked the still-laughing
Rubinstein. He caught the man by surprise, pushed him to the
ground before Rubinstein could act. He landed one good kick

in the Jew's ribs. It felt so good, so right! But Rubinstein only grunted in pain and then pushed himself up, easily. He stood on the balls of his feet like some street-brawling, bare-knuckle pugilist. Wolf launched a fist but Rubinstein deflected it easily. Then he slapped Wolf.

It was a slap the way you would administer a slap to a woman or a child. The way Wolf sometimes had to keep Geli in check. 'Punch me!' Wolf screamed. Rubinstein slapped him again, and the sound of the slap was swallowed into the foliage of the conservatory. Rubinstein reached for a desk drawer. Wolf tensed, expecting a gun. But all Rubinstein came out with was a wad of crumpled money. He threw the money in Wolf's face. 'Here,' he said. 'Take it. I said take it!' He slapped Wolf again, grabbed him by the neck, forced him to bend and catch the falling notes. His face was close to Wolf's own, breathing alcohol in Wolf's face.

'She's mine, not yours,' Rubinstein said. 'She has always been mine.' He said it gently; almost sadly.

He pushed Wolf away and stood there watching him, until Wolf left.

He walked away wordlessly; with each step he felt lighter and lighter. The maid waited for him outside the conservatory. She escorted him to the door. He passed the pile of suitcases. He thought he saw a figure standing at the top of the grand stairs, watching him. When he raised his eyes he thought he caught momentary sight of a pale beautiful face, heard the rustle of a summer dress, but then it was gone, perhaps had never been. A mocking final laugh, trailing into nothing. Outside it was dark and the clouds were amassed low on the horizon. The driver was still cleaning the car. He seemed to have been at it for hours. 'Noticed the bags in the hallway,' Wolf said. 'Going someplace?'

'Airport, mate,' the driver said.

'Flying?'

'Makes sense.'

'You know where?'

'What's it to you?'

Wolf sighed. 'Nothing,' he said, tiredly. 'It's nothing to me.'

'California,' the driver said, unexpectedly. He spat on the ground. 'Jews, right. Know it's over for them here. Whereas me, I got to find another job. Didn't tell the missus yet. What would I tell her? Got a small one at home, a lad. Still got to drive them to the airport tonight, don't I. Who did you vote for?'

'I didn't vote.'

'You should have.' He smiled, exposing his teeth. 'I voted for Mosley. Got to do what's right. Not a Jew, are you?'

'No.'

'Well, you look a bit Jewish, mate. No offence.'

Wolf glared at him. He'd had enough.

'Well, have a nice life and all,' the driver said.

'Yes . . . you too,' Wolf said. He walked away. Behind him, the curtain on the second-storey bedroom window might have twitched as she maybe watched him go. But he never turned to check.

Wolf's Diary, 22nd November 1939 – *contd.*

I was out of work. I was out of luck. I had two cases and I lost them both and I hadn't been too happy about either to begin with. Like the Rubinsteins' driver, I needed another job. Things bothered me, things I couldn't quite put my finger on: who my old comrades were working for, for instance. Hess had only been a link in the chain. Goebbels was another, higher up. But someone was above them all, in the place I had once occupied. Someone had pulled the strings to put me in hospital.

But who?

And where was Judith Rubinstein now?

I felt light-headed from the alcohol, but still, almost supremely, in control. My anger was hot, coiled inside me. I walked for a while. There wasn't much rain. The air felt expectant. It was quiet in Belgravia but in the distance I could hear shouts, chanting. I found an open garage.

'My car,' I said apologetically. 'It stalled. I think I ran out
of petrol.'

'No problem, mate.' The mechanic wiped his hands with a
dirty cloth and filled a bottle. The wireless was on and the
BBC was reporting live from Trafalgar Square, where Mosley
was speaking to an audience of thousands. When the
mechanic wandered off to put the money away I stole the
cloth. I daresay he wouldn't have missed it. I also swiped a
half-empty box of Swan Vestas. They were matches you could
trust.

I felt very calm. I retraced my steps. Townhouses towered
over me each way. It was very quiet: in this neighbourhood
there were special employees just to walk the dogs. The
Rubinsteins' house was dark. I didn't see the driver though
the car was still parked outside. I uncapped the bottle of
petrol and twisted the mechanic's cloth and soaked it in some
of the petrol and then jammed it into the mouth of the bottle.
I stared at the house. A light came on, on the second floor. I
wondered what she was wearing. I struck a match and applied
it, carefully, to the soaked cloth. It flamed brightly and for a
moment I saw myself standing on the street, holding the
makeshift bomb, reflected in the black gloss of the
Rolls-Royce.

The bottle arced through the air.

It hit the window and smashed through into the house, flaming
petrol exploding in a wide pattern over furniture and carpet,
paintings and wall.

A whoop of flame billowed out of the broken windows.

Wolf heard a scream. Heard a man swearing. The flames
climbed higher. He hid in the shadows and watched them come
tumbling out from the house, smashing open the door in their
haste to escape. The maid was wobbling and the driver was
cursing and swearing to quit and damn them all to hell, he was

going home, and then came Julius Rubinstein with a shotgun in his hand and finally Isabella.

She wore a sheer silk nightgown and her feet were bare. She looked young and scared. Wolf almost wanted to reach for her, in some perverse way he couldn't quite define she reminded him of Geli. Then Julius Rubinstein fired the shotgun into the air and Wolf jumped. Isabella laughed, a high-pitched, crazy sound that filled the night. Wolf saw her father's hand come to rest on her shoulder, pulling her close to him. Julius pulled open the passenger-side door of the car. He pushed Isabella in and shut the door on her and got in himself on the other side. Wolf couldn't see them inside the car. The house burned and the flames were reflected on the car's hood and there were sirens in the distance. The Rolls-Royce growled to life, then accelerated away. Wolf tracked it with his eyes. It moved fast, took a corner with a screeching of tyres, and was gone. In front of the burning house only the maid remained, too shocked to move. The box of Swan Vestas rattled between Wolf's fingers. He let them drop to the ground as he walked away from the flames.

Herr Wolf—

She was waiting, as though she always knew I would come. She would have haggled over the price but I gave her money to silence her. It was a lot of money for a whore. I led her by the hand to the door - your door. The bakery was shut, and it was but the work of a moment to unlock the door in the dark, when no one was watching. I don't know, she kept saying, I don't know. We stole up the stairs. I broke into your office. Here? she said. To me the place was enchanted. In the darkness there was the presence of you, in everything I touched there was magic. To her it might have seemed a blight, a place of decay, but she did not understand what you and I have.

Get on your knees, she said. She pushed me
down. Her hand reached into her bag and came out
with a black whip. It whistled through the air. I
said stay down! She slapped me, rocking my head
back. Is this what you want? she whispered. Is
this what you want?

Yes, yes. Everything was a fog. Take off your
shirt, she said. I threw it in a corner, and
shivered as cold air touched my exposed skin. Have
you been a bad boy. Yes, yes! She lashed me,
once, twice, and I cried out.

Is that what it feels like for you, too?

I knelt before her. But I needed, wanted, more.
When she lashed at me next I raised my hand and
grabbed hold of the whip and wrapped the leather
around my wrist and pulled. I caught her off-
balance and she stumbled and I caught her, rising.
My cockerel was on her skin, rubbing in an agony
of pleasure. I wrapped my arm round her neck. She
smelled so sweet. Listen, bitch, if you struggle
it will go worse for you, I said.

I didn't know she had a knife!

The whore stabbed me.

You fucking bitch! I yelled. I released her
with the pain and stepped back, confused. I stared
in horror at my own blood. She had stabbed me in
the ribs. I raised my eyes and she was standing
with the knife in her hand, and she was smiling.

You like that, do you? You like that? I
shouted. I lunged for my coat, for the knife
hidden there. She slashed at me with her own
sharp little knife, missed. I tried to get my
blade out but my hands were shaking. The coat was
crumpled in my hands. She kicked me, catching me
on the side of the head with her heel. I lost my
balance and landed on my buttocks, hard. She began

to kick me, viciously, and her heels tore chunks
out of my skin. I tried to curl into a ball to
protect myself. I was lying on the coat and I
felt something cold and hard and my hand closed
on the handle of my knife. Then I felt calm
again, in control. I stood up with the knife in
my hand.

13

Wolf was in a cheerful mood. He was humming a popular song without quite paying attention, then realised it was Marlene Deitrich's 'Falling in Love Again'. He continued humming and adjusted his fedora at a cocky angle. His cases were finished with, but so what? He had been paid. Who cared where the stupid Jew bitch Judith Rubinstein had got herself to? Today was the first day of the rest of his life. He came to his street but there was no one about. Even the whores were gone. Beyond he could hear shouts, see fireworks rise over the rooftops from the direction of the Thames. The hordes were out there, in Leicester Square and Trafalgar Square and Piccadilly, and thronging the Embankment and the wine bars and pubs. He went to his door and found it unlocked, the lock in fact jammed, inexpertly, and his good cheer evaporated. He pushed the door open and went in.

It was dark and he climbed each step with a slow and careful footfall; each step was like another level he was climbing, on top of some ancient and enormous pyramid, a once-grand edifice now reduced by centuries of neglect and misuse. The air smelled metallic. His shoes on the faded carpet made no sound. It was so very quiet. He could hear his own breathing, but nothing else. Nothing moved. He came to the landing and stopped. The door to his office was open. The taste of rust was in Wolf's mouth, on his tongue and in his gums. He pulled the door open all the way.

He went inside.

He saw it in snatches, not quite forming a full picture. The faint light from outside rippled on the walls and on the carpet, ancient light that had been traversing space for untold millennia and new light, born from the mysterious electrical processes housed within the streetlamp outside. The light illuminated the room in a chiaroscuro where shadows danced like the naked savages studied by Ernst Schäfer on his expeditions to prove the origins of the Aryan race. Arcs of bright fresh blood decorated the walls of Wolf's office. Some reached as high as the ceiling, some criss-crossed each other in strange hieroglyphs, a language of death and blood. A raincoat had been tossed to the corner of the room. There were dirty red palm prints on the floor around it.

Wolf watched the toes. The toes were long and slender and the nails were painted a fuchsia colour. Furniture had been overturned in the room and one chair was broken. A woman's high-heeled shoe lay on its side. Wolf couldn't see the other one. A woman's handbag, a bag he recognised, was upturned by the window and spilling out of it were dildos and a whip and make-up, blusher and lipstick, a wad of notes, keys, prophylactics, half a sandwich wrapped in wax paper, of the sort Herr Edelmann occasionally sold in the bakery downstairs.

There was a concavity in the floor where her head had been bashed, repeatedly, with cold fury, and he saw her hair, clumped with brain matter and blood, in delicate bunches like the stems of flowers. She was not like the first girl, cleanly arranged. She had struggled, had inflicted her own violence on her attacker, and was silenced, at last, for her transgression, for the crime of being a woman, or a prostitute, or for just being. Her murderer had lashed out blindly, repeatedly. Her head on the floor barely resembled something human.

There was the fading smell of semen, like wet mushrooms.

Having done this deed the killer had tidied himself up, had become a man amongst men once more. He had tidied his clothes and straightened himself and then he had dipped his finger in her blood and he had drawn a swastika on the wall, and then, beside Dominique's head, he had left Wolf a toy: a tin wind-up drummer.

Wolf picked up the toy. Idly, he wound the little key. He set the drummer on the floor and watched it march past Dominique's body, the tiny hands moving mechanically up and down over the drum, beating out a funeral dirge. It was the only sound in the room. He watched it go. It marched and marched.

On the desk was Wolf's typewriter and in the typewriter was a sheet of paper, neatly inserted. Wolf went round the desk and sat down in his chair. The keys of the typewriter were smeared in blood. He pulled out the piece of paper and read.

It began, *Herr Wolf.*

He read the letter, holding it at a distance and squinting at the hard black letters on the page.

The letter was a confession of a sort. It ended with a simple entreaty for the two of them to meet.

On the desk next to the typewriter was a ticket for the revue show at the London Hippodrome, dated for that night. Wolf picked it up, looked at it, turned it over, put it back down. As an afterthought he turned the typewritten page over in his hand.

Written on the back of the paper in an unsteady hand, with the same ink that only a scant time before had run through Dominique's veins, was a single word in the murderer's hand.

Run.

Wolf's Diary, 22nd November 1939 – *contd.*

The door downstairs crashed open. The sound, unexpected and terrifying, made me jump. My heart beat fast in my chest.

Could it be the killer, coming back?

A madman, I thought, dazedly. I was dealing with a madman. Not for the first time I wished I had a gun. A gentleman killed with bullets, the state with gas, Only a madman used a knife.

I listened to footsteps come labouring up the stairs. Stray light from the window bounced off an object thrown beyond my desk. It was a blood-covered knife. It must have belonged to the girl. It was the weapon she had used on the killer. I picked it up and sat behind the desk again, waiting. The footsteps reached all the way to the landing and stopped.

'Oh, it's *you*,' I said.

'Well, well, well,' Constable Keech said. 'What have we got here, then?' He stood in the doorway, his fat face covered in a sheen of sweat. When he grinned his big square teeth looked like coral reefs buried under a murky sea.

'I would like,' I said, 'to report a murder.'

Keech bellowed a laugh. He laughed genuinely, with big heaving breaths, his face turning redder and redder, his hands supporting his weight on his knees as he almost keeled over on himself. 'Would you now, shamus,' he said. 'Would you now.'

'I didn't do this, Keech.'

'Of course you didn't.'

'I didn't do this! You have to believe me!'

'Don't insult me, Wolf.' He straightened up, glanced at the corpse, lost his good humour. 'Jesus, Wolf. What did you do to that poor girl?'

'Someone is trying to frame me.'

'Well, they've done a bloody good job, then, haven't they! Get up. You're under arrest.'

'Fuck off, pig!' I was feeling panicked. 'How did you get here?' I said. 'How did you *know*?'

He shrugged. 'I got an anonymous call at the station,' he said.

'I'm being *framed*!'

'Come along, Wolf. You can explain everything at the station.'

'Is it that inspector again? Morhaim.' I spat out the name. 'The filthy Jew has been after me from the beginning.'

'Inspector Morhaim is no longer in the employ of the Metropolitan Police. And another word from you about him like this will get you some broken teeth to complain about.' He took out his nightstick and ran his fingers along its dark shaft almost lovingly. Still I didn't move from the desk. Hidden from Keech's view was the dead girl's knife.

'What happened to Morhaim?' I said. I was, genuinely, surprised.

Keech spat on the floor. 'He quit. It's not like he was popular with the men. And well, with your boy Mosley headed to Downing Street, I don't think it would have been long before he was pushed out anyway.'

'Now, are you going to get up from that chair there or do I need to make you?'

'Make me, pig.'

'Oh, I'll make you all right!' he said. He advanced on me, the nightstick raised. 'Look!' I said. I waved the killer's letter in my hand. 'It's all but a confession, it's proof I didn't do it!'

'Proof?' His stick came down on the desk, shattering the cheap wood. 'Proof?' He snatched it from my hand, looked at it, his fat lips moving as he read. 'You typed this.'

'No!'

He scrunched the killer's confession into a ball and tossed it in the corner. 'You're sick in the head,' he said. 'You know what they're going to call you? The greatest murderer since Jack the Ripper. You're not right, mate. You're not right at all.' And he brought his stick down once again, right on the typewriter, smashing it to pieces.

Keys flew in the air; a semicolon hit me in the eye. 'Damn you, Keech!' I said. I rose from the chair just as he strode past Dominique's head and reached for me, his stick descending a third time. I slashed him with Dominique's knife. The knife missed his face, grazed his chest. The nightstick caught me on the arm and a terrible numbing pain spread through me and I could barely breathe. The knife fell from my hand. I screamed, '*Scheisse!*' and raised my knee sharply, catching him unawares between the legs. Keech made a high-pitched hissing sound and fell, slowly. Somehow he was still holding the stick and he swung it as he went down, hitting me on the shin, the pain so excruciating that I screamed and went down, too.

For a moment both of us were on the floor facing each other like two lovers at the end of an intimate moment, looking deep into each other's eyes. 'I didn't do it, Keech. I didn't kill them!'

'I will . . . fucking kill *you*,' he said. He spoke with difficulty. He reached for me, those huge meaty hands, his fat fingers closing on my throat. Their weight was terrible. His thumbs found my windpipe and began to press. I reached desperately for the fallen knife, scrabbling for it, panicking, the pain growing impossible, my breath departing. I tried to fight him off; we were entwined on the floor, slick with the dead girl's blood. His body pressed on mine; he was so heavy I couldn't breathe. I thought, what a way to die. Then miraculously my fingers scrabbling in the blood on the floor found the sharp edge of the knife. It sliced the tip of my finger, and my blood mingled with the girl's. Slowly, slowly I moved my fingers until I found the handle of the blade. I was so weak I could not breathe, but I could do this, just as I had cured my blindness with my mind. The power came to me, for one last desperate act, and I thrust the knife into his neck; just so.

The blood came out of the wound hot; it spurted out of him. And still he pressed on my neck, and for a moment I blacked out.

I came to, only moments later. The pressure on my neck had eased – was gone. I could breathe. The air tasted so sweet. I blinked back tears. His face swam into focus. His hand was pressed to his neck, holding back the blood, but it spurted out of him nonetheless, running between his fingers. His eyes stared into mine, and I was terrified of him. I scrambled to get away from him, from the blood. It was everywhere in the room, his blood, my blood, the girl's blood, the murderer's blood. I slipped and fell in it. Typewriter keys were pressed painfully against my flesh, an A and an H. Keech said nothing, just watched me, the blood still pouring out of him. I pushed myself up until I stood, supporting myself against the desk, looking down at him. The knife was on the floor. I think Keech smiled. I think he said, 'Now they'll get you.' I walked backwards until my shoulder blades hit the wall and I stopped and stood there, breathing deeply,

looking about me at the room and the dead whore and the
dying policeman.

Keech was right, I realised, with dread.

I was a marked man, now. And there was no escape.

I watched him die. He died well. I will say that much for
him.

I picked up the ticket for the revue show off the desk. I
took one last look at the room. My office. I had been almost
happy there, for a while.

One dead copper, one dead whore. I was getting too old.
Everything hurt. I would miss my books most, I thought. But
books, like people, can always be replaced.

. . . And so into the night Wolf went, and a thousand lamps
glimmered in the dark, and the ancient light of a thousand stars
fought through the cloud cover to be changed forever by the
hard surfaces of the city; within its narrow twisting alien alleyways Wolf walked like an explorer on the surface of a foreign
hostile world, an invisible umbilical cord stretched from his past
to his present, stretched until it finally broke, unable to hold
him anchored any longer; and so he felt light of gravity, and
floating, like an astronaut in one of those glorious, colourful
American pulps. He pictured men on the moon, proud Aryan
raumfahrer: spacemen, voyagers. Pictured capsules of aluminium
floating through space, men inside them; pictured a lunar
landing, a man stepping out onto the alien dust, planting a
swastika flag where no man had gone before. Wolf walked
through the city that night as a man with no purpose, a man
whose life had taken the wrong turn, around whom history had
flowed a different way, taken a different course and left him
stranded in an island of unreality in the midst of that great river
that was time. He felt untethered. He did not know who he was
or what he would become.

On Shaftesbury Avenue the last theatregoers had come and
gone and the theatres were shut though their lights shone on.
The pavements were crowded with a festive restless mass of

people, shouting, drinking, waving Union Jacks and the cross of St George. Wolf was swept up in the current. His fate was no longer his own. He was carried by the tide of these English citizens the way a spectator may have been in one of his own rallies, in the old days. Down Shaftesbury to Piccadilly where a Blackshirt rally was in progress, a full military campaign, and the men in their futuristic outfits no longer looked ridiculous but serious and deadly. He was carried along through the throng down Haymarket and on to Pall Mall, where he saw a ring of policemen blocking the road and a clash between Unionists and Blackshirts spilling bloody and awkward across pavement and road, men with makeshift weapons of bricks and piping smashing at each other, blindly, in a rage, but silently, or so it seemed to Wolf, in a primitive battlefield such as between Spartans and Persians, and the cars in the street jammed against each other and were savaged, too, and he watched the battle escalate, drivers trying to escape, windows smashed, glass shards spilling on the road, skulls cracked, a vehicle set on fire, policemen shouting, someone firing a gun in the air, a stampede where men were trampled underfoot. Somehow he managed to get away, swept again in the tide, down to Trafalgar Square.

From just down the road, along Whitehall, a sudden silence spread out as Big Ben began to strike the hour. The first and then the second heartbeats of the old clock went almost unnoticed, at three the sound began to penetrate, at four and five the massed crowds quietened, at seven and eight the silence grew; at nine it was entire. Nine and then ten heartbeats Big Ben struck and they echoed over the ancient city, old and new, old and new like the harbingers of a new dawn. Time hung, suspended. On the podium by Nelson's Column, Oswald Mosley waited, his face sweaty, his black uniform replaced for this one occasion by a dignified three-piece suit from Savile Row. Two other men were waiting in the wings, only one of whom Wolf would have known, but Wolf stood a way away, at the Whitehall intersection, listening to the clock strike the hour like a drum. Eleven, old Ben struck, and the second stretched and stretched and in its expectant silence Wolf saw the city as he had never seen it, rising before him like a metropolis dreamed of by Fritz Lang: huge shining buildings rose amidst the squalor of old London, by London Bridge a shard of glass taller than the pyramids pierced the sky. From the City of London there rose a phoenix egg of metal and glass, and a giant wheel spun and spun on the south bank of the Thames like a mandala. This city of the future was brighter, brasher, awash in an electric glow which faded as he watched, the ghostly outline of this futuristic could-have-been slowly washing away. Wolf held his breath and Big Ben tolled, twelve, and one day ended, and a new day began.

Wolf's Diary, 23rd November 1939

The night erupted in a shower of fireworks. The air filled with the repeated sounds of explosions, playing out a moment after the formation of bright shapes in the air. The smell of cordite, magnesium and sulphur stung my nostrils. In the sky were the fabulous shapes of spinning rings and diadems and tailed chrysanthemum, crossettes and hearts and palm-shell fireworks. A band began to play, rather incongruously, Gilbert & Sullivan's 'He Is An Englishman'. The crowds around me cheered, faces red and teeth yellow and skin sickly white; they were cast in the lights and shadows of the exploding colours overhead. Demonic grinning faces all around me, a nightmarish vista of skulls seen through translucent skin, moving skeletons clad in sacks of blood. I hadn't even thought of how I must look, bruised, battered and covered in blood, mine and others', but I didn't think anyone even noticed. I pushed my way towards the steps of the National Gallery. I had to batter my way through people and every moment I half-expected a policeman to find me, to blow the whistle, raise the alarm. But no one would find Keech and the dead girl, surely, I thought, not until the morning at least. What I would do then I didn't know.

I watched the stage. Watched Mosley come on, smiling,

waving at the crowds, his arm extended in a Blackshirt's imitation of a Nazi salute. The man was nothing but a cheap copy.

'Victory!' he called out. The crowd erupted in cheer again but I could hear booing coming from the distance and turned my head to see a group of union demonstrators trying to push towards the podium and being repelled.

'Britain belongs to the British people once again!' Mosley's voice echoed over the crowd. 'We've won! This is the beginning of a new dawn! This is a new day for Britain – and for the world!'

Cheers. Boos. Fireworks exploding overhead, the booms coming a moment later, disorientating me. I felt sick and dry-heaved. I had not eaten in I couldn't remember how long. On the stage Mosley assumed a serious, studious expression. His voice took on dulcet tones. He said, 'His Majesty the King has asked me to form a new government and I have accepted.'

Silence. Overhead the last fireworks burst and died.

'I would like to discuss some of the challenges we are now facing.

'I believe we need a strong government, a stable, good and decent government that I think we need so badly.

'It has been more than six years since the Fall of Germany to international communism. Communism with its method of madness is making a powerful and insidious attack upon the world today. It seeks to poison and disrupt, in order to hurl us into an epoch of chaos.

'It has flooded our country with refugees. We have opened our borders, our arms, our homes to them, in friendship. And they came, in their thousands, and thousands of thousands. Our cities reek of their cabbage! Their children speak foreign tongues in our schools. They are draining our country of its resources, they are taking the very bread from our own people's mouths!'

Cheers. Fists raised in salute. I felt a cold chill I could not explain. And yet it was almost as if it were my own words he was using against me.

'I think the service our country needs right now is to face up to our really big challenges, to confront our problems, to take difficult decisions, to lead people through those difficult decisions, so that together we can reach better times ahead.

'Germany is not our enemy. Communism is. That, and the bankers behind it all. I think you know their real name.'

'Jews!' – 'The elders of Zion!' – 'Shylocks!' – 'Yids!'

'We must help Germany in its time of need!' Mosley said. 'Yes!'

'Get the foreigners out!' someone shouted. Mosley smiled. The smile faded. His eyes gazed out coldly over Trafalgar Square.

'This is a testing time,' he said, gravely. 'I have news, news we could not share before with you. At nineteen hundred hours today, Germany, with Russian help, has invaded Poland.'

Gasps. Shouts. A wave of shock running through the crowd.

'It is true.'

He waited. Drew out the silence.

'Our bilateral agreement with Poland dictates a response,' Mosley said.

'It is my first duty to you as your prime minister, to let you know that we are at war.'

Gasps, but also cheers. The mood was turning ugly. They were enthralled. They relished the idea of war.

'I would like to introduce you to an old friend of mine!' Mosley said.

I began to make my way through the crowd, up towards Leicester Square, but now I paused. Turned back.

'Germany *will* return to its former glory,' Mosley said. 'This I promise. We will fight for its release from the shackles of communist oppression!'

This was less joyfully received.

'I would like to introduce you to the head of the newly formed German Government-in-Exile: a man who loves his country, who wants to return the refugees from our streets to their rightful homes. A former member of the National Socialist party, the rightful winners of the last German elections.'

Somewhere behind that stage the American, Virgil, would be standing, smiling like the cat who drank all the cream. Somewhere there, waiting to make his entrance, would be the man behind it all, behind the white slavery and the people-smuggling rings, one of my old comrades, I was sure.

My replacement.

My fingers tightened into fists. Who could it be? Hess was dead, Goebbels ruthless but lame.

Himmler? Bormann? Heydrich?

'Together we will change the world!' Mosley pumped his fist in the air. 'Please welcome the rightful Chancellor of Germany – Mr Adolf Eichmann!'

'Who?' someone beside me said, bewildered.

'Who?' I screamed. A tallish thin man with a vulture's face and thinning hair came onto the stage and solemnly shook Prime Minister Mosley's hand.

'Who the fuck is Adolf Eichmann!' I said.

'Thank you, Prime Minister. You do me a great honour.'

'Eichmann? I have never even heard of this Eichmann!' I screamed. Heads were turning. 'Who . . .? How . . .!'

'You may not know me,' the man on the stage said. 'I joined the National Socialist party in '32, only a year before the Fall of Germany. Some of you may even remember our one-time leader, the man we called our Führer—'

'God damn you, Eichmann! Who is this imposter, this swindler!'

'But he was weak. And I shall replace him.'

'No one can replace me, do you hear! No one!'

More heads were turning my way but I didn't care. I did not know this man! He was nothing, a nobody! Did Dorothy feel this way when she finally discovered the great wizard was just some man behind a curtain?

'Germany has been taken over by Jews!' Eichmann said. 'But I have a solution! A final solution to the Jewish question. Mr Prime Minister?'

'Indeed,' Mosley said, smoothly. 'Mr Eichmann has some innovative and creative ideas, and we shall be discussing them thoroughly in the coming days. And for now—' he took a breath and looked mournfully at the assembled hordes. 'I regret to inform you that as of this moment I am declaring limited martial law. All non-registered foreigners will be collected and deported. All Jews will be designated hostile aliens and rounded up, to be either deported or placed in internment camps. We must cut out the cancer eating away at our society! Together we can do this! Together we are as one!'

'Together we are as one!' They all raised their fists in the air. They were saluting him, his power. A woman beside me whimpered, her thighs rubbing together as she climaxed herself to an onanistic orgasm.

This should have been *me* up there! The mood was ugly, and I was a foreigner alone and undocumented in this crowd of bloodthirsty British pigs. I had to get away!

I began to push again, to try and edge away, but the crowds closed on me and on the stage Mosley was speaking, shouting, cheering, and the band struck again, that ridiculous song from *H.M.S. Pinafore*, and a second bout of fireworks shot into the sky.

In the general confusion, at least, I began to make headway in my effort to escape, pushing through the crowds at last to reach Charing Cross Road. Bands of drunken men were forming into impromptu search parties, seeking out foreigners to round up and beat. Communists and agitators challenged them and fights broke out and policemen appeared like mushrooms and the whole thing was threatening to become one huge riot. Then I saw it.

The Hippodrome.

The club sat on the corner of Leicester Square. Charlie Chaplin had played there once, that vile man. It was a grandiose building, once home to a travelling zoo, from which it got its name; then it became a music hall and then a revue. I remembered the ticket in my pocket. The building was shut now, of course. I was being pushed closer to it by the turning tide, people fleeing the melee. The main doors were locked and I was shunted sideways, into Leicester Square, where a battle was commencing between Blackshirts and a group of belligerent, drunken Austrians. My people. I could have wept!

At last I came to the back of the building, and found the service entrance to the Hippodrome.

The chain holding the doors fast was broken.

It was dark inside the Hippodrome and quiet, the noise from outside abating almost instantly when Wolf shut the door. Metal surfaces gleamed in the dark. Pots and pans hung in orderly rows. All he could hear was the soft tap-tap-tap of water drops hitting the bottom of a sink. He tried to listen for movement, for signs of life, but there was nothing. The entire building felt oppressively *empty*. Wolf tiptoed through the kitchen. Somewhere inside the building, he was sure, a killer was lying in wait.

In a kitchen drawer, wide as the span of his arms, he found an assortment of sharp knives. He equipped himself with a chef's knife. The sound the drawer had made when he pulled it sounded very loud to him, and so did the rattling of the knives, and he went hurriedly on, through the service doors and into the theatre proper.

It was a magnificent place, though desolate in its abandonment. No players moved upon the stage. There was no magician to perform his tricks, no comedian to tell off-colour jokes, no dancing girls to flash a glimpse of thigh, no jugglers to astound with feats of the impossible, and no audience to applaud and laugh and gasp and jeer, as could be demanded by the occasion. There was nothing but a great barren silence. The wide stage stood to one side, draped in red velvet curtains, which were raised now, and before it the floor was set with tables for tomorrow night's diners. Overhead, the auditorium rose in four tiers, all sparkle and velvet and dark wood, steep stairs rising on each side. But all the seats were empty: there was no one in the house.

Wolf moved cautiously, quietly through the aisles. He stopped and listened, but still there was no sound. Was the killer waiting, watching? He stumbled against a chair in the dark. It fell over with a loud crash. Wolf said, '*Scheisse*,' softly.

He heard someone moving, high overhead. Craned his head upwards. Sudden white light hit him in the eyes, blinded him. He turned his head away. A spotlight illuminated Wolf, alone in the theatre. It fell on him from high above, from the gods. Wolf moved, and the spotlight moved with him, and he heard someone laugh; high above the world.

'Show yourself!' Wolf cried.

'I have been waiting a long time, Mr Wolf.'

There was something familiar about the voice but it was distorted, amplified. Wolf climbed onto the stage. He stood facing the empty theatre, one hand protecting his eyes. At last he thought he caught movement, but all he could make out was a shadowy figure in the gods.

'What do you want?'

Wolf moved. The spotlight followed. He paced the stage. His patience was being exhausted. He had had a bad night, a bad month. The whole of November had been a bit of a washout, really.

'I wanted you to see.'

The speaker sounded plaintive. As though Wolf had somehow let him down. 'See what?' Wolf snapped. He edged to the wings and then slipped off-stage. The spotlight tracked him but it couldn't follow him beyond the curtains. 'Where are you?' the shadow said.

Wolf crept behind the scenery. A magician's sawing-a-woman-in-half trick box, a clown's red nose hanging from a hook, a pastoral village scene with cardboard cut-out cows that looked good-naturedly at Wolf as he passed.

'I don't like this, Mr Wolf. Really, hiding won't make any difference. I mean you no harm. On the contrary, I am your friend.'

A prop gun, a mask like something out of a Venetian dance. Ah, there! A set of hidden stairs behind the stage, twisting and turning away, leading up. Wolf raised his head. It was a jumble of unsteady construction as far as he could see, hanging sandbags and rickety gangways suspended from the ceiling. But the stairs looked solid enough.

'Don't you *see*? This isn't who you are! When I first saw you I was in awe, I could not believe it was really you, but then I watched you, I observed, I am the watcher in the dark—'

The watcher in the dark? How ridiculous! Wolf thought. He climbed the stairs quietly, cautiously. They rose up, a service passageway that ran parallel to the paying customers' stairs that mirrored them. The man – this *watcher* – was somewhere above. Probably he would be in a technician's box somewhere. The spotlight moved across the empty stage, still searching for Wolf. The man was all the time talking, talking: Wolf wished he would shut up.

'. . . Fallen,' the watcher said. 'Reduced, debased! You who were the greatest of all men, now playing out the role of the lowest: a shamus, a private dick? I could not believe it, I was outraged. You had a *destiny*!'

What do you know about destiny, Wolf wanted to shout, you stupid little man. What do you know of real pain?

'And you just gave up! You were like a man who is sick, I finally realised. A man out of his senses, a man in shock. I had to wake you. I had to make you see. To face yourself again. So you could become the man you were always meant to be.'

There. The voice was close. Wolf could see the limelight now, and the vague outline of the man behind it, moving it. He gripped the knife tightly. He would make this fast. He was an orderly man and he was settling up all of his accounts.

'That's why I killed them,' the watcher confided; his words floated down to the empty seats, the unserved tables, the stage on which no clown or magician performed. He had an audience of one, this watcher, and he seemed intent, Wolf thought, on boring him.

How he abhorred bores!

'They were whores, they didn't matter,' the watcher said. 'Diseased prostitutes, you said so yourself. In your book. I have read it so many times. It changed my life. Where do you get your ideas from?'

Wolf crept the rest of the way up, low on the metal stairs. The man was just behind the wall of wood. *Where do you get your ideas?* Really? It was the stupidest question Wolf had ever heard.

'I needed you to see. I need you to wake up!' He sounded desperate. 'Don't you *understand*?'

Then he stopped speaking and Wolf, too late, tried to rise with the knife but he was, of course, too slow. A young man in a shabby suit stood on the other side of the divide, holding a gun which he aimed at Wolf. It was a Parabellum M17, a German pistol. Wolf remembered when it was first produced, in the closing years of the Great War.

'Drop the knife. Please.'

Wolf dropped the knife. They were suspended high in the air. Below them the theatre stretched in tiers, all lifeless, all expectant. It was quiet. So quiet.

'My father brought it with him as a memento from the war,' the young man said. 'The pistol, I mean. He always had much respect for the German soldiers. He said the German army was the best in the world, but it had been let down by its leaders. It's good to see you again, Mr Wolf. I am glad to see you well.'

'Oh, it's *you*,' Wolf said.

A small smile played on the boy's face. 'Yes,' he said, softly.

'I'm sorry, I don't quite remember your name.'

The smile disappeared. The gun wavered. 'It's *Alderman*! Thomas Alderman! We spoke on the *phone*! We met at Sir Oswald's party!'

'Mosley's man, right! I wondered where I knew you from.'

The boy's face was pale, his eyes too large, bloodshot. His

clothes were covered in gore and he held himself as though he were wounded.

'I visited you at the *hospital*!' the boy, Alderman, said.

'I wondered if that really happened,' Wolf said, softly. 'It seemed rather odd, at the time. I assume the nurse did as I asked her, and got in touch with Oswald?'

The boy looked genuinely confused. 'What nurse?' he said.

'How did you know I was at the hospital?'

'I looked for you everywhere! I was frantic with worry when you never returned to your office. I have been watching you. It's what I do, I watch, I listen, and no one sees me, no one suspects. No one *sees* me!'

'Alderman.'

'Yes!'

'What do you *want*, Alderman?' Wolf said. He was so very tired.

'I just want you to *see*!'

'I'm looking,' Wolf said. 'Put the gun down, Alderman. You're not going to shoot me.'

The gun wavered. 'I don't know . . . I don't know if I will or not. You can't tell me what to do! Don't you understand?' he said, pleadingly. 'I did it all for *you*. I killed them. *I* did it. So you won't have a choice but to become what you were meant to be. I didn't *like* to do it – well, not much.' An expression that was part sly smile, part grimace rose and fell on Alderman's face. 'And it worked, didn't it?' he said. 'The police, they will be coming for you. For the girls, and that fat policeman. What did you do to him?'

'I killed him.'

'You see!' the boy shouted in triumph. 'There is nowhere left to run! Admit who you are! Say it!'

The whole thing was grating on Wolf's nerves. 'I know who I am, Alderman,' Wolf said. 'I have always known myself. Now give me the gun, boy!'

'Say it!' Alderman screamed. 'Your name, say it!'

'Wolf.'

'No! Damn it, don't make me shoot you, I won't—'

Wolf stumbled against the low wooden door. It swung open into the box, catching Alderman on the knees, knocking him back. The boy lost his balance and his gun dropped from his hand. He tottered on the edge of the box, above the dark chasm of the stage. His face was beaded with sweat, white and grotesque. 'Help me!' His hand reached out in a mockery of a Nazi salute. Moved by compassion or some other, more nebulous emotion he could not quite name, Wolf reached for him; for just a moment the tips of their fingers met, touched. The boy's eyes shone wet. 'Adolf . . .' he whispered. And then he said, '*Heil* Hitler,' and, for just a moment, Wolf thought he smiled. Then he lost his balance and fell.

Wolf watched him fall. Alderman fell like a trapeze artist, sailing with a grace he had never possessed on the ground. Then he hit the railings of the lower circle with a wet sound and rolled ungainly downwards until he smashed through a table already laid out for tomorrow night's guests, crushing the china, scattering the silverware and coming to land, at last, in a broken heap on the Hippodrome's floor.

'Wolf. Adolf. It's the same fucking name, you dolt,' Wolf said. He turned off the useless spotlight. It was still shining, on the wrong spot, on somewhere where nothing had happened. Everything was clearer in the dark but not for Wolf, not any more.

He saw the gun lying on the ground and tucked it into his waistband at the small of his back. Then he stepped out of the box and began to descend the stairs, going slowly.

Back on the ground he went and looked at the boy. He stood over him for some time; what remained of him. He felt like a match, burning. A hot hate suffused him. 'I'm Hitler!' he screamed. He kicked the boy, and again, and again, his foot slamming into the soft unresisting flesh of the corpse. 'I'm Hitler! I'm Hitler! I'm Hitler!'

The dead ruined face stared up at him with mocking blind eyes. Wolf's own voice came back to him reedy and thin, lost in the high ceiling of the Hippodrome. He was no one. He was nothing.

'I'm . . .' he said. The theatre was quiet. The seats were empty and silent with disuse. There was no one to see him; no one at all. There was no one to hear him, no one to respond. There was no one to acknowledge him; there was no one to march to his tune.

'I'm a Jew,' he said, and laughed; but like Wolf himself, the sound meant nothing.

14

In another time and place Shomer builds doors; endless doors come down the production line: small doors, big doors, house doors, prison doors, dollhouse doors and cage doors, and oddly shaped doors that fit no blueprint Shomer can imagine. A row of skeletons work on the production line, skeletons bent over in the cold emptiness of the factory, skeletons still clutching their soup bowls and spoons between their legs so that they are not stolen, like some nebulous proof of their vitality, of their existence. Men die like smoke. Time ebbs and congeals like dirty, slushy snow. Suns rise and fall, days turn to nights, trains come to a stop, men die. Across this vast camp children still clutching their dolls are escorted to showers from which no water comes but gas and gassed they are taken out in wheel-barrows, arms soft and flaccid, eyes glassed, their mothers and fathers lifted up and placed before the *Sonderkommando* whose job it is to extract their gold teeth, search their cavities for hidden valuables, to shear their hair for the war effort, to strip the corpses clean.

It is the job of the *Kanada kommando* then to sort through the items retrieved, piles and piles of gold teeth, shoes, rings – for Canada is the land of plenty; it is the promised land, so much wealth piled up, so many dead, but if only you can steal the occasional item you could trade gold for an extra slice of bread, a bowl of soup that came from the bottom of the vats and not the top, for down in the depths there could be lurking a cube of grey meat, a speck of potato. But all that rich food runs through you, constantly, and it is the job of the *Shiessekommandos* to clean up the latrines, every day wading in so much liquid shit, an endless sea of it, running and dripping and collecting in great oceanic puddles, but there are worse jobs.

In the camp's various Joy Divisions, what we may also term *Lagerbordell* or camp bordellos, the women are branded with *Feld-Hure* on their chests, field whores they become in service of the guards and some favoured inmates, man after man they must satisfy, relentlessly, and any failure means immediate dismissal, and that in turn can mean only the ovens, preceded of course by the showers and the gas.

Women die like air. They are consumed like oxygen. They are as transient as breaths. And in what was once fields, men dig mass graves into which they themselves will fall.

And so Shomer builds doors, while Yenkl stands beside him, watching, as insubstantial as smoke. Moons traverse the sky from horizon to horizon and fall and rise, the planet turns, the trains arrive, and Europe is slowly running out of Jews.

And so Shomer builds doors, until his entire world is contracted into one rectangular shape, always hovering before his eyes, calling out, an impossible promise, until he reaches out to the handle just attached, and pulls.

The door opens, and Shomer steps through.

*   *   *

Into a house at rest. A hushed Shabbat calm descends when he enters. Avrom in his starched white shirt, Bina in her Friday dress look up at him across the table where the Shabbat candles burn. Fanya at the oven straightens with the loaf of bread in her hands, and smiles. '*Nu?*' she says. And he takes his place amongst them like a man still dreaming – already the details of that other place, that other time, are fading. And he blesses the wine as though in a dream.

And Shomer goes to the sink and fills a cup with water. He transfers the cup to his left hand and pours on his right, three times. He then transfers the cup and repeats the process, until his hands are washed clean. Returning to the table he ruffles

Avrom's dark locks, kisses Bina's porcelain cheek. Touches the back of his wife's hand, briefly. '*Baruch ata adonai*,' he says, 'Blessed be, God, king of the world, for bringing bread out of the earth.' The cobwebs clear from his mind with the prayer. He tears a piece of cholla, dips it in salt, takes a bite. Tears more pieces, dips them, passes them on, to his children and his wife.

They eat.

Peace descends on Shomer; it engulfs him; almost he wishes to leave the dining table and go to his sanctuary, his little office where the typewriter waits, to feel once more the keys beneath his fingers.

The children chatter. Fanya brings out chicken and potatoes from the oven. The smell makes Shomer's mouth water. He carves the chicken and Fanya distributes potatoes to the children. '. . . But I want the thigh!' Bina complains, and Avrom says, 'No, *I* want the thigh!' and Fanya tells them to hush. Shomer thinks of a book he was going to write, something new and full of light. When they are done he sits back and the candles flicker and cast shadows on the wall and one shadow, disturbingly, resembles a door. 'Look, Papa!' Bina says, pointing. She pushes back her chair without asking, her little face lifted in excitement. 'No, no,' Shomer says, an unknown fear makes him tremble. 'No, Bina—'

But she doesn't listen and the shadows deepen and etch on the wall a door. Shomer jumps up, his chair crashes to the floor, Fanya and Avrom are shadows at the table. 'No, don't—'

But his little girl reaches for the handle and she *pulls*—

The door opens and Shomer throws himself at her, knocking her away from the shadows, for a moment this place feels to him as warm as an oven. He stumbles and loses his balance. He totters on the threshold of this shadow door. Only darkness beyond.

He falls.

And steps into the streets of a city at peace. It is silent, he is somewhere in an English town, London, perhaps, in the deep time of night. To his left is a river. On the ground are buntings, beer bottles, discarded cigarettes, flags, the remains of fireworks, yesterday's newspaper in yesterday's grease, some chips still left poking out cold and oily.

He picks up the newspaper. 22nd November 1939. The *Daily Mail*. 'Mosley Projected to Win Election'. Shomer looks at it in wonder, lets it drop again. A cold wind. He walks along the Embankment. No, he thinks. This isn't it, either. He spots a door ahead and opens it.

. . .

Emerging into a wide corridor lined with unmarked doors on all sides. He opens one and finds himself in another corridor. He tries another door, walks through into another corridor. Another door and another corridor, and another, and another: Shomer is opening and shutting doors.

'No, that's not it. That's not it either.'

In this other time and place, Shomer searches for an exit.

*   *   *

Dawn found Wolf at the Greenwich docks. How he got there he couldn't say he knew. He walked aimlessly, had walked for hours through the night as Big Ben ticked away the hours, the sound growing fainter and fainter until it disappeared altogether and with it the outline of the city, too, had been erased, and Wolf found himself in a liminal space, a twilight world of ship hulls, boatyards, shuttered pubs and empty streets, the river first on his right, before he crossed, it must have been at Tower Bridge, though he could recall nothing of this transition from north to south, only the call of ravens, ancient stones, the passing of a barge laden with refuse from the capital, down below, as silent as a ghost, with ghosts in its wide wake.

The Thames on his left as London was abandoned behind and he entered a land less populated, empty pastures, factories silent in the pre-dawn dark, chimneys rising like admonitions into the sky, the river widening, the Isle of Dogs in its midst, the call of seagulls and the sour tang of tar, boats looming in the fog, a whole flotilla of them.

And as he walked he was no longer alone. Wolf was joined in that ur-moment between night and dawn by others. Silently they appeared, walking beside him, behind him, ahead: silent haggard figures, faces pinched and drawn, carrying suitcases and holdalls and babies and things: the detritus of lives, hastily packed together; and everything that couldn't be carried was left behind. In a sombre, ugly mood, they flowed along the banks to Greenwich: to the place where the meridians start. All about him they congregated and the fog parted before them, these exodii, and Wolf amongst them, one of them now: one of us, one of us.

At last then they came to Greenwich and through the sleeping town they went like the coming tide, flooding the narrow streets until they came at last to the river bank again and there, in silhouette against the sky, were the ships.

The largest of the ships was named the *Exodus* and it was a packet steamer, almost one hundred metres in length. Its name had been hastily changed: stencilled underneath the lettering was her old name, the SS *President Warfield*. Beside it were two smaller ships: the *Salvador*, flying the Bulgarian flag, and the *Taurus*, flying the Greek colours. The *Exodus* itself flew the Honduran flag, blue and white. There were men and women in uniform clothing waiting for them by the quayside and they guided the crowd as best they could, and all in silence, families with their luggage and their life at their feet waiting in the cold dawn of the docks to flee this island with a hope that had no guarantees. Amongst the officials Wolf saw a familiar face: Eric Goodman, the man from the Jewish Territorialist Organisation. Next they were divided into queues, though not in an overly ordered way. Wolf saw men of His Majesty's Immigration Branch standing around, and port officials, and sailors smoking and eyeing these refugees with pity or disdain or indifference.

For refugees is what they had become, Wolf realised, as is

the way of their people, and he in their midst, a wolf amongst the sheep, such as it were. Slowly the line progressed, in a makeshift booth before each ship there stood one man, one woman, each one holding clipboards and pens, slowly, slowly the line moved on.

Dawn came, the sun rising sluggishly, the fog like spider webs melting in the morning air. The honk of a steamer cut through the morning, the call of gulls, a baby cried nearby and was shushed.

Wolf shuffled forward with the rest. A little boy with a Jew's pinched, hungry face sidled up to him. He pulled at Wolf's sleeve. Wolf looked down. The boy wore overalls and a mop of unruly ginger hair. 'Mister, mister,' he said. 'Are we going to Palestine?'

'Fuck off, you little twerp.'

The boy grinned, revealing buck teeth. 'You ain't nothing, mister,' he said. 'You ain't worth shit.'

Wolf went to clout him but the boy hared back up the line, grinning cheerfully as he went.

The queue shuffled on. At last Wolf reached the makeshift booth. 'Your papers?' the woman said. She was short and stocky and had long brown hair in a bun. Wolf took out the identity document. 'Wolfson,' he said, emptily. 'Moshe Wolfson.'

The woman carefully wrote down the name in her list. She had neat, small handwriting. She noted the date and country of his birth. Smiled at him distractedly. At last, gave him a ticket, a grubby piece of cheap paper, stamped hurriedly with ink that had already begun to run. 'Good luck,' she said, softly. Wolf nodded. Then he followed his fellow Jews up the ramp and on board the *Exodus*.

Ship's Journal, 23rd November 1939

We left for sea at 10:25 at high tide. The *Exodus* led the way while the two smaller ships followed. A damp, unpleasant breeze. London receding in the distance. I won't miss the damn place much.

The ship overcrowded. Thousands on board. Number of latrines limited. The river opened on all sides, the banks seemed as distant and exotic as those of some unexplored land, filled with danger.

We move so slowly. No one has attempted to hinder our progress but the river is filled with traffic. Listened to the wireless, Mosley taking office at Number 10. The damned man has been nothing but a nuisance.

So many people. It is hard to breathe. Sat on the deck watching England roll by. It rained, then stopped. Played cards with a group of men, friendly enough. There are all sorts on board this ship, a Babel of Jews: black-clad chasidim mix with East End roughs and German refugees, and genteel English Jewry looking bewildered at this sudden change. I won three shillings. We all carry our money on our person at all times. Many children running around; they seem to regard this as a holiday.

Ship's Journal, 24th November 1939

Friday. An odd thing. When darkness fell many of the men were gathered in an impromptu minyan, the women grouped separately, praying and welcoming in the Shabbat, or *Shabbos* in Yiddish. Cholla bread was divided amongst us by the committee. These are the men and women who are behind all this. It is a well-run organisation, the plan must have been in preparation for a long time. They wear blue shirts to distinguish them from us passengers. Listened in on a Hebrew class. '*Shalom. Shalom.*' It means hello, or welcome, or peace.

Yesterday we cleared out of the Thames Estuary into the North Sea. We sailed along the coast, going past Margate to Dover, then made the crossing to France across the Channel. Now we sail hugging the coast still, the French countryside on our left, the Celtic Sea beyond.

I have been given some clean, though not new, clothes to wear. My blood-caked clothes are being washed. No one said anything. I was not the only one bloodied that night, evidently. Dozed below decks as the night was very cold.

Ship's Journal, 25th November 1939

Bay of Biscay. The *Salvador* and *Taurus* chug behind us with their own cargo of Jews. I miss my books. I thought of Alderman and how he seemed so impassioned about his cause. It all feels very distant now. Played cards but lost this time: two shillings.

Hebrew word of the day is *tapuz*. This means the orange fruit, which we are told is plentiful at our destination.

Seen by a doctor. Expressed surprise that I was still alive, considering the various bruises. I explained it has been a difficult month. He nodded sympathetically, patted me on the shoulder and moved on to his next patient. I took that as a good sign.

It's the Shabbat. Strangely peaceful. Several of my fellow passengers had brought a book or two each with them, and a makeshift library was organised. Success! Obtained Agatha Christie's *Death on the Nile*.

Ship's Journal, 26th November 1939

'I can't believe Jacqueline was the murderer!' I told the man who came to borrow the book after me. 'I did not see that coming at all.'

He glared at me and snatched the book from my hands. 'You bloody bastard,' he said.

How rude!

The steamer is making good time. We have passed the French coast and entered Portuguese territorial waters. No way to escape the ship – we dock nowhere.

Last night a woman gave birth to a baby boy; the whole

thing carried out quite garishly in the open. I miss having a
dog. Food is uninspired but adequate: we have supplies for
two weeks. Air is clear. There is something peaceful about the
movement of the ship, lulling me into the first instance of
calm I have felt in years.

Masturbated last night on my bunk thinking of Isabella
Rubinstein.

Ship's Journal, 27th November 1939

Approaching Gibraltar. The air feels warmer. Spain on our
left, Morocco on our right. Tangier. Made me think of Leni
and whether she ever finished making her film. It all seems
very distant now. A strange day, the mood subdued.
Towards lunchtime I took a constitutional on board deck
and, skirting a pile of thick rope lying quite dangerously in
my path, I thought I saw a face I knew. It was only for a
moment, across the crowded deck, so I could have been
mistaken.

I hope for both our sakes I was!

Ship's Journal, 28th November 1939

. . . 'I thought it was you,' he said.

The Mediterranean. Weather continues to grow warm and
rather pleasant. Crossed Gibraltar around midnight. I was on
deck, at the stern. A clear night, black-blue with a myriad of
stars.

Soft footsteps. I had been anticipating them. I turned,
affected a smile. 'Morhaim,' I said, with loathing.

'Wolf.'

We stood regarding each other in silence. The deck quiet,
we were obscured by upright pipes, carrying the stench of the
sleepers down below.

'So,' I said, at last.

'I won't ask how you made it on board,' he said. 'Or, in God's name, why!'

'Why are *you* here?' I said. He gave a short, bitter laugh. 'Where else would I go?' he said. 'My country has been devoured by vultures.'

I shrugged. 'We've all got problems, Morhaim.'

'You shit. Tell me something, *Wolf*. Did you kill them?'

'Who?'

'The girls.'

'You know damn well I didn't!'

'How many people *did* you kill?' he said, softly. 'How many *would* you have killed, had you been elected to office?'

'You want to play what-ifs, Morhaim?' I said. 'You Jews spend far too much time in your own imagination.'

He laughed. 'Us Jews,' he said. I did not like his tone, or what he was implying.

'So?' I said, again. '*Nu*? What do you want, *Inspector*?'

'Do you know who did it?' he said.

I shrugged. 'Some boy.'

'What happened to him?'

I didn't say anything and he laughed again. I don't think there was any real joy in his laughter. It was as if he had forgotten how to laugh. I looked at him and saw only a bitter, tired old Jew. He had no power any more.

'Don't,' I said.

He had a gun. It was aimed at me. I remember the night; it was so clear and, for a moment, quiet. A lone seagull flew in a parabola overhead. 'Give me one reason why not.'

My hand edged to the small of my back. 'I'll give you two,' I said.

Ship's Journal, 29th November 1939

Wonderful weather! Passing Sardinia. Hebrew word of the day is *sof*, meaning ending. Also *aliyah*, which means the immigration of the Jews to Palestine. Played cards, lost two shillings. I am beginning to smell – we all do. In the latrines an argument over who is a Jew, some suggestion not everyone on board may be kosher. 'Easy way to tell,' I said. Pissing against the wall in a row, we all had a good laugh. I looked at my Jew dick in my hand almost in affection.

Read Conrad's *The Secret Agent*. Have read better, by worse.

Ship's Journal, 30th November 1939

Listened to the BBC World Service on the radio in the afternoon. Disturbing news. Third assassination attempt on now-PM Oswald Mosley: a bomb hidden in Number 10. There is no confirmation yet if Mosley is dead or alive. Not that I care, much. Mutterings on board, concern for those Jews left in England – we lucky few represent but a small fraction of the whole.

Taurus keeps apace but the *Salvador* is flagging behind. Past Sicily, approaching Greece. Weather is balmy. Hebrew word of the day is *ley'da*, meaning birth.

Ship's Journal, 1st December 1939

Greece. A lot of small and rather pleasant-looking islands. We are heading towards Cyprus. Heard on the wireless that Mosley is in critical condition in hospital. Palestinian terrorists sought in connection with the bombing. A cheer on the deck. Saw the ITO man, Goodman, talking intensely to a woman who bore a strikingly familiar face.

'A Jewish woman sought in connection with the bombing worked as a maid at Number 10 under an assumed identity. The police appeal to the public . . .'

Went past Goodman and the girl. She had a humourless face, her father's cruelty. I smiled at her politely and doffed my hat as I walked past, with the sense of an ending. 'Judith,' I said.

'Do I know you?'

'No,' I said, and walked away.

Hebrew word of the day is *machaneh*, meaning camp.

Ship's Journal, 2nd December 1939

Skirted Cyprus. Palestine full steam ahead.

. . .

Opening and closing doors Shomer tumbles through half-worlds and fraction-worlds, 'No, this isn't it,' falling down trapdoors and out through endless corridors, 'No, this isn't it, either,' for how long he cannot tell, for there is no time here, where there is no space, until:

He opens the door and steps onto a beach. The sand is yellow, coarse. Dust fills the sky. The air is humid, warm, scented with citrus trees and late blooming jasmine. On the horizon the first star appears: Venus, which in Hebrew is called *Noga*, meaning light.

The night is quiet, peaceful. He looks up, to the darkening sky, as more stars come into being overhead. And for a moment it seems to him a woman and two children hover there, outlined in light, and that they're waving: but he can't be sure and in another moment they're gone.

The sea is calm. In the distance, the lights of a town. Shomer stands still, breathes in this wondrous air. 'This must be it,' he says to Yenkl; but Yenkl is no longer with him.

Shomer stands on the shore of that sea on that ancient land and looks out over the water. He sees a ship gliding into safe harbour as the sun fades in the east.

He stands there like a man suspended. Or, perhaps, like a man released.

. . .

The *Exodus* arrived in Jaffa as the sun was setting. They waited on board ship until officials came. An argument broke out. On the shore people gathered, waiting for them. At last something was decided, small boats came towards them in a fleet, shouts in Hebrew, Yiddish, Polish, German and English, a scramble to get off, along the wharves sacks filled with oranges awaiting export, stamped *Jaffa*.

On the shore they formed again into queues and there again waited their turn with the officials. The man waited in line meekly. When it was his turn he handed over his documentation and after careful examination a stamp was placed on the page. The man smiled his thanks.

'Welcome to Palestine,' the official said.

. . .

In that other time and place, the camp prepares to wake for another day of work and death. Beyond the walls, perhaps, the war continues. There is a rumour that the Red Army is advancing on the camp, intent on liberation, but will it be today, tomorrow, in an hour, in a year? The camp prepares for waking as it has done every day, in every block the inmates rise preparing for inspection. The prisoners rise but for the ones who had expired in the night. Slowly they shuffle, these skeletal men. Ka-Tzetnik wrote of Auschwitz, 'It was another planet', but later in life he went back on himself. 'Auschwitz was not created by the devil,' he wrote, 'but by men, like you, or me.'

. . .

In the morning they came for Shomer, but Shomer wasn't there.

THE END

THE END

HISTORICAL NOTE

In 1888, the leading Yiddish novelist Sholem Aleichem launched an extraordinary attack on the *shund* writer whose pen name was, simply, Shomer. This remarkable document, *Shomers Mishpet* ('Shomer's Trial'), ran to many pages, and categorised Shomer's writing as being 'ignorantly composed, poorly constructed, highly repetitious [and] morally bankrupt'.

Why Sholem Aleichem – the leading writer of his time – should feel the need to launch such a bitter attack on a humble purveyor of *shund*, or pulp fiction, is perhaps a mystery. Whatever the cause, Shomer – at the time a prolific author of hundreds of novels and plays – is now all but unknown, while Sholem Aleichem's place in literature remains assured.

This Shomer died, peacefully, in New York City in 1905. Thankfully, he never saw the Holocaust that was about to erupt some three decades later.

How does one write the Holocaust? In Chapter 8, two prisoners briefly discuss that question. Prisoner 174517 is, of course, Primo Levi, whose *If This Is A Man* (1947) remains one of the defining works of Holocaust literature. His 'opponent', prisoner 135633, wrote under the name Ka-Tzetnik (a word which means 'concentration camp inmate'), including the infamous novel *House of Dolls*, which first described the Nazi 'Joy Divisions', or camp brothels where women were kept as sexual slaves. Where Levi is cool and dignified, Ka-Tzetnik burns with the clear-eyed madness of a *shund* writer. His books were 'often lurid novel-memoirs, works that shock the reader with grotesque scenes of torture, perverse sexuality, and cannibalism,' noted David Mikics in *Tablet* magazine, adding: '*House of Dolls* is, unavoidably, Holocaust porn.'

During the 1920s, Adolf Hitler used the *nom de guerre* of 'Wolf' ('Adolf' means, literally, 'Noble Wolf'). Though countless books have been written about him, so much yet remains uncertain, shrouded in rumour and misinformation and propaganda. Certainly, it seems clear that he was an abused child; that his experience as a runner in the First World War led to that extraordinary scene (described in Chapter 10) where his blindness was seemingly cured by the psychiatrist, Edmund Forster; and that, though women were powerfully attracted to him, his relationship with them was far from simple.

Kershaw, in his vast, two-volume biography of Hitler, is surprisingly reticent about the question of Hitler's sexuality. While discussing the experiences recounted by Hitler's friend August 'Gustl' Kubizek (in *Adolf Hitler, My Childhood Friend*, published in 1951), Kershaw concludes that 'Later rumours of Hitler's sexual perversions are similarly based on dubious evidence. Conjecture – and there has been much of it – that sexual repression later gave way to sordid sadomasochistic practices rests, whatever the suspicions, on little more than a combination of rumour, hearsay, surmise, and innuendo, often spiced up by Hitler's political enemies.'

Indeed, in their highly entertaining and scurrilously gossipy *Hitler and Women*, Ian Sayer and Douglas Botting note that 'Investigating the private life and sexual inclinations of Adolf Hitler has been like trying to work one's way through an Elizabethan maze built on a tidal mudflat.' They go on, however, to discuss Hitler's 'copulation business' with some considerable, if often suspect, detail.

Many erstwhile Nazis weave their way through this novel. Of these, Josef Kramer (Chapter 2) was a ruthless concentration camp guard who was eventually put in charge of the gas chambers in Auschwitz, and later became the commandant of the Bergen-Belsen death camp. He was executed by hanging after the war.

Ilse Koch (Chapter 2) was known as 'The Beast of Buchenwald'. She was notorious for acts of violence and sadism against prisoners, and was accused of taking mementos off the corpses of her victims – including using their skin to make lampshades. She committed suicide in prison in 1967. She was also the inspiration behind the 'classic' Nazisploitation film *Ilsa, She Wolf of the SS* and its sequels.

Klaus Barbie (Chapter 6) was known as 'The Butcher of Lyon', where he was the head of the local Gestapo. He was known for torturing prisoners, including the use of electroshock and severe sexual abuse. Some prisoners were skinned alive. He was behind the deportation of some 14,000 Jews to the death camps. After the war, Barbie worked for American intelligence in its battle against communism. He emigrated to South America, and while there it was rumoured he was behind the eventual capture and murder of the revolutionary Che Guevara. He was finally extradited to France in 1983, and was convicted for war crimes in 1987. He died in prison.

As for the higher-up Nazis in this book – Hess was Hitler's long-time deputy; Göring, the founder of the Gestapo and commander-in-chief of the German air force (he was a decorated World War I ace fighter pilot); Goebbels his propaganda minister. Adolf Eichmann, whom Wolf fails to recognise in the novel, joined the SS in 1932. He rose quickly through the ranks, working for the Jewish Department of the SS. He was the recording secretary at the Wannsee Conference, in which the Final Solution to the Jewish Question was first formulated, and became the effective administrator of the Jewish genocide. He escaped to South America after the war but was captured by Israeli Mossad agents in 1960. He was put on trial, in Jerusalem, and executed in 1962. The author Ka-Tzetnik (revealed at that time as Yehiel De-Nur) famously testified during the trial, collapsing unconscious after delivering a short statement. He did not resume the stand (see Chapter 8 Endnotes).

One unexpected by-product of the Eichmann trial was the short-lived flourishing in Israel of 'stalag' novels. Published as pulp paperbacks during the 1960s, and featuring garish, lurid covers, they began with the infamous *Stalag 13*, by a 'Mike Baden':

the cover portrayed two female guards in skintight leather, cut to expose a great deal of cleavage, as they torture a male prisoner of war down on his knees. A string of such books – which featured sexual domination and torture of POWs by sadistic Aryan 'nymphomaniacs' – was published, available under the counter. They sold in unprecedented numbers, perhaps enabling many Israelis, for the first time, to talk openly about the great taboo that was the Holocaust. The pulp novels were themselves possibly inspired by Ka-Tzetnik's 1955 novel, *House of Dolls*, which was considered canonical, and became a part of the Israeli high-school curriculum. Whatever the causes, the relationship between desire and dominance, coupled with the power of taboo, continues to exert a fascination to this day.

In the margins of history one comes across, from time to time, remarkable yet obscure figures. Robert (Boris) Bitker (Chapter 8) was a militant Zionist, a Polish immigrant who worked in the film industry in Hollywood, fought in both China and Palestine and died in 1945 in San Francisco. In contrast, Leni Riefenstahl was famous as the golden girl of Nazi cinema. A close personal friend of Adolf Hitler, she created Nazi propaganda films such as *Triumph of the Will* (1935), which chronicles the triumphant Nuremberg victory rallies of the previous year, and *Olympia* (1938), which details the 1936 Olympic Games held in Berlin under the Nazis. She was never convicted of a crime and died of old age in 2003, when she was 101 years old.

Oswald Mosley, an admirer of Hitler, founded the British Union of Fascists in 1932. His paramilitaries, the Blackshirts, wore one-piece jumpsuits designed by Mosley himself. They are perhaps best remembered today for the Battle of Cable Street, in 1936, when they attempted to march on – and were repelled from – the mostly Jewish East End. By 1940 the organisation was outlawed: Mosley and his wife spent the majority of the war in London's Holloway Prison. His second wife was Diana Mitford. They married in 1936, at the house of Joseph Goebbels. Adolf Hitler was the guest of honour. Diana's sister, Unity, was a fervent devotee of Hitler, and for a time competed for his affection with

Hitler's mistress, Eva Braun. She remained in Germany as part of Hitler's close circle for five years before the outbreak of the war. She attempted suicide in 1939, returned to Britain, and died in 1948 of complications relating to the bullet still lodged in her head. She was 33.

The *Exodus*, *Salvador* and *Taurus* were all ships used by the Mossad Le'Aliyah Bet to illegally bring Jewish refugees from Europe to Palestine. The *Salvador* was wrecked in the Sea of Marmara in 1940, carrying some 300 refugees. The *Taurus* was the last refugee ship to operate during the war. It sailed in 1943 from Romania, carrying some 900 refugees. They arrived safely in Istanbul and from there caught the train to Palestine. The *Exodus*, famously, was stopped by British forces at Haifa harbour in 1947, and its cargo of some 5000 Holocaust survivors sent back to camps in Germany. My own mother came to Palestine on board a similar ship when she was two years old: she was born in a refugee camp near Munich after the war, to parents who had each survived Auschwitz. The majority of my family, on both sides, died in the camp.

Adolf Hitler finally married his long-term mistress, Eva Braun, in a private ceremony on the 29th April 1945, in the Führer's bunker in Berlin. They committed suicide, together, one day later, and their corpses were carried to the garden outside, placed in a bomb crater, doused with petrol and burned.

END NOTES

Chapter 1

1. *'She had the face of an intelligent Jewess . . .'*
Wolf is possibly echoing here the words of the crime novelist Raymond Chandler (1888–1959). We know he was fond of popular, or 'pulp' crime novels, though they comprised but a small part of his extensive library. See *The Big Sleep* (1939).

2. *'The Jews are nothing but money-grubbers, living on the profits of war . . .'*
See *My Struggle*.

3. *'I was so cold, and it was going to be a cold winter . . .'*
Wolf isn't wrong – the winter of 1939–1940 was the coldest in 45 years, with record temperature lows. Frost and fog were common in London. By January snow storms had hit Britain and the Thames froze for some eight miles between Teddington and Sunbury.

4. *'The painting on the wall showed a French church tower rising against the background of a village, a field executed in a turmoil of brushstrokes . . .'*
The painting is, possibly, *The Church of Preux-au-Bois*, a large watercolour dating to Wolf's time in Vienna before the Great War.

5. *'A personally inscribed copy of* Fire and Blood, *Ernst Jünger's memoir of the Great War . . .'*
Feuer und Blut's nationalistic ideology was an early inspiration for the nascent National Socialist movement. It was first published in Germany in 1925.

6. *'One could tell by the number of darkened windows how trade was going . . .'*

The incident is similarly recalled in the memoirs of Wolf's friend, August 'Gustl' Kubizek.

7. *'Whores. How I hated whores! Their bodies were riddled with syphilis and the other ills of their trade. The disease was but a symptom. Its cause was the manner in which love itself has been prostituted . . .'*
Wolf expresses a similar sentiment in *My Struggle*.

Chapter 2

1. *'Sometimes he thought he would drown in words, all those words . . .'*
'Books, always more books!' recalled Wolf's childhood friend, Gustl. 'Books were his world.'

2. *'[The Jews] were a parasitic race, preying upon the honest portion of mankind . . .'*
See *My Struggle*.

3. *'Wolf liked his women cute, cuddly and naïve, or so he liked to say at his more expansive moments back in Munich: he liked little things who were tender, sweet and stupid . . .'*
Wolf's friend Gustl quotes a similar sentiment in his memoirs.

Chapter 3

1. *'I respected my father, but I loved my mother . . .'*
Wolf says much the same in *My Struggle*, though in that earlier book he does not delve as deeply into the matter of his childhood and his father's subsequent death. That Elois was a violent drunk, and that the young Wolf felt freed by his passing, however, there seems little doubt.

Chapter 4

1. *'And yet worse was the time we had been approached in the street by an older man, on the corner of Mariahilferstrasse-Neubaugasse . . .'*
This incident is indeed also recounted in Gustl's memoirs.

2. *'There was this, too, about Gustl: he was a compulsive masturbator. At any given opportunity, in his bed, in his wash, behind his piano, sometimes at his desk in class or even on the corner of the street, his hand in his pocket, Gustl would relieve himself the way I had denied myself . . .'*

Wolf is perhaps being unkind here. Certainly Gustl had the normal impulses of a young man, and in his memoirs he recalls that Wolf, himself, did not seek physical release in this way. Perhaps, for Wolf, any kind of masturbatory impulse would have seemed excessive.

3. *'as the personification of the devil, as the symbol of all evil, assumes the living shape of the Jew . . .'*

Wolf expresses a similar sentiment in *My Struggle*.

4. *'"Marxism must be destroyed," Mosley said. "It is the poisoned ideology of the Jewish race . . ."'*

Perhaps unconsciously, Mosley is here echoing Wolf's own words (see *My Struggle*).

Chapter 5

1. *'In 1917, Lord Balfour wrote a letter to Baron Rothschild, in which he asserted British support for the establishment of a Jewish homeland in Palestine . . .'*

'His Majesty's government view with favour the establishment in Palestine of a national home for the Jewish people, and will use their best endeavours to facilitate the achievement of this object, it being clearly understood that nothing shall be done which may prejudice the civil and religious rights of existing non-Jewish communities in Palestine, or the rights and political status enjoyed by Jews in any other country.'

2. *'[Palestine was] then still in the possession of the Ottoman Empire . . .'*

Palestine fell to the British forces, commanded by General Edmund Allenby (1861–1936), by early 1918.

3. *'You were always steadfast in your hatred of them, Valkyrie . . .'*

Wolf is perhaps thinking of this letter to *Der Stürmer*, in which Unity wrote: 'The English have no notion of the Jewish danger.

Our worst Jews work only behind the scenes. We think with joy of the day when we will be able to say England for the English! Out with the Jews! P.S. please publish my name in full, I want everyone to know I am a Jew hater.'

4. '*The alcohol hit me like an upper cut from Max Schmeling* . . .'
Schmeling was a German boxer and heavyweight champion of the world 1930–1932.

Chapter 6

1. '*One day walking down the street he saw one of their number in the black Hasidic garb and he was plain bemused: was this a Jew?*'
Again, much the same instance is similarly recounted in *My Struggle.*

2. '"*Put a tenner on Bogskar for us, will you?*" he said . . .'
A good bet, as Bogskar went on to win the Grand National the next year. However, he was an unexpected winner, with long odds of twenty-five to one, so perhaps the tall man simply knew something the bookies didn't.

3. '*I was sunk in melancholy thoughts. Architecture affects me that way* . . .'
Though Wolf aspired to become an artist, he was rejected twice by the Academy of Fine Arts in Vienna, with the recommendation that he study architecture instead. Wolf, however, lacked the necessary academic credentials. He also lacked the money, and for a time lived in a homeless shelter, before settling in the men's dormitory on Meldemannstrasse 27.

Chapter 7

1. '*his conversation on the World Ice Theory, the* Welteislehre, *has always been fascinating and erudite* . . .'
Also known as *Glazial-Kosmogonie* (Glacial Cosmology), the idea came to the Austrian engineer Hans Hörbiger in a dream in 1894. It suggested bodies in the universe were composed primarily of ice, and was adopted by National Socialism as

an antidote to 'Jewish science', such as the theory of relativity.

2. '*I had been paid three hundred and fifty pounds from my British publisher, Hurst & Blackett . . .*'

   My Struggle. London: Hurst & Blackett, 1933. By 1939 the small firm had been subsumed by the larger publishing firm, Hutchinson.

3. '*It was the second time in a week that a Rubinstein was holding Wolf by the balls . .*'

   Various sources have claimed over the years that Wolf was in possession of only one testicle; but that has never been conclusively confirmed.

Chapter 8

1. '*That big fat oaf, Gil Chesterton . .*'

   G.K. Chesterton (1874–1936), was indeed a large man – he was over six feet in height and weighed some 21 stone. He converted to Catholicism later in life, and is best known as the author of the Father Brown detective stories.

2. '*The Zionist Congress sent an expedition to British East Africa . . . Unfortunately the expedition did not return a favourable report . .*'

   For further details see *Report on the work of the commission sent out to examine the territory offered by H.M. Government to the Zionist Organisation for the purposes of a Jewish settlement in British East Africa* (London: Wertheimer, Lea & Co, 1905).

3. '*We have no names. We have no parents and we have no children . .*'

   Ka-Tzetnik's testimony during the Eichmann Trial in 1961 lasted just 2:50 minutes before his collapse. He did not resume the witness stand. He said:

   'It was not a pen name. I do not regard myself as a writer and a composer of literary material. This is a chronicle of the planet of Auschwitz. I was there for about two years. Time there was not like it is here on earth. Every fraction of a minute there

passed on a different scale of time. And the inhabitants of this
planet had no names, they had no parents nor did they have
children. There they did not dress in the way we dress here;
they were not born there and they did not give birth; they
breathed according to different laws of nature; they did not live
– nor did they die – according to the laws of this world. They
were human skeletons, and their name was the number
"Ka-Tzetnik".'

Chapter 9

1. *'He had a long mournful lawyer's face and a lawyer's fidgety manners . . .'*
Roland Freisler (1893–1945) Nazi lawyer and judge. An officer in the First World War, he joined the Nazi party in 1925 and indeed, as Wolf notes, served as defence counsel for Nazi party members.

2. *'Murder is a frustration not just of the individual: it is a frustration of the race . . .'*
Wolf is, perhaps unconsciously, echoing Raymond Chandler again here, in an essay ('The Simple Art of Murder') written some time after the events depicted here.

3. *'I am working on a case that may be related. I need access to . . . a part of the Jewish community . . .'*
It is not clear, in view of later events, what Wolf was planning. Perhaps he was hoping to use Isabella Rubinstein's wealth and social influence, such as they were, to try to gain access again to the Palestinian networks, thus working the Mosley case. But he does not, unfortunately, record here the details of his plan.

4. *'You want me to work with you? Solving . . . crime? Like Nick and Nora Charles!'*
Nick and Nora Charles were a mystery-solving husband and wife team in Dashiell Hammett's 1934 novel *The Thin Man*, and in a subsequent series of films.

5. *'Albert Curtis Brown was my literary agent . . .'*
Albert Curtis Brown (1866–1945) was indeed Wolf's literary

agent in the UK, having taken on representation of *My Struggle* from Wolf's German publishers, for the English-language market. He founded Curtis Brown Ltd in 1899, representing Steinbeck, Faulkner and Mailer, amongst others, and growing the agency into one of the largest in the UK.

Chapter 10

1. *'Leni? Leni Riefenstahl? My God!' Wolf said . . .'*
Leni Riefenstahl (1902–2003), German actress and film director. She was a committed National Socialist; Wolf had always been an ardent fan of hers, and the attraction was mutual.
2. *'It wasn't even a* personal *rejection!'*
Stanley Unwin indeed received a copy of Wolf's book – but turned it down – around 1926. Wolf obviously bore a grudge.
3. *'The foul man had tricked me!'*
Professor Edmund Robert Forster (1878–1933) was much as Wolf describes him here. A Berlin neurologist and decorated war medic, Forster was put in command of the Pasewalk hospital, in charge of treating soldiers from the front diagnosed with being hysterics – what we would probably now call post-traumatic stress disorder (PTSD). He had little patience for the soldiers in general, seeing them as 'shirkers' from their duty. Treatment for such 'hysterics' sometimes included electric shocks and total isolation. Forster confined himself to a harsh, almost bullying attitude to his patients – an attitude which often worked. He treated Wolf during October–November 1918, successfully restoring the young soldier's vision with the method Wolf indeed mentions above – as unorthodox as it may seem.

Chapter 11

1. *'It was in the plain yellow dustjacket, like the books published by that Jew, Victor Gollancz . . .'*
Victor Gollancz (1893–1967) was a British publisher and

well-known socialist. He was born to an orthodox Jewish family in North London. In 1927, he founded Victor Gollancz Ltd, publishing works by George Orwell amongst many others. The yellow jackets were a distinctive brand choice for the imprint, which had existed for many years. It is quite possible Wolf's publishers had simply copied the design. The imprint continues to this day, though mostly publishing popular fiction, primarily science fiction and fantasy.

2. *'On her sickbed in Urfahr my mother lay dying . . .'*
A small village near to – and now a suburb of – the Austrian city of Linz.

3. *'I had been residing in Vienna at that time, attempting to enrol in the Academy of Fine Arts . . .'*
As noted previously, Wolf was not accepted into the academy.

4. *'"The Grosvenor Hotel, Victoria. And step on it!" The driver chuckled as though Wolf had said something funny . . .'*
It seems probable Wolf's English tended to incorporate elements of slang borrowed, sometimes inappropriately, from the kind of books he was reading. 'Step on it' – referring to a driver pressing down on the gas pedal of an automobile – dates some twenty years back and is probably of American origin.

Chapter 12

1. *'I was dressed in my beat-up old raincoat, a suit that's seen better days, scuffed shoes and a fedora that didn't quite fit me . . . I don't know how much Rubenstein's house was worth but my guess was plenty. I was calling on Jewish money . . .'*
Wolf is again, here, and perhaps unconsciously, echoing the words of the writer Raymond Chandler, specifically the opening scene of Chandler's debut, *The Big Sleep*. It is possible Wolf read the novel on publication – it had come out in the UK, published by Hamish Hamilton, in March of 1939.

2. *'The kind of boiseries to give Syrie Maugham heart palpitations . . .'*

Syrie Maugham (1879–1955) was a leading British interior designer; with her penchant for white, airy rooms, she probably would not have approved of the boiseries (ornately carved wainscoting) Wolf mentions.

Chapter 13

1. *'Who the fuck is Adolf Eichmann!'*
Adolf Eichmann joined the Nazi Party in 1932 as a member of the General SS. As such, he would have been unknown to Wolf at the time.

Chapter 14

1. *'Auschwitz was not created by the devil,' he wrote, 'but by men, like you, or me.'*
See Ka-Tzetnik, *The Code* (1987).

ACKNOWLEDGEMENTS

To my editor, Anne Perry, for turning this manuscript from an impossibility into a reality, my endless thanks.

To Oliver Johnson, Ellie Cheele, Fleur Clarke, Sharan Matharu, Naomi Berwin and everyone at Hodder for all your help and support.

To friends who at various times read the manuscript, offered suggestions, or just listened to my complaints: in no particular order my thanks to Shimon Adaf, Nir Yaniv, Rebecca Levene, Benjanun Sriduangkaew, Konrad Walewski, Tade Thompson and Nicola Sinclair. This book is better for your being there.

To my friend and agent, John Berlyne, who got it.

And to my wife, for putting up with me.

Virginia Andrews® Books

The Dollanganger Family Series
Flowers in the Attic
Petals on the Wind
If There Be Thorns
Seeds of Yesterday
Garden of Shadows
Christopher's Diary: Secrets of
    Foxworth
Christopher's Diary: Echoes of
    Dollanganger
Secret Brother

The Casteel Family Series
Heaven
Dark Angel
Fallen Hearts
Gates of Paradise
Web of Dreams

The Cutler Family Series
Dawn
Secrets of the Morning
Twilight's Child
Midnight Whispers
Darkest Hour

The Landry Family Series
Ruby
Pearl in the Mist
All That Glitters
Hidden Jewel
Tarnished Gold

The Logan Family Series
Melody
Heart Song
Unfinished Symphony
Music in the Night
Olivia

The Orphans Miniseries
Butterfly
Crystal
Brooke
Raven
Runaways

The Wildflowers Miniseries
Misty
Star
Jade
Cat
Into the Garden

The Hudson Family Series
Rain
Lightning Strikes
Eye of the Storm
The End of the Rainbow

The Shooting Stars Series
Cinnamon
Ice
Rose
Honey
Falling Stars

Virginia ANDREWS

BITTERSWEET DREAMS

SIMON &
SCHUSTER

London · New York · Sydney · Toronto · New Delhi

A CBS COMPANY

First published in Great Britain by Simon & Schuster UK Ltd, 2015
This paperback edition published 2016
A CBS COMPANY

1 3 5 7 9 10 8 6 4 2

Simon & Schuster UK Ltd
1st Floor
222 Gray's Inn Road
London WC1X 8HB

www.simonandschuster.co.uk

Simon & Schuster Australia, Sydney
Simon & Schuster India, New Delhi

A CIP catalogue record for this book is available from the British Library.

Paperback ISBN: 978-1-47113-382-4
eBook ISBN: 978-1-47113-383-1

Printed and bound by CPI Group (UK) Ltd, Croydon, CR0 4YY

Simon & Schuster UK Ltd are committed to sourcing paper that is
made from wood grown in sustainable forests and supports the Forest
Stewardship Council, the leading international forest certification organisation.
Our books displaying the FSC logo are printed on FSC certified paper.

For Gene Andrews,
who so wanted to keep his sister's work alive

BITTERSWEET
DREAMS

Prologue

Beverly Royal School System
18 Crown Jewel Road
Beverly Hills, California

Dear Mr. and Mrs. Cummings:

As you know, the school has been conducting IQ tests to better address the needs and placement of our students. We always suspected that we were going to get extraordinary results when Mayfair was tested, but no one fully understood or anticipated just how extraordinary these results would be.

To put it into perspective, this is a generally considered scale by which most educational institutions judge these results.

IQ scores of 115 to 129 indicate a bright student who should do well with his or her educational pursuits.

We consider those with scores of 130 to 144 moderately gifted and those with 145 to 159 highly gifted. Anyone with scores between 160 and 179 is recognized as exceptionally gifted.

Rare are those whose scores reach 180. We consider such an individual profoundly gifted. To put it into even better perspective for you, statistically, these students are one in three million; so, for example, in the state of California, with a population of approximately 36 million, there are only eleven others who belong in this classification with Mayfair.

Needless to say, we're all very excited about this, and I would like to invite you in to discuss Mayfair's future, what to anticipate, and what to do to ensure that her needs are fully addressed.

Sincerely yours,
Gloria Fishman, Psychologist

1

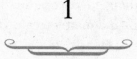

"For what you did, you belong in a juvenile home, maybe a mental clinic, but certainly not a new school where you'll undoubtedly be coddled and further spoiled, an even more expensive private high school than Beverly Royal," my father's new wife, Julie, muttered bitterly.

Even though they had been married for years, I didn't want to use the word *stepmother*, because it implied that she filled some motherly role in my life.

Her lips trembled as anger radiated through her face, tightening her cheeks. If she knew how much older it made her look, she would contain her rage. I did scare her once by telling her that grimacing too much hastened the coming of wrinkles.

It was the morning of what I thought would be my banishment from whatever family life I once could have claimed, something that had become a distant memory even before all this. I knew that few, least of all Julie, would think that mattered much to me. They saw me as someone who lived entirely within herself, like some creature who moved about in an impenetrable bubble, emerging only when it was absolutely necessary to say anything to anyone or do anything with anyone. But family did matter to me. It always had, and it always would.

I didn't have to go on the internet and look it up to know that a family wasn't just something that brought you comfort and security. It provided some warmth in an otherwise cold and often harsh and cruel world. It gave you hope, especially when events or actions of others weighed you down with depression and defeat. All the rainbows in our lives originated with something from our families.

In fact, all I was thinking about this morning was my mother, the softness in her face, the love in her eyes, and the gentleness in her touch whenever she had wanted to soothe me, comfort me, or encourage me, and how my father glowed whenever we were with him. How I longed for that warmth to be in my life again. Yes, family mattered.

True friends mattered, too, even though I had few, if any, up to now. Just because I was good at making it seem like I was indifferent and uncaring about relationships, that didn't mean I actually was. Students in the schools I had attended thought I was weird because of what I could do and what I had done, most of it so far above and beyond them that they didn't even want to think about it. I didn't need to give them any more reasons to avoid me, especially adding something like being a social misfit, which in the minds of most teenagers was akin to a fatal infectious disease.

I knew most avoided me because they believed I was too arrogant to care about anyone but myself. I mean, who could warm up to someone who seemed to need no one else? From what they saw or thought, I didn't even require teachers when it came to learning and passing exams. I was a phenomenon, an educational force unto myself.

Maybe I didn't need a doctor or a dentist or a parent, either. I already knew as much as, if not more than, all of them put together. It wasn't much of a leap to think I didn't need friends. I'm sure most wondered what they could possibly offer someone like me anyway. Besides, being around me surely made them feel somewhat inferior. They were afraid they would say something incorrect, and who likes to worry about that, especially when you're with friends? I would have to confess that I didn't do all that much to get them to think otherwise. Perhaps it really was arrogance, or maybe I simply didn't know how to do it. I didn't know how to smile and be warm just for the sake of a friendship. One thing I couldn't get myself to do was be a phony. I was too bogged down in truth and reality.

Julie moved farther into my room, inching forward carefully, poised to retreat instantly, like someone approaching a wild animal, even though the wild animal was in a cage. Thinking that was where I was made sense. If anyone should feel trapped and in a cage right now, it was I.

In fact, the more I thought about it, the more I

realized that wasn't much of an exaggeration. That was what I felt I was, and not just because of what I had done and what was happening today. I'd always felt this way. Deep down inside, despite my superior intellect, I sensed that people, especially educators and parents of other students, believed I was like some new kind of beast that needed to be kept apart from the rest of humanity, a mistake in evolution or the final result of it, and because of that, I was chained to something I'd rather not be, especially at this moment: myself.

As she drew closer, the sunshine streaming through my bedroom windows highlighted every feature of her face. I wished it hadn't. I was sorry I had opened the fuchsia curtains, but I had needed to bring some light in to wash away the shadows gripping my heart. I had no desire to look into Julie's hateful, jealous, dull hazel eyes. Sometimes they followed me into dreams, those envious, vicious orbs floating on a black cloud, invading my sleep like two big insects that had found an opening in my ordinarily well-locked and guarded brain.

I hoisted my shoulders and stiffened my neck as if in anticipation of being struck. My abrupt action stopped her, and she retreated a few steps. She fumbled with her cowardice. She never, ever wanted to look like she didn't have the upper hand in this house, especially when it came to confronting me. However, she never seemed to get the satisfaction she sought—at least, not until now, when I was most vulnerable, practically defenseless, but with no one to blame for that but myself.

"I don't care how smart people say you are. You never fooled me with your complicated excuses and fabrications concerning things you have done and said. Right from the beginning, I could see right through you as if you were made of clear glass," she said, more like bragging, to give the impression that she had some special insight that neither my teachers, my counselors, nor even my father had. She was always trying to get my father to believe that, to believe he couldn't be as objective about me as she could and thus was blind to my serious faults.

To emphasize the point, she narrowed her eyes to make herself look more intelligent, inquisitive, and perceptive. I nearly laughed at her effort, because she was so obvious whenever she did that and whenever she spoke with a little nasality and used multisyllabic words like *fabrications* instead of *lies*. She was the queen of euphemisms anyway, always trying to impress my father with what a lady she was, never without a perfumed handkerchief, the scent of her cologne whirling about her, her head held high and her posture regal. She loved giving off that aristocratic air, practically tiptoeing over the floors and carpets as if she floated on a private cloud.

I think Julie had long ago convinced herself that somewhere in her background and lineage there really was royal blood. She believed she was born with class and had inherited elegance and stature. Heaven forbid she heard any profanity out of my mouth or her daughter's. Didn't we know it was unladylike, made us look cheap and unsophisticated? She would go into hyperventilation and have to sit quickly, especially if it happened in front of my father, who would rush to her side to apologize for me, because he knew I wouldn't. He couldn't see that small smile of satisfaction sitting on her lips, but I could.

Why were men so easy to fool or so willing to tolerate phoniness just to sail on smooth water? What wouldn't they compromise to keep the pathways to their beds unobstructed? Were women really the superior sex? Was sex, in fact, a big disadvantage for men? Ironically, I had been thinking about writing a paper on that topic. Women seemed more able to avoid sex, hold off longer than men, and certainly use it as a weapon when necessary or a device to get what they wanted. I had read a theory that developed the idea that women craved sex with nearly the same intensity as men only when they were ovulating, while men craved it continually.

"I always knew you were very capable of being mean, evil, and selfish," Julie ranted. "Your intelligence doesn't make you any sort of angel. In fact, in your case especially, it's just the opposite. You're sly and conniving. We already know how effective you are at manipulating people, especially someone younger than you. You're just better at these evil ways than most people."

She waited for my reaction, but I just continued to stare at her as if she was some sort of curious form of life. It was getting to her, despite her claims of invulnerability.

"You don't intimidate me with that 'I'm better

than you' look. It hasn't happened to you yet, in my opinion, despite what others might think, but someday you'll get your just *desserts*," she concluded.

I finally had something to say. "From the way you're saying it, I have a feeling that you would spell that expression wrong," I said.

"What? What on earth are you talking about now? What expression?"

" 'Just *desserts*.' *Deserts* in the sense you mean is actually spelled with one *s*, not two. You're using that expression to mean I'll get my proper punishment."

She continued to glare at me but now with her mouth fallen slightly open, her salmon-pink tongue looking like a dead fish.

I straightened up, and I'm sure it looked to her like I was in front of a classroom, my classroom. I was a good inch and a half taller than she was, a little broader in the shoulders, but with just as small a waist, long legs, and just as ample and firm a bosom. Despite the fact that we had no facial resemblances or similar hair color, I was always afraid that someone who didn't know us might make the wrong assumption that we were actually related.

"*Dessert* with two *s*'s is the course in the meal that gets people excited and happy. And getting what you deserve might also mean you're finally receiving the accolades and rewards you've earned. That's certainly nothing to fear. But the expression does come from a playbook called *A Warning for Fair Women*. The exact quote in question is 'Upon a pillory—that the world may see, a just desert for such impiety.' It's spelled with one *s*, coming from *deserts* in the sense of things deserved. Understand?"

"Understand? That's how you treat what I say even after all you've done? Do you think I'm one of your dumb high-school classmates? Why, you pedantic little bitch," she said, spitting the words out through clenched teeth. "I bet you think you're so superior to the rest of us because of that computer you have for a brain and those bureaucratic school administrators who fawn over you as if you were the next Albert Einstein or something. They're just as much a cause of all this as you are, by encouraging you to think of yourself as . . . as someone who doesn't need to go to the bathroom or something."

I didn't change expression, even though I was laughing at her on the inside. My father wasn't home. He had an errand to do before we left, so he didn't hear her say all this, not that I thought he would have done much to reprimand her for saying any of it anyway at this point. I recalled the expression on his face yesterday when he didn't think I saw him looking at me. It was soaked in disappointment. Vividly recalling that look, I thought he might even agree with her now, every nasty and mean word. I imagined him nodding and putting his hand on her shoulder, not mine, to bring her comfort and whisper something to make her feel better and show her how concerned he was for her welfare. "Don't get yourself too upset," he might tell her. "It doesn't do anyone any good for you to get sick, especially now, in the middle of all this."

"I don't mean to be condescending," I said, with

just the quiet, matter-of-fact tone that irritated her heart. "You use the expression so often, Julie, that I thought you might want to know about it. I know how important it is for you not to look like a fool in front of your friends. Not that any of your so-called friends would know the difference anyway. If you surround yourself with mediocrity, you become mediocre," I added. "You probably think you stand out, but believe me, they pull you down, not that you had all that far to fall."

Her eyes widened, and her face reddened, with cheeks that looked like fully ripe red apples. She balled her fists and readied her vocal cords for screaming. I loved the way I was getting inside her and tying her already twisted little heart into tighter knots. For me, it was sweet revenge, and for the moment, it took my mind off the pool of trouble in which I was swimming, maybe drowning.

"It's not unlike another favorite expression of yours," I continued. I felt like I was on a roll, like a contestant on *Jeopardy*. "'The icing on the cake.' I notice you're always using it for negative remarks, like 'His wife's suing him for divorce is the icing on the cake.' It really is used more for positive comments. Think about it. Who doesn't like licking the icing on a cake?"

She continued to glare at me, as if hoping her fiery eyes would make me explode and drop into a pool of dust at her feet. She could do that so easily to her daughter.

"Is that what you do? You analyze all my

expressions?" she asked, amazed. "You judge my every word and do a critique behind my back?"

I shrugged and turned away. "Believe me, it's not brain surgery," I said, hiding my smile.

"What else have you criticized about me? Well? Let me have the whole bag of ugliness you're so capable of filling and flinging in my direction before you leave us. We already know some of the distortions and lies about me that you spread, and don't think I was ever unaware of what you told your father about me. You never understood how important I've become to him and how much we trust each other now. Well? Go on. What else? What other things have you told my daughter? You might as well get it all out before you leave."

I acted as if I didn't hear her anymore. I knew that was one of the things she hated the most. A woman like Julie couldn't tolerate being made to feel as if nothing she said or did mattered. She couldn't stand being ignored. Her ego would stamp its feet, pull its hair, and scream.

The truth was that most of the time, I didn't really listen to the things she said, even if I gave her the satisfaction of pretending I was listening. I didn't only do it to her. I could shut people out as quickly as I could shut off a light, especially someone like her. I didn't go into a trance. There was no faraway look in my eyes that would reveal that I was gone. It was almost impossible to know when I was listening and when I wasn't. Sometimes I imagined that I had two sets of ears and two brains. You know, like an extra hard drive in the computer that she thought was my brain?

My mind had a zoom lens. I could just focus on some interesting thing and cut out the distraction.

But this morning, unfortunately, I did hear her every mean-spirited word. To be truthful, I welcomed her verbal whipping, even though she was certainly no one to accuse anyone else of being mean and selfish and had no right to assume the role of judge and jury. If there ever was someone who should be restrained by being without sin before casting the first stone, it was my father's wife, Julie. It was lucky she didn't have a twin. She would have smothered him or her in her mother's womb just to be sure she would get all of her parents' attention.

But despite what she thought, I wasn't feeling particularly superior this morning. She was at me like this because she knew I was down and incapable of defending myself very much. That was usually when someone like her would pounce. I call them coyote cowards. They're parasites who will only swoop down on the small, wounded, or handicapped. Otherwise, they hover in the shadows, feeding their green faces on envy with hopes for your failures, waiting for you to become crippled and weaker but too frightened to challenge or compete when you weren't.

"I don't know how you will live with yourself," she continued. "If I were inside you, I'd scratch and kick my way out."

I turned and glared at her. Despite what she claimed, I knew I could frighten her with a look like the one I had now. I had practiced it in the mirror. It was a look I often employed at school. My eyes were like darts. I had the face of someone capable of sending out curses like emails.

Fear began to overtake her in small ways. She embraced herself quickly, swallowed hard, and took another step back.

"At last, we agree about something," I said. "If *you* were inside *me*, I'd rip you out. You know, like a bloody cesarean section." I held up my hands as though they had just been in a mother's womb and were dripping with blood down my arms.

She gasped, turned quickly, and marched out, holding her head high. She was always worried about what she looked like, even when she was alone and wouldn't see anyone else. However, frustrating and defeating her didn't give me as much satisfaction as she thought it had. I had long ago given up on baiting her and making her look foolish in front of my father, hoping it would open his eyes. I certainly had nothing to gain from it today. It was far too late, too late for many things. I was soaked in regrets.

I stood by the window in my bedroom, looked out toward the Pacific Ocean, and thought it should be gray and rainy today, at least. That would fit my mood, everyone's mood. I didn't pay much attention to the weather. Maybe that was because we lived in Southern California and took beautiful days for granted, or maybe it was because I spent most of my time inside, my face in a book or at a computer screen. I wasn't one of those people who stopped to smell the roses. We actually had beds of them out front, along with other flowers. If I stopped, it wouldn't be to enjoy the scent and beauty of anything but instead to examine the flowers, looking for some microscopic genetic change. I couldn't help it. As my teachers were fond of saying, and which was probably true, it was part of my DNA.

Moments after Julie had stopped bitching and left, I heard someone behind me and thought she might have returned to say something else that was even nastier that had crawled into her clogged brain, a brain I imagined infested with little spiders weaving selfish, hateful webs of thought. This time, I would face her down more vehemently, not with calm sarcasm but with what she hated: cold, dirty language. When I spit back at her, she would rush to cover her ears, as if my words would stain her very soul.

However, when I turned, I saw it was my thirteen-year-old stepsister, Allison. That surprised me. I was sure her mother had told her to stay away from me, especially this morning. She probably told her I had done her enough damage, and maybe, like Typhoid Mary, I would contaminate her further. "Stay in your room, and keep the door locked until she's gone," she surely had said. She was unaware of the short but honest and sweet conversation Allison and I had had the night before. Her mother was on her this morning, however. She wanted nothing to happen to change anything now.

Allison did look very nervous sneaking in here, but, like last night, she looked very sad, too, sad for both of us. She stood there staring at me.

"What is it, Allison? I thought we said our good-byes last night."

"I know, but I remembered something. My father gave me this pen the last time I saw him," she said, holding up a silver pen. "He said it was a special pen, one of the ones the astronauts used in space. You could write upside down or sideways with it, everything. I wanted to give it to you to use." She stepped forward to hand it to me.

"You want to give it to me? Why? Do you think I'll be upside down or sideways?"

"No," she said, smiling. "It's just a very special pen."

I looked at it. On the surface, it didn't look like anything terribly unusual, but I did make out the word *NASA*.

"Please take it," she said, waving it. She looked like she would cry if I didn't.

"Your father gave it to you? Are you sure you want to give it to me?"

"Yes."

"Why?"

"The words you'll write with it will be better than the words I'll write."

The way she said the obvious truth, with no self-deprecation or self-pity, made me laugh. In some ways, Allison was already head and shoulders above her mother.

I took the pen.

"Okay. Thanks. Who knows, maybe I will hang from my feet in my closet when I do my homework up there. Some people think I'm a vampire."

She smiled. "No, you're not. No one thinks that. You're too pretty to be a vampire."

"Pretty?" I glanced at myself in the mirror. I didn't feel especially pretty today. I thought my face was pale, my eyes dull and dim, and my hair unkempt. If anything, I looked more like some homeless girl wondering what in the world had happened that she should find herself so lost and alone.

"That's a nice color on you, too, turquoise. Remember? I made my mother buy me the same blouse, but it didn't look as good on me as it does on you."

"It will," I said. "You're going to have a nice figure, Allison." As hard as it was for me to say it, I added, "As nice as your mother's." What was true was true. Julie was physically attractive. If only she could be kept under glass like a wax figure, I thought, and not bother or hurt anyone else.

Allison smiled again. "Okay, see you when you come home for the holidays." She started to turn to leave.

"We don't get holidays," I said.

"Really?"

"I don't know. Things are very different there. I'll let you know."

"Will you? Really? I mean, let me know and not my mother first?"

"She'll know, even though the moment I leave, she'll have a moat built."

"A what?"

"Forget it. Okay. Like I said last night, I'll send you an email or text you."

"I know you said it, but will you really?"

"You sure you want me to do it, Allison? You

know you'll have to keep it secret from you-know-whom."

"I'm sure. Please, send me emails. My mother doesn't know how to use a computer."

I stared at her with a hard look. She knew why.

"I'll keep this secret. I swear," she said in a deep whisper, with her hand over her heart, and then turned and went to the door, checking first to be sure her mother didn't know she had come in to see me. She looked back, smiled, and then hurried away.

I put the pen into my bag.

My father's wife was in her glory, my father was in a deep depression, and my stepsister was terrified of breathing the same air I breathed.

How would I go about explaining all of this to anyone if I had trouble explaining it to myself? I thought I should write it down so I could study it all exactly the way I would study a math problem or a science theory, pause, step back, and analyze. Maybe if I did a full, intelligent, and objective review, I would have an easier time living with myself, not that it was ever easy to be who I was or who I was going to be.

Was I cursed at birth or blessed?

I suppose the best way to answer such a question is to ask yourself how many people you know your age or a little younger or older who would want to trade places with you, would want to have your talents and intelligence, or envied you for your good looks enough to accept all the baggage that came along with it.

Right now, in my case, despite my accolades and

awards, people like that would be harder to find than the famous needle in a haystack.

But the thing was that despite it all, I didn't even want to look. I didn't want to be validated, complimented, or even respected in any way.

I looked in the mirror again. Allison was right. This was a nice color for me.

I wondered, would anyone where I was going notice, and if they did, would they care?

I must have wanted someone to care. I did want to have friends, and I did hope that there was some boy out there about my age who would find me attractive.

Otherwise, why would I have taken so long to choose my clothes, the way a prisoner on death row might contemplate his last meal?

2

When the phone rang in my room, I thought it was probably my father giving me an update on the time we would be leaving, but it was Joy Hensley, my new and only best friend ever since I'd made an effort to help her with her anorexia, something her own mother hadn't been addressing properly. The school nurse wasn't effective, probably worrying about a lawsuit or something, and there certainly weren't any other girls at the school who would give her a second look or show any concern. I would have to admit that when I first considered helping her, it wasn't out of any particular affection for her. She interested me the way anything abnormal might. There aren't too many species that deliberately do something harmful to themselves.

Joy fit so many descriptions of potential anorexia sufferers. She was heavy when she was younger and thought being thin would win her more friends and admirers. I suspected that she was afraid of growing up; she wanted to be a preadolescent forever. In short, she was afraid of sex. Eventually, I was fascinated with what I could do to change or heal her.

"I really didn't say good-bye to you properly," she began.

"Is there a proper way to say good-bye, Joy?"

"You know what I mean," she said, and followed that with the jingle of a giggle she usually used when she was nervous or frightened.

"I'm beginning to wonder if I know what anything means, Joy."

"Oh, no. If anyone does, you do."

For months, I had tolerated Joy's exuberant compliments, knowing she was desperate to keep me as a close friend, but I had gotten so used to over-the-top compliments that I almost didn't react to them anymore.

For most of my life, people, especially teachers and other adults, were more interested in what I thought than in what I felt. It was as though being given almost supernatural intelligence deadened my feelings or diminished them to the point where they weren't necessary or important. If I was sad, I could think my way out of it, you see, and the only way I could be happy was to discover a new fact or add something to my encyclopedia of knowledge. That's what they believed about me. No wonder they saw me as some kind of monster, a brain creature who had microscopes for eyes. Despite how ingratiating and fawning Joy could be, I had no doubt she harbored some of the same feelings about me. Ironically, she was very fond of me, respected me, but was also at least a little afraid of me. Can you have a close friend with that combination of feelings about you?

"Is your new school more expensive than ours?"

"Yes, very," I said. "Julie was just complaining about that, as a matter of fact."

"I guess you'll meet more very rich kids, then," she said sadly.

"There are only fifteen students, if that many."

"Fifteen? It sounds more like just one class. How can that be a school?"

"I'll let you know," I said dryly.

I hadn't told Joy much about where I was going. She was one of those who were under the impression that I was leaving our school to enjoy better opportunities, and while that was probably going to be true, it wasn't what had motivated my father and Julie to agree to it.

It was true that Beverly Royal was a ritzy private school in Beverly Hills, which I had attended along with the sons and daughters of famous Hollywood actors, producers, and directors, not to mention wealthy business executives. Everything was new and clean, with the finest equipment and the latest technology. The over-the-top security, with metal detectors, surveillance cameras, and half a dozen security personnel, gave the students' parents a sense of comfort that was rare in, if not totally absent from, public schools. The teachers were among the highest paid and most likely the best qualified. Administrators at Beverly Royal liked to brag that while the lowest five percent of college graduates went into teaching, Beverly Royal hired only from the top five percent. Who would want to leave such a school voluntarily?

My father and Julie would deny that I was being sent to this new school as a kind of punishment. My father would deny it because he really believed it wasn't. Despite what my stepmother had just told me, she couldn't have me sent to some penitentiary or mental clinic. She was trapped. She had to put on an act and claim that I was being offered a unique opportunity, because she didn't want the scandal to grow. She was always very protective of her lily-white reputation. She was terrified that her friends would gossip about her the way she and they gossiped about other people.

Of course, in your heart, if you were me, you would know it was at least partly a punishment, and no form of sugarcoating would change that.

"So I guess someone like me couldn't get into your new school even if my parents wanted to spend the money, huh?" Joy asked. If I were going to just another private school, I had no doubt Joy would pressure her mother to put out the extra money and send her there, too.

"No, Joy. Despite what most of the others at our school believe, money can't buy you everything. You have to qualify, and the standards are very, very high, so high you need oxygen."

"Huh?"

"You know what I mean."

I was never falsely modest about myself. If

anything, I thought that would be futile. It would be like a blind person pretending he could see. I was what I was, and being modest and humble didn't change anything. I was profoundly gifted. The whole faculty and all of my father's and Julie's friends knew it.

Whenever anyone heard me called that, he or she would look at me and surely wonder, *What's so special about her? What's her gift?* On the surface, I supposed I didn't look different from any other girl my age, although I'd been accused of being very pretty. I say *accused* because for most of my teenage life, I had done relatively little to make myself look beautiful. Until recently, I had rarely dwelled on my hair, clothes, makeup, or jewelry. There had never been an actress or singer I wished I resembled. Unlike the other attractive girls in my classes, I never flaunted my good looks and figure, and I never flirted with or teased any boy.

But I did recognize that real beauty, natural beauty, didn't need to be emphasized or exaggerated. It couldn't be hidden, and perhaps that was the sort of beauty I possessed. I supposed I should be more grateful, feel more blessed, but the truth was, I hadn't yet gotten control of it the way I controlled most things in my life, and that made me nervous and insecure. A girl my age who was beautiful but didn't dwell on it or even realize it was always surprised at how others, especially men, treated her. She was always at some disadvantage, and I hated being at any disadvantage when it came to relationships with others my age, or actually, with anyone regardless of age, especially men.

People who heard I was gifted didn't fully

understand what that meant. They might expect me to get up and play Beethoven when I was only five or create a magnificent work of art. Those are truly gifted people, but they are gifted with a quickly and easily displayed talent. I'm different.

"I know, Mayfair," Joy said, with some discouragement in her voice. "You're a genius, and the school probably takes only geniuses."

"You know I hate that word, Joy."

"I know you do, but you are."

"A genius is someone who supposedly doesn't make mistakes. They are expected to be right always."

"You always are."

"Believe me, Joy, I'm not. Besides, people anticipate that great things will come from geniuses, and I'm not sure anything of great value will ever come from me."

"It will," she insisted.

My faithful friend, Joy Hensley, I thought. She was practically the only person I might miss, besides my father, of course.

"You're lucky," she added.

"Lucky?" Now I was the one to follow what I said with a jingle of a giggle.

"Of course. Look how much you know and how fast you can learn anything."

Joy didn't understand and probably never would, but when you're young and brilliant, especially if you're female, people think you don't want the same things so-called normal or average young girls want, like love and romance or even sex. From where do they get these ideas? Don't eggheads have hormones?

And why is falling in love unusual for someone who can solve the most complicated algebraic equations?

Maybe that's what made most boys hesitant about approaching me even though I was quite attractive, even having been called voluptuous. They thought that if they did get to make love to me, I would be analyzing them and then might reveal that they had premature ejaculation or something. What hurt a boy's feelings more than a girl thinking and saying he was poor in the sack? Why risk it?

"Yes," Joy insisted. "You are. Will you write to me as soon as you can?"

"As soon as I can," I said with a very noncommittal tone.

"I'll miss you, Mayfair. It's not going to be fun going to school anymore."

"I hope you have more self-confidence now, Joy. You're doing so much better. Don't let any of those bitches push you around."

"It wasn't hard when you were there to help."

"You've got to be on your own sometime, Joy. Just think about what I would do, what I might say, okay?"

"Yes, thanks," she said in a small voice.

Here I was giving someone else advice when I was the one who needed it the most. My self-confidence surprised even me now. What right did I have to do it?

"I've got to go, Joy. Still packing."

"Well, have a good trip," she said. "I guess you'll email me sometime."

"I said I would. I want to hear good things about

you. You know I don't like failure, and I've invested time and energy in you."

She laughed. "I'll try."

"Don't try. Do. Remember what I told you. What doesn't destroy you makes you stronger."

"I'll remember," she said.

After I hung up, I realized I'd been giving myself that advice, not her.

If my grandmother Lizzy, my mother's mother, was still alive, she'd be chiding me for showing even the slightest evidence of self-pity. I knew I took after Grandmother Lizzy more than any other relative, including my own parents. She had a way of saying things that not many wanted to hear. She would often say that something was "plain and simple." I appreciated her more than anyone else did, and when we looked at each other, we knew we were special. She wasn't gifted, of course, unless you would consider being bold and coldly truthful a gift. With all the phoniness raining down around us these days, maybe that could be a very special gift after all. She didn't understand my superior intelligence or what it would come to mean, but she tried to treat me as if I were no different from any other little girl my age. She didn't want to bring any unusual attention to me. Now that I think back to that, I realize how impossible a task that was for her.

There was no way I wouldn't attract unusual attention. I wasn't looking for it, but I couldn't help it. At three years old, I was reading on an eighth-grade level. When I entered grade school at five years old, I was already reading books meant for at least college sophomores.

I can still hear Grandmother Lizzy's rippling laughter when I astounded relatives with my recitations of famous speeches, world capitals, scientific facts, or math equations and then offered quotes from Shakespeare, not only reciting them from memory but also explaining them.

"The kid's a walking computer," my uncle Justin, my father's older brother, would say. He was the comedian in the family. He'd spin me around, claiming he was looking for the plug and wires. No one in my family loved me any less because I was so smart, especially not Grandmother Lizzy. I don't think anyone hugged me more or made me feel as precious, but grandmothers can be like that.

After I said something brilliant and Grandmother Lizzy would clap and then hug and kiss me, I'd look at my mother and see the love and pride in her face. There was nothing more protective than a real family, even for someone like me, despite what people like Julie thought. People like her thought that because you were very smart, you didn't need support, but I thought it was just the opposite. You needed your family around you, caring about you, even more. They cherished my being gifted. Maybe it made them feel that their family lineage was special. I didn't know, but I enjoyed their affection and soaked in their pride.

It wasn't that way when I was with strangers. Once you were labeled profoundly gifted in the educational system, you might as well have *weird* tattooed on your forehead. No one really wanted to be friends with you. Some were even afraid of you. Many thought I was like Spock from *Star Trek*, the one who knew everything but had no feelings. I thought they even expected me to have pointed ears or something frightening about my eyes, especially when I looked at them.

Often, especially when I was younger, I would hear things like "Stop looking at me, you freak."

How this made me feel would be no surprise. When I was younger, it was always harder, of course. Despite my brilliance, I still had to develop defenses, especially social defenses. I could think of clever comeback lines, but they wouldn't win me acceptance or sympathy. Maybe I would be feared and avoided, but was that something a young girl wanted?

Regardless, I had to develop a harder shell. Young kids especially enjoy seeing how they can get to other students, bring tears to their eyes. I don't know why it's truer for young kids, but the rage in bullying today clearly demonstrates it. They tried to bully me from the get-go, maybe because of all the attention I was receiving, but I frustrated them. It got so they believed I had no tears and couldn't cry, so they finally gave up.

Even though I had attended a fairly big school, as far as I knew, I was the only one at my grade school who had ever been formally labeled profoundly gifted after all sorts of testing. In fact, I had the impression that there had never been any student like me in the history of the entire school district, which included four other schools, as well as in the entire county. I used to wonder if one of the eleven others estimated in the state at the time were in Los Angeles, too, and what it would be like to meet one of them.

Would we both just know? Could we look into each other's eyes and see some rich pool of brilliance that only we and others like us could see? Were we truly like alien creatures that had been smuggled into the human population? I dreamed that someday we would all meet or maybe would deliberately be brought together by the government or some corporation. Everyone else would expect us to take over the world or do something significant.

According to what I had been told and what I had read, I would meet some others who were somewhat, if not exactly, like me very soon at this new expensive private school that Julie thought was much more of a reward than a punishment. But this wasn't exactly how I had imagined I would meet them. It felt like we were being herded together, corralled and contained.

Anyway, I didn't want to rule the world, especially this world. In my mind, despite how we could impress teachers and others and despite what they imagined we would invent or create or discover, we weren't really welcomed. People could tolerate us for a short period, the way they might enjoy a magician, but who wanted someone pulling rabbits out of hats all the time?

Maybe Julie would get her wish. Maybe my new school would turn out to be more of a prison, because in the end, what all these educators and other young people, even some parents, really wanted was to keep us apart, keep us away from their precious children, as if we could somehow ruin them with our intelligence. Maybe they thought we would teach them things that would make them more rebellious.

I had started to get these ideas from the moment the grade-school psychologist, Mrs. Fishman (I called her Fish Face because of her Botox lips), started treating me like a rare diamond and took credit for the discovery. Like that was hard to do. Whenever she could, she had me perform for teachers and administrators, defining words, reading high-school textbooks aloud, solving difficult math problems in minutes, or simply reciting some fact that others would need to discover on an internet site. Sometimes I felt like I was doing a little ballet but with facts instead of ballet slippers. I felt like a monkey performing when a bell was rung.

After I was diagnosed as being profoundly gifted, Mrs. Fishman brought my parents in to discuss what it meant. I remember overhearing my mother tell my father, "She's so excited about Mayfair, I thought she was having an orgasm."

For quite a while, I struggled with the comparison. I didn't have to ask my mother what *orgasm* meant. In fact, since I had become a good reader and an expert on my computer, I rarely asked her or my father questions or definitions of words. I've heard people say that computers and smartphones are running our lives now. For kids like me, unless your parents put some sort of lock on what you could see and read, nothing in the world was out-of-bounds or prohibited. I knew so many girls and boys who had gone to their computers to learn about sex. I bet you did. I bet you're doing it now.

Few did it when they were as young as I was at the time, of course.

But remember, I was profoundly gifted. I was one in three million. Can you even picture three million other people? Can you imagine looking at sixty thousand or seventy thousand people in a stadium and thinking, *There is no one here remotely as brilliant as I am*? And even if you did think that, can you imagine thinking of it not arrogantly but just as a simple fact? That might make me seem very cold, I know, but it wasn't something I chose to be.

Anyway, I learned that both men and women have orgasms and that it was an autonomic physiological response, which are big words for *you can't stop it if you've gone too far*. Parents were always warning their kids not to go too far, and this was the reason. When you were very little, they warned you not to go too far from the house. Well, this meant not to go too far from your self-control.

After I read about the word and understood the physiological activity, which is a fancy way of saying what goes on in the body, whenever I was with Fish Face, I would look for symptoms, especially something in her face to tell me it was happening, symptoms like her being flushed or breathing too hard. I even wanted to take her pulse and tried to figure out how I could get my fingers on her wrist. My intense concentration rattled her, and one day she finally asked me why I was looking at her with such an engrossed expression.

"When you glare at people like that, Mayfair, you make them feel quite uncomfortable. What is it about me that makes me so fascinating to you right now?" She sat back, waiting for something intriguing to come out of my mouth, something she could blabber about in the faculty lounge. Her face looked like a big saucer ready to catch all my gems.

"I'm studying you to see if you're having an orgasm," I said, as casually as anyone would say "to see if you are feeling okay."

Remember, this is coming out of the mouth of a five-year-old.

She turned a dark shade of red and looked like she would choke on her own saliva. Then she sat forward, entwining her chubby fingers, which made each arm look like it was holding on to a shoulder for dear life. Her lips were so tight that little white spots popped out in the corners, and her shoulders looked like they would rise higher and higher until her head sank down between them completely. I was quite fascinated with her reaction.

"We all know you're very intelligent, Mayfair, but you have to learn what is proper and not proper for a little girl to say," she told me.

"Who decides what is and is not proper?" I fired back.

She narrowed her eyes and nodded as if she was confirming a suspicion about me.

She had given my parents some booklets about profoundly gifted children, and one described them as "often argumentative, more like lawyers challenging words and comments." That definitely sounded like me, but it wasn't something I was conscious of doing. It was just natural to me to question and challenge anything and everything I heard or saw.

"Never mind that. Just think before you speak," she told me.

"I always do. I have to think before I speak. Don't you? Maybe you don't. Maybe that's why you say silly things sometimes." She had a habit of saying something she didn't mean to say and then pressing the back of her hand against her mouth as if she were trying to stop a leak.

At this moment, she looked like she was going to explode. Her cheeks ballooned, and her face went from red to white very quickly. "You can go now," she said.

After that little exchange between us, she didn't parade me about as much or ask to see me as much, and when she did, she was very formal and always on her guard, trembling in anticipation of something I might say that would embarrass her. I enjoyed her discomfort. Was I already showing some signs of meanness or disrespect?

Anyway, she had called my parents in again, this time to warn them about me. Suddenly, it was both a curse and a blessing to have a profoundly gifted child. That excitement she had first evinced was gone. She was full of new warnings, pointing out red flags like someone from homeland security.

"If you're not careful," she told them, "you'll lose control of her. Like conniving, manipulative little lawyers, profoundly gifted children find loopholes in all the rules you lay down. If you tell her it's time to turn off her lamp and you don't add 'and go to sleep,' she might turn off the lamp but switch on a flashlight and continue doing what she was doing."

"What are you saying? You're making her sound dangerous or at least like a burden," my mother countered. "Why this sudden change?"

For some reason, she didn't mention my reference to her possibly having an orgasm. Maybe she really was and was ashamed or shocked that I had discovered it.

"I'm just telling you what I know," Fish Face responded, a bit sullenly.

Both my parents were quite upset with Fish Face after that, and neither of them really heeded her words when it came to how they treated me or evaluated anything I did or said.

All of it was quite a learning experience for me, but then again, just about everything in my life was.

"The world is my classroom," I often said. Some people would smile, but most would look at me as if I had just stepped off a spaceship. "She really is Mr. Spock!"

I knew that calling the world a classroom sounded boring, but if there was one thing I never was, it was bored.

Maybe if I were once in a while, I'd have been happier or, as my stepmother said, normal, because I'd look for amusement instead of information.

"It's normal to want to have fun once in a while more than you want to have facts," Julie said one time.

She laughed and added, "That's been my life's motto, Mayfair. When in doubt, have fun, and you can't be any more normal than I am."

I wanted to reply, "If you're what is considered normal, I'm signing up for Abnormals R Us." But I wasn't quite at the stage where I would confront her head-on instead of subtly or with words and analogies she would never understand.

I did think, however, that something was missing inside me, something that might be necessary in order for someone to be happy with herself. It was true that I was not happy most of the time, and I was envious of girls my age who had far lower IQ scores but who looked like life was just one exciting roller-coaster ride full of screams and laughter, all happening while someone warm and handsome was holding on to you. I would think about that image very often.

I would think about it, but I wouldn't confess to anyone else that I lacked anything that important. I would come to realize that I was very attractive, and that bothered some girls because it seemed to them that I had everything: good looks, a great figure, a rich complexion, soft healthy hair, and brains. I was always so self-confident that I never dreamed a time would come when I would admit that anything was wrong with me, that something important was missing, especially to myself.

I guess I didn't know everything after all.

Even though I was profoundly gifted.

3

We were on our way to my special new school, Spin-drift. Somebody very creative, of course, came up with that name. Students there were supposedly the crème de la crème, the best of the best, and the purpose of the school was to get them to live up to their enormous potential so that everyone would benefit from their achievements.

Just in case someone considering the school for his or her child didn't understand the name, the booklet explained it: "Spray blown up from an ocean wave is called spindrift. It is expected that our graduates will spray the world with their brilliance." Can't you just see the faces of our proud parents? Who wouldn't want their child to spray the world with brilliance? Every word from their mouths would be dazzling.

From the booklet, I also knew that the motto above the main entrance read: "A brilliant mind wasted is a sin beyond redemption." The quote belonged to Dr. Norman Lazarus, a biochemistry research scientist whose discoveries included a drug to treat bone cancer. As our school psychologist and guidance counselor had explained to me, Dr. Lazarus had donated most of his profits to educational institutions. He established this special school for gifted students, which was his favorite project. I supposed the motto was intended to make us all feel guilty if we didn't live up to our potential. If you were brilliant and lazy, you were like a person who had a talent to play the piano beautifully but wouldn't take a lesson or touch a key. People who lacked any talent could really despise you for that and hate the fates that wasted their powers on giving you the talent.

I wasn't afraid that I would enter Spindrift and fail to meet anyone's expectations for me. I was afraid that I would enter the special school and fail to meet my own expectations. The implication was very obvious. I could almost hear my own father saying it again: "If you can't be happy here among your own kind, Mayfair, you'll never be happy."

My own kind? Even my father thought I belonged to a different species now.

I wasn't too happy and didn't expect that I would be the most pleasant new student. I was never good at hiding my displeasure, which goes back to my taking after my grandmother Lizzy. I should have taken lessons from Julie while I had the chance, I thought. Maybe that was really how you got along in this world.

I gazed out of the car window and saw that the few clouds streaming across the sky looked like white ribbons floating over a sea of Wedgwood blue. Whenever my real mother saw a sky like this, she would say something descriptive like that. She would often speak in beautiful metaphors, which were sometimes quite spiritual, even though she wasn't very religious. We would go to church only on holidays or for special occasions like weddings and funerals, but she believed in a holy spirit in us and around us.

She'd say, "Look, Mayfair, God is tying ribbons in earth's hair. Isn't she beautiful?"

"Why do you say 'she'? How do we know the earth is female, Mother?" I would ask.

My father would laugh and say, "What a kid. Look at what she thinks of at this age."

But my mother would stay serious and kiss my cheek or my forehead before running her fingers through my wheat-colored hair. She wanted me to wear it long then, and she enjoyed brushing it for me. I would look at her in the mirror while she sat or stood behind me, and I would study her face and wonder, *Do all mothers look at their daughters like this, with such pure love?*

I thought that as long as I had my long hair, I would have my mother's deep love. It had grown to reach halfway down my back before she died. After that, I chopped it down to just at the nape of my neck and did such a bad job that I usually wore a hat, even when my father took me by the hand to a beauty salon for repairs.

"We know the earth is female because of all that's born from her," she told me. "And you know mothers are the ones who give birth."

That was logical, so I accepted it. I always appreciated that my mother would try to be logical when she answered my questions, even when I was only three. She never ascribed anything to fantasy. Just as there was no bogeyman, there were no good fairies. Mothers do seem to know their children better than fathers do. She knew early on that make-believe wouldn't work with me.

When my father wanted me to believe in Santa Claus, I simply told him that it was physically impossible for one man to deliver gifts to all the children in the world on one night, much less keep a record of who was naughty and who was nice.

"Not even FedEx can do that," I said, and he roared with laughter.

"This kid's better than television," he told my mother.

"Don't you want there to be a Santa Claus, Mayfair?" my mother asked.

Of course, I did, but I just couldn't believe in him.

"You can't believe in something unless it's true," I said, and my father laughed again. He had such a wonderful laugh then, an infectious laugh that made anyone near him laugh along, including me.

"You poor dear," my mother would say, embracing me. "I hope you can find something wonderful to believe in someday without worrying about whether it's true or not."

"She will," my father promised her. "This kid will do it all."

He was so proud of me back then. If there was any possibility of taking me along with him when he visited someone involved with his public relations business or simply went shopping for something, he would. I knew even at age three that he was eager to show me off, almost the way Fish Face did, but I was eager to please him. And after my mother died, it was even more important to please him. In my mind, I was still pleasing her, too. It was as if part of her floated into him after her death. They were that close when she was alive, and that was as far as I would go in believing anything supernatural.

I was just as eager to please him now, but it had become more difficult, maybe even impossible, because once he married Julie Dunbar, I felt that the part of my mother that was in him had left. She'd have been the first to tell him, "There's not enough room in one heart for two lovers in your life, Roger."

She wouldn't sound angry or upset. She would be smiling softly, her voice gentle and kind. I missed that voice and that smile. All the mirrors in our ten-room Bel Air hacienda-style home surely missed that smile as well. Everything lost its glitter and gleam when my mother died. This was so much her home, down to her choice of every color, every floor tile, every cabinet handle, and every light fixture. Almost without comment, my father had nodded and approved everything she planned or wanted. He had that much faith and trust in her judgment, but more important, he had that much of a desire to see her happy. She was as important to him as she was to me.

Whenever I thought of myself becoming romantically involved with someone someday, I'd think of what my parents were to each other. The parents of so many girls I knew just seemed to be sharing a place to live. I'd overhear their daughters complaining about how much their parents argued. Doors were always slamming in their homes. Parents were often sulking, sometimes for days and even weeks. These girls hated to be home and looked for every opportunity to keep themselves away.

I never felt this way about my home when my mother was alive, and I couldn't remember any doors slamming, nor could I recall my parents being so angry at each other that one would sulk. If either upset the other, he or she became almost desperate to make it better. Love in our house wasn't a goal; it was a reality, the status quo. I could feel it, and that feeling gave me a sense of security. I loved being with them. It was because of them that I was less skeptical about people actually loving each other, caring more for each other than they cared for themselves.

I was always skeptical about almost everything in my life, from when I was an infant until now, but one thing I always trusted was my mother's hand holding mine. I knew she would rather have her arm separate from her shoulder than let go if I needed her. After she died, life without her was like a bird without a voice, just something that glided silently along, jealous even of the screech of a cat.

There were no birds singing now, and I knew a good part of the reason was my own fault. Julie wasn't all wrong. Just because you were brilliant, that didn't mean you couldn't do something terribly wrong, something that would hurt the one person you loved the most in the world. I liked to think that I had more control of my emotions than most people because I was so intelligent, but emotions really did come from another place. Anger and jealousy could be more like viruses eating away at you until you did something you regretted.

And I did.

All the way up to Spindrift, Daddy watched me in the rearview mirror. I saw the sadness in his eyes, but I also saw him anticipating my doing or saying something to show my resistance and maybe cause another serious blowup between my stepmother and me. I knew he was tired of being a referee, and frankly, I was tired of it, too. I wanted out of this game as much as he did.

I caught the hesitation and sadness in his eyes. At times along the way, I thought he was going to stop and turn around, even though I knew that if he didn't go through with this, he'd surely end up in a divorce. Julie had been through a nasty divorce, so she was a veteran of the marital wars and might be quicker to pull the trigger. It was always easier to do something the second time, although even for Julie, it had to be terrible to face the fact that it was difficult for her to hold on to a relationship. I had yet to hold on to any, even a silly little high-school romance, but I knew what disappointment a failure like that could be. No matter what, deep inside, you'd always blame yourself. Surely there was one more thing you could have done, could have said, one more thing that would have saved the relationship.

Although my father didn't say it in so many words, it was obvious to me soon after he married Julie that he was sensitive to the possibility of her eventually wanting a divorce solely because of me. That would be so unfair to him. He was as good a father to her daughter, Allison, as he could be, maybe too good. The blame for any problem between my stepsister and me would always be on me, "because you know better." Most of the time, he would say something like that to please Julie. I realized that was his sole reason and he didn't always believe it. My father had a good poker face, except with me. He knew I could see through any mask he put on.

He would be the first to admit that most things were not what they seemed to be. That was his business, after all, often putting lipstick on a pig. He had no false illusions about it. It was still a pig. Both of us pretended and put on an act for each other when he finally agreed with Julie that I should be sent somewhere far away.

The night before we left for the school, he had come into my room while I was packing and stood silently for a few moments watching me. I knew he was there, but I ignored him. Finally, I paused, and we looked at each other. I saw how difficult this was for him.

"What?" I asked softly.

"This is a really good idea, Mayfair. You need the challenge this school will give you," he said. "You need the personal attention and the chance to go at your own pace."

"Right," I said, even though both of us knew nothing had ever stopped me from going at my own pace and I always enjoyed personal attention when I needed it.

"And as your guidance counselor, Mr. Martin, says, it will be good for you to be with students with abilities like yours. You'll feel more comfortable, and you'll have some competition. You're the one who told me runners go faster when they have someone right on their heels."

"Fine," I said. "You're right. I'm wasting my time here with these Yahoos."

"Yahoos?" he said, smiling.

"In *Gulliver's Travels*, remember? They were disgusting, stupid creatures that resembled human beings."

He stopped smiling. "I don't like it when you're so condescending, Mayfair. Don't look down on people who aren't as brilliant as you are. A little humility is important, especially now," he said. "You should know why better than I do."

Even though he was right, I hated it when he saw something wrong with me. My fear was that perhaps he would love me less, although I would never admit to that fear. I believed that admitting to any fear gives that fear more power over you. "Stuff it" was my motto. I would never show that I was afraid of the dark or of being alone when I was little. And there wasn't another girl or even a boy who could make me cower and retreat. They could see the resistance in my eyes, and they'd usually be the ones who backed off.

But it was always different when it came to my father. I could defeat him in an argument, frustrate him with my logic, but it never made me feel any better. The truth was, it always made me feel worse.

I turned away so he wouldn't see my eyes burn with tears. I took a deep breath and nodded. "Yes, Daddy. I'm sorry. You're right."

"Okay," he said, and came up behind me to kiss me softly and pat my hair. I watched him walk away, slouching like someone in defeat. What had happened to all those wonderful predictions for me, for our family, when I was younger and something of a star not only at school but at home and everywhere we went as a family? I was sure he was wondering where he had failed and that he was troubled with the thought that my mother would be very disappointed.

I packed faster. I owed it to my mother to make it easier for him, I thought. I could just imagine her watching the two of us and looking disappointed in my behavior. That was all she ever had to do, look disappointed. I could practically feel her thoughts. *Don't hurt him, Mayfair. Please*, she would think. *It's not easy for him, either. Help him get through it.*

I was still trying to do that now in the car as we drew closer to Spindrift. I hid any displeasure or regret and acted quite indifferent about it all. I wasn't going to give Julie any satisfaction by pleading for mercy or promising to improve my behavior toward her. To me, promises were like colorful bubbles, pretty but quick to pop and disappear, especially if they came from someone like her. If she had half a brain, which I didn't think she had, she would be able to see through my false face, which I couldn't help but have. After all, as Shakespeare wrote in *Macbeth*, *False face must hide what the false heart doth know.* And when it came to agreeing to all of this with any resemblance of enthusiasm, I had a false heart.

She should have been able to see that easily. Didn't it take one to know one, and who better to see a phony than a phony? That was why my father couldn't see through her. He was too trusting and honest, despite the work he had to do. He was desperate for happiness since my mother's death. I didn't like it, but I had to forgive him. I had to make myself understand and accept.

My stepmother sat with her shoulders hunched up, which made the skin at the back of her neck crinkle like cellophane. She would lower her chin and cramp up tightly when she was nervous. I could imagine all the organs inside her crowding together like frightened mice. And when she was very, very nervous, she would hold her breath until her face turned red. Right now, it was as if she felt that if she made a sound or moved a muscle, it would all go bad, and my father would take my side, turn the car around, and blame it all on her. All the way home, she would think, *So close. There I was, so close to getting rid of her, and I screwed up.*

I knew the silence in the car was driving her bonkers, however. My father wasn't his talkative self. Julie didn't want the radio on, because the chatter made her even more nervous, and I certainly had nothing to say to her. I hadn't said anything to either of them after we had left Los Angeles. I was sure she thought I was just being spiteful, my old spoiled self. I wasn't, but I couldn't help my silence. Maybe I was sadder than I would admit, and I wasn't sulking as much as I was crying inside. But that was something I would never reveal to her.

Everyone talked to himself or herself. Perhaps I did it more than most people, because I had running conversations going as if my brain was on Facebook or something. It was probably another reason so many other students kept their distance at my old school. To them, I always looked as if I were on another planet, in another dimension, listening to some other voices. It bugged some of my teachers, because they thought I wasn't paying attention to their important comments, but when they questioned me to catch me so they could bawl me out, I always had the answer.

Was I very sad about leaving my home? I knew that any other girl would have looked back at the house and gotten all choked up inside. It wasn't only because of what the house was, an eight-thousand-square-foot, two-story Spanish-style hacienda in Bel Air, complete with a beautiful oval pool, a cabana with a built-in barbecue grill, and a clay tennis court. I'd heard my father say the house and the grounds were estimated to be worth upward of twelve million dollars. He bought it when he was promoted to CEO of Pacifica Advertising, which had contracts with major pharmaceutical companies and some entertainment firms. He was now a major stock-holder in the company, a fact I was sure was not lost on Julie.

I had mixed feelings about leaving, because I grew up in this house. My best memories of my mother took place in this house, and now I was being deported from it. *Deported* was the right word. How often I had felt like a foreigner now in my own home. But when I looked back and thought about it more, it was like cutting the umbilical cord again. I wasn't just separating from my father and my mother's memory. I was losing them. They were drifting off like smoke in the wind, falling behind as we drove on. I was never so afraid of being alone.

Nevertheless, I refused to let myself get emotional. I had talents and skills few people had, number one of which was harvesting the most value from any experience. What I had in that house I was taking with me. I was able to internalize all of it. I treasured all the memories, no matter how small or insignificant someone else might think they were. Not Julie, not the school administrators who had come down on me, no one could take any of it from me.

"How much longer?" Julie asked, as if she were being waterboarded.

"Not far now," Daddy said. He turned and flashed one of his rah-rah, sis-boom-bah, high-octane, successful-advertising-executive smiles at her.

"You sure you know where you're going, Roger?"

"He has it on the GPS," I muttered. "If he makes a wrong turn or something, it will let him know."

She ignored me, but my father said, "Mayfair's right. We can't get lost."

"I don't trust those things," Julie said, and I laughed a little too loudly for her. She didn't trust the GPS because she couldn't grasp how to use it. The one in her car was never turned on. She had trouble with a television remote. It was a wonder she could work her blow-dryer, and if it did get too hot and shut off, she'd scream, "Roger, the electricity in the house is off!"

"Try to figure it out yourself, Julie," I would tell her. "How can the electricity be off if the lights are on?"

Just like back then, she glared at me angrily now in the car and then turned quickly away. I didn't have to wonder what she was thinking. She had made that perfectly clear many times. Almost from the day she and my father had married, she'd always accused me of ridiculing her in one way or another. Why should it be any different even after what I had done? I was irretrievable, unrepentant, and impossible to change or improve. You didn't just give up on someone like me, she might say. You shook her completely out of your memory. I was sure she was chafing at the bit just thinking of the free rein she would have in our house now, never worrying about any comment I might make about something she had done or wanted to do.

The midafternoon Southern California freeway traffic suddenly began to swell. Somewhere along the highway artery, there was a blood clot, I thought. We slowed to a crawl. It didn't bother me. Whenever we were on the freeways and traffic slowed to a crawl or came to a standstill, I would continue reading or researching something on the internet. My father had bought me my first laptop when I was just a little more than three, and later he made sure I was always hooked into a satellite or had a PDA so I could get onto the internet. Whenever we had company and someone asked a question no one could answer, he would turn to me and say, "Mayfair, why don't you look that up for us?"

Like a father watching his son in a Little League game, he'd sit back with pride and watch me, at three or four years old, get the right website and come up with the answer, usually in less than a minute.

I was on the internet now, researching the community where Spindrift was located. It was in the Coachella Valley, just outside the small city of Piñon Pine Grove, named for the piñon pine trees that populated its borders. There were some small factories providing building materials and one that made store racks, plus some industrial farms. Not exactly an exciting new community, I thought, but I didn't exactly enjoy Los Angeles, either. I rarely visited the museums or the parks.

Researching the community and the school, I was quite content with the delay, but I knew the traffic jam put butterflies and worms in Julie's stomach. If anyone wanted to get this over with as quickly as possible, it was she. I imagined the only reason she'd come along was to make sure my father didn't change his mind. Of course, she acted as if she was concerned and cared about me, at least for his sake. She was concerned, all right, concerned that I would somehow be rejected at the door and end up back at home with Allison, who had been left behind with the maid. After what I had done, the faster and the farther we were separated, the better it would be in Julie's eyes.

"How do people do this every day?" Julie asked, nodding at the traffic.

"Is that a hypothetical question?"

"What?" she said, turning around to me again. She had to struggle to make it look like a painful effort. She was that tightly wrapped.

"*Hypothetical* means you really don't expect a specific answer. You ask it to begin a conversation, a larger discussion. Do you want an answer?"

She stared a moment. "You have an answer?"

"People do this every day because they have little choice, Julie. Their jobs are far away from their homes. They want their kids to go to better schools. They want to live in safer neighborhoods. The commute and all this traffic on weekends to get to malls or stores," I said, waving at the cars in front of us, "are the trade-off. It's probably far worse on weekday mornings and late afternoons."

She dropped the corners of her mouth and pressed her lower lip under her upper one. "Well, I couldn't do it," she said.

"You don't have to do it. You don't even have to shop for food."

"Mayfair," Daddy said, with that little upturn in his voice to indicate that I should go into retreat.

I knew that the whole episode at school, including

what had recently occurred between me and the girls I called the "bitches from *Macbeth*," had exhausted him. He looked like he had aged years. He was afraid of any conversation between Julie and me continuing for more than a few seconds. He was quite aware of how easily I could belittle her in any argument. I was always good at winning arguments, whether it be with her or with my teachers.

My father had said that ever since I could talk, I had questions and, soon after, good answers, even before I began to read. When he was first dating Julie, he told her quite a bit about me. He wanted to prepare her. In fact, she'd said that some nights, I was the sole topic.

"He's so proud of you," she had told me the first time we met at our house. They were on their way to a charity event, and he had brought her to the house first, explicitly to meet me. He'd asked me to put on something nice and brush my hair.

Anyway, from her tone of voice, I had understood that she wasn't terribly happy about my being so much the center of my father's life. I didn't mind that I was the big topic of discussion when he was courting her, but he had built me up so high in her eyes that she was quite nervous about meeting me the first time. I enjoyed her being so tense. It was like shooting fish in a barrel.

"How pretty you look," she began. "Did your daddy pick out that dress for you?"

"No. I pick out my own clothes," I said.

"Really?" She smiled. I could see it was quite

forced. She really didn't like the dress I had chosen. She glanced at my father, who shrugged. "Well, maybe you'll let me help you choose a dress next time you need one," she said.

"Why would I do that?"

"Mayfair!" my father said.

I gave him one of my innocent looks, and he shook his head in frustration. I really was innocent back then. I was looking for some reasonable response. Was she a clothing expert? What was her justification for the offer? Why would she care so much about how I looked? These all seemed to be logical questions, and my comment hadn't been meant to show disrespect or hurt her feelings. It was meant simply to get an answer that made sense.

However, I could see in her eyes that I had hurt her feelings. I didn't care, and I could admit that I was actually a little pleased. Of course, I would soon realize that my reaction had been natural. Any child, even one who was unafraid of showing her feelings about something, as I was, would naturally make it evident that she resented another woman replacing her mother, not that she ever could. It was merely a pathetic attempt at it.

"Your father's told me so much about you," Julie continued. "I feel as if I've known you for years."

"Does anyone really get to know anyone, even after years?" I asked.

"Pardon?"

"People change so much," I said, eyeing my father. "You never know when they'll do something completely out of character, or the character you thought they were."

His eyes were full of warnings. He knew how sharp and biting I could be, even at that age.

"Oh, well, I suppose. I mean, I don't really mean I know you yet, but I hope in time we'll get to know each other and be more comfortable with each other," Julie said, fumbling for the right words.

"I know a little about you. I know you have a ten-year-old daughter and you were in a bad divorce," I said.

She looked at my father as if he had betrayed a confidence they held dearly between them. "Yes," she admitted, "it was unpleasant."

"Well, there you are," I said. "My point."

"Pardon? Your point?"

"You obviously never really knew your husband if you ended up in a divorce. Either you or he changed so much you had to get a divorce."

She stared for a moment as if she were looking at someone who spoke a foreign language and then looked to my father for a rescue. It was clear she had never had someone as young as me say such things to her. He shook his head at me, smiled slightly, and then declared that they had to get going.

"I look forward to seeing you again, Mayfair," Julie said before she left, holding out her hand.

"Why?" I asked.

She held her breath, puffing out her cheeks and then pulling her hand back, saying, "To get to know you better, of course. I also would like you to meet Allison."

"Okay," I said, with about as much enthusiasm as someone going to the dentist.

She turned to leave, and my father leaned toward me to whisper, "We'll talk later."

Afterward, when we did talk, he made it clear to me that he really liked Julie and thought she would be good for both of us.

"I'd really appreciate it if you would make an effort to get along with her. Any relationship requires some compromise, Mayfair. Besides," he said, "we always wanted you to have a younger brother or sister."

"Don't you know which it is? Allison sounds like a girl."

"Mayfair, stop it," he said. Whenever he gave me his warning to behave, he lifted his eyebrows and pressed his lips together so hard that the blood would leave them.

When he started to spend nights at her house, I knew the marriage was inevitable. I tried to accept it, running through reasons and motivations, but I knew I never would.

The night he'd come into my room to tell me he had proposed to her, I was in the middle of researching the various theories about Hamlet and why he took so long to avenge the murder of his father. It was almost as if something powerful had arranged for me to be reading *Hamlet* coincidentally at that time. I had just read the lines, "A second time I kill my husband dead, When second husband kisses me in bed."

I didn't look up from the paper I was writing.

"Did you hear me, Mayfair?"

"Yes, Daddy. You're standing only a few feet away."

"Well, can you at least acknowledge it, please?"

I turned around and looked at him. "Are you sure you want to marry her? Marriage is a very serious commitment."

He nearly laughed. "I think I know what I'm doing, Mayfair, yes. Don't tell me you didn't think this day would come."

I nodded. "Are you drawing up a prenuptial?"

He shook his head. "What?"

"It's just sensible nowadays, Daddy, especially with your net worth and the fact that you're going to marry someone who has been through a divorce. She might have trouble with long-term relationships."

"Don't worry about it. I'll take care of it," he said. "Why am I talking about this?" He shook his head as if he could restart our conversation. "Can you please make an effort to get along?"

"I can," I said. He was asking only for an effort.

"Thanks." He turned to start out and then stopped. "This doesn't mean I don't miss and love your mother, Mayfair."

"That's not something you should tell me, Daddy. It's something you should tell Julie."

I didn't think I would ever forget the hard, cold look on his face. "She knows," he said before leaving.

For a moment, it was as if he had taken all the air out of the room with him.

But I didn't cry.

I returned to *Hamlet*.

We're all in a play, I thought. We all seemed to have roles assigned to us even before we were born. I knew I did. Whether I liked it or not, I was on a stage. The curtain was open, and the lights were on.

Who knew how the play would look when the final curtain was drawn?

4

I had met Allison a few times before my father married her mother, of course. I thought she was a mousy, frightened little girl, but that was just a first impression. In the back of my mind, I stored the thought that she was Julie's daughter. She had to have inherited some of her conniving, a little of her phoniness. The innocent, meek look could very well be a deception. Besides, my father was now going to absorb a great deal of her mother's attention and love. She was probably as unhappy about it as I was, and maybe she would do more to sabotage the relationship than I would. I hoped so.

Julie must have prepared her for meeting me. She was polite but very cautious.

"My mother told me you were very smart," she had said, sounding like it was a criminal offense. "I get mostly Bs."

"Bs sting," I said. "Go for As."

"What?"

Figure it out yourself, I wanted to say, but I just laughed.

She looked at me suspiciously. "None of my friends get all As, and the girls I know who get all As don't have many friends," she said.

This is going to be really something, I told myself. *I'll be living with a Barbie doll for a stepmother and a ditzy tween who thinks she might catch intelligence from me and lose her friends.* Later, because of who and what she was, it would be easy to use her as a way to get back at both the man who abused me and my stepmother, with whom I eventually shared a mutual dislike.

Fortunately, my father and Julie decided not to have a big wedding, so I didn't have to go through all that business with dresses, flowers, pictures, guest lists, invitations, and menus. They were married by a judge and took a week in London as a honeymoon. Allison stayed with an aunt. I was fine by myself with our maid looking after the house and keeping an eye on me, although I could tell that I intimidated her as much as I did anyone else. She spent most of her time avoiding me. She wasn't afraid of me. I was just too different from the teenage girls she knew, her two nieces and their friends. She was always promising to have them come around to meet me. Maybe my father had put her up to it, but she never did, and although I think I would have liked it, I didn't encourage her.

My father called from London during their honeymoon only once. Whenever he was away on business trips that took a week or more, he always called me two or three times, at least. Anyone would tell me that a man on his honeymoon shouldn't be calling home much. Maybe he knew my mind was already cemented when it came to my opinion of Julie back then. I imagined she would make a face or a comment if he mentioned he was thinking of calling me.

I could just hear her. "Why? She's no child, Roger, and she's more intelligent than the two of us together. Don't baby her. She might even be insulted."

Insulted? It wasn't a thought he would have had, but perhaps she put it into his head and that was why I didn't hear from him again until he returned.

I would never have been insulted by his showing me concern. I never was when he went on other trips. I knew he had confidence and faith in me taking good care of myself and the house. He wasn't calling because of that. He was calling because he loved me. I was good at reading people right from the first time I met them. Daddy used to say half-jokingly that I would be an incredible detective. For a few weeks, he was on a real streak when it came to that, talking about forensic law enforcement, CSI stuff, and even international law enforcement. Like all parents, he probably needed the comfort of knowing there was an endgame here, some target or goal for me to achieve, a goal he could understand, that anyone could. Otherwise, what was the point of all this intelligence?

To me, Julie was a simple read. She was one of those insecure people who needed to be constantly reassured of her importance and was threatened by anyone sharing her stage. From what I already knew about her before she had even moved in to live with us, I thought she would even be jealous of the attention my father paid to *her* daughter.

After spending more time with Allison, I came to the conclusion that she was merely shy and battle-fatigued from what must have been a nasty home life and living in the shadow of a self-centered mother. Julie was surely the kind of mother who flaunted her good looks and made her daughter feel she would never be as beautiful. Maybe that was part of what had destroyed her first marriage. I listened between the lines whenever I heard her describing it, and I felt confident that her ex-husband had grown tired of being married to someone who was more in love with herself than with him. I wondered when my father would grow tired of that, too.

From the details I learned from Allison when I was able to get her to talk about it, the fights between Julie and her ex-husband had bordered on physical. I easily imagined Allison behind a closed door with her hands over her ears and her teeth clenched, half expecting the ceiling to come falling onto her head. I had read sociological and psychological studies on domestic turmoil to do a paper for my history teacher, so I knew that when parents went at each other like that, their children feel they're also being pulled apart. If the children are very young at the time, they actually can develop medical problems, such as trouble with digestion, and learning disabilities.

While reading about all of this domestic turmoil

and its effect on children, I felt like screaming. Could parents be so blind that they couldn't see what they were doing to those they supposedly loved? The truth seemed to be that people hurt those they claimed to love more than they hurt those they didn't. I listened and overheard stories other students told about their home lives. To me, it was very clear what was happening and what the results would be. When I mentioned some of this to my father once, he brightened and said, "Maybe you should be a psychiatrist, Mayfair, a child psychiatrist. You'd be great."

I'd be great at anything I did, I thought. That wasn't the point. What was obvious was that my father needed me to be aiming at something tangible, something he could cite. He couldn't explain that his daughter was going to be a student for most of her life, maybe a philosopher. Everyone else's daughter was going to be a teacher, a lawyer, something in the fashion industry, perhaps a doctor. Something.

All of this, my life at home, my father's expectations, my teachers, and the pressures other students subtly put on me, made me want to scream. Often, I was in the school library when this urge came over me. Imagine what that would have done, what it would have added to the image I had at school. The librarian, Mr. Monk, already thought I was something created in a laboratory. The speed with which I went through books seemed to frighten him. He was a tall, thin man with glassy gray-blue eyes and very thin light brown hair. Whether I imagined it or not, he seemed to step back whenever I approached the desk, as if he expected I might throw a book I was returning at him because I found it poorly written or something.

After having done the paper on domestic crisis, I was sure I could diagnose Allison's problems. She seemed to be a classic example of what could result, which was why I wasn't sympathetic as much as I was curious about her. It was as if a good case study had been delivered to my doorstep. My father wasn't too far off with his latest suggestion for my career. Anything to do with psychology was intriguing, so I was happy to have the opportunity to study something firsthand.

In the beginning, I approached her the way a good therapist might. I wanted to know how much her parents' nasty divorce had destroyed her emotionally. I formed my questions carefully. I wanted to see if she had any talents, abilities that her mother had stifled. What would her feelings be about my father and her relationship with him? Would she see him as an interloper, someone who didn't have any business being in their lives, or would she see him as a wonderful change, a hope?

My father mistook my interest and my talks with Allison for a desire to make her feel like my sister. Maybe that was really a part of it. Maybe he was right that I had always wanted a younger brother or sister, but as he and I already knew, forming relationships, any relationships, didn't come easily for me. I had little faith that they ever would. So, in the beginning, at least, Allison was simply another specimen under my microscopic gaze. I admit I had a tendency to treat most of the girls I met the same way, and consequently, building friendships was very difficult, if not impossible. I had always been like this, but it was even worse after my mother's death. It wasn't entirely my fault.

When I entered junior high school, my teachers often separated me from my classmates every chance they had, putting me in small rooms or in the library to read and work on my own, so even then, I never had much of a chance to have a best friend or, for that matter, any real friends. Maybe the real reason I had so much trouble making friends, trusting people, or committing to a relationship was the pain I had suffered when I lost my mother. I was afraid of losing someone else, wasting my affections. Because I was so intelligent, most people misread my reactions to my mother's untimely death.

My mother had died instantly one morning in our kitchen. The autopsy later showed that she had suffered a cerebral aneurism. I was nine and sitting at the kitchen table at the time. I didn't freeze and start to cry when she collapsed. I called 911, and as calmly as I could, I told the operator that my mother had fallen over her bowl of cereal and was unconscious with her eyes wide open.

"I got her down on the floor and gave her CPR," I said, "but I can't revive her. I think she has had a stroke."

I knew exactly what a stroke was. One of the first books I asked my father to buy for me was a medical book. I loved diagnosing illnesses. My father was

always amused at how I interpreted symptoms whenever he or my mother had an ache or pain, but I was
not yet set on being a doctor and already, even at only
nine years old, wondered if I would be good with patients. I could see them complaining about me for not
having a good bedside manner. "She treats me like I'm
a specimen and not a person," they would say.

See? I could admit to my problems. Right from the
days when I could first read and write, I knew that if
you weren't honest about yourself, you would never
improve or grow.

After I had called 911, I kept myself from crying,
because I knew I had to get the correct information out
quickly. Then I called my father and basically told him
the same thing, but this time, I did begin to cry. Until
the paramedics and my father arrived, I sat on the floor
beside her, holding my mother's hand, struggling to
think of something else I might do to help her. I could
almost hear her telling me to stop pretending, because
she was already dead and gone.

"You know better, Mayfair. Concentrate now
on helping your father get through this," she would
certainly say. "He'll be leaning on you, even at your
young age. And he'll be worrying so much about you
now. Comfort him. Be warm and loving, Mayfair. I'm
depending on you."

My father was there minutes after the paramedics
had arrived. He stood off to the side, holding me, as
we both watched them work desperately. I knew she
was gone, but my father clung to hope. He was surely
thinking, *This can't be happening*, while I was thinking

of how it had happened, what had gone wrong in her body. When the paramedics shook their heads, my father pressed me tighter to him. I put my arms around him, and we walked out behind the stretcher to watch them put my mother in the ambulance.

My father always claimed that I was holding him up. The strength in my arms was what kept him standing, and the look in my eyes kept him breathing.

All through the funeral, my father never stopped telling people how I'd had the foresight to call 911 before calling him and how I had performed CPR. He assured them that I knew exactly what to do. He was probably still in shock himself and kept himself from breaking down by bragging about me. I found it interesting how people wanted me to describe what had happened in as much detail as I could. It was as if that made them feel better or they thought it would help me get through it. I knew almost all of them were surprised at the cool explanation of the physical details from someone my age, but I would have had to confess something. Ever since I was a little girl, ever since Fish Face, I enjoyed shocking people and seeing the expressions of amazement on their faces.

At least I had a sense of humor about something, right?

Anyway, later on, when my teachers informed Daddy and Julie that I had to be separated from the others more often because I was disruptive, challenging things they said or asking questions that were beyond the subject at hand (at first, they thought I had ADD and was unable to concentrate; later they realized I was merely bored), Julie was embarrassed. She surprised me. She wanted my father to persuade them not to do such a thing. They had the discussion right at the dinner table in front of me, as if I weren't there.

For a moment, a small, slight moment, I thought she really cared about how this would affect me. Was she capable of being concerned for me? Then she continued to talk, and that thought died a swift death.

"Separate her? It sounds like they're afraid she'll contaminate the other students. I have many friends with children in this school, Roger. There'll be talk. It doesn't make us look too good, and it makes me wonder about her relationship with Allison, whether I should be worried or what?"

My father didn't see it that way, but Julie pointed out that Allison was going to grade school at the same school and would eventually have the same teachers I was having.

"You know how teachers are when they have the younger sisters or brothers of students who gave them trouble. They think it's a family trait or something."

"She's not really giving them trouble, not in the sense you mean, Julie," he said patiently.

"It's the same result. Your name gets soiled."

"Soiled?" I said, looking up. "You mean made dirty or disgraced?"

"What?"

"Okay, Mayfair," my father said quickly.

"But this is a stupid discussion, Daddy. Allison and I don't share any genetics. Why would my teachers transfer their feelings about me to her?"

"You can still have an influence on her," Julie said quickly.

"The teachers won't make that connection so quickly. Allison doesn't have the same last name. My father hasn't legally adopted her."

"He will someday," Julie said confidently. "Her father will not oppose it, believe me."

I looked at him. *Give her our name?* It simply hadn't occurred to me. As long as she had her father's name, she was still a stranger, sort of a guest, but that would certainly change if she had my last name, too. And what a mean thing to do to her father, I thought.

"Yes," Julie went on. "You think of everything, but you didn't think of that. You shouldn't have been so annoying in class. Teachers don't forget."

"It's not the reason they gave for moving me out of the classroom," I said. "They know I'm beyond what the class could achieve already. It wasn't fair to me, and it wasn't fair to them."

She simply smirked. The principal might have done better if he had told her I had bad body odor. Despite what my father said, she took it hard. She made him feel guilty, too. She kept harping on what their friends would say. She had married into this family. Her favorite expression about me at home whenever she and my father discussed my school situation and the special way I was being treated by my teachers and the school administration was, "She won't grow up normal."

I couldn't help but correct her. "You mean, I won't grow up to *be* normal, Julie. Or you could say I won't grow up *normally*. Adverbs and nouns," I added, "have different destinies in sentences."

"What? What did she say? And when are you going to make her call me Mother? I'm so embarrassed when she calls me Julie in front of other women, and it's a very bad influence on Allison. She's starting to call me Julie, too. I had to slap her this morning."

Allison was nearly eleven at that time, and I was almost fourteen. I wasn't just reading Jean-Paul Sartre and Albert Camus, which was Greek to my classmates, but I also read science books like *Lives of a Cell* or *The Evolution of Amphibians* and graduate-level sociological and psychological essays and discussions. I was fascinated by everything in my textbooks and never at a loss for a new question, even if it was about something my teachers would not be presenting for months, maybe years. I was that far ahead in my reading and my thinking.

Despite what I had told Julie, I knew in my heart that the real truth was that my teachers shoved me out of the classroom to escape from me, not to make things better for me or the rest of the class. They weren't programmed to work as hard as they would have to work if I remained in the room. Calling what I was doing independent study was just a fancy way of saying, "Get her out of my hair."

They were all probably happy that I had been taken completely out of their school, I thought now as we drove on to Spindrift. There was no longer a possibility of having me as a student, of being challenged and made to look inadequate in front of the other students. Some of them were probably saying they had suspected that someday I might do something as outrageous as what I had done. They might even cite some notorious people who were highly intelligent but had done bad things, just so they could justify their antagonism for someone they had to admit was mentally advanced, someone they should normally cherish and nurture.

"She'll probably end up working for some clandestine organization like an even more secret branch of the CIA," one of them would say, and most of the them would nod.

As we drew closer to Piñon Pine Grove, Julie primped her hair and checked her makeup. She never could understand why I didn't care more about my appearance. She actually encouraged me to wear lipstick and paint my toenails and fingernails when I was eleven. Many of the girls in my class were doing just that.

One of the happiest but soon to be frustrating days she spent with me was instructing me in how to put on makeup at her vanity table. I was there because I didn't want to disappoint my father. Allison stood off to the side, watching jealously. I would have gladly given her my seat and let her take my place. My mind kept drifting back to the calculus problem I was attacking in the twelfth-grade math book I was using, so I was inattentive. I was sloppy about putting on fingernail polish.

"Whenever you have no interest in something, you rush it and mess it up," Julie complained, moaning as if I were ruining one of her precious works of art or something. "Maybe some of your grade-school teachers were right. You have ADD."

"No. They were wrong. They've admitted that. They're not the best judges of the problem, despite being teachers."

"How could you say that? They were your teachers."

"You need to be a doctor to diagnose it properly, and many teachers use it as a convenient excuse for why students don't pay attention to their boring presentations of material. Don't you recall having teachers like that? My father does."

She stared at me a moment, at a loss for any way to argue, which was something she desperately needed to do. "I don't care. That's not the point I'm making," she said. When she became frustrated, she always wagged her head, which made her upper torso wag, too. Sometimes she did it so hard I thought she might fall off her chair.

I sighed deeply. "Okay, Julie. What is the point you're making?" I asked.

"Don't you want to look pretty? You have a very pretty face, your mother's eyes, and if you brushed your hair properly, it wouldn't look like a rat's nest."

"Have you ever seen one?" I asked her.

"One what?"

"Rat's nest."

"Oh, Mayfair. It's just an expression."

"Yes, but do you know why people use it? You should know what you're saying when you say something, Julie."

She shook her head and muttered to herself, "Why am I even trying?"

"We compare messy things to a rat's nest because rats build their nests from an assortment of items, including anything that attracts their interest. Their young defecate in them before they're old enough to leave the nests and sleep in their own mess."

"Oh, my God, that's disgusting."

"Maybe then you don't mean to compare my hair to a rat's nest," I said.

She lowered her chin to her chest and stared down sadly at her makeup, all her wonderful new powders and creams, the special scissors, and the variety of brushes, all that beautification magic. She looked like she was about to burst into tears. I must say, from the time my father married her until that moment, I had always found her as curious as I would a new insect. She rarely read a book. She collected fashion and celebrity gossip magazines like a squirrel storing acorns and spent half her day getting ready to go to lunch with other women like herself and the rest of the day talking about what they had talked about at lunch.

Was she a product of evolution going in a different direction?

"I remember when my mother first permitted me to wear makeup and instructed me in how to do it," she said softly, sucking back her tears. "I was very excited, and when I went downstairs to show my father, he looked like he was going to cry. 'My little girl is becoming a young woman,' he said. I was sad and happy at the same time."

She turned to me, narrowing her eyes as if she were the one looking at a specimen under a microscope, and not vice versa.

"Doesn't any of this excite you or interest you at all? You must have some reaction to it, right?"

"It's curious," I admitted.

She looked at Allison to see if she understood anything I was saying, but Allison stood there with that habitual smirk of hers. Unfortunately, she had her mother's ugly habit of dropping the corners of her mouth.

"Curious? What do you mean, curious?" Julie asked.

"We make fun of primitive people for coloring their faces, but here we turn it into a high domestic art form."

"What? You're saying putting on makeup makes us primitive?"

"Consider the whole picture, Julie. Television commercials imply that if you use their products, you'll be as beautiful as the models. They airbrush them and touch up their faces in magazine advertisements and photographs. It's dishonest and makes every girl, every woman, frustrated and unhappy with herself. Look at Allison. She's dying to get to this vanity table, and she's only in the fifth grade. You should take that television set out of her room. It's a carnival."

"No!" Allison cried.

"Don't change the subject, Mayfair. Don't you want to use makeup, wear lipstick, and have your hair look nicer?"

"Not particularly," I said. "At least, not now. I'm not in any mating season."

"Mating season?" She looked like she would cry again.

"I want to use makeup," Allison said. "I want to look nicer now. Let me."

Julie shook her body as if she were throwing off water like a drenched dog. "This is giving me a headache," she said. "I wanted to do something nice for you, and you're giving me a headache. Curious, primitive . . . I've never heard any young girl talk like you do."

"It's interesting, that's all I'm saying, Julie. You know, it wasn't that long ago that girls were forbidden to wear lipstick until they were at least eighteen," I told her. "Think about the changes in social mores that have occurred not only over the past century but over the past decade. There are girls in high school now with tattoos on their necks, breasts, and rear ends, and their parents didn't stop them. Girls wear rings in their noses, their navels, and their lips. They punch holes in their cheeks. Now, there is a tribe in Central Africa—"

"Stop!" she cried, and popped out of her seat with her hands over her ears. Both Allison and I were a little shocked at her burst of frustration. She relaxed and regained her composure, because Allison was looking at her wide-eyed. I might have been smiling. "I need to see about dinner," Julie said. "Either finish putting on your nail polish or wash off what you've done." She scrunched up her shoulders and left her bedroom.

I looked at myself in the mirror. I did have my mother's green eyes, slightly almond-shaped. I had naturally long eyelashes but still didn't understand why Julie coveted them so. My nose was slightly longer than I would have liked, but it was straight, and I had full grapefruit-pink lips that I knew Julie also coveted. Whenever she complimented me on my rich, smooth complexion, she sounded like she was complaining. I knew she thought my beauty was wasted. She wasn't alone. I had heard that sort of comment bitterly made by other girls in school from time to time. I wasn't unappreciative of my good looks. I just wasn't as absorbed with them as she and the other girls were. Maybe that was a fault. I was thinking more about it lately.

My menarche came later than for most girls, but once it had, my body began a determined march to maturity, led by full, perky breasts. I read everything I could get my hands on in articles or books that discussed the subject of female development, and then I analyzed my own reactions to my budding sexual desires. I even thought about keeping a journal about my own development, but I decided there was really nothing unusual enough about me to warrant the effort.

That was the way I was.

I analyzed everything I did or started to do and determined how much time and energy I should spend on it.

Like this makeup thing.

It was easier to wash off the three nails I had painted, give my hair four or five quick brushes so it wouldn't fall over my eyes, and then get back to my calculus.

"You're being ungrateful to my mother," Allison said. The word *ungrateful* was in practically every other sentence her mother tossed in my direction.

"Do you know the meaning of gratitude, or are you just parroting your mother?"

"Don't call me a parrot!" she screamed, and walked out when I began to laugh.

However, there was no question that Julie saw all that as another example of my deliberate failure rather than appreciating what she was trying to do for me. She complained to my father at dinner.

"After all," she said, "I'm making the best effort I can, Roger. I offer to take her to get new clothes, new shoes, anything, but she shows no interest. She has to meet me at least halfway."

He nodded and told me I should be more appreciative. He tried to sound stern, but I knew he hadn't reprimanded me enough to please her. She sulked her way to bedtime.

I suppose what I eventually did to Allison and her English teacher, Mr. Taylor, in a way pleased her, despite how she reacted. It finally turned my father against me and justified her constant complaining about me.

Right now, it was the only reason for any regret, the only reason for my telling my father I was sorry.

But let me explain how I happened now to be in my father's car, with my bags in the trunk and my stepmother, at the prospect of getting me out of the house and out of her hair, practically panting like a dog about to be untied and let free to run.

5

I have this tendency to compare Julie to animals often. I remember thinking she must have charged like an elephant in heat at my bedroom door one Sunday afternoon a few months ago. First, I heard her footsteps pounding on the hallway floor. Most of the time, she wore sharp-heeled shoes that clicked over the Spanish tiles, but this particular day, they sounded more like the rat-a-tat of a machine gun. She was moving that quickly and determinedly. Then I heard the rattling of the doorknob, and when I didn't respond instantly, I actually saw the hinges strain. Adrenaline must have been pouring out of her ears.

I had looked up reluctantly from *The History of Western Civilization* to pay attention. I was nearly finished with the book and hated the interruption, especially if it was Julie doing the interrupting. Most of the time, it was about something so minor or insignificant that I could barely listen.

"Why is this door locked?" she screamed. I

envisioned her putting her lips to the hinges to be sure her voice carried through. "Mayfair! I know you hear me. Don't pretend you're asleep!" She slapped the door with the palm of her hand so hard I was sure it turned bloodred.

"Coming!" I shouted back, but I took my time. I took so long, in fact, that she rattled the handle again, this time so hard I thought surely she would break it, which only made me take longer. I stood there and let her shout my name one more time and slap the door again before I unlocked it.

When I opened it, she was standing there breathing hard, her shoulders rising and falling with every deep, quick breath, her face looking like she had been in direct sunlight too long. She was so upset she'd permitted strands of her dark brown pampered hair to pop up like broken guitar strings and her mascara to run. Her lips trembled as the rage washed over her face in small tremors. I was waiting for her to explode and shatter herself all over the walls and the floor.

In her hands was a book I had lent to Allison. She opened it and held it up with two hands in front of herself like a shield so that the cover was facing me.

"What's wrong, Julie?" I asked in a calm, almost sweet-sounding voice.

"What's wrong? What's wrong? How dare you give this book to Allison!"

"I didn't give it to her. I lent it to her."

"You know what I mean. Why would you give her this book?"

"She's more than thirteen years old now, Julie.

Four girls in her class are pregnant. They all probably have mothers like you, terrified to mention S-E-X. You should be thanking me. That happens to be a well-written book on the subject by a renowned expert in the field, presented in a clear, simple manner so someone her age can understand it all easily."

"Thanking you?" She swallowed hard. "Thanking you? A clear, simple manner? You call this simple?"

She turned the book around, flipped some pages, and held up a drawing of a naked man and a naked woman in the missionary position. She turned it back to herself and read, " 'The missionary position is a male-superior sex position in which the woman lies on her back and—"

"I know what it is, Julie. The problem is that Allison doesn't, or she didn't. I hope she got through most of it before you confiscated it, which I think was a mistake."

"Of course I confiscated it. I'm her mother!"

"I know you're her mother, but what world do you live in? Do you think Allison hasn't watched soft porn with her friends, French-kissed at parties, had a boy's hand in her blouse and in her pants?"

She recoiled and then shot back like a rattlesnake. "That's absolutely disgusting. Of course she hasn't. I'd know if anything of that sort happened."

"How would you know?" I asked. "You treat her like she's never menstruated."

She opened and closed her mouth without making a sound.

"If you're not going to permit her to read it, may I

have my book back, please? I'm doing some research on the fruit fly and want to make some comparisons."
I wasn't, but I thought that was a funny thing to say.

She didn't. She thrust the book at me. "You can be sure that your father is going to hear about this," she said.

"Hear about it? Sex? I think he knows about it."

"You know exactly what I mean. Don't be . . . be . . ."

"*Facetious*? I think that's the word you're searching for," I said. "It means joking inappropriately, perhaps to satirize or show contempt."

She did what she usually did when she couldn't get the best of me. She nodded repeatedly and looked like one of those toy dogs people placed in the rear windows of their cars. I felt like reaching out and putting my hand under her chin to stop her before her head rolled off.

"I don't understand you," I said in an even calmer voice. "Didn't you want to know these things when you were your daughter's age? Aren't you happy that there are better ways to learn this stuff than listening to misinformation other girls spout in bathrooms or sneaking terrible sex books into your room and reading them under the covers?"

"Allison is . . . is . . ."

"What? She's probably masturbated. Are you saying she is a virgin? Are you absolutely sure? And what if she loses her virginity inappropriately? Wouldn't that upset you more? When you calm down and think about it later, you will definitely thank me," I said with that stone-cold confidence that assured most people that I was right.

Her eyes looked like two balls lit up in a slot machine. I felt like reaching out for an invisible lever on the side of her head and pulling it down. If I got two bloodred pupils, her mouth would open and spill out silver dollars. She opened and closed that mouth, and then she spun on her heels and walked away with her back hoisted like a flag on her iron-pole spine. I envisioned smoke streaming out of her ears.

I closed my door quietly and returned to my book. Usually, I could turn Julie on and off like a light switch, but for some reason, this latest confrontation between us annoyed me more than usual. I had trouble shutting it out of my mind, and it wasn't because I felt any sense of guilt about it or was worried about how my father would react.

My stepsister, Allison, was, in my view, very immature for a girl her age living in California in the twenty-first century. I really did believe I was doing her a favor. It was one of those rare times when I did something in this house without the initial purpose of annoying Julie.

Like most mothers, Julie wasn't even measuring her daughter in terms of herself at this age, recalling the questions and concerns she'd had. Worse, it was as if these mothers believed nothing had changed since they were teenagers. Information for those who sought it was accessible much more quickly and easily. They either were ignorant of or ignored what their daughters could learn on the internet, what sorts of materials they passed around and discussed, and what their personal experiences with boys already were. Had she even ever heard of friends with benefits? Didn't she know the birth rate among teenagers? Didn't she go to the movies or know about sexually explicit films deliberately targeting girls her daughter's age? I could rattle off statistics that would make her head spin. I could have wiped the floor with her if she hadn't run away.

Although I tried, I was unable to shut it out of my mind. Maybe it was because I wasn't happy about my own romantic life, which was a zero. Even though I was good at pretending that it didn't bother me, acting convincingly as if I wasn't interested, it did bother me. It bothered me a lot, and I was very interested. If my mother were alive, I'd have someone to talk to about it. I certainly couldn't talk to Julie or my father, and at this time, I hadn't connected with Joy and still had no girlfriend with whom I could spend hours on the phone, not that Joy was ever a great source of comfort or information for me. I didn't even have anyone to email frequently. There was just no one yet whom I trusted enough to reveal anything more than the weather report.

I couldn't remember when I was last invited to a party or when other girls in my class asked me to do something with them. It was probably a few years, and back then, I was only invited because of my father and his business relationship with the parents of the girl. When I arrived, I could see that no one cared to talk to me. The parents of the girl whose house it was most likely pushed her to be civil to me, and she was barely that. It wasn't difficult for me to see the lack of sincerity.

The girls who finally did talk to me did so on their own initiative, speaking to me as if they were with some foreigner who had just barely learned English. The questions they asked gradually got more and more annoying as their confidence grew. I'm sure they saw how uncomfortable I was getting. Perhaps I wasn't so hard to beat after all. Maybe if they were good enough, they could bring me to tears or send me running from the room. Then they could gather in a clump and giggle as they congratulated one another.

"How come you don't ever have a party at your house or hang with anyone at the mall?"

"Don't you think any of the boys are good-looking at our school?"

"Are you afraid of boys? Is that what happens when a girl is so smart?"

"Who do you dream of being with, at least? What actor?"

"What sorts of fantasies does someone like you have?"

They fired the questions at me so quickly I couldn't answer one. Finally, they stopped and waited.

"There are some good-looking boys at our school," I said. "But when they open their mouths to speak, their faces fall off for me."

"Huh? Fall off? How can someone's face fall off?" Willa Marley asked me. I remembered her question because I could see that she wasn't quite sure whether I was speaking literally or figuratively. Perhaps I did know something about some sort of disease that caused a person's face to fall off.

"It just slides off his skull," I said casually. "Like hot melting butter sliding off a pan."

"Ugh."

"That's not true. That never happens. You're just afraid of boys, aren't you?" Victoria Walters asked. I remember how small her eyes were, beady, how they seemed to retract while her nose grew pointier, and how her mouth twisted, with her lips becoming pale.

"I'm certainly not afraid of boys. Why should I be? Do you think they have some magical powers they hold over us? I'm not afraid of sex, certainly. It's not a disease, and it doesn't require a great deal of intelligence to perform it."

"Perform it?" Victoria said, and laughed with the others as her chorus. "Do you do it on a stage?"

"You're defining *perform* too narrowly."

"Huh? Just answer the question."

"Yes, I'm just as interested in boys and sex as any of you are. I'm just not as obvious about it. I don't walk around with my tongue hanging out like some of you."

"Maybe you should," Victoria flung back at me. "Maybe then you'd attract someone."

They all laughed and shook their heads but still peeled away like frightened birds. I watched them go off into corners to tell the boys about me and laugh. I told myself it didn't bother me. After all, I had gotten the best of them, hadn't I? Who cared what they thought?

But sometimes I did feel like a potted plant, bored and unhappy, just waiting for someone to care enough to water me.

Lately, I felt invisible in my school when it came to boys anyway, even though I had been returned to regular classes. That came as a surprise. I didn't know it at the time, but both my father and Julie had gone to the administration and requested that I not be separated from the rest of the students when I was in high school. The guidance counselor, Mr. Martin, agreed. He said it was damaging to me socially.

"She has to grow as a person and as a student," he said. "I hope she considers joining one of the clubs or going out for drama, something that will help her have social intercourse."

"That would be wonderful," Julie said. "We worry a great deal about her."

I had heard all about it afterward. My father told me about some of the things they'd said when he came into my room to explain why he wanted me returned to classes so I could be more of a regular student. How would I explain to him now that everyone, including some of my teachers, looked right through me most of the time, whether or not I was in a regular classroom? Actually, it was more difficult than ever for me to function within the normal classroom structure. I was happier working on my own. Being in regular classes held me back.

As far as socializing went, I couldn't force myself on the rest of the students, either, by joining a club or a sport, even if it was something like chess club. No one would want to play against me, and all of them would resent how I left them in the dust. The envy and resentment would only be compounded. How could I describe the situation without sounding like I was whining?

Despite how much he loved me, my father would have to face facts, and some of those facts were that other students either were disinterested in putting in the extra effort to make friends with me or simply afraid of me or badly put off by me. We couldn't depend on my teachers doing anything to help, especially those who knew they were incapable of motivating me very much and saw me as evidence of some failure on their part. It was very clear to all that I could do very well without them. Why should they have any concern for me?

I couldn't blame them entirely. The school day was already overwhelming them, with growing class sizes even in our expensive private school and the disciplining they had to do, without adding special attention to someone like me, perhaps special lesson plans or one-on-one sessions. They were struggling to keep up with their normal responsibilities. Watching them and how they were weighted down soured me on ever pursuing a teaching career of any kind.

Yet I wasn't going to disagree with my guidance counselor about all that he was trying to do. It wasn't difficult to see what a miserable school life I was having, if it could even be called a school life. I might as well be attending school on a deserted island or maybe in a monastery where everyone had taken a vow not only of silence but of lack of sight. Never look at each other, and, especially, never look at me.

After I was forced to return, it got so that in class, no matter what subject it was and what we were doing at the time, I could read whatever I wanted even while the teachers were talking. None of my teachers ever bothered me or reprimanded me for it. I had yet to get a grade lower than 100 in any of my subjects. If I ever did pay attention or raise my hand, it was because my teacher had done or said something incorrect. It got so that they looked frightened if I showed any interest in what they were saying. They tried to ignore me, and if they did so long enough, they knew I would put my hand down and go back to what I'd been doing.

There was nothing a teacher hated more than being corrected by a student, especially one like me. Some reluctantly said thank you, but most brushed over it as if it were just a small glitch, not worth more attention. Lately, it had gotten so that even the other students resented me for doing it, as if I had no right to ruin their image of their brilliant teachers.

I had met few teachers so far who would put their egos behind their interest in truly educating someone. Those who did were more secure about themselves and didn't mind a student teaching them, too.

One of them, my tenth-grade English teacher, Mr. Madeo, said, "You're always a student, even when you become a teacher. Once you think you know it all, you're a puppet, with ignorance pulling the strings. Don't stop asking questions, Mayfair."

The point is that the attitudes of most of my

teachers toward me spilled over onto my classmates. They, too, avoided talking to me, even nodding at me in the hallway. I usually sat alone in the cafeteria. Others could accidentally bump into me in the hallways and act as if they had bumped into the wall itself. No one apologized. Sometimes my father brought Allison and me to school on his way to work. Other times, Julie had to do it, and she usually picked us up. If I wanted to go somewhere else, I called a taxi. None of the students who drove ever asked me to go somewhere with them. This was supposed to be the year that I got my driver's license, and my father was getting me my own car. No one even mentioned it now. Like most teenagers, I thought that once I had my license and a car, I'd gain in popularity. I didn't want to admit to myself that it was a motive for getting my license and my own car, but it was.

Of course, I told myself that those kinds of friends wouldn't be sincere. They would use me and make me feel foolish for trying to win their friendship that way. I wondered why other girls and boys my age didn't see all the phoniness hovering around them. Maybe they didn't want to see it. Maybe that was the solution: ignore the truth so that you could feel happy. Perhaps, deep down, that was what my father was doing when it came to Julie. No one who fools himself wants to be reminded of it.

I looked at the book I had given Allison and reread some passages describing foreplay and orgasm. Even though the other girls in my class never spoke to me about anything social, I couldn't help overhearing them talking in the locker room before and after PE or in the cafeteria when they sat at a table close to mine. Most of them struck me as airheads, but I was still somewhat fascinated by the discussions. It surprised me just how much intimate stuff they would reveal.

"He got behind me, put his hand under my blouse, and said I should let him pretend to be my bra," Joyce Brooker told the others one afternoon. "While he kissed me on my neck."

"And?" Cora Addison asked when there was too long of a pause.

"My father came home early."

She was doing this in her own house? Maybe that made it more exciting. Would I want to be alone with any of the boys in this school at my home, in my room? How would I feel if Julie or my father burst in on us? Embarrassed, titillated, or just annoyed at the interruption?

"He got his hands out just in time, but . . ."

"But what?" Denise Hartman asked.

"My father looked at my face and knew something. He didn't say anything, but he told my mother, and she gave me a lecture. I don't know what would have happened if my father hadn't come home early," Joyce admitted. "And I still don't know what will happen next time, despite my mother's lecture."

I thought it was a stunning confession. The others looked mesmerized, lost in their own fantasies, wondering if they would surrender completely, even if it wasn't safe sex. It was written on their faces. They were excited just by the possibility.

As was I.

A similar thing happened whenever I read information about sex and then thought of myself, just as I was doing after my confrontation with Julie about Allison. I'd see myself with a boy, even with a teacher. It wasn't that I grew frightened as much as I grew nervous and unsure of what I would do. The only time I felt as if I were skating on thin ice at school was when it came to boys, talking to them, reacting to their rare flirtations or approaches. Being scientific about it or pointing out that I knew what they were up to was the only way I could be comfortable, but what boy liked that? It was like tearing off their masks or telling the emperor he was naked, that he wore no clothes.

It was clear to me that boys were more comfortable with girls who were either really dumb about it all or good at pretending to be. Boys needed their egos pumped up more than girls did, I concluded. But what other girl would even care to think about it as much? Many times, I was tempted to say something to one of the girls after I overheard a conversation she had been having with a boy she apparently liked. I felt the need to warn her, to guide her, as if she and I were on the same team, but one look at her face told me that I would have my advice or concerns for her thrown back into my face.

"What do you know about it?" she would surely snap at me. "You have the love life of a mannequin." It would bring a crowd of gawking onlookers, who would surely enjoy my being taken down. I wasn't going to put myself in that sort of jeopardy. It wasn't worth it.

However, I was as guilty as Julie when it came to imposing how I felt on Allison. I knew she was thinking about boys constantly now, and I had offered her the book thinking that knowledge would make her feel as comfortable and as safe as it made me feel. Of course, I knew that she would be titillated by it, especially the graphics, just like I was, even though I knew in my heart that it wouldn't be enough. She wanted her romance novels and enjoyed toying with her own emotions. She didn't want to explore in a classroom with a health teacher. She wanted to explore in the rear seat of a car or in a bedroom when no one was home. What I had to offer her would educate her, but it wouldn't satisfy her. I knew that. I knew because it wasn't satisfying me.

Once, when my father was trying to step into my mother's empty shoes and give me some advice about boys and dating, he told me I shouldn't depend on my superior intelligence when it came to physical relationships.

"Just because you're miles above the guy you're with, that doesn't mean you won't lose control, Mayfair. Lots of smart people get into trouble. It happens so quickly sometimes that you don't even know it. You know the drill."

I was acting as if I were listening with half an ear, but I was totally absorbed by what he was telling me. "Drill?"

"Sure. You're at a party. You want to be one of the girls, so you drink or do whatever, too, and then you go off with someone, and you go too far."

"Oh, Daddy, please," I said. "I'm not Suzie Bubble Brain."

"Don't be arrogant when it comes to your emotions, Mayfair," he warned. "Aside from those who were forced into it, I bet there's not one pregnant teenager who didn't know the consequences but did it anyway. Regrets come too easy."

"Okay," I said. "I get the point." I just wanted him to stop, not because I didn't appreciate his concern for me but because he was nudging places in my brain and stimulating thoughts and feelings that frankly frightened me.

All my life, I felt I had complete control of everything and everyone around me.

Sex was an area where I knew I might not.

He shrugged and smiled, holding up his hands. "I've done my duty," he said.

I thought of all that as I thumbed dreamily through the sex manual I had given Allison. I found the graphic drawings and some of the photographs with detailed explanations more than just interesting. They were fascinating, because I was able to see myself in the drawings and some of the photographs. It was like getting on a roller coaster. I was sure that Allison, even though she was much older than I had been when I learned all this, had similar reactions and feelings.

Actually, despite how Julie had reacted, I still was hoping that Allison would come to me and we could talk about it, the way two real sisters might, but Julie wasn't going to let that happen if she had any say about it, especially now. It had gotten to where she was frightened of me herself, not just for Allison. It had been gnawing away at her for some time now. I could feel it. This was why she was at my father so much, demanding that he rein me in as if I were a wild horse, complaining about the influence I could have on Allison. She was champing at the bit to complain every chance she got now, and I was sure she believed she had finally found the in-house scandal big enough to get me severely reprimanded, maybe turn me into a meek and obedient stepdaughter. I braced myself for the inevitable confrontation.

An hour after he had come home from work, my father was knocking on my door. When I opened it, he just stood there shaking his head, a look of great disappointment on his face.

"Okay, Mayfair, exactly what did you do now? Julie is fit to be tied."

"Now, there's a good idea."

"Stop it."

"She's being ridiculous, Daddy," I said. "I didn't give Allison a porn magazine, you know."

"What did you give her?"

"I gave her a scientific, informative manual written by a college professor."

I went to my bed and got the book. I handed it to him, and he opened it and thumbed through some of it. "Kind of graphic stuff," he said. "Where did you get it?"

"I bought it over the internet."

"Didn't they ask your age?"

"That's not a work of pornography, Daddy. It's

a scientific discussion about sex. Besides, what is my age?"

"I'm not talking about your mental age, Mayfair."

"What's more important? Days? Months? An accumulation of years? There are twenty-year-olds who shouldn't be driving or drinking and certainly not having unprotected sex and becoming parents."

"Okay, okay," he said, handing the book back to me. "I'm not going to debate you about that. However, you have to remember that Julie is Allison's mother. She should be the one who decides what she reads, not you. You want to give her something, you ask her mother first. Do you understand? Do you?" he followed when I didn't respond.

"It's not brain surgery."

"Don't be smart, Mayfair."

"You know, there's an interesting word, Daddy, *smart*. If someone just overheard you saying that, they'd think you were a bad father. Don't you want your daughter to be intelligent?"

"Stop it, Mayfair."

I would have, but I couldn't stand him always taking Julie's side, so I continued lecturing him, instead of crying or screaming. "*Smart* also means witty but often in an insolent way, and that's what you mean, I believe. *Smart* can also mean fashionable, as in 'That's a smart-looking suit.' We also hear it used to mean accomplished, talented, as in 'He's a right smart ballplayer.'"

We stared at each other.

Then he shook his head and walked out, closing

my door softly. I had frustrated and defeated him again, but I didn't feel good about it. I flopped onto my bed and looked up at the ceiling. Sometimes, maybe more often than I'd care to admit, I hated myself. It was as if I couldn't stop myself from being who I didn't want to be, who they expected me to be.

I should have known then. If I couldn't stop myself, how could I really do anything about the future I really wanted?

No wonder I was in a car being taken away like someone who was going to a mental clinic.

6

Before all this, there were many people, even many other students, who thought I was a lucky girl. I had a wealthy father, I lived in a beautiful house, I was attractive enough to draw the envy of other girls and the interest of men who didn't know me yet, and I was a super-brilliant student, a rock star in the educational system. Because I would never let them, no one ever saw the other side of me, what I might admit now was the tragic side. I didn't want to give anyone the satisfaction of knowing that I wasn't as perfect as I was thought to be. I had come to rely on that image, depend on it to get me through any crisis, whether it was of my own making or not. I should have known it wasn't going to be enough.

Only my high-school guidance counselor, Mr. Martin, had an inkling about what I was really feeling about myself, what my weaknesses and deficiencies were. When I had first entered high school, he really did try to get me to join some extracurricular activity like the drama club. He gave me a copy of the school play to read and told me I would enjoy the experience. Even though I thought he might be right, I resisted. I didn't want to be on any girls' teams, either. It wasn't because I didn't like plays or sports. To be honest, I was afraid of the interchanges I would have with the others. Simply put, I was afraid I wouldn't be able to be a teenager after all, and I had yet to fail at anything in my life. Nevertheless, Mr. Martin was persistent, reasonable, and logical. He would call me in to talk with him periodically, stop me in the hallways, or repeat the advice whenever he had an opportunity to speak with my father especially.

"I know they see you as someone very different, Mayfair, and that's why they don't warm up to you," Mr. Martin told me, "but maybe if you join something and they get to know you better, they won't be so put off by your intellectual achievements."

"I don't care that much about making friends here, Mr. Martin," I said. I couldn't argue with his premise, so I tried a quick escape.

But he wasn't buying it. "Yes, you do," he insisted.

Finally, he gave up, even though I was sure that he could see in my face that I didn't mean what I told him. I wasn't always as good at hiding my feelings as I thought I was, especially from someone trained to see through the fog of excuses and fears.

Of course I would have loved to have a best friend, someone else to talk to, to share my intimate thoughts and feelings. Of course I wanted to giggle and laugh over silly things and talk for hours about things that didn't matter. But I wouldn't admit it, and I wouldn't do anything to make it happen.

Frustrated with me, Mr. Martin became intrigued with the possibility of my being accepted at the country's most prestigious colleges. While still in high school, I had been able to take a number of college classes and had enough credits to enter most universities as a junior. We had a meeting about the situation, but my father wasn't happy about Mr. Martin's priorities. He was afraid I was moving too quickly. On the other hand, it was difficult to argue against Mr. Martin's point that I was wasting my abilities.

"I know she's bored with her classes here," he told my father. "Her teachers are doing the best they can for her, but another year in high school, at least one like this, might not be the best choice."

"I'm not worried about her mental development. I'm worried about her social development," my father replied. "I mean, you were the one who brought up the problem of her not developing fully as a person if we kept her separated from her classmates. We agreed and insisted that she be put back into regular classes. Why isn't it helping?" he asked.

I was surprised to hear him say that in front of me. He sounded frightened about it, frightened that I would never be a fully rounded person and never be happy. Although he did try to get me to do some of the things Mr. Martin and some of my earlier teachers had suggested, my father never gave me the impression that he thought there was anything actually freakish about me. He was always proud of my accomplishments, but since he had married Julie and she was constantly complaining about me, he began to look at me differently.

And because he was doing that, I started doing it, too.

Hours after my tiff with Julie about lending Allison the sex manual and my sarcastic reaction to my father, I looked at myself in the mirror and thought about all this. Suddenly, I began to wonder if I really was as pretty and as sexy as some of the other girls in my class. Maybe those who gave me compliments weren't doing it simply to be nice. Even Julie had, reluctantly or not, complimented my features and expressed some envy.

Maybe it was because of the way Julie had come after me for giving Allison the book on sex or maybe it was the way my father was seeing me now, but whatever the reason, I decided to do something I hadn't much done up to now. I decided to improve my appearance to see if that would make any difference at school. Perhaps I could stop being seen as part of the woodwork, fading into the hallways and the backs of classrooms. Maybe I could sparkle, too, and from something other than my intellectual capacities. Perhaps this would lead me to socialize and be the more well-rounded person everyone seemed to want me to be. I had to start somewhere if I was going to attempt a change, and my looks were the most logical and easiest place to begin.

Whether I liked it or not, Julie was the expert when it came to that, I thought, and one thing I knew was to go to the best source for the information you wanted and needed. If I ignored her, I'd be just like any fool who refused to face facts, scientific truths, just to satisfy his or her prejudices.

I surprised her at dinner that night. She was still pouting over my giving Allison the book and my comments when she had come to reprimand me. She wouldn't look at me. Her jaw looked frozen. It wasn't uncommon for her to go into such a determined sulk so she could extract more sympathy from my father, but I could feel it was more intense. My father looked at me, practically pleading for me to mend fences.

"I want to apologize," I began.

"Oh," she said petulantly. She still didn't look at me. She was capable of childlike tantrums and could sulk for hours, if not days, until she got her way.

"Yes. A while back, I was ungrateful when you went out of your way to help me with makeup."

"What?" She looked at my father. Of course, both she and my father were expecting a different apology.

"You do all that so well," I said. "I should have paid more attention to the lessons you were trying to give me." Giving her any compliment was like swallowing spoiled milk, but I did it.

"Well, I did try to help you."

"Maybe you can show it all to me again. And I would appreciate your suggestions about my hair."

"Your hair?"

"I know the clothes I wear are blah, too," I admitted. "You're right about the colors I choose. Almost all of my clothes are not in fashion and don't flatter my figure at all."

She straightened up and nodded. "Exactly. I've tried to get you to see that, and . . ."

"You have. I was foolish to refuse your offers of

help. I should appreciate that there's someone like you so easily available to me to give me good advice. I hope you are still willing to do that."

Even though this wasn't the place my father had hoped I would go, he was beaming. Allison, however, was staring at me with suspicious eyes. I was stealing away her mother's attention, her mother's concentration on her when it came to these things, but Julie enjoyed being in the spotlight.

"Well, thank you for saying that."

"The point is, I've come to the logical conclusion that I need some help with this."

"Of course you do, and that's nothing to be ashamed about."

"I'm not ashamed," I snapped.

Her smile began to fade. Allison started to smile.

Can't she get anything right? I thought. I softened my tone again. "I'm simply admitting that it's an area in which I am deficient, an area in which you obviously have great expertise."

"Exactly. I've been tutored by some of the best cosmeticians and hairstylists and have followed fashion studiously all my life."

"She must like somebody who's not paying attention to her," Allison piped up, smiling with suspicious eyes.

My father looked from her to me. "Oh?" he said.

"No, that's not it," I said.

"You don't have to be afraid to admit you have a crush on someone," Julie said, enjoying my discomfort for a change. "If you have someone special in mind, it's better if you describe him a bit."

"There isn't anyone special." I looked at Allison. "If there was, I wouldn't need to be coming to you now, Julie."

"Well, there will be," she assured me. "You have the natural beauty that makes it easy to work miracles."

I could see that Allison wasn't pleased with her mother giving me compliments. I wanted to lean over and assure her that I wasn't looking for them, that I couldn't care less about what her mother thought of my looks, or me, for that matter, but I kept myself in check.

"Right after dinner, we'll do another lesson in makeup, and I'll look at your hair again." Julie sat back and looked at me as if seeing me for the first time. Then she nodded to herself. "As you often say, it's not brain surgery."

Oh, how she was enjoying this, but for me, it was like going to the dentist. It had to be done.

"I think we should make an appointment with my hairstylist this Saturday, after which we can do some shopping and see if we can make some real improvements in your wardrobe. You'll need new shoes, too, and a few decent purses. I think she needs a more feminine-looking watch," she told my father.

"Of course. I was going to get her one for her birthday, but . . ."

"You can get her another, something more special, perhaps. I think I know what you need, Mayfair."

"Thank you," I said.

"Can I go, too?" Allison asked.

"No," Julie said. "I don't want to be distracted.

I shop for you all the time, and besides, it won't be much fun for you to stand there and watch me buying things for Mayfair and not you."

Allison seemed disappointed, but she also looked at me with real envy, and I couldn't remember her doing that before. It didn't bother me. Actually, it made me feel a little better, even a little lightheaded.

My father looked like a weight had been lifted off his shoulders. I didn't want him to get too excited and happy about this. Once I had gotten what I wanted from Julie, I didn't intend to do much more with her. She would never replace my mother, and I would never call her anything but Julie. In my eyes, she was simply a good source for this particular information. I'd put her back on the shelf afterward, just as I put back a library book or clicked off a website.

However, days later, I couldn't deny that I was happy about the changes she had made in my appearance. She did have a good hairstylist, who complimented me on the health of my hair. Julie stood by and oversaw it all, concentrating on the smallest details and making me feel like some sort of celebrity. I had to admit that the cut she and the stylist chose did change my whole look, and that change began changes inside me, too. I could feel a growing confidence that came from the way others in the salon looked at my metamorphosis from someone with potential to someone who could invite cameras.

From the salon, we went to one of Julie's favorite boutiques. Everything was quite expensive, all created by one designer or another. She made me try on and model a few different styles, discussing every one with the store's sales manager, a French woman who obviously knew more than she did. At the end of the day, I had a half dozen new outfits and pairs of shoes. She even took me to get some costume jewelry, especially earrings, and made sure I had a nice watch. I had never wanted to get my ears pierced, but I clenched my teeth and agreed to have it done. I kept reminding myself that she knew better than I did about all this and it was a sign of ignorance to deny it for personal reasons.

My father brightened in a way I hadn't seen since I was very young. He didn't say it in front of Julie, but when he saw me later, he told me that for a moment he had thought my mother had returned when I had stepped into the house after my makeover.

"You have all her wonderful qualities, Mayfair. Julie's done a good job of bringing them out."

What he said made me feel good but surprisingly brought tears to my eyes. Was this physical change unchaining emotions I hadn't seen or felt for years?

I was very nervous about going to school now. Never, no matter what I did or how I was treated, was I uneasy about walking into the building. I could be indifferent to anyone and anything. But when I returned to school that Monday, I did feel quite different. Not only was my hair cut and styled, but I was dressed like a girl my age dressed, and the makeup I wore, as Julie had said, highlighted the most attractive features of my face. Those girls in my class who were jealous of my good looks to start with were absolutely beside themselves with envy now. That was easy to see and also quite pleasing. Before this, there wasn't a girl who felt threatened by me. In their opinion, my looks weren't enough to overcome the way I was viewed by boys and by other girls. Now things might be different.

I couldn't help being nervous and doubting the wisdom of what I had done. To calm myself, I told myself that it was just another sociological experiment, and I tried to analyze it that way, but as soon as I began to get second looks from boys in the corridors and classroom, the scientific, analytical approach died, and I was suddenly and finally a teenage girl whose heart began to pitter-patter with every smile tossed in her direction.

Ironically, however, it wasn't one of the high-school boys who made me feel sexy and attractive; it was one of the younger teachers, Allison's English teacher, Mr. Taylor, or Alan, as he would want me to call him later on.

He was standing in his classroom doorway when I entered the building and started for my homeroom. He knew who I was. Faculty members gossiped about their students, and I was confident that I was frequently the topic of their conversations. Whenever he had looked at me before, there was little or no excitement in his face. Like most of the teachers, he wasn't interested in having much of a conversation with me. Few wanted to know what I was researching or reading, and if any did ask, he or she would nod and smile, clearly revealing that I was into areas beyond them, reading books they didn't even read in college, but that wasn't true today for Mr. Taylor.

At six feet two inches tall, with thick, rich light brown hair and cerulean blue eyes, Alan Taylor was the most attractive male teacher in the school. He was only twenty-five and still a bachelor. All the unmarried female teachers were vying for his attention, but as far as I knew, none had won his interest. He had one of those movie-star perfect faces that hovered between handsome and pretty because of his high cheekbones and perfectly shaped nose and mouth. His good looks were complemented by his tennis-pro figure and confident posture. Just like I knew I was brilliant, he knew he was physically striking. The high-school girls who swooned over him all wondered why he was "just a teacher" and not at least on television.

"Hey there," he called to me as I started past his room.

I paused, a little surprised. "Yes?"

"What did you do with your hair?"

"I donated it," I said.

"What?"

"They use it to make wigs for women who suffer baldness during chemotherapy."

He stared a moment and then laughed.

I didn't, but that didn't discourage him. He stepped toward me, looking me over even more closely. I felt more self-conscious and had the surprising urge to bring my arms up and around my breasts as if I were topless, but I resisted. His smile now made my heart do flip-flops. I fought to hold it back, but I could feel the heat go up my neck and into my face. He took so long to speak, seeming to enjoy just looking at me, that I had to say, "What?"

He laughed again. "I don't mean the hair you had cut off. I mean you've changed your appearance."

"There's a little chameleon in all of us," I said. "You know, blend with your surroundings to survive?"

He widened his smile. I knew he was struggling to think of a response. I didn't wait. I saw no reason to linger, so I walked on to homeroom.

But I knew he was watching me all the way, and it was a different feeling knowing a man was looking at me not as a phenomenon but as a woman. I was more conscious of my body, the way I moved, even how I turned toward the classroom.

I looked back and saw that he was still looking my way and smiling. There were still feelings traveling through my body that I had longed for. I tried to contain them, but they were like wild horses that had seen an opening. My breath quickened. He nodded at me, holding his smile as if he knew I would imprint it on my memory and recall it whenever I wanted.

The moment I entered my first class, I noted the way the others were looking at me and chattering. Gossip about me already had gone through the hallways and into every homeroom. I didn't think anyone looked at me all morning without taking a second look. My history teacher, Mr. Leshman, actually called on me twice and didn't seem to mind when I went on to elaborate on the answer and get into another topic. It actually interested him, and he and I were almost alone in the room for the remainder of the period.

When lunch started and I went to the cafeteria, I quickly realized that I wasn't going to be sitting alone. Carlton James, one of the better-looking senior boys, broke away from his friends and started toward me the moment I sat at a table. From the way the others were smiling after him, I imagined some sort of a bet had been made or some sort of a challenge, and Carlton had accepted it.

"Are you a new student?" he asked.

When I had fantasized using the pictures in the sex manual, I had seen myself with him in some of the illustrations, but I would never admit to myself that I had a crush on him or anything that juvenile. And I certainly had never done anything to give him reason to think so.

"Why? Are you the official greeter?"

"I can be," he said, and slipped into the chair across from me.

Despite how much I wanted to like him, his youthful male arrogance put me off. I felt like tossing my container of juice at his wry smile. I simply didn't like being in the company of someone who had more self-confidence than I did. Perhaps that was a compromise I would have to make if I were to get into any relationship successfully. He nodded at his friends, who were still looking our way and grinning like idiots.

"What, did you draw the short straw?" I asked.

"Huh? What short straw?"

"You never heard that expression?"

He shook his head. His smile weakened.

"It was one of my grandmother's expressions." I smiled, thinking about her.

"What's it mean?" he asked, regaining his composure, obviously hoping it meant something that would please him. He couldn't imagine my saying anything otherwise, especially with the warm smile on my face.

"When a group of people decide that one of them has to do something unpleasant, they draw straws, and the one who gets the shortest straw does it."

"Oh, well, I'm not doing anything unpleasant," he said, widening his smile again. "Why would you think coming over here to talk to you was something unpleasant anyway?"

"I was born with a suspicious nature. So you're here. What do you want to talk about?" I asked.

"Just . . ."

"What?"

His smile began to fade. "Just saying hello. You know."

"Hello," I said. "Now what?"

He lost his smile completely. "What are you, gay?"

"Why do you ask that?" I was really curious, especially since I had done so much to make myself attractive to boys, or at least I thought I had.

"Because, well . . . you're, like, not interested," he said, obviously feeling good about coming up with the word and the idea. "Am I right?"

"You haven't done or said anything interesting yet," I told him. "Maybe you're just relying on your good looks. That will take you just so far in this world."

"Huh?"

"No one's ever told you that?"

He smirked, looked back at his friends, and then leaned toward me. "You're a big brain, right?"

"The size of your brain isn't what makes you intelligent." I looked around the cafeteria. "There are some very big heads in here on very stupid people."

He laughed. "Okay, how do I get you to help me with my intermediate algebra?"

"Is that why you came over here?" I asked, feeling disappointed.

"No, but I thought it might be a good start."

I smiled. That was clever, I thought, more clever than I would have thought him capable of being. "No, that doesn't work. You have to ask something you really care about, talk about something you want to talk about, not something that might just get you by."

"You sound like a dating instructor. You know, like one of those websites that's supposed to help you find someone compatible."

"You use them?"

"Absolutely not," he said, a little insulted. He straightened up. "Do I look like someone who needs to use them?"

"Looks deceive," I said. He stared at me. "Okay, you don't."

He smiled again. Then he raked the room with his eyes to be sure he was the center of attention before turning back to me. "Okay. Here's something I really want to say. What are you doing after school today?"

"Why?"

"Maybe you can come home with me and give me

some pointers about how to talk properly or something. I'm open to improvements," he said. He looked back at his friends again.

I nodded at them. "What do you win if I say yes?"

He laughed again. Then he gave me his best sexy smile. "I won't know until I get you over, right?"

That made me smile. Maybe he wasn't as dull as I had expected him to be. Yet I hesitated. I had never, ever been alone with any boy, let alone in his home. I thought about some of the conversations I had overheard in the girls' locker room. Would I have similar experiences if I went with him? I felt like a schizophrenic person arguing with herself. The feminine part of me was urging me to say yes, but that part of me that made me feel older, more mature, and far superior was telling me to say no.

I was tired of listening to that part of me.

"Where do you live?"

My not saying no immediately pleased him so much that I couldn't help but widen my smile. He looked more like a little boy to me now, a harmless, excited little boy. I was obviously making his day, and that did make me feel good. I was a big enough prize.

"On Camden," he said. "Ten, fifteen minutes at the most. And I'll take you home whenever you want," he quickly added. "I drive a BMW 335 hardtop convertible. You probably saw it out there in the lot."

"BMW? What's that stand for, Big Man's Wheels?"

He laughed. "I like that. You're pretty clever. I had a feeling you might be fun to talk to. Those idiots back there thought we'd have nothing to say to each other."

"Because they have nothing to say to each other? Nothing meaningful?"

"Yeah, I guess. No, I mean . . . I don't know what I mean. I just knew you would be interesting."

"How did you know?"

"Do you have to always ask questions?"

"That's a question."

He looked frustrated again. "I just knew, okay?"

"I'm impressed. Do you even know my name?" I asked him.

"Sure. Mayfair, like the boat that brought the Pilgrims, right?"

"No." I shook my head, not hiding my disappointment. "You're right that my name is Mayfair, but you're thinking of the *Mayflower*. The ship, not the boat, that brought over the English separatists from Plymouth, England, was the *Mayflower*. It docked in Plymouth. You must have been asleep during that history lesson."

"I'm asleep during most history lessons," he said. "Sorry. Mayfair's just as nice. You're not named after another ship, too, are you?"

"Mayfair comes from the annual fortnight-long May Fair held in London."

"No kidding," he said without any real interest.

"Do you know what a fortnight is?"

"A night at a fort?"

"No," I said, laughing. "It's a unit of time equal to fourteen days. It comes from Old English."

"You mean, like that Beowulf story we had to read in class?"

"Yes, exactly, only they don't have it in Old English in your textbook."

"Yeah, Mr. Lofter read some of it in that Old English. Dumb," he said. "No one knew what the hell he was saying. I don't know how anyone could talk like that."

"Old English was spoken in England and southeastern Scotland between the fifth and twelfth centuries. It's also known as Anglo-Saxon. It has a Germanic heritage in its vocabulary, sentence structure, and grammar. It can sound quite interesting, almost musical, when it's read correctly."

"Jeez, are you always like this?"

"Like what?"

"A teacher," he said, making it sound like a curse word.

"Are you always this reluctant to learn anything?"

He stared at me a moment and then leaned back, turning to look at his friends, who had lost interest in us and were laughing and talking with other girls. They looked lighthearted and relaxed. Then he looked at me again, this time with regret. "I just remembered I have to do something for my father after school today. Maybe some other time, when I'm hungry for knowledge," he said, getting up.

Disappointment surged through me and curled under my breasts.

He paused and leaned toward me with his hands on the table. "But it was nice studying with you," he muttered, and walked away.

I watched how his friends greeted him with

laughter. He shook his head and spoke, describing our conversation from his perspective, and then they all looked my way and laughed again, especially the girls.

Yahoos, I thought.

They surrounded me. If I wasn't careful, I might catch the disease of ignorance. That's what I told myself, but deep inside, I did feel a sense of disappointment and defeat.

Before the bell rang to end the lunch hour, I left for the library. I wasn't even going to bother to go to math class. My teacher, Mrs. Samuels, would simply check with the librarian later to see if I had gone there. I wanted to go on the computer and see what I could find on the mating habits of primates. I had told my science teacher that I was going to do a paper on the subject, and he'd looked very interested.

I was almost at the library when Mr. Taylor appeared, seemingly out of nowhere. It was almost as if he were lying in wait for me.

"Hey," he said. "How's your day going?"

"Like a blur," I said, and he laughed.

"Where are you headed?"

"The library. I'm doing a research paper."

"Come into my room for a while. I've got a free period," he said, shifting his shoulder. "C'mon. I'm not going to bite you."

"Why?"

"A little intelligent conversation," he said. "I'm starving for it. I spend most of my day talking to junior-high students. Don't you know this is the front line in the big battle called education?"

"What about the other teachers? Don't you talk to them?"

He shrugged and smiled wryly. "I said *intelligent* conversation."

I looked back when the bell rang. The students would be bursting out of the cafeteria like a herd of wildebeests in seconds. Half of them would knock into me. Maybe that, more than my curiosity about Mr. Taylor, made me turn in his direction. Whatever the reason, I did.

I'd always wonder if it wasn't something meant to be, not that I believed in fate or fixed destiny. If I did, I couldn't be much of a scholar, because it was too easy to fall back on that rather than study and do research for an explanation, but I couldn't help secretly hoping it was fate.

That way, all that had happened to me, to Allison, and especially to my father wouldn't have been my fault, not my fault at all. All the blame and guilt would fade, and I would be the object of sympathy, not anger and disappointment. But deep in my heart, I knew that to hope was to dream, and to dream was to deny what was real. Maybe that was all I had ever wanted to do. Maybe I was guilty of everything I had accused most other people of doing.

I wasn't profoundly gifted after all.

I was profoundly dumb.

7

Mr. Taylor went behind his desk and put his feet up. I stood just inside his classroom doorway with my books cradled in my arms. I wasn't about to fool myself. It wasn't the prospect of having any sort of intelligent conversation that brought me into his room. I had really come in because I was far more interested in how a mature man thought of me than I was in how one of the boys in my class thought and behaved. I already felt a difference in my own reaction. It was more exciting, because his flirting and my responding seemed like something forbidden. After all, he was a teacher, and I was a high-school junior. There were all sorts of news stories about teachers who exploited their young students, even female teachers seducing young boys.

I did think to myself, however, that if we weren't who we were, it would be different. Suppose it were a couple of years from now. If I were a woman six or seven years younger than he was, and he were a businessman and not a teacher, no one would think anything of it. People could say a teacher had an unfair advantage over a student. He or she had great powers of influence. Students supposedly looked up to and listened to their teachers. That was certainly true for most.

But I had gone through almost all of my school years and never really been influenced by a teacher. I didn't need any teacher to encourage me to study or be responsible about my schoolwork. I didn't need any teacher to inspire me to have interests in science or math or English or history. If anything, I occasionally found myself inspiring one of them. How many times had I heard one of my teachers say, "You know, Mayfair, you have me thinking like a college student again"?

I certainly wasn't looking for their compliments. Nothing I did would change, whether they gave me a compliment or not. Maybe that was the arrogance I would be accused of possessing. To me, it was just a simple truth.

There were teachers I respected, of course, but many I didn't respect. I didn't do anything disrespectful to them. I was simply indifferent. In those teachers' classes, I looked beyond them to the challenge of the work.

Still, there was no way around this. I was standing there fantasizing about a teacher and actually hoping he had some fantasies about me. For the moment, at least, I was in exciting new territory, certainly more interesting territory than I was in with Carlton James in the cafeteria. If I had too many more experiences like that, I would probably give up on boys altogether, I thought.

"Sit. Take a load off," Mr. Taylor said.

He put his hands behind his head and looked at me. There was something about the way his eyes moved over me that made me hesitate. I told myself I was feeling the natural instinctive fear a female had of a male. I had read enough about it to know what it was.

Then I told myself to stop being so damn analytical and enjoy this. *You can analyze it later. For now, just soak up the experience. You've never been with a man who looked at you more as a woman than as a brilliant brain. You don't have to romanticize about it. You're really here, and he's really here looking at you and saying these things to you.*

"You've got to learn how to relax, Mayfair," he said. "You're too intense about everything."

"How do you know that?"

I was never in his class. He had come to teach junior-high English when I entered ninth grade, nearly three years ago. Allison had him for English now, but I really had no contact with him.

"I watch you, see you moving about the school. When you walk through the hall, you barely look right or left. You don't let anything distract you. I never saw anyone as intense. A bomb could go off, and you'd keep going in the direction you were headed if you had some purpose, some goal to fulfill," he said, and widened his smile. "Not that there's anything wrong with the way you walk," he added.

"What's that mean?"

He looked thoughtful for a moment. Did he realize he already had gone too far? I regretted coming back at him so fast and hard. He shrugged, took his feet off his desk, and leaned forward. "Well, you move with a great deal of confidence. Great posture," he said. "Even now, standing there, you don't slouch like so many of the girls your age do. I have to tell you that you fascinate me, and I don't mean because of your off-the-charts IQ scores." He nodded. "The way someone walks can tell you a lot about that person."

"I'm not conscious of it," I said. "I don't think about walking like that. Walking is a habitual action. We might be conscious of it occasionally to impress someone, but generally, we don't think about it. Everyone has a unique way of walking."

"Exactly. That's my point. It's part of who you are. Insecure people have a far different way of walking from secure people, and you don't look at all insecure, ever."

"What's wrong with that?"

"Nothing. Stop challenging every comment I make. Relax," he repeated. He paused and leaned back again. Then he nodded at me and smiled. "Until today, I didn't think looking this way was important to you," he said, holding his right hand out, palm up.

"Looking what way?"

"Attractive. I don't mean to say you weren't a very pretty girl before, but now you have your hair styled. You're wearing makeup. Quite intelligently, I might add. And you're wearing clothes that complement your figure. You don't mind me telling you these things, do you?" he quickly asked.

"Mind? No. I just didn't expect it."

He shrugged again. "Why not? I'm no hypocrite like some of my fellow male teachers who will swear on a stack of dictionaries that they don't lust after any young, beautiful teenage girls."

I think I was more surprised than he was at my smile. "I don't doubt it. I'm just surprised to hear you say it."

"Hey, we're all human," he said. "When I see an attractive woman, I don't pretend I don't see her just because I'm a junior-high English teacher. Which reminds me." He lifted a pile of papers. "Spot English grammar quiz. It's good to give them. Keeps the kids on their toes, but I hate correcting them. Care to help?"

"I really do have to get to the library, Mr. Taylor. I have a paper I want to finish this week, and I have lots of reading left to do."

"Oh, too bad. Well, maybe when you have time, you can stop by once in a while after school and help me with some of this dull work, huh?"

"Why would I want to do dull work? You shouldn't think of what you teach as being dull."

He laughed. "I knew it would be an interesting challenge talking to you, Mayfair. You really are a breath of fresh air for me."

"Why is that? What makes me so fresh?" I knew I was asking too many questions and challenging him too much, but I couldn't help being interested.

"You're not distracted with yourself. I think that's why you didn't do all these cosmetic things until now. You have your feet on the ground. You're head and shoulders above your peers, and I don't mean just because of your IQ. There's something very mature about you. I can have a conversation with you." He paused, stood up, and came around to the front of his desk to sit back against it, folding his arms. "I bet you wouldn't mind speaking to someone more mature, either. You must be starved for meaningful conversation at this school."

"That's not why I come here," I said. Instinctively, I brought my books up against my breasts. The way he was looking at me made me feel as if I were standing naked in front of him.

He shrugged. "Maybe not, but everyone wants some social contact with other people. I've noticed you don't have all that many friends here. You don't join any clubs or teams. You don't sit with anyone in particular in the cafeteria or walk with anyone in the hallways. You don't even talk to other students at the lockers in the morning. You float through this place as if you're on the way to somewhere else."

"You sound like you're watching me all the time."

"As much as I can," he said with that disarmingly soft smile again.

His honesty didn't shock me as much as it excited me. Again, I felt myself smile as if there was another part of me taking me over. I didn't want to resist.

"Actually, I overhear the students gossiping from time to time and pick up things the guidance counselor says. No one's saying anything terribly negative about you," he quickly added. "It's just comments, observations."

"I'm sure," I said dryly. "They all have my interest at heart. I confuse them."

"I'll say that's true, but you don't have to explain to me why you don't socialize much with your classmates. As I said, I know you're head and shoulders above them. Miles ahead of them, in fact. I'm sure what they do, what interests them, is unimportant to you."

I wanted to say that wasn't completely true, but I didn't. I didn't want to continue standing there talking to him. His words and the way he continued to look at me were starting to make me unsure of myself. I think it was because he was touching places inside me that I usually protected, like my loneliness. Now I thought it was a mistake to play with him like this, to allow myself to have such fantasies.

"I've got to go," I said, and turned toward the door.

"Okay. Please stop by anytime you want to talk or take pity on a poor junior-high English teacher buried in drudge work. Even though I love my subject matter, there's still drudge work," he added quickly. "No matter what exciting thing you end up doing, you'll see there's always the drudge work."

I glanced back at him. He held that licentious smile. It sent a tremor of excitement through my breasts. I felt myself blush.

When I had woken up this morning excited about my new look and how my classmates and other students would react to me, what was furthest from my mind was how the best-looking male teacher in the school would react. How did I miss that? I hated not anticipating something, especially something directly related to me. Although I would have had to be blind or completely oblivious not to have noticed him before, I never dreamed my changed appearance would mean that he would be the one I would draw out.

The one thing I hated most was surprise. I spent most of my time researching, investigating, and understanding everything I saw, did, and touched. I was always prepared, but I would be the first to admit that I wasn't prepared for this. He nearly had taken my breath away.

This whole experience had me confused, not just about him but also about myself. I hated anyone causing me to be unsure about myself. It rarely happened at school, but I wasn't leaving his room because I was dying to get to the library. As hard as it was for me to admit it, I was leaving his room because I was a little frightened of my own reactions.

I was acting and thinking like one of those girls in my class whom I ridiculed.

I hurried out and didn't look back, but just like before, I instinctively knew that he was standing in his doorway watching me walk away.

And he wasn't interested in my good posture, either. I had first thought that this skirt Julie had chosen was too snug and too short, but it was the way many of the other girls were dressing. Give the devil her due. Julie knew fashion, knew how to be attractive. She had captured my father's interest and his heart, hadn't she? What good did it do me to deny it?

I did almost nothing in the library. I couldn't get the conversation I had with Mr. Taylor out of my mind, nor could I stop thinking about the way he looked at me. When the bell rang and I left to go to my next class, I anticipated him being in his doorway waiting for me to walk by again. At first, he wasn't there, and I felt a combination of relief and a little disappointment, but before I'd passed his room completely, he appeared.

"How'd your research go?" he called out to me.

"Fine," I said, only glancing back at him.

"Best posture in the school," he called after me, and laughed. I kept walking, walking faster but smiling to myself.

I was thinking so hard about him that I completely forgot about the incident in the cafeteria with Carlton James. It wasn't until I went to PE class that the consequences of that disappointing conversation were brought home to me. I was just getting my uniform on when Joyce Brooker stepped up behind me.

"We heard you blew off Carlton today," she said.

I turned and looked at her. I couldn't remember the last time she had spoken to me or I to her. She was probably the prettiest of the girls with whom she hung, or I should say clung. They always looked more like a clump of girls clinging to one another than a group of close friends.

Joyce had almost doll-like facial features, stunning green eyes, and thick amber hair. She had the

best figure, too, but she behaved just like someone
who knew all this would behave. Talk about a walk,
I thought, recalling Mr. Taylor's comment about me.
Joyce didn't walk; she moved as if she were on a fashion model's runway. If any of them would go on to
become Miss California, it would be Joyce. I could
just see her answering the final question.

"If you could have one wish, what would it be?"

"A better cell phone." Or maybe she'd realize she
had to at least look serious and mature and say, "I
would want to see an end to poverty." Even though
she didn't know a single poor person.

Sometimes I felt a little envious of her, but I
smothered that feeling as quickly as it showed its face.

"He never got on," I told her.

"Huh?"

The other girls joined her. They were like pigeons
waiting for me to cast some peanuts.

"I couldn't have blown him *off*. He never got *on*."

She laughed and looked at the others. "Well, he
tried, didn't he?"

"If so, it was a pathetic attempt," I said.

"Pathetic? Carlton James? I think it might be you
who's pathetic for rejecting him. Unless, of course,
you're seeing someone outside the school. Someone
older, maybe? Someone in college? Figures that someone with your brains would probably be dating a college boy, maybe even a graduate student."

"Are you?" Cora Addison quickly followed. I always thought she had a face like a fox's, because it was
so narrow, and her nose was so pointed and long.

I gave them all a big smile. "I never realized my comings and goings were of so much interest to all of you. I guess I should be flattered. You're interested in someone other than yourselves. I didn't think that was possible."

"Curiosity, not interest," Denise Hartman corrected. "We can't help wondering if being so intelligent means you have no love life. Men don't like brainy girls."

"There's no basis in fact for that sort of conclusion, Denise. The least intelligent organisms conjugate."

"What?"

"I'm surprised you're not familiar with that, being closer to an amoeba than a primate."

"Excuse me," she said, with her right hand on her hip. "Can you talk English?"

"Is that what you speak? It's difficult to tell."

"Very funny."

"You didn't answer the question," Joyce said.

"Was there a question? I'm still not finished translating."

"Ha-ha," Cora said. "Forget her."

"No," Joyce said, not giving ground. "The question was, are you seeing someone on the outside, and is that someone older, maybe much older?"

I half wondered if someone had reported my private conversation with Mr. Taylor or had overheard him talking to me in the hallway. Was that what she was fishing to find out?

"That's two questions," I said.

"Well, give us two answers."

"Do you write the social column here?"

"Sort of. So?"

I slipped on my sneakers and looked at the three of them. "I still don't understand why this is so important to all of you. Don't you have any lives of your own? Do you have to use other people's lives for your kicks and highs? Live vicariously?"

"Forget the big words. You don't have anyone, do you?" Cora said with a wry smile. "That's why you're not answering us. You've probably never had anyone."

"Any boy, at least," Denise said.

The two others brightened.

"Yes, that's it, isn't it? You're gay. That explains why you rejected Carlton and why no one has ever seen you with a boy anywhere."

"Believe what you want," I said. "Unlike you, I couldn't be less interested in what you think or do or what anyone in this school thinks or does, for that matter."

"Carlton's the best-looking boy in school. He could have any girl he wanted," Cora said, mostly to the other two. They nodded. "Why would she reject him if she wasn't gay?"

"Come to think of it, now that you've brought it up, Cora, I've seen the way she looks at us, especially in here when we're undressing," Joyce said.

"Oh, really? How do I look at you?"

"Like a boy looks at us."

I smiled. "You have misjudged me, girls. I am studying you, but I'm in the middle of doing a research paper on lower forms of life, and your resemblances to single-cell organisms are too remarkable to ignore. Carlton James might be the subject of every adolescent girl's wet dream to you, but he doesn't fit my criteria. I require more than a handsome face. I have to be with someone who can do more than talk about bubble-gum cards."

"Wet dream?" Denise said.

"Look it up," I said, and walked out to the gym.

The only reason I continued to take PE was my belief that it was important to get some physical exercise every day. I enjoyed the warm-up Miss Hirsch put us through, all the exercises, but only halfheartedly participated in the games, especially basketball. Whatever team I was on, the members hardly passed the ball to me. I didn't care. I was more interested in running up and down the court. Sometimes I didn't even notice who had the ball.

The three bitches from *Macbeth* ignored me for the remainder of the period and afterward in the locker room. What Joyce had been asking about my seeing someone older did make me a little more self-conscious, and I deliberately avoided walking near Mr. Taylor's classroom. I hurried out of the building at the end of the day. Allison was already waiting for her mother to take us home.

"You probably got a lot of compliments today, huh?" she asked me.

"I didn't notice," I told her.

"Yes, you did." She stared at me and almost reluctantly added, "You look very pretty now, Mayfair. Even some of my friends said some things about you, some nice things."

Why take it out on her? I thought. "Thank you, Allison. And yes, I did receive compliments."

"I knew you would. My mother will be very happy about it."

"That's good. It's good she's happy about something," I muttered.

I looked back as other students poured out of the building. The three bitches from *Macbeth* looked my way and then laughed as they piled into Joyce's SUV. I had hoped that my answers had discouraged them from having any more interest in me and what I did and didn't do, but as it turned out, my responses had resulted in quite the opposite reaction. I wouldn't learn about it until that night, however.

When Julie picked us up, she had almost the identical question waiting on her lips.

Yes, I had received compliments, I told her, and yes, I felt better about myself. She drove with a smile of self-satisfaction planted on her face all the way home. But thanks to the bitches from *Macbeth*, that would quickly disappear later.

Just before dinner, I could feel that something was up, but I didn't pursue it. When we all sat at the table, she didn't say much to either Allison or my father and avoided looking at me. My father went on and on about how much he enjoyed my new appearance and then talked about some big new business achievements. The whole time, Julie kept herself from looking at me. She seemed to be in very deep thought about something.

Maybe she thought I didn't show enough appreciation, I concluded, and left it at that, but about a half hour after dinner, my father called me on the intercom from the den and asked me to come down. When I walked in, I found him and Julie sitting on one of the leather settees. Both of them looked rather glum.

"What's wrong?" I asked.

My father nodded at the settee across from them. "We'd like to talk to you for a few minutes."

I hadn't done anything with Allison, nor had I spoken much to her since the sex manual incident, so I was curious about what would turn their faces into prunes.

"What's this about?" I asked after I sat.

My father looked to Julie, giving her permission to begin.

"Lauren Hartman is a good friend of mine. Maybe *was*," she added, glancing at my father.

"So?"

"You know her daughter Denise."

"I know who she is. I don't have enough interest in her or her friends to know any of them, Julie. Please stop the dramatics and tell me what this is all about."

"Lauren is very upset with something Denise and the other girls told their mothers."

"They're all pregnant?"

"This isn't funny, Mayfair," my father said.

"I don't know what it is, so I don't know if it's funny or not, Daddy."

"They claim you've been . . . I have trouble even saying it," Julie said, shaking her head.

"Write it out, then," I said.

"Mayfair."

"Well, I'm not going to sit here all night waiting for the dramatics to end, Daddy. What is it, Julie? Speak your piece or forever remain silent."

"They claim you've been watching them undress in the locker room," she rattled off quickly.

"What?"

"They said you admitted to doing that. They also said that one of the most popular and good-looking boys in the school showed interest in you, after I helped you with your hair, makeup, and clothes, and that you showed no interest in him at all. You drove him away after he issued an invitation to spend some time with you, as a matter of fact."

"Is that it?"

"Isn't that enough?"

I looked at my father. "You believe this stuff, the implication she's making?"

"Why shouldn't he believe it? You have no interest in going to parties or on dates, and we know you've been invited to some parties in the past and turned down the invitations."

"They weren't really invitations, and I know they were offered reluctantly and not sincerely," I added, looking at my father. I knew both he and Julie had engineered some of the most recent ones.

"What was the point of my doing all this for you," she said holding her hands out toward me, "if you're not going to take advantage of it? The money spent, the time and effort, why do you want this if you're going to avoid opportunities and drive away any interest in you? When I was your age, I couldn't wait for the weekend. You seem to be disappointed that school isn't seven days a week.

"And," she added after a pause, "you showed Allison that disgusting book that has a whole chapter on masturbation, even showing techniques."

I simply glared at her. Inside, my stomach felt as if a hive of wasps had broken and in their fierce anger they were stinging every organ in my body.

"As Julie said, Mayfair, Lauren's daughter claims you didn't deny their accusations," my father said. "Is that true?"

"Of course I didn't. I didn't take them seriously. I wouldn't take anything they said seriously and waste my time answering them. Who do they think they are, anyway? If there weren't any mirrors in the girls' room, they wouldn't go to the bathroom. They'd all be constipated."

He continued to stare at me. I saw a different look in his face, a mixture of worry and fear.

"You don't really believe any of this stupidity, do you, Daddy?"

"What either of us believes isn't important right now," Julie said.

"Excuse me? What my father believes about me is very important," I said.

"You're missing the point."

"That's because there isn't any."

"Let her speak, Mayfair," my father said, his voice full of fatigue and defeat.

"Okay, Julie. Speak. What else do you have to add to this idiotic conversation?"

"It's not so idiotic anymore. The other mothers are getting together and going to the principal to complain about you."

"Complain? You have to be kidding."

"I'm not kidding. They are worried about their daughters' . . . security."

"Security?" I looked at my father. "What am I now, a sex terrorist?"

"Joke about it all you want, but you can't even begin to imagine how embarrassing this is for me. For us," Julie quickly corrected. "I ask again, why did I do all that to help you with your appearance if you weren't interested in boys? Were you trying to get some girl interested in you? It's best if you tell us the truth."

"I'm not going to give any dignity to these stupid questions by answering them. Those girls never liked me. They know what I think of them. They would say anything they could that would hurt me." I stood up. "Believe me, I have more important things to do with my time right now than sit here and talk about what those girls say or think. Thinking is too high a process for them anyway."

"Mayfair," my father called as I started out.

"What?"

"You know that if you have these inclinations, you can tell us, right?"

I looked at Julie. She had her right hand over her heart as if she were about to recite the Pledge of Allegiance, and she was holding her breath. I was tempted to say I was gay just to see her have a heart attack.

How could she face her high-society friends at their lunches and charity galas? Maybe she would pack up and go, I thought. That was the biggest motivation for me to admit to it, but then I looked at my father and retreated.

"Of course I would tell you," I said. "If it's a fact, it doesn't do any good to deny it. I know I can say anything to either of you and always have. Right now, I'd like to say good night," I added, and walked out.

I left Julie stuttering and hyperventilating, but I didn't feel good about it. It didn't give me the usual satisfaction. I felt nauseated and tired. Despite the brave and angry face I had put on, I was crying inside. Look at how Julie had twisted up my father, I thought. She was insidious, inserting herself in the smallest of ways in the beginning, making changes in our house, the decor my mother had created. It was as if she thought she knew the pathway to get her out of my father's memory. She hated my mentioning her now. I had no doubt that if she could, she'd confiscate the pictures of her I had in my room. I knew my father and mother's wedding picture had been stashed in some carton in a closet.

Before Julie had come into our lives, something like this would have made my father and me both laugh. Neither of us would have worried about what the other parents thought of us or especially me. Although he wanted me to be more well rounded, my father used to believe that a very busy social life wasn't a priority, either for him or for me. It was different now. Julie had him rushing around to one social event after another. Everything was different now, and that difference was painful.

I knew this wouldn't end quickly. She was certain to moan and groan to my father about how worried she was about my influence on her precious little daughter, Allison. I realized that things would only get worse. Without telling my father, she was probably going to warn Allison not to undress in front of me or report to her immediately if I touched her. It was all very sad, but my sadness quickly turned into rage, rage against those girls in school, rage against Carlton James, whose ego I had bruised and who was surely encouraging the rumors about me now, and rage against Julie, who was like a sponge soaking up the gossip and then squeezing it out at my father's feet. She wouldn't stop until she drowned us both.

Unless I could find a way to stop her.

8

No one said any more to me that night, and my father didn't bring up anything about it while he was taking Allison and me to school, but you could have cut the air between us with a knife. The silence was that thick. I could see the curiosity in Allison's face. What was happening now? Apparently, Julie hadn't said anything to her yet, but despite what she might have told my father about protecting her daughter's innocent ears, I was confident that she would. It did occur to me that she actually believed it all.

I was angry enough not to put on the makeup Julie had shown me how to use and not to wear any of the new clothing she had helped me pick out, but I thought I would be cutting off my nose to spite my face if I did that. My hair was now my hair. There was no change possible, and besides, if I did revert to what I had looked like, I was sure the three bitches from *Macbeth* would see it as some sort of a victory. Maybe they would think they had forced me to come out of the closet or something and go bragging around the school about that.

When we arrived at school, my father let Allison get out first and then reached for my hand. "Just be careful how you handle this," he told me. "I know you're angry, but don't make it worse than it is."

"There's nothing to make worse, Daddy. Talk to your new wife, and tell her to chill out."

"Stop calling her my new wife, Mayfair. We've been married nearly three years."

"Whatever," I said.

"Watch yourself," he warned. "Your attitude isn't making any of this easier."

I watched him drive off and thought I was losing whatever I had left of him. Now it seemed so long ago when he had such pride in me. I could barely remember that wonderful smile on his face, that great laugh that once turned our dark days into bright sunshine. It was almost another lifetime.

Despite my bravado, when I looked at the school entrance, I hesitated. Knowing how well these girls could spread stories through their texting, phone calls, and emails, I was sure many more students were talking about me. It was like walking into a giant spider's web. Mr. Taylor was right about my ability to ignore my surroundings generally, but this was different. I could easily imagine the smug smiles, the gleeful eyes, and the waves of whispers following my every move. Yet turning and running would be just what they wanted me to do. They would be so satisfied, and so would Julie, I thought, despite the act she put on for my father.

Of course, I could stare down any of them if I chose to do so or ignore any comment. I could look right through them all. After a while, there would be nothing different about my school day here. However, I was certainly not naive enough to think that this would all go away quickly. I didn't believe they would go through with their threats, but Julie was right about the other mothers. I didn't think she knew it at dinner, but apparently, they had made an appointment with the principal this morning. Looking out the window in my first class, a window that faced the parking lot, I saw them all arrive, gather in the parking lot, and march toward the front entrance. To me it looked like they were carrying hatchets.

As I had suspected, the three bitches had begun spreading their rumors even before the day had ended yesterday and during the evening, and they were at it in a full-blown assault this morning to complement their mothers' meeting with the principal, Dr. Richards, who had a doctorate in education administration. Normally, I got along well with him, because, like Mr. Martin, our guidance counselor, he treated me as someone special and was somewhat in awe of my achievements. Many times, he'd make a point of seeing me in the library or the cafeteria to find out what I was currently reading or working on, and I could see that he sincerely enjoyed some of our conversations. But I knew that administrative positions, especially those in private schools like this one, were very political appointments. The parents who were wealthier and more powerful were usually big influences, many serving on the board of directors. Even though my father was very important, I didn't expect Dr. Richards would stick his neck out to defend me.

And boy, did the three bitches know that. They strutted with an air of confidence through the halls, attracting other students like flies to flypaper. There was so much whispering that it created a breeze, or more of a whirlwind. I could easily imagine how they were elaborating on our confrontation in the locker room and how Carlton was embellishing it with his interpretation of our conversation in the cafeteria.

I hadn't seen Mr. Taylor yet. I did pass his classroom once, but he was busy with some of his students. Because he was in the junior-high wing, I didn't think he was up on what was happening in the belly of the senior high, where all the lies and distortions were being digested.

Toward the end of third period, I was called to the principal's office. By now, almost every student in the senior high had heard something. Instead of everyone looking through me or ignoring me, now they were all watching me carefully, looking for some break in my armor of indifference. Maybe it was my imagination, but I thought even some of the teachers were looking at me differently, perhaps anticipating some sort of breakdown.

I was shocked to see Julie waiting in Dr. Richards's office. She had to have arrived after the bitches of *Macbeth*'s mothers. The mothers were gone by now, but Mr. Martin was in Dr. Richards's office waiting for me, too. For a moment, I stood in the doorway glaring at Julie. She looked like she had been crying. That didn't surprise me. She could turn on her crocodile tears as easily as turning on a faucet.

"What are you doing here?" I demanded, since my father wasn't with her.

"Come in, Mayfair," Dr. Richards said firmly.

Dr. Richards was a tall, lean man. He wasn't ugly, but he had hard, sharp facial features and rather ordinary brown eyes. Like most people who were taller than six feet four, he had a tendency to slouch. When he stood up to come around his desk, I couldn't help but think of my conversation with Mr. Taylor and his comment about my posture.

"Please," Dr. Richards said, extending his long arm and his hand toward the chair across from Mr. Martin and Julie. He took the chair beside the settee and sat across from me, too. They had a pot of tea, cups, and some biscuits on a tray.

Isn't this cozy? I thought.

"Would you like some tea? There are some biscuits, too," Dr. Richards said.

"No, thank you. High tea is a little later in the day for me," I said.

Julie smirked and looked away as if facing me nauseated her.

"Okay. It seems we have a little situation here," Dr. Richards began.

He glanced at Mr. Martin, who nodded. Everyone who cherished his or her job had to be in lockstep. That was for sure. When Julie turned back, she looked ready to burst into tears again. She took a very deep breath, looked up at the ceiling, and pressed her lips together to show us all how difficult this was and how hard she was fighting to keep her composure. If I didn't know her, I'd feel sorry for her, too, I thought.

"If it's a little situation, it shouldn't be much of a problem," I said.

Neither man smiled.

Julie shook her head slightly. "She's always like this," she said. "Smart remarks."

"Why did you call her and not my father?" I demanded.

"We called your home," Dr. Richards began.

"Your father is at a very important meeting today," Julie said. "I called him and told him I would handle this."

"Handle? What's there to handle?" I asked Dr. Richards.

"Some accusations have been made against you. Frankly, it's not important whether these accusations are true or not. We're not here to find that out."

"Why *are* we here?" I asked.

"We don't want you to be unnecessarily disturbed. We know how important a good, stable setting is for someone like you," Dr. Richards said.

"Someone like me?"

"You know what we mean, Mayfair. You're doing great work on your own. Everyone is proud of your accomplishments, your test results, the reactions from potential colleges . . ."

"What is it you want, Dr. Richards?" I asked. "It's

not necessary to set me up for some unpleasant conclusion. Get to the point."

"Can't you show some respect for your elders?"
Julie snapped.

"I thought I was being respectful by making whatever this is less painful by getting it over with, like a
root canal or something," I told her.

"She's right, Mrs. Cummings," Dr. Richards said.
He turned back to me. "I'll get right to the point. We
think that for the remainder of the year, you can be
excused from PE. Miss Hirsch can give you some sort
of exam later on and give you a passing grade." He
smiled. "I don't imagine you're particularly excited
about PE class, anyway."

I looked from him to Mr. Martin. So this was their
politically correct, diplomatic solution to an unpleasant problem. I felt certain that Dr. Richards had already promised the mothers of the three bitches that I
would be removed from PE and therefore any physical contact with their precious daughters. I stared,
shocked for a moment, fearing a scream in my throat
and thankful that it just stayed there. I swallowed it
back.

"Excused from exercise?" I asked as calmly as I
could manage. "No, *au contraire*, Dr. Richards. I think
exercise is very important. Didn't you ever hear that
expression, that healthy minds and healthy bodies go
hand in hand? My brain isn't in a glass case. It's in a
body that needs to be kept strong."

"Oh, yes, of course, you're right. Well, I suppose
we could arrange for you to use the gym when it's

free and . . ." He looked at Mr. Martin, who nodded quickly.

"Yes, there is an afternoon period when it's free."

"Good," Dr. Richards said. "It's yours along with whatever equipment you want to use."

"Isn't that dangerous? If I hurt myself without supervision, I mean? Julie might start a lawsuit."

"Don't be ridiculous," she said. "Frankly, under the circumstances, I think it's a good solution. My husband and I will sign any permission slip you need," she added for Dr. Richards. He smiled.

"Really? How surprising," I said. "So, let me understand this, Dr. Richards, understand exactly what's happened here. Some self-absorbed airheads make a ridiculous accusation against me, and the solution is to avoid confronting them, to accept what they say as true, and to find a way to please them and their carbon-copy mothers?"

No one spoke.

I looked at Julie. "This is the way you're representing my father and our interests? You'll sign a permission slip without conferring with him?"

"He doesn't need this sort of distraction right now, Mayfair. He has a lot on his mind with his business. None of us needs this distraction, and the solution is simple and avoids any more unpleasantness. Why be so obstinate?"

"I haven't found anything terribly unpleasant yet," I said. "Except the fact that I'm being judged without any sort of hearing concerning the evidence. I should at least get a trial by ordeal. Burn my hand and see if it heals in three days or something. If you want to go backward in the pursuit of justice, there are so many ways."

"Please, stop this. You know what I mean, what they mean. Why make this difficult when there's a good solution?"

"Good for whom?"

"The girls have agreed not to say another word about this," Dr. Richards said.

"There aren't any words left to say. They've said it all. They've embellished their disgusting and hateful stories so much that you'll have to wear boots to slosh through the hallways now."

"Then this will end it, get it off the front burners," he said.

"Front burners? That's an apt analogy, Dr. Richards, but I'm afraid it's already cooked."

"Please don't make this any more difficult," Julie begged, trying hard to sound as if she was really concerned about my interests. "You certainly don't care about these girls, and PE as a class is not important to you. You can exercise in our gym at home if you want. You don't even have to use the gym here at all. She can have more time to do her own thing, right, Dr. Richards?"

"Yes, that's true."

"So the conclusion here is that I should be grateful?"

No one spoke.

"You're not in the least bit curious about whether what the girls are accusing me of is true?" I asked Dr. Richards.

He smiled that plastic, political smile that administrators must practice in front of mirrors so they'd be prepared to confront boards of directors. "I think it's best we follow the military lead. Don't ask. Don't tell. Why get into such a sensitive topic? No one benefits."

"That doesn't exist anymore, and it wasn't a solution for the military anyway."

"We just want to stop it," Mr. Martin said. "Calm the atmosphere and protect you, too."

"But I just told you. They've already been spreading their lies, and they have done it in spades."

"They'll stop now," Dr. Richards said, putting on his firm face. "I can assure you of that."

"Just conduct yourself properly, and the nasty rumors will evaporate," Julie said. "Am I right?" She looked at Dr. Richards, and he smiled again and nodded.

"Precisely. I'll bring each of the girls involved in this matter into my office and spell it out to them very clearly."

"There, see?" Julie said.

I shook my head. "You're pathetic."

"It's not like you're going to run for class president," she said, sharply now. The dam had broken. There was no telling what else she would say. She was on a roll. I could see how pleased she was with herself and the solution. She might even be able to keep her friends.

"No, Mayfair has bigger things to do than that," Mr. Martin said, trying to sound like an appeaser. "You don't want to be distracted by this nonsense."

"No, I don't."

"Good," Julie said. "Then it's settled." She pounded her words down like a judge pounding a gavel to end all arguments.

She stood up quickly so there would be no question that this hearing had ended.

"Thank you very much, Dr. Richards, Mr. Martin. My husband and I appreciate the way you've handled this. Mayfair, be a good girl, now," she said, flashing a cold smile that would freeze someone's heart, and headed for the door. "I'll see you at the end of the day."

"No," I quickly replied. "I have something important after school. Just come for Allison."

"Fine," she said. She flashed another smile at Dr. Richards and Mr. Martin and then left.

"You come see me if you have any more problems with this," Dr. Richards said, returning to the chair behind his desk. "Or come see Mr. Martin."

"Yes," Mr. Martin said. "Anytime."

I rose to leave, feeling my legs half turn to lead. At the door, I turned back to them. "You didn't do those girls any favors today, Dr. Richards," I said. "You taught them that lying, being mean, is okay. They'll keep doing it until they hurt someone more than they hurt me, and they'll eventually hurt themselves."

"Don't you worry, Mayfair. We're keeping our eye on them. I'm letting them know my feelings about this. They'll behave themselves."

I smiled at them the way an adult would smile at a child who had said something very silly. "Why is it that the easiest person to fool is yourself?" I asked.

Neither replied.

I walked out. The bell had rung, and students were rushing to their next class. I felt like I was floating. I think I was in more pain than anger. I even felt like crying, letting my face flood with tears, and that surprised me. Tears did begin to burn my eyes as I fought them back. I stood still for a moment and took deep breaths to calm myself.

How could I have become the victim here? How could these tiny-minded, mean-spirited girls get the better of me? How smug would they be? I thought I looked like a clown now in my new hairdo, my new clothes, and these damn earrings in my pierced ears.

"Hey there," I heard. One look at the expression on Mr. Taylor's face told me he had found out about all this. He looked like he had been waiting to speak to me, in fact. "Keep your chin up. Stop by my classroom after school."

It was hard to understand why I would consider doing that. All I really wanted was to get as far away from this place as possible.

However, my father hadn't been here to protect me, Julie had practically brought the rope with which to hang me, and the school administrators were hiding behind closed doors, congratulating themselves on how they had squirmed out of a potentially sensational event and kept their lily-white reputations unblemished.

Who was there for me now to talk to?

"Why?" I asked.

"Just do it," he said sharply. "I'm on your side," he added, and then winked and walked away.

Before the end of the day, news about how I was being handled spread faster than the original rumors and lies. I did my best to ignore the smug smiles, but I couldn't subdue the anger raging inside me. I wasn't planning to have lunch in the cafeteria, but a girl in my class, Joy Hensley, tugged at my arm when the bell rang.

Joy was at least twenty pounds underweight, a classic anorexic. I wondered how she even had the energy to walk. Shrunken on that skull of hers was actually a pretty face starving to be fleshed out. Her eyes were a tired, dull gray, and her dark brown hair looked dry, with split ends. She was only about an inch shorter than I was. I often wondered about her, because she was probably ignored just as much as I was, for obviously different reasons.

I think the whole time I had been here, I had spoken no more than two words to her. If anything, she seemed more afraid to approach me than most people did. I had the feeling she thought I might say something even more devastating than the nasty comments other girls made. I once witnessed her being dressed down mercilessly by Joyce Brooker and Cora Addison in the locker room. They mocked her small bosom and the way her ribs pressed against her skin.

"What's your mother's food bill?" Joyce had begun. The question really took Joy by surprise, because Joyce sounded very interested and not critical.

"Why?"

"We're doing a survey for the school."

"I don't know," Joy said with the familiar look of panic on her face.

"Twenty cents?" Joyce asked.

"What? No."

Cora stepped up on her right side. "Why don't you eat?" she asked as if she cared. "Are you being used as a model at some medical school because the students can see your organs so easily?"

"No," Joy said, and tried to turn away.

"Are you getting help from the UN?" Cora asked.

"What?"

"You know, that organization that helps feed starving people all over the world?"

"No," Joy said.

"Would you like a cookie? I have an extra double chocolate chip."

"No, thanks."

By now, other girls had joined them and stood by smiling. They were like a pack of coyotes getting ready to kill and feast on a small rabbit. Joy looked around and saw that they were all feasting on her discomfort. She held her blouse up in front of her and searched for some escape route, but there was someone standing everywhere. "Leave me alone," she said.

"How do you pee? Don't you have trouble sitting on a normal toilet seat? You could fall into the water," Joyce said, and there was a roar of laughter.

I stood back, watching them as if I was observing another social ritual.

"Your mother shouldn't have to pay for gas when you're in the car with her," Cora said. "It takes energy to move weight, and in your case, a breeze could do it."

Joy shut down. She just stood there now, accepting

one derogatory comment after another, her eyes closed. When no one could think of anything more to say, they all moved away. She stood frozen for a few more moments and then hurried to get dressed and out of the locker room.

I hated what they had done to her, but I didn't particularly care to go to her defense. She had mental problems that created her physical problem, I thought. I knew she had lost her father in a terrible auto accident. I had overheard other students talking about that, but I wasn't eager to burden myself with someone else's psychological baggage at the time. I felt sorry for her, of course, but I didn't see any value in having her friendship.

"What?" I asked her now, surprised at how aggressively she had grabbed me.

"Can I talk to you, have lunch with you?"

"What about?"

"What happened to you," she said.

"Nothing happened to me."

"You're smarter than all of them, so I just wanted to know what you were going to do to get even," she said.

"What makes you think I care enough to do that?"

"I hope you do," she said. "They had no right to spread those stories about you, even if they're true."

I widened my eyes.

"I mean," she continued, "there's nothing wrong with you if they're true, right?"

It was as plain as day. She suspected that she was gay and was hoping that I was, too, or maybe that I could convince her that she wasn't. She was also hoping that somehow by avenging myself, I would be avenging her, too. "You're right," I said.

She smiled.

"Even if it was true, but it's not."

I decided to go to the cafeteria after all. Joy kept up with me and was right at my side when I entered. I looked around the room. There were many eyes on us. Conversations stopped and then started.

"I'm hungry," I said. "I didn't think I was going to be, but suddenly, I am." I went to the food line.

"I'll save you a seat over there," she said, nodding at a table.

"I doubt that you need to save it," I said. "It'll be there."

She smiled. When I got what I wanted, I went to the table. She had brought her own lunch, which was just a small plain yogurt and an apple. She started to eat her yogurt as if she had a sore throat. I could tell she wasn't even going to finish it.

"I watch you a lot," she told me.

"Watch me? What's that mean?"

"I mean, I see you working on other things in class and see how you work in the library by yourself. Nothing seems to bother you."

"Nothing here, maybe," I said. "I don't want to give them the satisfaction of thinking I care. Understand?"

"Yes," she said with disappointment.

"Time is important. You don't want to waste it on them. Work on improving yourself, helping yourself," I said. "Forget about them."

She nodded. "You're very pretty," she said. "I overheard them talking about you recently, and they were all very jealous. It must be nice to have people jealous of you for something."

I put my sandwich down. "Look, Joy, I'm no one to give anyone advice when it comes to social happiness around here, but the worst thing you can do is fall into a pit of self-pity. Get a hold of yourself. Gain some weight. Is your mother addressing your problems?"

"Addressing?"

"Getting you medical help?"

"Oh. No. My mother just tells me to finish my dinner, but she doesn't say anything when I don't. She always gives me too much."

I shook my head. *Too much to you*, I thought, *but probably just enough to anyone else*. "Okay. I'll do some research for you and get you information to give your mother. She has her head in the sand. You should be seeing a therapist, at least."

She laughed. "My mother would be terribly embarrassed if I did that."

"She's not embarrassed about you now?"

She lost her smile.

Suddenly, I thought of something. I looked around the cafeteria and saw the way some of the girls and boys were whispering and looking at us. How well known was it, I wondered, that Joy was gay? Had she had some sort of experience with someone else from school?

Possibly what I was doing now by sitting and talking with Joy was confirming the rumors the bitches from *Macbeth* had spread.

"I have to go," I told her, ironically not even coming close to finishing my own food. "I have something to do before my next class." I rose.

"Can I call you?" Joy asked.

"What for?"

"To talk," she said.

"I don't have time to talk on the phone," I told her, and took my tray to the trash bin and the shelf for trays. I didn't look back when I left.

What am I doing? I thought when I was halfway down the hall. I stopped. *It's like I'm running away. I'm letting them push me around.* Why was I fleeing from Joy? I was so angry at myself. *Damn them.* Maybe I would find some way to get back at them after all.

I was in deep thought about it for the remainder of the afternoon. Every chance they got, one of them would say something nasty close enough for me to hear. I didn't react to any of it, but I was fuming inside. By the time the last period ended, I felt like strangling someone. I had told Julie that I was doing something after school. I needed more time before confronting her, especially in front of my father. It was then I remembered Mr. Taylor's invitation and went to his room.

9

"Please, close the door," he said when I stepped into his classroom. He smiled and loosened his tie. "I need a break from the racket. Sometimes I wish I were teaching in a school for mutes."

He wasn't wrong about the racket. The students were leaving the building. Most of them always acted as if it were a fire drill, especially the junior high. They charged at the doors like prisoners released, their screams and shouts bouncing off the hall walls.

I closed the door.

"Glad you decided to stop by," he said. "I was hoping you would."

He got up and took one of the seats at a student desk. Then he patted the desk beside him, and I took that seat. Now that I was here, I felt very foolish and nervous. Why had I come? He was a junior-high English teacher. What did I expect to gain? Was I flirting? Was I so thick when it came to any of this that I wouldn't recognize what I was doing? Could he see it?

It was like I had swallowed a ping-pong ball whole and it was bouncing in my stomach. Oddly, I hadn't felt nearly as nervous in Dr. Richards's office, and he was someone who was trained to strip me mentally. Somehow, though, when Mr. Taylor looked at me, I felt naked.

"So, I hear through the grapevine that you're having a particularly bad day," he began.

"I'd say the school's having a worse day than I am."

"Well, whether you like it or not, you're part of the school. Tell me what happened, what really happened. By the time anything gets to this wing of the building, it's quite distorted, I'm sure. What actually caused all this commotion?"

Commotion, situation, whatever word was used, didn't do it justice. I looked down at the floor. His asking me about it stirred my rage the way a wild beast that had finally quieted down might burst into an angry roar when poked. My body tightened with the frustration I felt. He misread my silence.

"I'm not looking for juicy gossip," he said. "I know some of my colleagues feed on that, but I have a feeling you weren't treated fairly, and this whole thing, what's happening to you, is more important than gossip."

"Treated fairly? You've been here long enough to know that fairness is not the first consideration, not in a school where donors put in enough money to get their names on gyms and pools. Justice comes in only one color here, green."

He laughed. "Okay. What happened?" he asked, softening his tone. "How did this start?"

"How did it start? What happened was that I didn't turn into melting butter when the school's Don Juan, Carlton James, lowered himself to approach me in the cafeteria and suggest that we get together at his house after school. I believe his idea of a get-together is literally that. He thinks it's all about plugs and sockets."

He widened his smile. "That's very good. Plugs and sockets. I would have loved to be a fly on that cafeteria wall when he came on to you. I know who he is, of course. Girls trail behind him, waiting for him to drop a smile in their direction. They scoop it up like beggars hoping for a handout of love."

"You have time to notice that sort of thing?"

"I'm just being observant. We're all supposed to be observant. It comes with the job description. From what you're saying, I gather he struck out completely and left with his head in his hands."

"It was more like a balloon losing all its air. And I think he had more than his head in his hands."

"I'll bet," he said with that wide grin again. "He met more than his match when he tangled with you. And then what happened? I mean, how did it lead to all this?"

"Simple. Not being one who gracefully takes rejection, Carlton fanned the flames of hot gossip that were obediently and loyally spread by the three bitches from *Macbeth*, gossip that would make him look better, too."

"Three bitches? Not the three witches?"

"The witches at least had a purpose in Shakespeare's play, prophecy. These three just stir the pot of frogs and newts."

He shook his head. "I love it. So who are they?"

"Joyce Brooker, Cora Addison, and Denise Hartman."

"Oh, yeah. Now that you mention it, I have heard them mumbling, 'Fair is foul and foul is fair,' in the hallway. So they were the ones who mixed the witches' brew, went home, and told their parents you were making unhealthy sexual advances on them?"

"On them, I can't imagine any sexual advances possibly being healthy," I said.

He laughed again. "What fools to take you on. So?"

"We had some words in the locker room. They were trying to find out . . ."

"What?"

"If I was seeing someone from outside the school."

"Are you?" He raised his hands when I looked hard at him. Was this something he should be asking? "Just trying to understand the whole picture. Whether you are or not isn't my business. I will say I had that suspicion myself. Not that I'd blame you," he quickly added. "You're so far ahead of the boys here they probably look like tykes to you."

"Am I?"

He tilted his head. "I could tell that just from talking with you for a few minutes, Mayfair."

"I'm not seeing anyone from outside the school, anyone older," I said. "Nevertheless, they started to accuse me of being interested in *them*, assuming that if a girl turned down the school's heartthrob, she had to be gay. They accused me of paying too much attention to their naked bodies."

He unbuttoned the top button of his shirt. "I see. That's it? That was enough to cause all this commotion?"

"Mothers rushing to the defense of daughters in danger can be very persuasive, especially if their combined net worth is more than that of most third world countries."

"And what ruling has come down from the high command?"

"I'm excused from PE for the year and banned from the girls' locker room, where the alleged incidents took place. This is called a politically acceptable compromise because it's assumed I didn't want to go to PE."

He shook his head. "Makes you look like the bad one here."

"Tell me about it."

"Your parents approved of that?"

"Only my father's new wife appeared at the hanging."

"And put up no argument when they made that so-called compromise?"

"She probably cowrote it."

"Oh, I see. I'm sorry."

"That's all right. I didn't anticipate much more. Nothing to be sorry about, Mr. Taylor. I'm actually not brokenhearted about missing PE classes, and avoiding the locker room might prevent athlete's foot."

He laughed again. "Call me Alan," he said. "When we're alone in the building, I mean." Then he turned very serious. "I know that it's painful for you to see these other girls get it over on you, but joking about it doesn't help really, does it?"

"I suppose I can say it keeps me from crying, so it's the better choice."

"This sucks," he said, surprising me with his burst of anger. "It's why I keep thinking about looking for a job in a public school. There, everyone's equally abused. If there's anyone who deserves the full respect and support of this school's administration, it's you, Mayfair. I know for a fact that they brag about you whenever they can."

"Yeah, well, they will probably stop doing that. Politically risky."

He moved his hand close to mine, and before I could pull it back, he put his over mine. "You're putting on a good show, Mayfair, but I'm sure you feel as if you're all alone here, left to drift any which way, especially now. I've heard the talk about you in the faculty room. No one feels up to the challenges you present. You have to be pretty frustrated with how you're treated in and out of the classroom."

"If I gave it any real thought, I guess I would be."

"I'm sure you think about it. I don't have your IQ," he continued, "but I was pretty much at the head of my class in high school, and that cost me some popularity. It's stupid, but I intimidated some of the other students. I can't even begin to imagine how stupid you make your classmates feel."

"I don't have to do that. They do it for themselves," I said. "Stupidity is on sale here every day."

"You do have a great sense of humor, Mayfair."

"Sense of irony. There's a difference."

"Right, right."

He still had his hand over mine. Suddenly, he looked down at our hands and began to gently play with my fingers. I wanted to pull my hand away from his, but I didn't want to embarrass him or make him feel bad. I was enjoying his sympathy for me, maybe too much.

"There's no reason two people, two adult people, and that's what I consider you, an adult, can't treat each other like adults even in a place like this. I'm not your actual teacher here. For all practical purposes, I'm just like someone else you might meet on the outside. I wish you would seriously consider me your adult friend. That's what I would like to consider you."

Slowly, I pulled my hand back. "Thank you," I said.

"I mean it. I'm serious when I say that sometimes I feel as if I'm on an island here. Knowing that I have you to talk to occasionally will be something to look forward to."

"I'm not the best at making small talk, Mr. —"

"Alan."

"Alan."

"We won't make small talk. I promise. So," he said, glancing up at the wall clock, "I guess you missed your ride home. Your stepmother usually picks up you and your stepsister, Allison, right?"

Was there anything about me he didn't know? I guessed he was looking at me every chance he got.

"Bus duty," he said, seeing the puzzled look on my face. "I have to watch the critters board safely."

"Oh. Right. No, I didn't miss it. I told my father's new wife not to wait for me today."

"Why do you keep saying 'new wife'?"

"I'll never think of her as anything else."

"I see. No love lost, as they say."

"No love lost."

"Did you tell her not to wait after I asked you earlier to stop by? I mean, I'm flattered you remained after school, but . . ."

I saw where he was going. He thought I really wanted to see him, that perhaps I was hoping or expecting that he would take me home. "No. I had already made different plans," I said. I stood up. "Thanks for the talk, Mr. Taylor."

"Alan, please, when we're alone," he said. "Hearing you call me Mr. Taylor makes me feel older than I am."

"Okay. Thanks, Alan."

"I could give you a ride if you need one," he said, standing. "It's not a problem. I just have a few more things to do here, and . . ."

"That's all right. I've already made other arrangements," I said.

The disappointment on his face reminded me of Carlton James's reaction in the cafeteria. Young or old, when men didn't get the reaction from a female that they wanted or expected, they all looked the same, like little boys told to put away their toys and go to sleep.

"Wait," he said, and returned to his desk. He jotted something on a piece of paper and brought it to me.

"That's my home phone number. It's unlisted. Kids are always pulling prank calls on teachers, but you can call me anytime you want, day or night, Mayfair. I'll be there to listen, and if you want me to come get you or anything, you just call. Anytime."

Anytime? I wanted to ask him if he had a life away from this building. Didn't he have a girlfriend? How could he be so good-looking and not have a line of beautiful women at his door? Why would he be available anytime? Would it be ungrateful of me to ask?

Another thing occurred to me. Had he ever given his phone number to any other female student? Suddenly, everything about him became important. Was this his first teaching position? If not, why did he leave the first one? Where was he from? Did he have family in Los Angeles or somewhere else in California? Brothers or sisters? Had he ever been married or engaged? What sorts of friends did he have? Were they all teachers? How would he explain giving so much attention to a high-school student?

Since most of the girls here didn't talk much to me, I was at a disadvantage when it came to knowing these sorts of things about our teachers, but I did want to know more about him, if not for any other reason than to be careful.

It was so much easier for someone to get lost out there when a school was located in a city, especially one as large as Los Angeles. My imagination began to run a bit wild. Maybe after he left the building, he turned into a serial killer or was part of some sex cult.

And then I paused and thought how ridiculous it

was of me to imagine such things. It showed how this place was getting to me. I was beginning to think like some of these airheads. If any school did a good background check on its employees, it would be this one. The rich could afford paranoia, and this school catered to the wealthy.

"Thank you," I said, and put the paper with his number in my purse.

"I'm here for you," he said. "Remember that."

I nodded. He watched me leave. I closed the door behind me and walked slowly down the hall toward the front exit. I heard his door being opened, but I didn't look back to see if he was watching me walk away. It made me too self-conscious about my body. I felt as if I were in a summer thunderstorm.

Hot lightning sizzled around my heart. No man, no boy, had ever touched me the way Mr. Taylor just had. When he put his hand over mine and began to play with my fingers, it wasn't a fatherly gesture or just a friendly one. It was pure, raw sex. I could feel the heat moving through his hand and into mine. It stirred me. Fight back as hard as I tried, I couldn't keep the tingle from traveling like electricity up and down my spine and into my thighs and breasts. All sorts of sexual images flashed like lightning bolts against the darkness of my deepest thoughts. The images I had shown Allison created a stream of erotic pictures resembling a trailer for a movie with the title *Mayfair Cummings Loses Her Virginity*.

But there was thunder, too, loud crashes of warning hammering at my heart. Alan Taylor was a young man, yes, but no matter how I tried to rationalize it away, I was still legally a minor, and he was an adult with an influential position when it came to young women at the school. Besides the legal and ethical aspects, I had to confess to myself that he had an unfair advantage. He was a man of some experience who easily saw my vulnerability. How seamlessly he could make the transition from concerned faculty adviser to my first lover if I didn't heed the sound of thunder. But did I want to?

I really hated being vulnerable and innocent, because I was at a disadvantage. All the books and articles about sex that I had read did not prepare me for these feelings. I hated that more than anything. Information was always my steadfast protector, my God. I worshipped with encyclopedias, not Bibles, but here this was failing me.

And that made me angry, but to be honest, I wanted to be angry. Anger helped me avoid dealing with my inner feelings. How dare Mr. Taylor take advantage of me at one of my weakest moments? He knew I wasn't going to run to the principal or to my father to tell them about him. He certainly knew I wouldn't tell Julie. On top of what had just happened to me because of the three bitches, my creating another scandal would be too much. I wouldn't have any credibility, and it was no good to pretend that didn't matter. I still had to attend school here, and my father still had a life in this community. There was nothing to do right now but ignore what I could ignore and concentrate on my studies as usual.

I walked out and away from the building. I didn't want Mr. Taylor to see me get into a taxi after he had offered to drive me home. I sensed that he wouldn't take that as a rejection so much as a challenge. He would want me to understand that I didn't have to be bashful or embarrassed to ask him for help. Ironically, my refusing his offer would only encourage him more.

And yet I would be lying if I didn't admit to myself that I was more than flattered by his attention. The woman who had blossomed inside me couldn't help but continue to wonder what it would be like to be with such a good-looking adult man. I had read and understood enough to know that it would be quite different from being with Carlton James, even though Carlton saw himself as every girl's dream lover.

Carlton would go at it all too quickly, clumsily. The book I had given Allison explained the mechanics well. I knew that males often cared only about pleasing themselves and did so before the female even got started. In short, I knew Carlton wouldn't take lovemaking as seriously as a man like Mr. Taylor surely would or, at least, should. With Carlton, there would be no real romance, just groping and satisfying egos. For most of the girls, if not all of them here, that would be enough, but it wasn't enough for me. I wasn't looking to neck in the back of a movie theater or be with a boy in the rear of his car. Alan Taylor would know that, had to know that, otherwise he wouldn't have taken the risk of talking to me like this and making the subtle proposals he was making.

Shouldn't I be more attracted to that, to someone

who saw me for who I was, someone mature enough to handle this forbidden relationship?

When the three bitches accused me of being gay and making them uncomfortable in the locker room, I was angry, of course, but I couldn't deny that I had wondered about myself from time to time. I learned that it wasn't an uncommon thing for someone young to consider.

Maybe I *was* gay.

Maybe I *was* looking at those girls in the locker room.

I had read up on this once, and comments in a psychological abstract returned to me. If you thought back to your earliest memories and realized you'd always been different, you might be gay, but that didn't necessarily mean you were. However, I couldn't deny that I've always been different. I certainly didn't fit the stereotype of a gay woman, but not fitting a stereotype doesn't mean it's not true. And Albert Kinsey, a pioneer in human sexuality research, had determined that many people were in between.

Teenagers often felt strongly about members of their own sex and were aware of the attractiveness of someone of their own sex. I was keenly aware of how attractive Joyce Brooke was, but again, that didn't mean I was gay.

Did I drive Carlton away because his aggressiveness threatened me? Was I really turned off by him, or was I turned on too quickly and completely? Did I know in my heart that if I had gone with him to his home, I'd be unable to stop him from seducing me? Maybe deep down inside, that was what I really wanted, and I was afraid of myself more than I was of him.

Was I conflicted about Mr. Taylor for the same reasons?

Was Julie right? Was I infatuated with books and articles about sex because I was unsure about my own sexuality? I fantasized about boys. Wasn't that enough?

These thoughts kept the summer storm alive inside me. I didn't even realize how far I had walked until I reached the strip mall, where there were restaurants, a drugstore, a dry cleaner, and a mailing outlet. I'd call for a taxi and have the driver pick me up here, I thought, and walked toward the Italian restaurant.

Just as I stepped onto the sidewalk, I heard a car horn and turned to see Mr. Taylor pull into a parking spot. He waved and got out quickly. "What are you doing here?"

"I was going to meet someone here," I quickly replied.

"Oh. Secret date, huh?"

"Something like that. Maybe it was too secret."

He smiled and stood gazing at me with his hands on his hips. "Long walk from the school. Either you or your date were being very careful," he said.

"You're reading too much into it. Besides, walking is good for thinking, and right now, I have a lot of thinking to do."

"That it is. I don't do enough of it, of both. By the time I get home, I'm mentally drained from being on the front lines. That's what I call the junior high, the front lines. My students are like little hand grenades. When the bell rings to start class, it's like someone pulled the pin. I don't open my mouth before hands go up asking if what I said was important and should be put in their notebooks. There's enough energy in the room to launch a satellite into space."

"Sounds exhausting."

"Mentally, it is." He nodded toward the other restaurant, which was really more of a bar. "The truth is, I sometimes stop there for a while to have a drink and come back to earth." When I didn't say anything, he added, "Only one drink, of course."

It occurred to me that if he was going to stay here for a while, he would surely see the taxi arrive to pick me up. *Get out of this, genius*, I told myself.

Unless, you don't want to get out of it.

The summer thunderstorm inside me was gone. I felt more relaxed, maybe simply because I was out of the school building. Out here, I did feel as though we were equals of a sort. He was still a teacher, but he was never my teacher, and there were no administrators watching us from doorways.

"You're really not meeting someone, are you?" he asked, tilting his head a bit to the side and narrowing his eyes when I hesitated. "You just wanted to run away."

"I suppose," I said.

"Don't blame you." He looked at the bar and smiled. "How about we take a ride and look at the ocean? Nothing more calming than the sea on a day like this," he said. "Unless, of course, you're supposed to be home. I wouldn't want to be responsible for your getting into more trouble."

"I don't have to be anywhere," I said. "My father stopped putting curfews on me years ago."

"I bet. So?" He moved to the passenger side of his car and reached for the handle.

This was it, I thought, that great moment of decision. Should I fall back on being a teenage girl, or should I step forward and be a woman? For most of my life, I was so self-confident. I thought I would always make the right decisions, because I was so well informed and so perceptive. What I didn't count on, what I didn't consider, was what the woman in me would demand. Sometimes that had little to do with anything more than pure, raw feelings. "Okay," I said, and got in when he opened the door.

10

He got in very quickly, as if I might change my mind. Then he smiled, started the engine, and backed out of the parking space. Both of us glanced at the cars that rushed by, to see if any of the school administrators were driving past. I told myself that this was still very innocent. He just saw me walking along and offered a ride. They would certainly believe I had left the building in a rage.

"This looks like a new car," I said, running my hand over the leather.

"It is. I got it four months ago. I inherited a little money when my father died. He had remarried and left most of his money to his second wife. He had taken on the responsibility of raising her son, too. The kid's fourteen and a couple of handfuls, as I understand it. I haven't been close to the boy and probably won't see either of them given my father's passing."

"So you're an only child, too?"

"As far as I know," he said, smiling. "My mother wondered."

"What happened to her?"

"She died when I was in my teens, pancreatic cancer. She was just forty-five. I wasn't much older than you are. Chronological age, that is. I understand your mental age is off the charts."

"The latest research suggests that our brains never stop growing as long as we use them, learn new things, and keep challenging ourselves."

"Yes, I think that's true."

"And your father remarried, too."

"See? We have a great deal in common," he said. "Now all I need is fifty more points on my IQ."

"Believe me, you're better off not having them," I said.

"You feel that way now, but . . ." He looked at me. "And you won't change your mind later," he said, and we both laughed. I felt my body soften and defrost from the icy numbness that had overcome it most of the day.

He made some turns and headed west. As we drove along, he began to tell me more about himself. He was brought up in San Francisco, went to college in the Midwest and then took his first teaching position in a public school in Los Angeles. When the opportunity arose to teach in our private school, he jumped at it.

"I'm not making as much money, but I'm a lot happier with the class size, despite how I sound when I talk about it. At least the parents are involved.

Maybe too much," he added, obviously thinking about my day.

When we reached the Pacific Coast Highway, he pulled into the parking lot at the Will Rogers State Beach.

"You ever just walk on the beach?" he asked me.

"Rarely."

"You up for it now?"

"Yes," I said.

I really hadn't done it since my mother had died. Julie hated the beach, because the sun gave her wrinkles and the sand got into everything, including her hair. Consequently, my father never took us. Allison went with her friends occasionally, but, like her mother, she was too finicky to enjoy it and always came home complaining.

We got out of his car. There was a soft, cool breeze coming from the southwest. In the distance, I could see what looked like a cargo ship sliding along the horizon. Off to the north toward Malibu were two small sailboats. We're attracted to the sea because it takes us out of this world, I thought, off the land and far from our troubles and worries. I envied the ones on the sailboats.

"It is beautiful out there," he said, seeing how I gazed longingly at the soft blue in the distance.

"Yes."

"Ever sail?"

"No."

"I have a friend with a boat. I go out with him once or twice a month. Maybe I'll take you along sometime."

I looked at him as if he were promising to run off with me or something.

He laughed. "I will," he insisted.

We walked on.

"So, have you thought much about what you want to do? What you'll major in when you go to college? I bet you want to be a doctor, huh?" he asked as he walked.

"No, I don't think so. Maybe I'll go into bio research. I'm not sure yet."

"No hurry, I guess. I'm sure you're interested in many things. You just have to find the one that holds the most passion for you."

"Is that what you did?"

"Me? I thought I would write the great American novel but woke up days later looking at the same blank page. I enjoy teaching, though, when I have good students. At least at our school, we don't have the sort of discipline problems they have in public schools, and I don't have to spend so much time just getting the class civilized."

I laughed.

"Feeling a little better?"

"Yes," I said.

"You know, it's better if we take off our shoes and socks." He paused to do it, and so did I.

We went close enough to the water to get our feet wet.

"Yow, that's cold!" he cried, and retreated. I stayed with it a bit longer. "Aren't your ankles getting numb?"

"Maybe," I said. "I can't feel them. Does that have anything to do with it?"

He laughed, and I joined him on the softer sand.

For a while, neither of us spoke, and then I asked, "Do you have a girlfriend?"

"A couple," he said, smiling. "No one I consider serious. I'm in no rush."

"Don't any of them consider *you* seriously?"

"Maybe."

"That doesn't matter?"

He told me about a romance he had in college and how it had gone sour when his girlfriend went out secretly with a friend of his. "I guess that's made me gun-shy," he said.

His apparent honesty and willingness to talk about himself put me at ease, maybe too much at ease. When we were back at his car, he took out a towel he had in his trunk so we could wipe the sand off our feet and out from between our toes. He insisted that I sit so he could do my feet.

"Better rub them and get the circulation back since you spent all that time in the cold ocean."

"It's not that bad," I said, but he insisted.

"Nice feet," he told me. "You forgot to paint your toenails."

"I didn't forget."

He smiled, did his own feet, and got back into the car. "Still feeling better?" he asked.

"Yes, thank you."

"The magic of the sea," he said. "As long as you don't put your naked feet in it at this time of the year.

Actually, the Pacific is never warm enough for me unless I'm down in Mexico, way down."

We rode along quietly for a while, and then he slowed down.

"You have to get home?"

"I told you. I have no curfews, day or night."

"Right. I live right up here," he said. He looked at his watch. "What do you say to our getting a pizza and eating it at my apartment? I have a patio that looks out at the ocean. Of course," he said when I didn't respond immediately, "if that makes you uncomfortable . . ."

"No, it doesn't."

"Great."

He took that to mean yes, and I didn't say otherwise. He asked me what I wanted on the pizza and then called his favorite takeout place and ordered it with some salads. His car had Bluetooth, so I heard the conversation and understood that they knew him well at this restaurant.

"As you can tell," he said, "I'm not much for cooking. My best recipe is takeout. What about you?"

"I toy with it sometimes, but we have a maid who does most of our cooking and baking. We've had a few, actually. Julie, my father's new wife, as you know I like to call her, is hard on servants. She wears them down the way a driver who keeps his foot on the brake pedal wears down brake pads."

He laughed. "You sure come up with surprising comparisons."

"Not that surprising to me," I said.

"I bet. You really do fascinate me, Mayfair."

Normally, when someone said that to me, I shrugged it off. I had gotten used to hearing it, but the way he said it reached deeper inside me and stirred me sexually.

Our pizza was almost ready when we arrived. I waited in the car while he went in to get it. I had to admit it smelled delicious when he returned with it. Minutes later, we pulled into his apartment building's underground garage. He told me to leave my books in the car.

"That way, you won't forget anything when I take you home," he said.

"I never forget anything," I said, but I left them.

We went to the elevator and up to the eighth floor. He had a very nice marble-floored apartment with a living room that had a patio facing the ocean. I looked around. He didn't have any family photos up or photos of any women. The artwork was the sort you could pick up in a department store to work into your decor. I did see that he had his college diploma framed. While I was gazing about, he put on a Three Tenors—Luciano Pavarotti, Plácido Domingo, and José Carreras—CD.

"Is that all right?" he asked. "It's not rap or rock."

"I listen to it often," I said. "I enjoy many operas."

"Figured you might."

Was I that easy to read and predict? Was that because I wasn't as impulsive and reckless as most girls my chronological age?

He got our pizza ready and called me into his

dining room, which, aside from the china cabinet and one small table with a miniature grandfather clock on it, was also spartan. I saw a bottle of Chianti on the table.

"I'd rather have wine than beer with my pizza. Do you drink wine?"

"Occasionally," I said. I really hadn't drunk much wine. "Julie, my father's new wife, fancies herself a wine connoisseur, but she doesn't know the difference between a syrah and a pinot noir."

"You know about wine, too?" he asked.

"There are five basic types: red, white, and rosé; what is called fortified wine or dessert wine, which has extra alcohol; and sparkling wine and champagne. She buys sparkling wine and calls it champagne. Real champagne has to come from the Champagne province in France. I believe it's a trademarked name."

He stood with the opened bottle of Chianti in his hand, his mouth slightly open.

"And you know all this without drinking much of it?"

"I know about nuclear energy, too, but I've never created it or built a bomb," I replied.

He laughed, shrugged, and poured two glasses. "Well, I've gone this far. I might as well corrupt the morals of a minor who knows more about it than I do and give you some wine."

Maybe because he said that more than anything else, I eagerly drank the wine. I drank it too quickly, emptying my glass before his was a quarter empty. He poured me another. While we ate, he asked me more about my family life. "So tell me, why do you keep calling Julie your father's new wife? It sounds as if they just got married, but from what you're telling me, it's been years."

"She'll never be anything more to me," I said. "I don't care how many years they stay married."

He nodded. After we ate, he poured another glass for each of us, and we went out onto his patio to watch the sun setting.

"If you want to call home and let them know anything, go ahead," he told me.

I glanced at him. Was he testing me? Did he really mean I could tell them I was at his apartment having dinner and wine with him? The small smile on his face told me that he knew I wouldn't.

"It's not necessary," I said.

It really was necessary, but I wanted my father to worry. I wanted him to know how unhappy I was about what Julie had let Dr. Richards do to me. Let them believe for a while that I might have run off in a rage.

We finished the bottle of wine. It seemed to me that I had drunk most of it, because I drank faster than he did, and he kept filling my glass. He brought the empty bottle and the glasses in, and then I stood up, expecting he would now take me home. I remember feeling so relaxed. It was as if my whole body had turned into a down pillow. He met me in the living room, and for a moment, he just stood there looking at me. Maybe I really heard him say it, or maybe I was imagining it from the look in his eyes, but I walked up to him after I heard, "You have no idea how pretty you are, Mayfair, especially with a little flush in your cheeks. Don't let anyone tell you otherwise."

I'll always regret not doing this if I don't, I thought, *so I think I will.*

I kissed him. When I leaned back, I saw his look of surprise.

"I'm sorry," I said. "I didn't mean—"

"No," he said, putting his finger gently on my lips. "You meant it. It's all right."

Then he kissed me, but not like I had kissed him, not a quick snap of my lips against his.

I closed my eyes and still had them closed when he stopped. He didn't let go of my shoulders but brought my lips to his again, this time pressing a little harder. I felt his tongue press into my mouth. For a moment, only a moment, I thought I would tear myself out of his hands and rush to the door, but when his right hand went to my waist and his lips moved down to the side of my neck, I heard myself moan and felt my body soften even further.

"You're so beautiful," he kept whispering. "So beautiful."

He put his left arm around my waist and then his right arm under my legs and lifted me as if I were a little girl. I didn't protest. I had no doubts about what he was doing, but I didn't resist. Instead, I rested my head against his chest, and I could feel how that excited him, quickened his heartbeat. He carried me to his bed and lowered me gently.

My thoughts were spinning and tumbling over

one another in my head. He stood there looking down at me.

"Do you want it to stop?" he asked.

I shook my head. Then I watched him slowly undress, his eyes never leaving mine. It was as if his hands belonged to someone else. He loosened and took off his tie, dropping it to the floor, where he dropped his shirt, his pants, and then his underwear. He stood completely naked, enjoying the way I looked him over and reacted.

"Should I?" he asked, kneeling beside the bed and fingering the buttons of my blouse.

"Yes," I whispered. I hadn't had someone else undress me since I was three, and my mother would stand aside and watch how carefully I took off my clothes, folding them neatly.

I watched his face, the movements in his lips and his eyes, as he slowly, almost as if he wanted to tease himself, slipped my bra off me. He stared down at me so intensely.

"It's not a pot of gold," I said, and he laughed.

"To me, it is."

With continued surgical skill, he finished undressing me, taking his time to make little discoveries about my body, a dimple here, a birthmark there, the smoothness of my skin, and the soft rise of my breasts as my own breath quickened.

The wine kept me just a little confused, but I was thinking like someone who was observing and not participating. It was almost as if I were watching a medical procedure. I was fascinated with his every move, how he continued stroking, kissing, and exciting me, and then how he stopped, remembered his protection, which was just as much my protection, and returned to me, again feasting on me with his eyes first.

"You're like a Greek goddess," he said, and took his time kissing every part of me, moving down to my toes and then up again, pressing between my thighs, moving over the rise of my stomach and nudging my breasts ever so gently with his lips.

I felt as if I were sinking into the mattress, oozing out of my body. Any thought of restraint was crushed to bits the moment it raised its head or began to voice itself. Every picture, every description of this moment that I had read and seen, did it no justice. How foolish I was to believe I knew anything about my own body when it came to what was now happening to me. I thought this was why sex education in school was such a weak fortress against passion and desire. The teacher shouldn't be using textbooks. He or she should be reading from great novels that aroused their readers. Sex education should bring students real-life scenes and then describe what should or should not be done.

I did nothing to stop him, and when he was in me, kissing me, chanting about his pleasure and my beauty, I let myself fall back into the rush of my own exquisite sensuality until I began to ride one wave of pleasure after another. I was embarrassed by how I moaned and cried. Actual tears streamed down my face. My heart was pounding so fast and hard it seemed like one long beat. When it all ended, I felt as if I were still dangling in space, until my blood calmed and I fell back into myself.

Without speaking, he rose and left the bedroom. I lay there, still naked, trying to recapture my normal breathing. Finally, when I had, I began to dress slowly, almost reluctantly. I watched the doorway, hesitating, hoping he would return to make love to me again, but to my surprise and disappointment, he was also dressed when he returned. He had his hair neatly brushed and looked as if he had nothing to do with what had gone on in his bedroom, almost like he was surprised to discover me in his apartment.

I hurried to dress myself now.

"How are you doing?" he asked.

"All right," I said.

"You surprised me. I really thought you were a virgin."

"I am. I was," I said. "I've never been with anyone like this. Do you want me to describe the female anatomy and why I didn't bleed?"

"No, no," he said, smiling and shaking his head. "That's a little too much information right now. Why don't you get refreshed in the bathroom while I clean up out here, and then I'll take you home. Curfew or no curfew, I'm sure you've got them wondering by now."

I didn't say anything. I went into the bathroom and looked at my flushed face. I brushed my hair, ran a cold washcloth over my forehead and cheeks, and then finished fixing my clothes. I still felt a little dazed.

He was waiting anxiously when I stepped out of the bathroom.

Because this was the first time I had been with any man, I wasn't sure what to expect. Would he start a review of our lovemaking to tell me how wonderful it had been? Would he offer some sort of apology, perhaps for moving too quickly? Would he ask me to be sure to keep this a secret? Would he say or do something to make absolutely sure I was all right with what had happened between us?

All these thoughts seemed very reasonable to me, but he acted on none of them. Instead, he began talking about the apartment, how long he had been in it, what the other tenants were like, and where he would really like to live. In his car, he went on and on about the commute to school and how it took him nearly twenty more minutes on some days.

I had to keep reminding myself that we had just made very passionate love. Was this normal? Was I making too much of it? Was that a sign of immaturity?

"One thing you can never anticipate in Los Angeles is the traffic. There's no rational way of figuring it out. Why Tuesdays are busier than some Mondays drives me nuts. You have your license yet?" he asked.

"No. I'm getting it this year," I said.

"You'll see what it's like. I know teenagers can't wait to drive, to have their own cars, but it's not long before you realize you were better off having someone drive you places."

Suddenly, I'm back to being a teenager, I thought. How could he turn it on and off so easily? I certainly didn't think of him as one of our school's teachers, not anymore.

"You have to give me directions. I have a vague idea where you live, but . . ."

"Turn up here," I said. "It's a faster way."

"Right. You okay?"

Finally, something that referred to what we had done, I thought.

"I'm fine," I said. "Maybe just a little tired."

"I bet. You've had one helluva day."

I looked at him. One helluva day? It was almost as if we had not gone for the ride to the beach, had the pizza and made love in his apartment, almost as if we were back at the strip mall and he was taking me directly home.

Does sex linger longer in the mind of a female than in that of a male? Perhaps that was it.

I knew what "wham, bam, thank you, ma'am" meant. Males satisfied themselves and then, as if that was all there was, left the scene. That wasn't lovemaking. That was love *taking*. In my way of thinking, it was as if they had mailed a letter with no address. They just wanted to put an envelope into a slot and leave. Whether it had any purpose or meaning wasn't important.

"What are you going to tell your parents?" he asked when I showed him our driveway. Although he tried to disguise it, I knew he was worried.

"I don't have to tell them anything."

He looked at me skeptically. "Come on. You didn't go home after school. Look at the time," he said.

"My father will just assume I went to the city library, and Julie won't even ask. I've done that before, or I've gone to museums without telling them ahead of time. If anything, Julie might be upset that I came home at all, especially after today. I'm sure she's been going on and on about how much of a strain it's been on her."

"What about dinner? Surely they'll be wondering about that."

"I told you. I've done it before and had something to eat nearby."

He nodded. I saw the way he was keeping his head tilted when he pulled up in front of the house. "Well, if they see that I brought you home, you can tell them I just bumped into you accidentally and offered you a lift."

"That's exactly what you did do," I said. I gathered my books.

"Well, I hope I helped you forget the bad time you had in school."

"What bad time?" I said, and he laughed.

"Take care of yourself, Mayfair," he said. It sounded like we would never see each other again.

I thought that was what you were doing, taking care of me, I wanted to say, but I didn't.

I just closed the car door and started for the front entrance of my house. I turned to watch him drive off, and then I took a deep breath and went inside.

Despite all I had told him and the brave face I had worn, I had no idea what really awaited me.

11

"Where were you?" my father demanded the moment I entered. He popped out of the living room, with Julie trailing behind him like a puppy. I looked at her first. If she was in any way concerned about how my father would react to what had been decided at school, it didn't show in her face. She was putting on an act, wearing the expression of a mother who had been wringing her hands with worry about a child.

"Your father has been beside himself," she said when I didn't answer immediately.

"I would have thought he would be beside you," I said.

"Don't get smart, Mayfair, and don't give me a lecture on the word *smart*, either. Where were you, damn it? After what happened today, you would think you would have come directly home."

"After what happened today, anyone would expect me never to come home. Daddy, didn't she tell you what she let them do to me?" I asked, practically shouting at him.

My father rarely saw me lose my temper. I had always relied more on sarcasm and good arguments. I had always believed that letting your emotions get control of you put you in a weaker place, but right now, I couldn't help myself. The events of the last few hours had confused me and twisted me up inside. I was feeling so many different emotions at once. It was a kaleidoscope of feelings. I had gone from anger to depression to elation. Now I had returned to anger. Julie's feigned face of concern put me over the top. I could barely contain myself. I felt like charging at her and slapping her and wiping that mask of false concern off her.

My father relaxed his shoulders and lost some of his aggressiveness and outrage. "As I understand it, it was a sensible compromise avoiding any more unpleasantness for you."

"Avoiding unpleasantness for me? The only one who avoided any unpleasantness was Julie. Exactly how do you think those bitches are going to describe this to their friends in school? Are they going to tell them that I got the best of them because I don't have to take PE but I still get credit for it? Or are they going to make a big point of the fact that I was ripped out of the girls' locker room because I'm most likely gay? You're a big-shot advertising man, Daddy, how would you present this situation to the eagerly awaiting public?"

I continued, "Imagine a billboard with me on it being dragged by my hair out of the locker room and the bitches laughing. Got that image in your head?

Thank Julie for it, and then consider what it was and will be like for me in that school." I headed for the stairway.

"But we thought . . . I mean, I thought you'd be happier not having to deal with those girls every time you had PE, Mayfair," he said.

"Happier?" I turned to look at them. My father looked concerned, even a little sorry. Julie looked worried. Perhaps he wouldn't like her solution after all. I took a deep breath and continued to look wounded. I could put on a performance, too, even better than hers, I thought, if that was what it took to win back my father.

"Maybe it is my fault," I said. "It's been so long since I've been happy about anything. I probably don't recognize the feeling anymore. Besides, I wasn't afraid of dealing with them. What are they but vapid, self-absorbed Barbie dolls who spend most of their time agonizing over their choice of lipstick?" I looked so directly at Julie that someone would have to be blind not to see the connection I was making. "No, happy is not what I feel, Daddy. What I feel is betrayed, betrayed by the people who should have my best interests at heart and not their own."

I paused. I saw that my father was feeling worse every second, but I wanted him to feel that way. I wanted him to feel absolutely terrible.

"If you had been there, it might have turned out differently," I said in a softer tone. "You used to always be there for me, Daddy. I needed you today. I needed someone to defend me. My mother would have been there."

He looked up at me with as much sadness in his eyes as I had seen there since my mother's death. I started to feel sorrier for him than I did for myself. The truth was, I really didn't care what the bitches from *Macbeth* thought and said. I was angrier with Julie than I was with them. And I was angry with my father for giving her so much control over what happened to me.

But there was nothing more I could do about it right now. And I didn't want to dwell on the bad and the ugly. I wanted to think about Alan Taylor. I wanted to relive my time with him. It was still so fresh.

"Just forget about it, Daddy," I said. "It's not too important in the scheme of things. I'll live, and all the precious reputations have been saved."

"Did you have dinner?"

"I grabbed something."

"Where were you?"

"City library," I said.

Normally, I wouldn't lie to him. I had never done anything I didn't feel I could justify or defend, but this was quite different. If I began to analyze it, I was sure I would have trouble justifying and defending it to myself.

He nodded.

"I'm going to take a bath and read," I said, and continued up the stairway.

As soon as I turned down the hallway, Allison burst out of her room. Her shiny new braces glittered in the hall light. Girls her age weren't as upset about their braces as girls used to be, because every six weeks, when they went in to have them tightened, they could change the color. When that was mentioned at dinner one night, I had told my father that good advertising could make a root canal desirable, and he had laughed. That was one of our happier moments, the kind of moments that seemed rare now.

Allison wore an oversize nightshirt with a print of her astrological sign, Virgo, spread over her budding breasts and belly. Her birthday was August 24. The English translation of *Virgo* is "virgin," and for a moment, having that astrological sign in my face seemed like poetic irony.

"I'm glad you're home," she said. Those weren't words I heard her utter often.

"What do you want?" was my natural question. I wasn't disappointed. She was happy to see me because she needed something, but in this house now, that wasn't unusual behavior.

"I need help with this math assignment. It's brutal."

"Brutal?"

I had to smile at the hyperboles she and other girls her age often used. They were so dramatic, so over-the-top. Everything that happened to them, whether it was a pimple or a dead iPod battery, was tragic, practically fatal. I couldn't recall ever being like that. Although I mocked them, at times I envied them. They seemed to be able to sidestep every really important task or decision. Moaning and groaning, throwing up their hands, and bursting into a downpour of tears, they fed on adult sympathy and usually got their way. Maybe I could learn something from them after all.

Parents, especially today's parents, would do absolutely ridiculous things to placate their teenagers, including driving back miles to school to bring them an AA battery or a cell-phone charger. Later they would complain to other parents about it, but those parents would confess to doing similar things. Sometimes I felt like a modern-day Alexander de Tocqueville, analyzing society the way he analyzed American democracy. I was smart enough to do it, but it left me feeling like an outsider. Where did I belong?

"Let's see it," I said in a tired voice. I wasn't exaggerating. I was really feeling exhausted.

"Thanks!" she cried, and led me to the desk in her room.

Julie had spared no expense in setting up Allison's room, from its four-poster canopy bed with a headboard of embossed cherubs to the recently installed vanity table with a mirror straight out of a *Snow White* illustration. I half expected to hear *Mirror, mirror, on the wall, who's the fairest of them all?* automatically recited every time she stood or sat in front of it. She had a computer table and a desk and a walk-in closet that was twice the size of mine. We had similar en suite bathrooms, all marble, with whirlpool tubs and large stall showers. Of course, Allison, like me, had her own telephone, the difference being that she used hers. Mine was almost a table decoration. Most of the time, it rang only when my father called me, and lately, he hadn't done much of that.

I looked at her assignment. To me, it was the equivalent of one plus one equals two.

"This only asks you to find the fourth angle of a quadrilateral, Allison. It's basic addition and subtraction. It's far from brutal."

"I wasn't paying attention today," she confessed. "I don't remember what a quadrilateral is."

I sighed. I could never be a good teacher, I thought. It took too much patience. "A quadrilateral is a polygon with four sides or edges and four vertices or corners."

She grimaced as if I had just fed her a bitter herb. "What's a polygon?"

"Didn't you listen to anything?"

She shrugged. "Mr. Bissel talks too fast. He teaches to the kids who are really smart and forgets the rest of us."

I nodded. She was probably right. Most of the teachers I had were the same way. They looked for the easiest way to get through their classes, and ignoring the students who didn't grasp concepts and ideas quickly enough was the most convenient method.

"A polygon is simply a plane figure bounded by a closed path or circuit. It's two-dimensional, length and width. So, here, this rectangle is a polygon," I said, drawing one. "This problem tells you that the sum of the four corners is three hundred sixty degrees, right?"

"Uh-huh."

"So, just add up these three corners, which equals two hundred seventy, and subtract that from . . . ?"

"The three hundred sixty?"

"Exactly. What's the answer?"

"Ninety."

"That's it. You do the same thing with the other five problems, Allison."

"And the last one?"

"That just asks you to find the area of a square. Didn't he show you this, at least? You just multiply the base times itself."

She shrugged again. I couldn't believe any teacher would be that lackadaisical.

"What were you doing in class today?"

Her face flushed with guilt. *Today.* I should have known. Why wouldn't it all have filtered down to the junior high? The school had a total population, grades seven to twelve, of just more than nine hundred students. And everyone was in the same building.

"Someone was talking about me?" I asked.

She nodded. "I didn't encourage them," she said quickly, "but they kept passing notes to me, asking me stupid questions."

"Like what?"

I saw how reluctant she was to answer. Instead, she went to her book bag, opened it, and took out three slips of paper to hand to me.

One read, *Does she watch you take showers or baths?*

Another asked, *Does she want you to help her masturbate?*

The last one simply asked, *Does she kiss you on the lips?*

"Well," I said. "It looks like you've become quite popular. Everyone will want to be your friend to be the first to learn some gossip."

"I didn't tell them anything. I told them they were all stupid."

"Did you tell your mother about this?"

Again, she looked guilty. "I didn't show them to her. I just told her a little," she confessed.

"What did she say?"

"She said she wanted me to do my best to ignore them, but . . ."

"But what?"

"But to tell her if anything like *that* ever happened."

"Do you think it would?"

"No. You're just very smart. You're not like that. Right?"

I nearly laughed at her uncertainty. "Right, Allison." I gave her back the notes. "Save these. We might need them as evidence someday."

"For what?"

"A lawsuit."

"Really?"

"Really," I said. I started to leave.

"Mr. Taylor said something like that to me today, too."

I turned back. "Mr. Taylor?"

"Uh-huh."

"What? What did he say?"

"He saw that I was upset. I sit right up front. He's always looking at me to see if I understand things or if I'm unhappy. He gives me special attention."

"Does he? So what did he say, Allison?" I asked more firmly.

"When the bell rang, he told me to stay behind a

moment, and then he said he'd heard some nasty rumors were being spread about you and that I shouldn't pay them any attention. He said those spreading them would get themselves in big trouble. He's the nicest teacher in the school, and the best-looking. I know he likes me a lot," she added.

Something about the way she said that sounded an alarm. "Likes you? What do you mean?"

"He likes me," she said. "He's always looking at me and smiling and stuff."

"What stuff?"

"Just stuff," she said, and sat at her desk. "Thanks for helping me, Mayfair. My friends think you do my homework all the time, especially when I get a high grade. That's why I try not to ask you too much."

"Forget your friends. If you don't understand something, you ask me. They're just jealous."

"That's what I thought."

I hesitated a moment as she worked on the remainder of the math problems.

"Right?" she asked, showing me her answers.

"That's it. Look, Allison, I want you to tell me what else Mr. Taylor says to you, especially over the next few days, okay?"

"Why?"

"I'd just like that. I help you with your homework, don't I? You can do that for me, can't you?"

"Okay," she said.

I started out again.

"Mayfair?"

"What?"

"You're not really like they're saying you are, right?"

Look how easily someone's reputation can be ruined, I thought. Often, just being accused of something made you guilty. Most people weren't going to be bothered with proof. Here was my stepsister, who had lived with me for years, already thinking it was possible.

"I already told you no, but stop looking so worried. Even if I were, it's not anyone else's business, and people who are like that are still good people."

I thought of something that I knew would bug her.

"Why? Are you feeling that way about yourself?"

"No!" She grimaced and shook her head vehemently.

I laughed. "See how easy it is to make you sound guilty? Don't grow up with your mother's middle-class prejudices," I said. "If you can help it, that is."

She just stared at me. I knew I was taking her too high too quickly.

But as the poet Robert Browning wrote, "A man's reach should exceed his grasp, or what's a heaven for?"

Arrogant of me, but I thought that if Allison hung around me, enough might rub off to make her at least a decent student, if not a decent person. Julie was worried that I might be a bad influence on her. *I'll be an influence on her, all right. I'll get her eyes open wide enough to see what a hypocrite her mother is.*

But I wasn't thinking about Julie now. I was thinking about Alan Taylor. Did he single out Allison because of me? Was he paying too much attention to her? At her age, she was far more vulnerable than I was, and today, I thought, I was most vulnerable.

I ran a bath and soaked in it, not because I felt unclean or spoiled after having been with Alan but because it relaxed me and let me think. What bothered me the most was the idea that I had allowed myself to be a victim today in so many ways. It began in Dr. Richards's office and ended in Alan Taylor's bed. I wanted to blame my troubles in school on those bitchy girls and Julie, but did I let it happen? Could I have been shrewder and more intelligent about how I had handled it all?

Did I throw myself at Alan Taylor willingly, or did I fall into a trap, all the while thinking I knew what I was doing? *I'm smarter than he is. I'm old enough to understand and handle myself*, I had told myself.

Was I suffering from what the Greeks called *hubris*, excessive pride, the fault that would bring tragedy to the arrogant? Had my super intelligence turned me into too much of a snob, a smuggie? Did I deserve what was happening to me after all?

One of my grade-school teachers, Mrs. Schumer, once voiced something to my parents that I thought she regretted immediately afterward. They were talking about my superior intellect, the wonders I had performed in second grade, and Mrs. Schumer said, "I wonder if it's a curse or a blessing." She looked at my parents' faces. This was something they had heard before from Fish Face, and they didn't like it then.

Mrs. Schumer quickly added, "Of course it's a blessing. Look at what she will be able to do. Why,

I imagine someday, I'll be reading about her accomplishments."

She spoke as quickly as she could to override her previous utterance, but I saw it was too late. It had already taken root in my parents' minds and would flower into more and more doubt as time went by.

It had taken root in me, too. It grew like a wild vine, reaching deeper and wider inside me.

As I lay there in my bathtub filled with soothing bubbles and bath oil, these thoughts, these memories, streamed behind my closed eyelids.

And minutes later, when I opened my eyes and looked at myself in the mirror, I saw that I had been crying. Not realizing that I had been until I looked at myself was more frightening than anything.

It was truly as if there were someone else in me, a second Mayfair, who was always trying to emerge, to pop out of me and cry, *"I'm the real Mayfair Cummings, not you. I want to be normal. I want to have fun, do stupid things, eat the wrong things, make happy mistakes, laugh at dumb jokes, wear silly clothes, flirt with vapid boys, cheer my lungs out at football games, eat popcorn and watch a goofy Simple Simon raunchy movie, and neck and pet in dark corners at house parties where we all drink too much or smoke pot or take other stuff and feel like rotten apples in the morning but laugh about it on telephone calls that go on and on until our parents scream at us to get off and do something worthwhile like clean our rooms and pick up all the clothes scattered everywhere.*

I'm the real Mayfair Cummings, not you. I'm

putting you back in the box and stamping it "No longer at this address."

I put my hands over my ears as if I really did hear my second self, and then I took some deep breaths, got out of the tub, and got ready for bed.

There was a knock at my door.

"Not another problem, Allison," I called.

The door opened. It was my father.

"Oh."

"Hey, May," he said when he entered. He hadn't called me that for a long, long time. I couldn't recall when he had first started, but it was his most affectionate greeting. "Hey, May." Sometimes he would just say it, smile, and go on to do whatever he had to do, but it always made me feel good. Once he composed a little rhyme that he would often sing for me.

Hey, May, what do you say?
Hope you had a very good day.
If not, someone's going to pay.

It made me smile and made my mother laugh. Now it seemed so long ago; it felt more like something I had watched on television or read in a book. Maybe it was just wishful thinking, a little fantasy.

I pulled myself up on my pillow and watched him come to my bed and sit at the foot of it, just the way he used to before he married Julie.

"Sorry about what you went through today. I intend to give that Dr. Richards a piece of my mind tomorrow."

"Don't bother. It won't help. They're all probably right. I'm better off away from those girls."

"I would have been there, but there was a major screw-up at the firm, and . . ."

"Don't knock yourself out about it, Daddy. It's over. I didn't expect that Julie would stand up for me, and she lived up to my expectations, that's all."

He nodded. "She thought she was doing the right thing."

"Believe what you need to believe," I said.

"I know it's not easy for you, hasn't been, but . . ."

"Let's just go to sleep, Daddy."

I lowered myself again. He got up and fixed my blanket. I kept my eyes closed and then felt him kiss me on the forehead. He brushed my hair. For a moment, I was afraid he might notice the change in me, sense that I had been with someone, but that was probably the furthest thing from his mind.

"Good night, May," he said. He turned off my lamp.

" 'Night," I said.

I heard him leave and close the door softly. For a while, I just lay there in the dark. I was worried that I wouldn't fall asleep, that I would stay up all night thinking about this roller-coaster day, but when I finally did close my eyes, it was as if I had fallen into a coma. I didn't dream; I didn't remember getting into bed. The light of morning surprised me the way a spotlight might catch a burglar stalking a target. It took me a few moments to realize that it was another day and I would face even more challenges, more than I, with my super intelligence, could ever imagine.

My father was quieter than usual in the morning. He always had things to say to Allison. Sometimes I thought he was sweeter to her than he was to me, but I excused that by thinking she was so much younger and more insecure. I couldn't remember being as insecure as she was, and I supposed my father never thought I needed as much reinforcement, but that didn't stop me from feeling sibling rivalry. In short, I was jealous, something I never imagined I would be.

"I'm sorry about all this happening to you, May-fair," he said when we'd arrived at the school. "Let's just let things calm down for a while and then talk about it some more, okay? The three of us can have a family meeting."

"I don't need things to calm down to talk about them, Daddy. But I know you do," I said. "Or should I say, Julie does, which has become the same thing, unfortunately."

He didn't like that, and he didn't answer. I closed the car door and followed Allison into the school. Probably the thing I was most curious about this morning was the way Alan Taylor would look at me and what he might say. Like all homeroom teachers, he was at his doorway. Dr. Richards wanted his teachers always keeping an eye on the students as they passed through the hallways, especially in the morning. That's what Alan meant when he told me that being observant was in the job description.

He saw me coming toward him, but he didn't smile, nor did he acknowledge me in any particular way. Instead, he started to talk to a seventh-grader and turned his back on me. It gave me the strangest feeling. I wasn't angry as much as I was confused. It was almost as if I had dreamed everything that had happened between us.

Two periods later, I had another opportunity to walk past his classroom, and once again, he was in the doorway. This time, he looked at me, but it was as though he had never spoken to me and didn't know anything about me. It was the look someone would give a total stranger, an empty glance, his eyes shifting quickly toward someone he did know, and then a smile and chatter.

Perhaps he thought it was too dangerous for us to be seen talking to each other now, I thought. That had to be it. Why else would he ignore me today? Maybe, just maybe, someone had seen us together, and he was trying to show Dr. Richards that there was nothing to it.

The school day was passing quickly. I was bored and distracted in every class, and during math, I read nearly all of *Crime and Punishment*. I wasn't a speed-reader like those people trained in the Evelyn Wood methods. There was a trade-off between speed and comprehension. Long ago, during some educational psychological testing, it was determined that I had another gift associated with my super intelligence. It was the ability to gulp thousands of words and process them instantly. It was not uncommon for me at age five to read a book a day and understand each and every word, and those were books read by adults.

When the bell rang at the end of the period that I knew was the one right before Alan Taylor's free period, I strolled down to his room to see if he would beckon for me to come in. He was just leaving when I approached. He turned and saw me. I anticipated at least a smile this time. There was no one else in the hallway, but he turned again instead and hurried off toward the faculty room. I almost called to him but choked back his name and watched him disappear around the corner.

What could possibly be the reason for his ignoring me completely?

I debated remaining after school so I could confront him, but I didn't. Perhaps it was better that he find a way to contact me safely, I thought, and went out to get into Julie's car with Allison. I sat in the rear, where I normally sat, and, as usual, didn't offer a word of conversation. Julie looked more nervous than usual.

The day had turned quite overcast. A storm was blowing in from the north, and that meant rain was very possible, and the temperatures were dropping. The weather fit my mood now. I almost welcomed it.

"You were pretty hard on your father yesterday," Julie finally said, after we had been riding for a while.

I didn't respond, but Julie was one of those people who always had to have the last word.

"I know you're a very intelligent person, Mayfair, yes, probably a genius, but you really need to work on your people skills."

"And what are people skills, pray tell?" I couldn't help but ask.

"You probably don't know this," she said, "but I took a course in people skills."

"No, I didn't know there was such a course. Where was it given? The mall, Saks, Nordstrom? How many times did you have to take it to pass?"

"You're not funny, Mayfair. I happen to get along very well with most people, no matter what position they're in or how important they are. And you want to know why?"

"I have a feeling you're going to tell me, no matter what, so why?"

"Because I show people that I care about what they say and who they are. I keep an open mind. No matter what you accomplish in your life and what honors you receive, you're still going to have to communicate with others."

"I'm impressed, Julie. That's two out of three."

"Two out of three what?"

"Complete sentences. The first was an adverbial clause, what we call a sentence fragment. Allison knows what I mean," I said. "I've helped her with her grammar homework."

Allison looked at me, frightened that I was somehow turning her into an ally against her mother.

"Okay, be like that. I tried. You never gave me a chance to be a friend to you, a mother. I am your father's wife, and that's a fact that can't be denied. I love that man. I'm warning you. I won't sit back and let you hurt him."

"Don't worry about it," I said. It was a weak thing to say, but there was no doubt in my mind that she had greater influence over my father now than I did, maybe than I ever had. I hated the fact that he was a man and, like most, was vulnerable to a good-looking woman. He needed that, maybe as much as he needed me, if he did need me.

My eyes stung with tears that I wouldn't release. Now that I thought more about it, I hated the idea that in my father's eyes, Julie would care for him, protect him, more than I did or perhaps more than I could.

"And despite any of this, all that's going on in this house," she continued, almost under her breath, "Allison is going to grow up normal, because she will permit me to be her mother, to be her friend and give her the benefit of my experience. She's going to have friends and go on dates and go to parties and go to college."

"And get married, live in a house with a white picket fence, and have other little Allisons," I said.

"Exactly." She nodded at me in the rearview mirror. "Exactly. And as much ridicule as you toss over it, normal relationships give you the best chance at being happy."

"Like your first one?"

"You're just trying to hurt someone else because you feel hurt," she said.

I turned away, folding my arms and leaning against the window. Sometimes Julie's arrows hit their targets. That one did.

The rain began to fall. The monotonous sound of the wipers began.

Allison turned around to look at me, then quickly turned back so her mother wouldn't think she felt sorry for me in any way.

Right now, I didn't need her to do that anyway. I didn't need anyone to do it.

I was feeling sorry enough for myself.

12

When my phone rang that night, I thought there was a real possibility that it was Alan Taylor. I had given him my private phone number because I had hoped he would be calling me to arrange our next rendezvous. I had explained that he could risk a phone call because I had my privacy at home. When we had walked on the beach, I had talked about my life after my mother had died and especially after my father had remarried. By the time the evening was over, Alan certainly knew what I thought of Julie and how disappointed I had been in my father for marrying her and catering to her so much. During our dinner, I had described how little I had to do with her and even with my father at this point. I'd made it sound as if I lived in my own cave in our house.

Maybe he was calling to explain his behavior toward me in school, I thought. I was ready to accept any excuse and believe any reason he had, as long as it wouldn't prevent us from seeing each other again.

Our lovemaking had been the centerpiece of my day-dreaming.

I practically tore the receiver off the cradle, but as soon as I heard the voice of the caller, my heart felt like it had dropped into a sinkhole. It wasn't Alan. It was Joy, my new best friend whether I liked it or not. I had followed through on one promise to her. I had gotten her a good deal of information about anorexia, its symptoms, causes, and treatment. There was even a list of possible therapists in the area. I had put stars next to the names of the ones I thought might be most helpful. She had promised she would give it all to her mother, and I gave her my private phone number in case she or her mother had to ask me a question about any of it. Now I regretted it.

"How are you?" she asked.

"I saw you today, Joy. You know how I am. I'm fine."

"No, you're not, Mayfair," she said with uncharacteristic authority. "Is something else bothering you?"

"Why would you ask that?"

She was quiet.

"Were you watching me again, following me all day?"

I wondered if she had seen how many times I deliberately passed Alan Taylor's classroom and how I looked toward him, anticipating some personal recognition. If she had seen my face, she might have noticed my disappointment. Was she smart enough to suspect anything?

"I just want to be able to do something for you,"

she said. "You're trying to do something for me. My mother was impressed with the information you gave me. We had a talk. She admitted other people have said something to her about me. I will be seeing someone, one of the names you put a star next to."

"Good. Good luck."

"What about you?"

"What about me?"

"Are you sure there's nothing going on? Are those girls annoying you? Did someone say something to you, Carlton James or anyone?"

"No, and if they did, it wouldn't bother me at all. You should know that, Joy."

"I know. That's why I really thought it might be something else."

"There's nothing you can help me with, Joy."

"Oh. So there is something bothering you, but it's something I can't help you with?"

"No."

"You're sure?"

I was surprised that she hung on to my exact wording. Maybe I was rubbing off on her. "Don't be a nag," I said, and she laughed. I thought about her for a moment. She was such a lost soul. She was trying desperately to have a friend, to be needed, and to contribute something of value. I didn't have to be so hard on her right now just because I was hoping for Alan Taylor to be calling. "Thanks anyway for offering," I added, which I knew made her happy.

"If you ever need a friend for anything," she said, "please choose me."

"Okay, Joy."

"I mean it. Promise?"

"Yes, I promise. Look, I've got to go," I said. "I left a physics problem on the stove."

"What?"

"I'm just kidding, but I do have some reading I want to do tonight. Thanks again for calling."

"Okay," she said. "See you tomorrow. 'Night."

I hung up.

I couldn't imagine how she could help me with anything, especially Alan Taylor, but I had to admit to myself that it was nice hearing her offer, nice knowing someone was caring enough about me for whatever reason to sense that something wasn't right with me. I wondered what she would do if I really did confide in her. She probably wouldn't tell anyone at school, but she might tell her mother. Why take the chance? What would I gain? She certainly didn't have the experience to offer me any sensible suggestions. Besides, it required too much trust. As sad as it seemed, I doubted I would ever meet anyone in whom I could invest such confidence. Even my father had fallen into the realm of doubt.

Nothing was very different during the remainder of the school week and the beginning of the next. The bitches of *Macbeth* finally seemed to be bored with me and my apparent lack of interest in them. I imagined that everything surrounding the episode in the locker room discouraged them. I wasn't acting destroyed by it. There wasn't enough excitement in it anymore. Little did they know that my silence and further withdrawal from everything in the school had less to do with them and more to do with Alan Taylor, but there was no doubt in my mind about what they would do if they knew about that.

Alan continued to ignore me, to do everything he could to avoid looking directly at me, and he didn't say a word to me, even though there were a few opportunities for him to do so. I couldn't get myself to approach him and force him to acknowledge me. It felt too much like begging for attention, and besides, Joy was practically attached to me whenever she could be. It was like I had given birth to a second shadow. She had begun to see a therapist and was making some progress. I didn't want to do anything to detract from that. I knew my interest in her, albeit more scientific than emotional, was an important reason for her effort to recuperate. She wanted my approval. Right now, she was the only one who wanted that.

I thought about waiting around for Alan after school a few times but decided not to do it. I even wondered if he was waiting for me to do what I had done the first time and not go home with Julie and Allison but instead walk down to the strip mall and wait for him, where he had first picked me up. One day, I actually did that. He never followed me. In fact, I was sure I saw him drive right by, not even looking my way or, if he did see me, quickly turning away. In the end, I had to call a taxi.

My reaction to all this surprised me. I thought I could be more mature about it. After all, he had treated me like a mature, sophisticated woman and probably expected that I would behave accordingly. I could shake off the disappointment and go on as if nothing had happened if I put my mind to it, couldn't I? I certainly wouldn't become some lovesick teenager ready to toss herself off a bridge. But despite the confidence I had in myself, I felt myself sinking deeper and deeper into what I recognized as a serious depression. I no longer wore any makeup, didn't do much with my hair, and returned to wearing the clothes I had been wearing before Julie added to my wardrobe. Maybe I was punishing myself for being so naive and vulnerable, but I hated to come to that conclusion and think of myself as the kind of foolish, innocent young girl I often accused my classmates of being. If Julie got wind of this tryst between Alan Taylor and me and my reaction afterward, she would surely gloat.

I could see her now, lecturing my father, telling him how she could easily have predicted that something like this would happen to me. "The girl wouldn't listen to anything I said. She was always too high-and-mighty to take my advice. Oh, no, what does someone like me have to offer? What does someone like me know? Of course you should be proud of her academic achievements, Roger, but you've even said it yourself: a person has to have more than a high IQ to be a complete person, and Mayfair is far from a complete person. The fact is, she's socially immature, otherwise how could a thing like this have happened? How could a young girl living in our home be so . . . so . . . inadequate when it comes to relationships and permit herself to be taken advantage of like this?"

My father would just sit there soaking up her criticism and feeling like a total failure as a parent. Julie's hold over him and over me, for that matter, would grow tenfold, and who was really to blame for it?

Me, that's who.

It didn't matter that a teacher was involved and would take the brunt of the blame in the legal sense. He was an adult, and my chronological age made me a minor, but victims weren't given a pass all the time, even minors and especially females when it came to male abuse or exploitation. In some countries, women who were raped were punished, too.

The conclusion was almost the same everywhere. Somehow, for some reason, we always shared the blame, or to some people, we were solely responsible. We did something to tempt the male, and besides, we were spoiled now, damaged property. It was a lose-lose situation.

You'd practically have to go into the federal witness protection program to get a new start, to be innocent, pure, and fresh again in everyone's eyes.

Besides, if there was any girl who was supposed to be smart enough to avoid such a trap, it surely was me, the girl whose IQ was so far above anyone else's that it floated close to the Pearly Gates.

I had no intention of permitting this sort of criticism and ridicule to happen to me. I wasn't going to break down and cry about how a teacher seduced me, go running to Dr. Richards or Mr. Martin about it. What a field day the three bitches from *Macbeth* would have with that. They would tell every boy in school, and every one of them would approach me with some nasty suggestion. Life would be more of a living hell than it was now.

No, swallow it all back and plod on, I told myself. *Just try to keep yourself as busy as possible. That way, you'll worry about it less and less and stop pitying yourself. Eventually, it will all dissipate like smoke.* Of course, that was easier said than done.

How many times did I stop reading to think about what was happening? How often did I simply sit there staring into space before I realized what I was doing?

Nothing seemed to be important anymore. I was experiencing all the symptoms of deep depression. I knew it, too, but like someone sitting in a car without brakes careening down a mountainside, I couldn't prevent what was happening to me. I could only sit there and wait for the crash.

Thinking about all this made the world seem even darker and darker.

I felt like someone in quicksand who knew she was sinking but couldn't reach out for help from any of these adults and so-called professionals.

However, because I had so little contact with my teachers and fellow students, ironically no one but Joy took any particular notice of my depression. The others must have thought my silence, my self-imposed solitude, and my unhappy face were normal for me. My invisibility had grown too effective. I could collapse on the hall floor, and the other students rushing to class would step over me. Maybe they would even step on me without noticing.

Joy never stopped asking what was bothering me. She called often, and although she pretended to be calling about herself, with some question about her condition, she always brought the conversation back to me. It almost made me laugh aloud to think that someone so out of the mainstream was so observant, so sensitive to me, that she could see the subtle differences. It finally occurred to me that she really did care about me and wasn't simply trying to give herself some meaning and importance. Ironically, I was the sister she had never had. She had tuned herself in to the frequency over which my moods and feelings flowed, just like a real sister might.

Finally, I admitted to her that I was disappointed in someone.

"Who?" she asked instantly.

"I think it's better that I don't mention his name."

"Oh, so it's one of the boys at school," she concluded. "Well, he has to be blind and stupid."

"I'll get over it," I told her. "It would help, though, if you would stop asking. It keeps me thinking about it. Understand?"

She nodded quickly, grateful for the tidbit. Confiding that much in her didn't change my behavior in school at all. If anything, it made me think I had to be more careful, even a little more withdrawn.

I knew that Julie was quite satisfied with my further withdrawal. I didn't criticize or oppose anything she did or said in the house, any changes she got my father to make. As soon as I was home from school, I went into my room and stayed there until dinner.

My father was particularly busy at this time. There was one crisis after another at the company because of some bad economic news involving two of the pharmaceutical companies he represented. He was occupied with trying to pick up new business and was traveling more than usual for meetings in the Midwest and on the East Coast. We simply weren't talking to each other as often as usual.

The first hint anyone else at school had of my new mental state was my failure to turn in any required work and my not putting down a single answer on any test. I'd hand in the papers untouched. At first, some of the teachers thought they had given out too many tests and I had an extra copy or that I had lost my homework. They couldn't conceive of my not handing something in when it was due.

However, when they asked me about it, I simply said I didn't hand it in.

"Why not?" they asked.

"Sorry, I haven't done it," I said, without a note of regret.

The expressions on their faces ran the whole gamut of reactions from indifference to surprise and finally to a reprimand and a lecture telling me not to underestimate the importance of their classes.

It amused me how some of my teachers took my refusal to do any work so personally. I realized they saw it as a result of my arrogance. They believed I never thought of them as important enough to add anything to my education. I could see it in their eyes. How dare I belittle them and their subject matter and embarrass them in front of the other students by failing or ignoring their assignments and tests?

Whatever any of them said to me in these lectures went in one ear and out the other. I saw the expressions of glee on the faces of other students who overheard us. Sometimes I nodded and looked like I understood and might even get back to the way I was. They could take credit for saving me or something. But more often than not, I simply walked away without speaking and without changing expression.

Finally, one afternoon, Mr. Martin called me to his office to ask me what was going on. He had five different referrals now and probably had ignored them as long as he possibly could, hoping I would get back on track and make them all superfluous. Ever since my confrontation with the girls in the locker room and the subsequent meeting in Dr. Richards's office, Mr. Martin looked uncomfortable in my presence. He barely nodded at me in the hallway and rarely took time to speak to me the way he often had before the locker-room incident. It was as if he had been enclosed in ice.

The moment I entered his office, I could see how nervous and uncomfortable he was. "Mayfair," he said, holding the five referrals up like a poker hand. "What is all this? What's happening here?"

"I don't know what's happening here, Mr. Martin. I wonder who does."

"What kind of an answer is that, Mayfair, especially from you?"

"I don't know," I replied. "Most of my life is spent answering questions these days."

For a moment, he just stared at me. I could almost hear the wheels turning in his mind. I was normally a big challenge for him, but something like this involving me of all people threw him completely off kilter. I was sure he had told the principal and others that he wasn't trained to deal with a student like me as it was, because of all my special problems. Who here was?

"Is it what some of your teachers think? You think the work's too insignificant now and not worthy of your attention and efforts?"

"I suppose it's significant enough for most of the students," I said. "Although teaching intermediate algebra and calculus to some of them is like driving around with no place to go. How long can you do it before running out of gas?"

"You're not making any sense to me, Mayfair, and you're worrying a number of people here who are really concerned about you. You might not believe it, but there are many people here who think you are someone very special, someone we should do our best to satisfy and prepare for the world out there."

"The world out there?"

He looked at the referrals again and then back at me. "Aren't you feeling well? Is there something you should tell the nurse, maybe?"

I nearly laughed. "I don't have female problems, Mr. Martin, and I'm not pregnant."

Mr. Martin was a fair-complexioned man to start with. He had light brown hair and freckles that looked like spots of carrot juice on his cheeks. When he blushed, his face became so red he looked like he had a terrible sunburn. It made his green eyes practically luminous. "I didn't mean that," he said. "Is there anything, anything at all, you want to tell me?" He sounded desperate, actually interested. It was tempting.

Where would I begin? I wondered. Should I start with my need to be more accepted, surrendering to the female in me, and going to Julie for assistance, something that took away all my self-pride? Or should I begin by explaining how easily I was taken in by the school's most eligible and desirable bachelor? Maybe compare myself to the story of the fox and the hen? Despite how the parable turned out, who could fault the fox, and who didn't laugh at the naive hen? How could I do that? And besides, even if I was ready to tell someone, was he the person I should talk to, especially after he had sat in that office with Dr. Richards when the mothers of the bitches from *Macbeth* complained and then let what happened to me happen?

I realized just how much I missed my mother. For any girl, there were certain problems and subjects she felt more comfortable discussing with her mother and not her father or a best friend or anyone else. After my mother died, I did depend on my father more than most girls depended on theirs, but most of my life, I was able to analyze and solve my own issues and not bother him. Maybe that was arrogant, but I couldn't help thinking that no matter what, I could take care of myself better than anyone could take care of me, now and forever. But I really did need my mother. I needed to be cuddled and petted and told everything would be all right. When parents did it, you believed it.

Why did death have to be so damn final?

Why couldn't I at least pick up the telephone and call my mother in the great beyond and ask her advice?

Did I even believe in the great beyond?

I'm getting childish, I thought. *I'm losing my famous self-control.* Next thing I knew, I'd be sleeping again with my old stuffed teddy bear, the earliest gift I remembered my mother and father buying me. It was in a box, a symbolic coffin, in my closet. I put it there the day my mother died. I even dreamed of going to her grave, digging down to her coffin, and putting the bear in with her so she wouldn't be lonely.

I really was a child once. When my mother died, I became my father's little girl, at least for a short while. And I couldn't say I did that only for him. I needed his affection almost as much as he needed mine. I felt a little like that now, maybe more than a little. I battled not to burst into tears in Mr. Martin's office. I swallowed them back and balled my hands into fists so tight my nails cut into my palms and my knuckles turned bloodred.

I will not cry, I chanted to myself. *I will not cry. None of these people will ever get the satisfaction of seeing me cry.*

"No," I told him. "There's nothing I want to tell you."

"It doesn't have anything to do with your other problem, does it?"

"What other problem? I thought Dr. Richards brought that to a complete and satisfactory end. Both of you had it all under such control, remember?"

He nodded. I could see it in his face. He was thinking, *So this is the game you're playing with me?* "Okay, Mayfair. I'm going to have to discuss this with your parents."

"I don't have parents. I have only a father," I said.

"You may return to class," he said, "but please, feel free to come here to talk to me anytime you want."

He said that so often, probably at the end of every conversation with every student, that I wondered if it wasn't a recording inserted in his brain by some hypnotist.

Of course, when he called my house, Julie took the message and then embellished it when she called my father. I was sure it had given her the most pleasure anything had given her all day. The administration of the school actually calling to complain about my scholastic work? They were desperate for help, and therefore they verified her view of me. If they, educational professionals trained to handle and help young students, had so much trouble understanding me at school, what she and others considered my world, how could she be blamed for failing me at home?

She did such a good job on my father that he postponed an important business meeting to come home early. She was very clever about it all, too. When she picked up Allison and me, she never mentioned Mr. Martin's call and how she had panicked my father. I even wondered if Mr. Martin had decided to wait to see how our little nontalk affected me. After all, he and the other professionals were being paid to handle the problems at school. In a private school like ours, they did all they could to avoid laying any concerns on the parents of these privileged children. The last thing they wanted to hear was something like "Why am I paying all this money to send her here?"

Allison had been invited to a classmate's birthday party this coming Friday. The mother was one of Julie's garden party crowd, and of course wealthy and therefore, in Julie's mind, very important. She wanted to be sure Allison had a new dress and matching shoes. That was all she talked about during the ride home; she had already gone to her favorite boutique and set aside a few things for Allison to try on. She wanted Allison to have her hair done on Friday after school and had made an appointment.

"You'll have a manicure, too," she said. "You show your friends how much you care about them when you spend time on what you will wear and how you will look at their parties. It's simply good etiquette. And," she added, mostly for my benefit, I'm sure, "it's very nice that you are invited to parties, the more important parties."

Allison glanced at me to see my reaction. I just smiled at her. She looked grateful for that. Lately, she had been trying to get closer to me. She asked me even more questions concerning her schoolwork. Even after I gave her answers or helped her understand something, she lingered, hoping, I was sure, for me to say something personal. Julie usually gave her a look of reprimand if she saw that she was spending too much time with me. All that did was make Allison nervous. The truth was that despite her friends and going to parties, Allison was as lonely as I was. I sensed that she missed her father and couldn't condemn him as completely as Julie would like. It always would be a source of tension between them.

Julie was destroying her own daughter, I thought, and she didn't even know it.

Maybe, in the end, she would destroy me, too.

13

I was surprised to see my father's car at the house this early in the day, but then I thought about my meeting with Mr. Martin and imagined that he had reached him at work. I was still thinking that Julie didn't know about it.

"Oh, Daddy's home," Allison said, glancing at me. "He's never home this early."

Julie was watching me in the rearview mirror. "He's waiting for you in the living room, Mayfair. I called him immediately when I received the call from Mr. Martin," she said with a cold smile. "Allison, I want you to go up to your room. This is something Mayfair's father and I have to discuss with her and her only."

Allison looked to me immediately, but I gave her no hint of anything. In fact, I tried to look as uninterested and bored as I was with most things her mother planned. She got out quickly and hurried into the house.

"Couldn't wait to call him, could you?" I asked Julie as she started after Allison.

"Of course. He'd be more upset if I had waited."

When we entered, I hesitated in the hallway. I had no idea what I was going to give him as an excuse for my new academic suicide. Of course I was expecting him to be very angry, especially after the way Julie had surely presented it all to him, but he surprised me.

"Hey, May," he said when I stepped into the living-room doorway. "C'mon in. I came home to talk to you."

I nodded at him and sat, still holding my books in my arms. Allison had already gone upstairs. Julie sat beside him on the settee, doing her best to look like she really was concerned. *Why is he so blind?*

"Julie tells me that the school contacted us today," he began.

"School? How does a school contact someone?"

"No games, okay? Your guidance counselor, Mr. Martin, phoned. Julie called me to tell me, and I called him back as soon as I could. Apparently, you have been on some kind of academic strike or something, and no one can understand why. So, why?"

I looked away. There were so many other ways he should have known I wasn't happy, but it was always my schoolwork, my intellectual achievements, that drew his attention first and foremost. Didn't he notice the changes in me, my clothes, my whole demeanor? Didn't he think it had something to do with deep emotion and not something intellectual? Was he that oblivious to my feelings?

Maybe in his mind now, I was what my uncle Justin had once called me in jest, nothing more than a walking computer. Maybe he thought I plugged myself into the internet when I went to sleep, and kilobytes of information began flowing into my brain like a blood transfusion. Maybe he had given up on thinking of me the way a father would think of his daughter. I had metamorphosed into some alien creature living in his home.

Daddy, Daddy, I heard myself cry inside like a little girl feeling herself fall into a dark and frightening dream. *Can't you see me anymore?*

"It's very confusing to all of us, Mayfair," he continued. "As far as I know, you were free to follow your own interests as long as you did what was required, and that was never much of a challenge for you. Is this all because of what happened with those girls?"

First Mr. Martin and now him, I thought. Everyone always looked for the easiest solution.

"I told you. I couldn't care less about them and all that now. I'm not starving for friends and invitations to stupid parties. I don't care if I ever make the social page," I added, looking pointedly at Julie.

"But what happened to change your feelings about all that? You did ask Julie to help you with your clothes, your makeup and hair, and—"

"I thought it was important. I was wrong. I realized how vapid I was in danger of becoming."

"Vapid?" Julie said.

"Dull, insipid," I defined. "No one's ever called you that?"

"Stop it, Mayfair. We're here to talk about you."

"Yes, we wondered why you stopped taking care of yourself," Julie said.

"We?"

"Julie and I did discuss it, Mayfair."

"I wouldn't exactly refer to it as taking care of myself," I said.

"You know what we mean, Mayfair," my father said, looking disgusted with me.

"I came to the conclusion that it wasn't the most important thing."

"But feeling good about how you look is important," my father followed. "And I saw that you did feel better about yourself. What happened to change your mind about it? Obviously, it's affecting more than a potential social life now. Is it boy trouble?"

I didn't say anything. Why didn't he ask me this earlier? Why did it take a call from the school to open his eyes? He glanced at Julie, who kept her lips pursed and her face stiff. She didn't look at me; she just continued to face forward. I felt like getting up and slapping her to knock that mask off her face. I almost did. Maybe my father saw that in me, because his expression became a little fearful.

"No," I said sharply.

"Because if it is, that's nothing to be ashamed about, and Julie could—"

"I'm not ashamed! And I wouldn't go to Julie even if I was!"

They were both deadly quiet, almost of one face. I could hear the miniature grandfather clock on the mantel ticking, or was that the beat of my heart?

"Look, Mayfair," he said after a deep sigh, "I'm not someone who is comfortable pretending he knows more than he does or trying to do things he knows he's not qualified to do. We have a situation here, and—"

"There's that word again, *situation*," I muttered. "And that other word, *we*?"

"Yes, we, Mayfair. We're all part of this family, and when something affects one of us, it affects all of us. Now, getting back to what I was saying. I recognize there's a problem that is more serious than I first thought, and I want to do something about it."

"Like what?"

He hesitated for a moment. Julie looked at him, anticipating. "I think you should see a therapist. For a few times, at least," he quickly added. "As I said, I'm not qualified to do that sort of work, and neither is Julie. We readily admit it, but we care about you, and we're worried."

"So you want me to see a therapist," I said. "You think that would solve the situation?"

"It's a start, Mayfair. Many people, good people, successful people, are in some form of therapy or another. Life is very complex today. You're a unique individual, and you have problems and issues most people don't have, that most couldn't possibly understand."

"Because I'm so unusual?"

"Whatever," he said. "The problems are there because you are an exceptionally intelligent person. Everything in this life comes with its own baggage."

"Baggage? So now you think it's a curse, is that it?" I asked him.

"What is?"

I was disappointed that he didn't remember having once been told that I might be cursed or I might be blessed with such superior intelligence. "Nothing," I said. I stood up. "Okay. I'll see a therapist. It might be interesting. Let me know when I have an appointment."

"You have one tomorrow," he said quickly.

I spun around. "Tomorrow? What sort of therapist has an opening so quickly?"

"One of Julie's friends is good friends with a highly regarded therapist, Dr. Burns in Santa Monica. And—"

"Oh, one of Julie's friends? Maybe she is really one of his clients and not one of his friends. Therapy is in vogue, I know. It's right under getting a facial on the list of priorities for her friends."

"You're not funny, Mayfair. Your appointment is at two o'clock," my father said firmly. "I have a car and a driver arranged to pick you up at school and take you home. I'd do it myself, but I have a full day."

"Therapy car service. Probably a booming business around here," I said. "Fine." I started to leave.

"You don't believe us, I know," Julie said, "but we are very worried about you."

"Oh, I believe it, Julie. I'm just not convinced you both share the same reasons for it. Well," I said, looking at my father, "maybe that's no longer true."

My father looked at me sternly. "Two o'clock tomorrow, Mayfair," he said.

I glanced at Julie. She nearly smiled. I hurried out and up the stairs.

Allison had her door open and quickly turned from brushing her hair and looking in her Snow White vanity mirror when I approached. "I could hear some of it from the top of the stairs," she confessed.

"Good. Then I can verify that I didn't imagine it," I said.

She grimaced. "I'm sorry you're not feeling well," she said.

"That's funny," I said.

"What's funny?"

"You're the only one who is sorry." Of course she was confused, but I had no patience or interest in explaining it to her.

"What's wrong with you? Why do they want you to go to a therapist?"

"I'm round, and I can't fit into the box."

"What?"

"I don't feel like talking about it right now, Allison," I said, and went into my room. I didn't sulk like a child, but I kept to myself as much as possible for the remainder of the evening.

Julie didn't say a word to me in the morning. My father told me he would be very interested in hearing about my first therapy session as soon as he was able to give me his full attention. I told him I would make a full report in triplicate if he wanted it.

"I hope you take this seriously, Mayfair," he said. "Or at least give it a chance."

I didn't respond. Maybe I did need therapy. Maybe

he was right after all. I mean, didn't I push Joy into going into therapy? This might be one of those "Physician, heal thyself" sorts of things. Even therapists needed therapy.

Later, in school, I suddenly became a little paranoid about it, however. There were other clues. It seemed to me the bitches of *Macbeth* weren't ignoring me anymore. In the halls, in classrooms, and in the cafeteria, they were looking my way, smiling and whispering. Maybe they had overheard some of my teachers talking about me, or maybe Mr. Martin's secretary gossiped about our meeting and my behavior. Another very likely possibility was that Julie had discussed me with Joyce Brooker's mother, perhaps even telling her that I was going to see a therapist. Joyce Brooker's mother might even be the therapist's client.

If that was true, these girls could tell everyone how right they were about me. "See? She really is crazy. We told you so."

Something more was definitely going on. I could sense it. Carlton James wore a look of deep self-satisfaction. He, too, whispered to his buddies and looked at me while doing so. Then he strutted with pride and threw me a condescending smile that said, "You should have accepted my invitation, bitch. Now look at where you are."

Even Joy looked at me differently. Her "Are you all right?" now seemed planted.

"If you ask me that one more time, I won't talk to you again, understand?"

She nodded.

"Don't," I said, as she started to explain herself. "Just forget it."

She bit down on her lower lip and followed me around in silence. I thought I saw her talking with Cora, one of the bitches, between classes. Why would any of them give her the time of day? Maybe she was promised something, like an invitation to a party, if she spied on me and got them some juicy gossip to spread. My paranoia was exploding. I had to get hold of myself.

However, by two o'clock, I told myself it didn't matter that I was paranoid. I was convinced Joseph Heller's famous quote from *Catch-22* that "Just because you're paranoid doesn't mean they're not after you" was true, especially for me. All that I believed was happening was really happening. My stepmother, Julie, had sabotaged me at school. Whether it was true or not, I convinced myself that it was at minimum a credible theory.

I saw Allison in the hallway and pulled her away from her friends.

"Did your mother know you overheard the conversation with me in the living room yesterday?" I asked her. "Well?"

She nodded.

"Did she tell you not to say anything in school or to any of your friends?"

"No," she said. "I only told . . ."

"Don't tell me. It doesn't matter," I said, and left her.

In a way, Julie had done me a favor. My self-pity

turned into raw rage. By the time I got into the car to go to Dr. Burns's office, my strategy was formed. I was tired of being the victim here. My old self was returning. I could feel the surge of energy and glee.

I'll show my father's new wife how to play this game, I thought.

Dr. Burns had a small but very comfortable and bright office. There was a large bay window in his lobby that faced the ocean, so the afternoon sun beamed through the translucent curtains and tinted windows. There were two dark brown leather settees that faced each other, with a glass table between them. Everything was immaculate and neat, including the artificial flowers that were strategically placed to supplement the brightness and warmth. The light blue walls had framed prints of country scenes, fields, rivers, and mountains. Everything was designed to make someone feel relaxed and safe, including the elevator music piped in but kept so low it was almost subliminal.

His secretary sat in a small inner office with a window facing the lobby. I could see the file cabinets, copy machine, fax, and printer behind her. She had a name plaque that read "Sylvia Jones." I thought she was about Julie's age but less plastic-looking. She was even permitting some gray strands to infiltrate her neatly styled dark brown hair.

"I'm Mayfair Cummings," I said.

"Yes," she said, smiling with that superficial warmth surely designed to let the doctor's clients feel relaxed and calm about the fact that they were here to see a therapist, that they were admitting something wasn't right with them. "I'll let Dr. Burns known you're here. He's just finishing up a phone call."

"Don't I have to fill out anything?"

"No, dear. Everything's been done."

Probably by Julie, I thought. Maybe even a year ago.

I went to sit, but before I could, the second inner office door opened, and Dr. Burns called to me.

"Hi there," he said.

If a director were looking to cast an actor for the role of a modern-day psychotherapist in a play, he'd have chosen Dr. Burns. It reinforced a theory of mine that people often grew to look just like people expected them to look. Dr. Burns, who probably was no more than forty, was the new hip psychotherapist, with long black hair, wearing jeans and a light blue long-sleeved denim shirt with the sleeves rolled up to suggest he was going to get down to real work. He even had a small diamond stud earring.

In honor of Dr. Freud, maybe, he had a neatly trimmed goatee and a pair of wire-rimmed glasses that rested on the bridge of his nose. He looked to be about my father's height but much slimmer in build. I thought he had almost feminine hands. He extended his right hand, and I took it to shake, but he held on to mine and stepped back to have me enter his office, not letting go until I walked in and he could close the door. Maybe he was afraid that after taking one look at him, I'd turn and run. Perhaps he had potential clients who had done just that.

I gazed around. He had a large, dark-cherrywood

desk, a window that also looked out on the ocean, and another behind his desk with the drapes drawn closed. There was an oversize chair in front of his desk, walls of filled bookshelves, and only one picture, a print of the famous *Christina's World* by Andrew Wyeth. It showed a young woman lying in a field and looking like she's crawling or wants to start crawling toward a gray house on the horizon.

Dr. Burns saw that I was looking at it. "All my clients love that painting," he said. "Everyone has a different interpretation about who she is, why she's lying in the field, what's in the house."

"And you use that to analyze them?"

"Sometimes," he said, smiling. "Should we use it for you?"

"Won't work. I know the history of that painting. Wyeth saw a young woman with a paralyzed lower body crawling and was inspired to do the painting. He used his wife as a model for the girl's torso, even though she was much older than the girl depicted."

"You can still find some meaning in it, can't you?" he said, indicating that I should sit in the large chair as he moved behind his desk.

"I just told you what it was."

"You're very literal. Please, sit," he said when I continued to stand.

"What?" I said, looking around. "No couch?"

He laughed. "That chair has a lever on the side, and you can sit all the way back with your feet up. How's that?"

"Perfect." I sat and tried the lever.

"Don't fall asleep on me. I've had that happen more times than I care to admit."

"Then don't bore me," I said, sitting up again.

He smiled, but not as widely or as deeply as he had the first time. "Okay. Let's see if I can avoid that." He said, looked at a file on his desk. "Mayfair Cummings, nearly seventeen years old, with quite a remarkable school history. You're in very good physical health, I see."

"How long have you had all that information?"

"Oh, a little while. Preparation is important, right?"

"That's not preparation. That's anticipation. Maybe even a little plotting."

He laughed and sat back. "Okay. Let's not go through the mental fencing. I have no illusions about being subtle with you. I know how intelligent you are. You might know as much about my work as I do. Your parents are concerned that you've hit a wall of unhappiness with yourself, and we're here to see if we can understand the cause and do something about it."

"Father," I said.

"Pardon?"

"My father is concerned. His new wife, Julie, has her own agenda."

"Oh? Which is . . . ?"

"She couldn't care less about my academic achievements. She wants me to fall in line, be what she calls normal, so I don't corrupt her daughter with independent thinking or distract my father too much from paying attention to her."

"I see."

"No, you don't. You haven't heard enough, and you haven't asked the right questions yet."

"Okay. Let me try. What makes her think you're not normal?"

"I don't dwell on my appearance, my clothes, my hair. She tried desperately to get me to do that, to be more like her. For a while, I tried it, but I felt like a phony. So in her mind, I'm not normal. I don't have a boyfriend or go to parties, and I'm still a virgin." I thought I'd add "still a virgin," even though it was no longer true. It was important to my strategy.

Dr. Burns looked sufficiently shocked. "She doesn't want you to be a virgin?"

"Let's say she wants me to be more interested in sex than I am," I said. "It's clearly very important to her, and anyone who is not as interested in it as she is would be abnormal in her way of thinking."

"What has she done or said to get you to believe this?"

"She's tried to get me to look sexier, wear low-cut blouses, shorter skirts, push-up bras, more makeup. She's even tried to get me to enjoy orgasms."

He stared and sat forward. "I don't understand. How did she do that?"

"Told me how she enjoys sex, masturbation, and then . . ."

"Then what?"

"Bought me a vibrator."

"She bought it for you?"

"Yes. My father doesn't know about it. I haven't used it yet. She keeps asking."

I saw his look move from skepticism to thought-fulness. Then he wrote some notes and nodded. "Well, let's go back a little. How do you feel about the boys at your school?"

I smiled to myself. *He's buying it*, I thought. "There are some I think are good-looking, but they haven't shown interest in me. I suppose I'm a little shy. Julie makes me feel bad about that. Sometimes I wish I could please her just to get her off my back. She's tried giving me hints about how to be more enticing, how to flirt, stuff like that. I feel funny about it, but I can't tell my father these things, so I feel a little trapped. I suppose this has all been weighing on my mind lately, gotten me depressed. I didn't want to worry my father, but I just haven't figured out how to explain it to him. He's so devoted to her."

"I see."

"Yes, now you might have enough to begin to see," I said.

"Maybe you should consider psychology as a career."

I shrugged. "Maybe," I said. "I have been think-ing about that, but let's see how well you do with me first."

He laughed and leaned forward. "Tell me more about this pressure your stepmother is putting on you," he said. "I notice you don't call her that. You said"—he looked at his notes—"your father's new wife, but haven't they been married for years?"

"Well, she'll always be new in my eyes. He was married before."

"And your mother died. You resented Julie right from the start, then?"

"Classic. Of course. Any child doesn't want to see her mother completely replaced, forgotten. I think I handled it as well as could be expected. I'm not troubled by that anymore. My father made a decision he thought was best for us both, and that's that. It's just that . . ."

"Yes?"

"With all this concentration on boys and sex, she seems more like an older sister to me or an older girl-friend."

"Go on about that," he said, nodding.

I continued, elaborating on the details I had planned to describe as vividly as I could, describing evenings when she came to my room to tell me about her own sexual exploits, explaining how it would make me stronger to have such experiences and help me decide when it came time to settle on one person.

"She said it wasn't fair that boys were expected to have many girlfriends, many sexual experiences, but girls who did the same were frowned upon, labeled with nasty names."

He nodded and took lots of notes, scribbling away for practically the entire session.

It was going just as I had planned.

14

"Well?" my father asked. "How did it go with Dr. Burns?"

He had come to my bedroom. I was lying on my bed and reading *The Art of Persuasion*. I was surprised at just how many techniques had come to me instinctively when I was in Dr. Burns's office. Ironically, I thought, my father would be very proud of me under any other circumstances. I was in his world of advertising and persuasion, a world where the truth was easily twisted or completely buried.

Julie wasn't home when I returned. She had taken Allison to try on outfits for another party, so she couldn't give my father a preliminary report concerning how I looked or acted after my therapy session. I had planned on giving her a little of her own medicine, phony smiles and sweetness.

I lowered my book. "I like him," I said. "He has a good sense of humor, and he's not heavy."

"Heavy?"

"I don't mean his weight, Daddy. You know, too demanding, pushing, getting too quickly into your head."

"Oh, right. Well, what about progress? You think you can make some with him?"

I nodded. "He helped me see some things. I won't deny that it's good to have someone who wants to listen to you, even if he gets paid to do it."

"Well, as I said, someone who is trained to help is important," my father said. "As you always tell me, a little learning is a dangerous thing. Go whole hog."

He really couldn't see how unhappy I was about all this, I thought. It wasn't that long ago when he could sense something was bothering me with just a look or a few words. I wasn't inscrutable when it came to him. I wouldn't even try to fool him back then. Maybe Julie was influencing me more than I would willingly credit her for. After all, I had a master of disguise right under my feet. Learn from your enemies, and distrust your friends enough not to be disappointed. That had become one of my new rules of life.

"I couldn't agree more. Amateur psychologists don't do anyone any good."

He smiled with relief. "I'm not an amateur psychologist. I just don't like to see you unhappy, Mayfair."

"I don't like to be unhappy, Daddy," I replied, and he laughed.

"Maybe we'll all go out to dinner Friday night, huh?"

"Allison has another one of her socially important parties. Julie will want you to take her and pick her up."

"Oh, right. Well, we'll figure it out," he said.

"I'm sure we will," I replied. *As long as it fits what Julie wants*, I thought.

He nodded, smiled, and left. I looked at the empty doorway and wondered for a moment if I was doing the right thing with Dr. Burns. I could lose my father completely. We were alienated enough from each other as it was without me adding to it, but it was too late. I had gone too far. I was confident of what would happen next, and sure enough, it did.

Julie did not ask me anything about my therapy that night at dinner or the following morning on the way to school. It wasn't that she was afraid to ask or didn't want to know. I had a different sense of it. Something told me she was confident that she would know everything whenever she wanted.

When I arrived at school, I continued to feel this new sense of energy that had been born out of my anger. I returned to the vigorous pursuit of my academics. I aced a math test, answered questions in social studies, and got into such a deep discussion with Mr. Feldman about *Huckleberry Finn* that it seemed as if there was no one else in the classroom but us. He was very happy, even exhilarated. He told me he felt like he was back in college, discussing great literature with his professor. Half of the class hadn't even read the portions he had assigned.

He said a nice thing to me. "For one bright moment, I remembered why I had gotten into teaching in the first place."

The result was electric. Before the day had ended,

my teachers had reported my academic resurrection to Mr. Martin, and he was eager to show how effective he had been, even with someone like me. I knew he especially wanted to please my father. Before the day ended, he had obviously called Julie and reported to her. She commented about it when she came to pick up Allison and me.

"I was pleased to hear you've returned to doing well in school again, Mayfair. I'm glad I recommended Dr. Burns to your father. Therapy can be helpful," she said.

"Yes, it can be. You should try it yourself," I told her, and her look of self-satisfaction evaporated.

The real result, however, my intended result, occurred after I had two more sessions with Dr. Burns, elaborating even more on what I had told him the first time, providing practically pornographic details.

It was one of Julie's girls' nights out, and she had gone to dinner, which was supposed to be followed with a movie, but instead, she had come right home. She made quite a dramatic entrance.

Allison rushed in to tell me. "My mother's back early," she said, gasping.

"So?"

"I was downstairs watching television, and she came home very upset, slamming the door and crying."

"Really? Think she had a fight with one of her vapid friends?"

"What's vapid?"

"Ask your mother."

She looked at me strangely and then returned to

her excited report. "I don't know if she had a fight with anyone. She wouldn't let me stay there with her and Daddy," she said. "She told me to go up to my room, and Daddy agreed."

Julie had insisted that Allison call my father Daddy, both as a way of killing any relationship she might still have with her real father and as a lesson to me, for I still refused to call her anything but Julie. Nevertheless, Allison was always a bit hesitant to do so when she was alone with me. She thought I might resent it, when, in fact, I was more unhappy for her father than for myself.

"I never saw her so angry and upset, even when she had bad fights with my father," she told me.

"Well, I'm sure it's nothing terribly serious. Women get hysterical over small things sometimes. It's part of being a woman," I said.

"It is?"

"According to most men," I added. Allison was lost. I smiled to myself and returned to my computer.

I was intrigued with some experiments being carried out at Oxford University involving the transplanting of human brain cells into monkeys to improve their intelligence. Out of the corner of my eye, however, I saw that Allison was quite shaken and didn't want to leave my room. Julie must have gone quite over the top, I thought, frightening her own daughter with her antics.

"You can stay here and watch television, if you want," I told Allison. "Just keep the volume low."

"Okay."

She turned on my television and sat watching it. Fifteen minutes later, my father arrived. He asked her to leave us alone. She glanced at me and then turned off the television and hurried out.

"You frightened her, Daddy," I said. "She's frightened enough as it is over how her mother apparently behaved. The child has enough damage from Julie's bitter marriage and divorce. She should be the one seeing Dr. Burns. As a matter of fact, if—"

"Forget Allison for the moment, Mayfair," he replied sharply, and closed the door. He just stood there looking at me and shaking his head.

"All right. What is it now?" I asked, and turned completely around in my computer desk chair.

"Why did you make up all those lies about Julie?"

"Excuse me?"

"The things you told Dr. Burns," he said. "Absolutely crazy lies."

"How do you or anyone else know what went on between me and Dr. Burns? Are you telling me that Dr. Burns violated the confidentiality between himself and his client?"

"I'm not interested in that, Mayfair."

"Well, I am. Do you think I would have been so forthcoming if I thought he would gossip about me? What did he do? Call you? Call Julie?"

"How she found out isn't important."

"Stop saying that. If anything, you should be on the phone with your attorney and not up here talking with me. He told one of her friends, didn't he? What, is he having an affair with her?"

He just stared at me.

I smiled and nodded. "That's it," I said. "It makes sense. That's why Julie was able to get me the instant appointment. Her friend's having an affair with him. I can see it now. He revealed things about my therapy session while he was sleeping with her, and she couldn't wait to tell Julie, right?"

He sat, looking overwhelmed. "You've misinterpreted everything. Julie's concern for your looks and your social happiness isn't out of some mean motive. She's beside herself. She was only trying to help you so you'd be happier and we'd all be happier. You know she's gone through this terrible marriage and horrible divorce. Her former husband belittled her, had affairs, and even brought a woman into their home, into their very bed, while she was away. She's trying so hard to have a happy marriage now, a happy family. I'm so disappointed in you, Mayfair." He looked down and shook his head. "I really don't know what else to do. A vibrator! To tell Dr. Burns she bought you a vibrator?"

He sighed deeply and rose.

"Needless to say, your therapy is over. Nothing will change until you want it to. That's clear. I've forbidden Julie to make any more efforts."

He stood for a moment looking at me.

"I don't know you anymore," he said, and walked out slowly.

I had never seen such a look of disgust in my father's face. She had played him well, I thought. She had him in her complete control now. Why wasn't he angry about how she had manipulated me into this therapy session, where she knew she would find out everything about me and use it against me? It wasn't right. I was being abused. Why wasn't he defending me, outraged about what had happened to me? Why couldn't he see that I had simply turned the tables on her?

Maybe it was hopeless. If anything, I hated her more than ever. She was down there sobbing, and he had probably returned to her side, holding her and comforting her, when he should be up here comforting me. Maybe if he had done that, I would have told him more, told him about Alan Taylor, and the loving ties that were splintering between us would have grown stronger again.

He'd be my father.

I'd be his daughter.

There was a tiny knock on my open door. Allison had returned, still looking very frightened. "What happened?" she asked. "Why was Daddy so angry? Are you in trouble? Is my mother still very upset?"

"It was just what I told you. One of your mother's friends said something unpleasant to her that upset her. She'll be all right. Don't worry about your mother. She'll always be all right."

"I wish everyone thought I was grown-up enough to know about everything," she said, sitting on my bed. "I know about a lot of stuff my mother doesn't know I know about."

"I'm sure you do."

"When you're not home yet and she can't see me, I read some more in the book you gave me."

"Oh? Well, that's good."

"If you're going to fall in love, you've got to know about that stuff."

"That's very adult of you, Allison. I thought you were old enough to appreciate it. That's why I gave it to you and was disappointed when your mother took it away from you."

She beamed. I never realized how much my compliments meant to her. "Do you think someone my age could be in love?"

"I don't know if age has much to do with it. Why? Do you think you're in love?"

"I don't know. Maybe. Jamie Baron says that when you are in love, you can't think of much else, and sometimes you look dopey."

"Jamie Baron sounds dopey."

"You never fell in love, right?"

"No."

She looked disappointed.

"Why is that important, Allison? You're who you are, and I'm who I am. We don't have to have the same feelings and thoughts about everything. In fact, you don't have to have the same feelings and thoughts as your friends do, either. You'll end up being a clone if you're not careful."

"What's a clone?"

"An exact replica with no independent thought. In short, a nobody." I wanted to add "like your mother and her friends," but I thought I had gone far enough.

She shrugged. "I just thought that if you fell in love, you'd know more so you could tell me for sure.

I trust you. I mean, you know so much that I would believe what you said."

"Well, I don't have to be in love to tell you that it has to be something that lasts longer than a week."

She nodded. "This has lasted all year, practically," she said as if she was in a confessional booth.

"You mean for you?"

"Yes."

"It also helps if the person you fall in love with falls in love with you."

"And wants to be with you a lot?"

"Yes, of course."

"And likes to touch you?"

"Exactly."

"And smiles and looks bright every time he sees you . . ."

"Now you sound as if you could write an advice to the lovelorn column," I said. "You going to see this boy at the party Friday?"

"Oh, no."

"No? Why not?" I grimaced. "I get it. He's not what your mother calls popular or acceptable. Is that it? He wasn't invited."

She pressed her lips together.

"Well?" I pursued. "Which is it?"

"None of that. He wouldn't come to a kids' party."

I sat back. "Wouldn't come to a kids' party? Who is this mysterious lover of yours?"

She pressed her lips together again. She certainly could look just like her mother at times. "I can't tell you," she said, and slipped off the bed. "It's a very big secret, the biggest secret of my life."

"That's more reason to tell me. Something that big could mean big mistakes, too. Who is it?"

"Allison?" we heard.

"My mother's calling. I'll see you later," she said, and hurried out.

Why was I wasting time listening to an adolescent's fantasy? I asked myself and returned to my research on the internet.

The following day, I could see that Julie's new approach toward me was going to be simply to ignore me. She didn't mention a thing about my conversation with Dr. Burns, nor would she talk to me or look at me unless it was absolutely necessary. Maybe she thought that if she acted like this, I'd break down and apologize to her. I knew she was hoping for some reaction, because after a while, the silent treatment was ricocheting back on her. It was too uncomfortable in the car and at the dinner table. However, she was too proud to play the victim. She was more comfortable on the attack, and she was at least smart enough to know where I was most vulnerable.

The day after that, she finally turned to me in the car and said, "You have no idea how much you've hurt your father, Mayfair."

I didn't respond, but she had launched her attack, and every chance she had, she repeated it and other accusations.

I was an unnatural child.

I didn't appreciate anything she and my father were doing for me.

I had never given her a chance.

I was resentful from the beginning, and actually, despite my high intelligence, I was very immature.

The best one was "Everyone has hardships to bear. You have to be more considerate of that."

I didn't have to ask her to elaborate. She was off and running.

She had a horrible first marriage and had to provide all the parenting for her daughter. Allison might not be a quarter as intelligent as I was, but she was a decent, good girl. They had a wonderful, trusting relationship compared to what I had, and what I had or didn't have was my own fault.

My ability to turn her off the way I used to seemed diminished. Something had weakened me in that regard. I felt like putting my hands over my ears. It seemed to be the only way, either that or shout back at her until she stopped.

Over the next few days, there was no doubt that my father was more upset with me than he had ever been. He acted like someone defeated and devoted more and more of his time to his work. I knew he was trying to find ways to avoid me, avoid the tension in the house.

In school, I had completely stopped trying to catch Alan Taylor's attention. I no longer even glanced his way, and I avoided passing his doorway. What had happened between us seemed so much like a dream now that I began to wonder if I had fantasized it all.

Finally, after another week had passed, I was going to the library just after his free period had begun, and

I had to pass his room. Just as I drew close, he stepped out.

We were alone in the hallway. There was no way to avoid each other.

"How are you doing?" he asked.

"Are you talking to me?"

He smiled. "Listen, I know how it must seem to you, but I thought it all over that night. We both crossed a line, and it's better if we pretend nothing happened."

"Better for whom?"

"Both of us." He hesitated and then added, "Probably more so for me. I'm thinking of getting engaged, by the way."

"I thought you didn't have a serious girlfriend."

"I didn't think it was as serious as she did—does—and after a while, I realized she was the right one for me. You'll be all right," he added. He flashed a smile and walked away.

I'll be all right? What, was he comparing what happened between us to a common cold or something?

I stood there watching him and wondered why he had to be my first experience. Why couldn't I have been with some intelligent, good-looking college boy, at least, the sort of boy the bitches suspected I might have been seeing? Even if that had ended disastrously, I wouldn't feel as much like a victim as I did right now.

When I glanced at myself in the glass of a trophy cabinet, I cringed at the expression on my face.

"Stop feeling sorry for yourself, damn it," I told my image.

As Suzie Bubble Brain loved to say, "Cry me a river. Build a bridge and get over it."

I started to walk on but stopped with surprise when I saw Allison standing in the girls' room doorway, which was just across the hall from Alan Taylor's classroom.

"Hey," I said. "Why are you just standing there like that?"

"I was watching you talk to Mr. Taylor."

"So?"

She shot away and walked quickly toward her classroom.

"Allison?"

I hurried to catch up with her when she paused. When she turned back to me, I saw she had tears streaming down her cheeks.

"What's wrong?"

"I heard what he said to you."

A chill ran through me. "What did you hear him say?"

"He said he was getting engaged," she replied, and turned to walk away a little faster, flicking the tears off her cheeks as she did so.

He thought he was getting engaged? Why was that so devastating to her? What was I missing here?

I walked slowly to the library, thinking about her and Alan Taylor, and when I entered the library and set my books on a desk, it hit me. I didn't realize I was laughing out loud until Mr. Monk called out to me sharply. The other students all looked up, surprised.

"Sorry," I said, and sank into my seat, wondering

just how far along and how deep Allison's fantasy went.

That little discussion we had about love in my room the other night now made more sense. This was why the love of her life wouldn't attend her girlfriend's birthday party. If Julie knew what sort of fantasies her precious, perfect daughter had, she surely would have heart failure. Maybe she'd even agree to send Allison to see Dr. Burns.

Again I laughed, but this time to myself.

I turned on the computer and took out my notebook. I was still doing research on the transplanted human brain cells and some of the statistical results that were being posted. How ironic, I thought, that scientists not only in England but here and in most industrialized and technologically sophisticated countries were doing research in an attempt to improve and increase intelligence in animals instead of all these human airheads. One of these days, I might get a call and be asked to donate some of my own brain cells.

That, too, brought a smile.

But something was nagging at me about Allison and her fantasy. She was so overly dramatic. I knew girls her age often were, but there was something different about her, something more. I paused and recalled the exact conversation we had, and then I felt my eyes widen.

How did that conversation go?

"It also helps if the person you fall in love with falls in love with you," I had told her.

"And wants to be with you a lot?"

"Yes, of course."

"And likes to touch you?"

"Exactly."

"And smiles and looks bright every time he sees you."

Likes to touch you? She did say that. How much of this *was* fantasy? I wondered.

I was at a disadvantage. Unlike most girls who went through puberty, I never had a crush on a teacher. I never idolized a rock star or a movie star. I never swooned over anyone. What were you supposed to feel and think? How far was this to go before it became ridiculous, even dangerous? I'd seen other girls break out crying for no apparent reason and then discovered it was because some boy or some teacher looked at them the wrong way or didn't return a smile as warmly. I never paid much attention to it, but this was different. At least, it felt different. Maybe, just maybe, I wanted it to be different.

I watched the clock and left the library about a minute before the bell to end the period would ring. I waited just outside the door of Allison's classroom. She came out talking with some of her girlfriends, but she still looked despondent. When she saw me, she stopped and said something to the other girls. Normally, I rarely spoke a single word to her during the school day after we had arrived, and sometimes I said nothing to her all the way home.

"Are you waiting for me?" she asked.

"Yes. I'll walk with you to your next class. Hang back, so the ones with big ears aren't so close to us."

"What? Why are you waiting? What do you want to talk about that's so important?"

"When you were in my bedroom and we were talking about love, you meant Mr. Taylor, right?"

She kept walking until I grabbed her arm.

"You meant Mr. Taylor, right?"

She looked around to be sure no one was close enough to overhear us. "Yes," she said. "Are you going to tell my mother?"

"What for? Besides, she wouldn't believe anything I said now, anyway. Stop worrying like a child, Allison. You're having grown-up thoughts. You're maturing, developing. You'd better act grown-up now and catch up with your body. Girls who don't are usually the ones who get themselves into trouble."

She looked at me, impressed, and nodded.

"I'm really the only one who's close to you who understands these things. You know that, right?" I asked.

"I guess," she said.

"Don't guess. Know it. I gave you the right things to read and always will."

"I know."

"You're right to be worried about your mother hearing about this. She'd have a nervous breakdown, and it would be your fault. When you were in my room, you said he likes to touch you. Were you making that up?"

"No."

"Don't lie to me, Allison. I'll find out," I said, grabbing her arm at the elbow and stopping her. She couldn't look me directly in the face. "You made all of it up, didn't you? You just told me those things to seem older, more sophisticated, right?"

"I *am* more sophisticated," she said with defiance. "He thinks so, too."

"Who does?"

She turned and looked down the hallway. Alan Taylor was standing in his classroom doorway as usual. She didn't say his name. She simply nodded in his direction for me and kept walking.

I looked at him, too. He seemed worried.

I caught up to her again and grabbed her arm, a little harder and tighter than before. She cried out. I pulled her farther away.

"You hurt me, Mayfair."

"That's nothing. Stop behaving like a child, now." I looked at Alan Taylor again. "Have you been telling me about Mr. Taylor? Was he the one you said loved you and touched you? Tell me, Allison," I said, with as determined and angry a face as I could manage.

"Yes," she said.

"Yes." I glanced at him again. He was still standing there watching us. "What are you saying? Have you ever been alone with him?"

She looked down.

"Just tell me. It's very, very important, Allison. Have you been alone with him?"

"Yes," she said, pulling her arm away.

"When?"

She kept walking.

"When, Allison?"

She paused and turned back. "I'll tell you later, maybe. Or I'll show it to you."

"Show it? What's that mean? How can you show it?"

"I wrote it all down," she said, and kept walking.

She was walking toward Alan Taylor. He was watching us closely. I stopped her again. "You wrote it all down?" I said under my breath. "Wrote what?" I couldn't raise my voice. We were too close to him now, and he was obviously very interested in whatever we were saying to each other.

"Everything," she replied.

"Everything?"

She walked away quickly.

Alan stepped aside to let her enter the classroom but kept his eyes on me. Maybe he heard what she had said.

I felt like a dozen firecrackers were going off inside me.

15

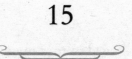

I couldn't concentrate on much else for the remainder of the school day. Of course, I couldn't talk to Allison again about it while Julie was driving us home. I'd had no other opportunities to pull her aside in school, so I had to hide my interest and as usual pretend to be in some deep thought about something too far above Julie to mention.

"Where did you write those things?" I asked Allison after we arrived home and went upstairs. I couldn't help lunging at her as soon as I had the opportunity.

"What things?" she asked, coyly now. Did she think she had something over me because she had something I wanted to know very much? Or did she realize the implications of what she had said and regretted it?

"You know what I'm talking about, Allison. I'm talking about Mr. Taylor. Don't try to be your mother and act like you don't know what's going on when you do."

"My mother doesn't do that."

"Okay, she doesn't do that. Where did you write the things about Mr. Taylor?"

"I wrote them in my diary, but I can't show it to you."

"Why not?"

"No one is allowed to read my diary. Not even my mother. I'm sorry I said anything about it. Leave me alone," she replied, and went into her room. Before I could respond, she slammed her door closed.

I should have thought she'd write something like that in her diary. Now she was embarrassed. I had never kept a diary. I did keep a journal when I was her mental age and for a while after, but it was filled with scientific observations of my experiences with insects and animals and very little about my feelings about them or about people.

When my father first married Julie, I started a journal about her. I was like an attorney building a court case. I kept track of every unpleasant thing she said or did. When I realized that nothing I wrote would please or perhaps even interest my father, I tore the pages out and burned them.

Somewhere I read that girls keep diaries because they can express their innermost thoughts without having to worry about anyone's reaction. Some analysts believe it's a form of therapy, a cheap form. Maybe I should have kept a diary about myself like Allison's diary. It's cathartic. It gives you relief. You get all the inner pain and tension out.

And I surely had a lot to get out. And I certainly didn't do it with Dr. Burns.

I had seen Allison writing in her diary only once and was so uninterested I barely paid any attention, but at least I had a good recollection of what it looked like. It was a leather-bound ruby-red book with a gold clasp. I imagined she kept it in her desk drawer, and I was sure she was writing in it right now, crying her river but building no bridge to get over it. Like most of the overly dramatic teenage girls around me, she wallowed in her own sadness even without an audience. At least she could feel sorry for herself if no one else would.

However, the depth of Allison's depression surprised me as much as it did Julie and my father. She was so unhappy at dinner that she barely ate a thing, and no matter how her mother prodded her with questions, Allison would not reveal the cause of her unhappiness. Unfortunately, Allison glanced at me during the questioning, and her mother became even more suspicious.

After dinner, when Allison had left for her room, Julie pulled me aside. "Did you say anything nasty or unpleasant to her that would make her so unhappy?"

"What would I say? What are you going to find wrong with me now?"

"Do you blame your father's disappointment in you on me? Is that what this is about? Because if it is, you have no right to take it out on poor Allison."

My father stood off to the side, looking meek but waiting to see what I would say. Years ago, he would have told her the idea was ridiculous and not to bother me with such a question.

"No," I said, glancing at my father. "I blame his disappointment in me on him."

My answer took them both by surprise. Julie's eyes nearly exploded, and he looked like he was in physical pain.

Before either of them could respond, I went upstairs and, like Allison, slammed my door shut. I didn't have a good night, either. It was uncharacteristic of me, but I sulked and raged inside myself. I didn't do any significant work and couldn't read. I watched a few minutes of television before shutting that off in disgust and just lay in bed, staring up at the ceiling. I felt tied up in knots, frustrated with myself as much as with everyone else.

We were so much better off before my father married Julie, I thought. Of course we both missed my mother. Because of who I was, what I could do, people might believe I missed her less. Some of that was understandable. Being a man, he was more lost and lonely. I could understand why a man as young as he was at the time had a need for a relationship with a female. I just couldn't understand and probably never would understand why he chose a woman like Julie. Maybe he should have had a heart-to-heart talk with her exhusband and learned what the divorce was about from his point of view. People like to find out who drove the used car they're considering and what they thought of it before they buy it. Why couldn't he have given a new wife at least as much thought and caution as a used car?

I didn't get more than a few hours of sleep. My father had to leave very early for a business trip. Julie took one look at me at breakfast and did her best to avoid looking at me after that. She was quieter than ever in the car, and with Allison still acting depressed and me behaving like a clam in a shell, it was more like riding to a funeral than to school.

"Remember, I'm going to Lisa's house to study for tomorrow's history test and have dinner," Allison told Julie just before she got out of the car.

"Oh. Right. Call me when you want to be picked up, but don't make it too late, Allison."

She finally turned to look at me.

"I'll be here to pick you up," she said.

"Don't bother," I said. "I have things to do after school and will take a taxi home."

"Oh. Well, then, I'll do some shopping down in Newport Beach with some friends," she said. I could hear the relief in her voice. She didn't have to be alone with me, even for fifteen minutes. I could shut her out easily, but it was a relief for me, too, not to have to bother.

It was an unremarkable school day for me, except that every time I saw Allison, she continued to look despondent. I noticed that when her friends were laughing, she wasn't even smiling. How could a fantasy about a teacher, even one as good-looking as Alan Taylor, cause a girl Allison's age to be so depressed? Why couldn't she see how ridiculous it was, and why would it take her so long to get over it? I felt sure she had fantasized about other teachers, boys, rock stars, and the like. She had gotten over them.

Could it really be that it wasn't a fantasy? Was

Alan Taylor's involvement with me simply part of his characteristic behavior? People, especially young girls, had the incorrect idea that only unattractive men took advantage of young girls. But I knew that it had nothing to do with their looks; it had to do with their mental state. Maybe, even for Alan Taylor, older women were too much of a challenge, too threatening, and this claim about his impending engagement was all a cover story.

Too curious now to ignore what was happening with Allison, I decided to go right home after school. It wasn't the first time that the behavior of other teenage girls interested me. I couldn't help feeling like an outsider. The things that made them laugh and cry, seized their complete interest and devotion, were mostly meaningless and silly to me. I took time to study and analyze them, knowing all along that it was a way to analyze myself. What was I missing? Why had my super intelligence made me so different? Did I enjoy being different?

Julie was gone for the day with her friends. My father was away and wouldn't be home until dinner. Our maid had left. The house was dead quiet. It was my house, but because of what I wanted to do, I suddenly felt like an intruder.

After I put my things away, I went to Allison's room. I wanted to read that diary, but I was surprised not to find it in her desk drawer. I had to be careful rifling through her things. I didn't want anyone to know, especially Julie, that I was doing this. I could just imagine the issue she would make of it.

It wasn't in any of Allison's dresser drawers, not even under the clothes, and it wasn't on the floor of her closet or on the shelf in it that was stacked with her board games. I checked her old toy box, with its dozens of small dolls and discarded electronic games, and then, frustrated, I even looked in the bathroom cabinets. If I hadn't seen her writing in it, I would believe she had made it up.

Did she carry it with her always? She probably did, I thought. Many girls her age probably did that. They were all afraid of forgetting to write down some major event in their lives, like their dreamboat boyfriend casually brushing against their budding breasts or something.

I was about to give up when I glanced at her shelves of children's books. Why hadn't I realized that for Allison, her diary was as important as a world-famous title? There between *Alice in Wonderland* and *The Wonderful Wizard of Oz* was the gold-trimmed, ruby-red leather binding. How appropriate that it was located between two of the world's most famous fantasies, I thought as I plucked it off the shelf. I listened to be sure no one had come home yet, and then I sat at her desk and opened the diary.

The first page was titled "My Life by Allison Cummings." Although my father still hadn't legally adopted Allison because her real father wouldn't give up custodial rights, Julie insisted that she go by his name. She was Allison Cummings now. It wasn't legal, but Julie told her it would look dumb to use her real father's name. I didn't know whether that bothered

Allison very much or not. She never said, and I never asked her.

From the dates on the pages, I realized she hadn't begun to keep this particular diary until early this year, but she began by recalling her feelings and thoughts after her mother had married my father and they had moved into our house. I was almost as interested in that as I was in what she had written about Alan Taylor.

Her writing was simple but surprisingly grammatical. Of course, she began each section with "Dear Diary" and dated it as if she were writing to someone who would actually listen or care. I suppose in the diarist's mind, she was sending a letter off into something like cyberspace. It was all floating out there but never touched by any other eyes.

What seized my attention, of course, was her opinion of and feelings about me. She liked my father very much and even thought he loved her almost as much as her real father loved her. I could understand that. My father did have a warm, wonderful smile. It was why he was so successful in business. I, however, was another story.

Dear Diary,

> *I always wanted to have a sister, even a brother, but when Mommy told me Mayfair was to be my new sister, I wasn't very happy.*
> *The first time we met, she was very polite, but she looked at me so hard with those scary*

eyes that she made me feel funny. She was very quiet and read even when we were all in the car or in a room together. She never asked me any questions or came into my room.

I remember she wouldn't let Mommy kiss her.

She still won't.

She didn't even kiss her father that much. He always kissed her, but she never threw her arms around him and kissed him like I would kiss Daddy.

I like her father very much. Someday I'll just start calling him Daddy, I'm sure. He'll probably love me more than he loves Mayfair, because I won't hesitate to kiss him or let him kiss me.

Maybe her daddy is sad about having a daughter like her. Maybe he pretends he's happy that she's so smart. Maybe he wishes he had a daughter more like me.

Mommy always thought Mayfair was very strange. She told me her father said she was more intelligent than any other student in the whole school. She told me Mayfair might be smarter than any student in the whole state and that we have to forgive her if she seems different because she's always thinking.

She's still that way. She can't help it.

Her brain won't stop.

Mommy said she thinks Mayfair even thinks when she sleeps and doesn't dream.

Dreams can't fit in her head because it is so crowded with thoughts and facts.

Mayfair never had a doll or at least never showed me one or told me she had one.

Mayfair doesn't have any real friends. Even now, I never see her talking with any girls except one girl named Joy who looks like she just got out of a third world country where people are starving to death. I don't think many girls or boys call Mayfair unless they need help with something in school. She usually doesn't get invited to other girls' houses after school or on weekends. I don't think she's ever hung out with friends at the mall or gone to a movie with them.

I can't remember if she was ever invited to a real party, but she doesn't seem to care.

Mayfair reads books Mommy can't read.

Mayfair never tells me about boys she likes.

She never wants to do anything with me. I asked her many times to do things, even just go for a walk, but she's always too busy.

But she is really very smart, even smarter than my teachers.

I ask her to help with my homework. Sometimes she does, and sometimes she's too busy.

I don't know why she's too busy. She is either on the computer or reading or writing things.

No one makes her do it. She does it because she wants to.

Mommy thinks she does it because she can't help it. Her brain makes her do it.

I still wish I had a sister.

Mayfair is like having another adult in the house. She doesn't even want to go to the movies with me and tells me every movie I want to see is silly.

Mommy says Mayfair might be the smartest kid in the whole world, but she would rather have me for a daughter and that secretly her father wishes the same thing.

She said Mayfair will never be happy. She said she wanted to see if she could help her.

That was when she tried to show her how to put on makeup and fix her hair.

Mayfair wasn't very interested, and Mommy gave up.

Here's what I remember about Mayfair when I first came to live with her and her father.

She never spilled anything at the table. She never ate too much or too little, and she always wiped her lips after every sip of what she was drinking.

She didn't care about her dresses or her shoes very much.

She never had a nightmare or cried.

She smiled sometimes, but it wasn't a big smile, and I can't remember when she laughed at something I laughed at.

> *She asked Mommy questions that made Mommy want to get away from her.*
>
> *Everything in her room was always neat. She liked taking care of her own room and didn't like the maid doing much in it.*
>
> *She never told her father that she loved him in front of me.*
>
> *I don't remember him going into her room much and never to tuck her in at night.*
>
> *I remember thinking that maybe she was made in a laboratory and she wasn't a real girl.*
>
> *She was in some of my nightmares.*
>
> *That's what I remember about Mayfair when I first came to live here in her and her father's house.*

I stopped reading for a moment. Nothing Julie had told her really surprised me, but reading Allison's impressions of me did give me pause. I loved my father more than she thought I did. Her mother had filled her with these ideas. The idea that she thought she could replace me in my father's eyes was disturbing. Maybe it was just a little girl's dream, that of a little girl who really didn't have a full-time father, but it still bothered me.

A second realization was how much Allison wanted me to like her and for her to like me. She really needed a sister. My father wasn't wrong when he said I wanted a sister, too. I wouldn't let myself get close to Allison. It was too much like accepting Julie. I didn't have to wonder why Julie never had any more children. Her husband probably realized that bringing

another one into the world with her would be unfair
to the child, maybe unfair to the world.

I looked at the diary again, this time flipping
through the pages that described more about her early
years with my father and me, how much she missed
her own father back then, and what she thought about
her new school, her new friends, and our house itself.

I was beginning to be discouraged and imagined
that she had made up what she told me on the spot.
She never had written about Alan Taylor, or at least
not in her diary. But then I turned a page and saw the
title: "The Day My Life Began."

Again, I listened to be sure no one had come home
yet. The house was still as quiet as before, and I felt
like a real intruder. My eyes returned to her writing.

Dear Diary,

Mr. Taylor looked at me differently today.
  I wasn't wearing a training bra anymore.
  And I had my first period last week.
  He knows I'm a young woman now.
Mommy said I was.
  *I think he knows how much I like him. He
always spends extra time with me, and today
when he stopped at my desk, he put his hand on
mine and kept it there the whole time while he
talked to the class. I saw how my girlfriends were
looking at me, all of them excited and jealous.*
  *I had a hard time listening to what he said.
My heart was beating so fast. Then he ran his*

hand over the top of my head and down the back of my hair as he walked away.

I thought about him all day, and whenever I walked past his room during the change of classes, he was standing there and smiling at me.

He was looking only at me.

His smile was only for me.

Dear Diary,

Today Mr. Taylor put his hand on my waist when he leaned over to read my composition.

I love his aftershave lotion.

He brought his face so close to mine we almost touched cheeks.

I know he likes me more than any other girl in his class, maybe all his classes.

He spends more time with me and never touches any of the other girls.

And he always waits for me in his classroom doorway so he can see me and smile at me when I go to other classes and pass his room. Today he even called to me and said, "Hey, how are you doing, Allison?"

I almost couldn't talk. I said, "Fine," and he laughed.

I love his laugh.

Dear Diary,

I knew it. I knew he likes me a lot and would find a way for us to be together more.

Today he asked me to come in during his free period and help him correct some quizzes.

How did he know I had study hall and could be excused?

He checked and made sure. He wouldn't have done that if he didn't really like me and want only me helping him.

My heart was pounding again when I walked into his classroom. He asked me to close the door, and then he told me to sit next to him at his desk. He put a chair there for me.

When I sat, he told me how much he liked the way I was wearing my hair and how much he liked the clothes I wore. He said the skirt I was wearing looked especially soft. He took some of it in his fingers and said, "Yes, this is very soft."

He didn't let go of it. Instead, he moved his hand under the material and kept saying it was the softest material he had ever touched. When he lifted it some more, he looked at my legs and said they were very pretty.

He touched my thigh and said my skin was so soft, too.

I didn't say anything. I wished he would kiss me, but not on the cheek, on the lips.

And then he moved his fingers up my thigh and touched me between my legs.

He wanted to know if I liked that, and I said yes, and he lifted my panties away.

Then he kissed me on the lips.

He told me he liked me very much because I was more grown-up than the other girls.

And I told him how much I liked him, too.

He said he wasn't all that much older than I was and the difference in ages between many wives and husbands was either the same or even more than the difference between us.

He had me move closer to him.

He moved his fingers all over me, and I closed my eyes.

Afterward, he said we should correct some papers just in case anyone asked.

Then he told me to come back on Thursday.

Dear Diary,

On Thursday, Mr. Taylor locked his classroom door after I came into the room.

Then he took me into the book closet at the rear of the room, and he kissed me again.

He wanted to take all my clothes off, and I wanted him to do it.

When I was naked, he kissed me everywhere and told me he knew he would keep loving me.

He said our love would get stronger and stronger as I grew older, and even when I was away in college, he would still love me.

And when I came home from college, he would take me out.

By then, no one would think it was wrong, and we would get engaged.

He said the most pleasure in the world for him would be watching me grow into a more beautiful woman.

Afterward, he had me get dressed quickly. He told me he didn't want us to do much more just yet.

He said we had to go more slowly, and I had to get more prepared.

He said he knew just how to do it and that I shouldn't worry about the details of sex.

Dear Diary,

I've been with Mr. Taylor almost ten times now. He said that we have to think of a way to meet outside the school.

He said he would think about it and I should think about it.

It's hard because it's such a big secret.

I wouldn't even tell Mayfair, even though she knows most everything and would make the best suggestions.

*I promised him I would never tell anyway,
and he said that if I broke a promise to him, he
would never love me again.*

*Today I wrote his name nearly five hundred
times in history class. No one knew because I
didn't write his whole name. I wrote, A--n T---or.*

Dear Diary,

Mr. Taylor and I finally met after school.

*I was at my friend Lisa's house, and when
her grandmother left, I told Lisa about Mr.
Taylor. I couldn't help it. I was bursting with
it and had to tell someone I trusted. She swore
first on her brother's, mother's, father's, and
grandmother's lives that she would never tell
anyone. After that, I told her everything, and
she believed me, and I left.*

*Mr. Taylor knew what time I would leave
and came by in his car.*

I got in, and we drove around just talking.

*Then he stopped by an old deserted house
he knew, and we parked behind it where no
one could see us.*

*I took off all my clothes, and this time, he
took off all his and we just held each other.*

*He said it would be good for me to know
about men, and he told me how to touch him.*

I didn't want to tell him, but I knew a lot already because Mayfair had given me a book to read, and I was reading it even after my mother took it away.

He said we still had to be careful because I could be spoiled and ruined if I went too fast.

I saw what sperm was, and then we got dressed quickly and he dropped me off back at Lisa's house.

Lisa wanted to know everything that happened. I'm glad I have a friend like her, but I saw she was a little jealous. I made her swear again on everyone in her family's lives never to say anything, and she did.

I promised her that if she was true to me, I would always be true to her and I would tell her more when it happened.

Then my mother came.

Dear Diary,

A terrible thing happened today. I can hardly write it, but I had to write it.

I heard Mr. Taylor tell Mayfair that he was going to get engaged.

I think my heart must have stopped.

I'm sick to my stomach.

> *Now, when he sees me, he doesn't act any*
> *differently from how he acts with the other*
> *girls in the class.*
>
> *I don't want to hate him, but I can't*
> *help it.*
>
> *I feel like running away or dying. All I*
> *do is cry when I'm alone, and when I'm not,*
> *I cry inside.*
>
> *I think I'll cry for the rest of my life.*
>
> *Only Lisa knows and understands why I'm*
> *so sad.*

I closed the diary and sat there.

Were these just the fantasy ramblings of an adolescent girl? They convincingly described the slow and deliberate approach of a sexual predator, the gentleness, singling her out, touching her innocently at first, just the way he had first touched me, and then the credible advances. Look at how easily he had turned himself on to me and then turned himself off when he had gotten what he wanted. Reading her diary made me feel as if I had been violated again.

I went from being fascinated by it all to blind, bloody rage.

Allison was just the type of girl who could be easily victimized. She was searching for a father figure since her parents' divorce. My father was providing something for her, but it wasn't really enough for a girl who was just blossoming into her full female emotions. The first part of her diary described someone desperate for significant, loving relationships. Julie certainly couldn't compensate for what Allison was missing, and I hadn't done much of a job of it.

Alan Taylor had pounced on her the way he had pounced on me.

Of course, it reinforced my opinion of Julie, too. How could any mother miss all this? A mother as self-centered as Julie could. I stared at the diary. Yes, to anyone else, it might just be the ramblings of a love-sick teenage girl fantasizing, but to me, it was as good as a legal brief.

I had to help her, I thought, and in doing so, I would get my own revenge and justice.

I laughed to myself, because an added bonus would be shaking Julie out of her tree of selfishness, arrogance, and insensitivity. Maybe then, maybe finally, my father's eyes would be opened and the hold she had over him would evaporate.

I knew just what I had to do for Allison and for myself.

I never liked believing in the power of coincidence or fate, but even I had to admit that something, maybe the spirit of my mother, had put me in a position to do what had to be done.

And I would do it.

16

Maybe I should be a writer of fiction, I thought as I sat in my room after putting Allison's diary back on the shelf. I loved to plot. The obvious occurred quickly. I couldn't reveal that I had sneaked into Allison's room and read her diary, and whether it was my pride or something more, I couldn't get myself, even now, even with this added potential evidence, to tell my father and especially Julie why I had a good reason to believe what Allison was claiming. For now, maybe forever, that would have to remain a deep secret buried in the darkest place in my heart. Too often, the messenger gets punished for the message, anyway. Julie would accept no favors from me. That was for sure. She would find some way to blame me and convince my father that she was right. At a minimum, she might point to the things I told Allison and the book I gave her to read.

"You put sex in her mind and all this has resulted because of it," she might say, as ridiculous as that was.

Suddenly, I would become the biggest influence

on Allison, and whatever I would have done to her, I would have done out of some meanness, some anger against her mother. Look at what I had done with Dr. Burns, how I had used him. Nothing I did was by accident. I was far too intelligent to do anything accidentally.

I could hear it all now.

No, this had to be done more subtly. It was a matter of planting seeds and using the system, which had also let me down when it came to what the bitches of *Macbeth* had done to me. This truly looked like the way to get back at everyone.

And I knew just how to start.

After Julie had picked up Allison and brought her home, Allison went directly to her room. I waited a few minutes and then knocked on her door. She was getting ready for bed and was already in her pajamas.

"I need to talk to you," I said. "It's very important." I closed the door.

She sat on her bed and waited with a look of concern. "What is it?"

"I know you're upset about Mr. Taylor. You have a right to be upset. What else did you hear him say to me besides telling me about his engagement?"

"Nothing else," she said. "I mean, I wasn't listening until he said that word. Engagement."

"Okay. Did you talk to anyone about what you heard him say to me?"

She started to shake her head.

"You'd better not lie about this. It's very serious. I'll tell you why, but you have to tell me the truth."

She looked sufficiently frightened.

"You told your best friend, Lisa, right? If I had a best friend, I probably would have told her, too. Well?"

She just stared at me.

"Look, Allison. You know you can trust me, and you know I'm smart enough to help you if you get into big trouble."

"Why would I be in big trouble?"

"Just tell me the truth, or I'll turn around and walk out of here. I mean it," I said sharply. "Did you tell Lisa or anyone else about Mr. Taylor, about being in love with him and his being in love with you?"

She still hesitated.

"You're luckier than I am, because you have a best friend you can trust, don't you?"

She nodded.

"Okay. Did you tell her anything about Mr. Taylor?"

She thought for a moment and then nodded.

"Do you know what happens to people, especially young girls, who make up stories about their teachers and what could happen to their parents?"

She shook her head.

"For starters, all sorts of legal troubles and lawsuits, not to mention what would happen to your mother's and my father's reputations. Now, if you didn't make up any stories, you wouldn't get yourself or your mother and my father into any trouble. Did you make up any stories about Mr. Taylor, stories you might have told Lisa?"

She shook her head quickly.

"Are you sure, Allison? This isn't some kid's game, now."

"I didn't make up any stories," she said. "Besides, I wouldn't even try to lie to you, Mayfair. You're too smart to fool about anything."

I widened my eyes. *Forget the compliment*, I told myself, *she does sound credible*. "What makes you think Mr. Taylor liked you so much that you would think he loved you?"

I saw that she was reluctant to answer.

"Did he favor you in class, touch you?"

She nodded.

"Did you help him correct quizzes or something with no one else in the room but you and him?"

She widened her eyes. "Yes."

"Did he touch you then? Tell me," I demanded.

She nodded. She looked like she might start crying, so I decided to stop.

"Okay, okay. Don't be frightened. You have nothing to worry about. You just listen to me. Even if you elaborated on something that happened between you and Mr. Taylor, embellished what happened a little because you wished it was more like that, don't ever say you made up any stories, understand? No matter what, don't ever say that, because once you say one thing is not exactly how it happened, they'll believe that nothing was, understand?"

"Okay. But why? Why are you asking me all this and saying all this?"

I paused and sighed as if it were a great effort for

me to talk about it. "I heard lots of gossip today. I think some of the older girls wanted me to hear it. Did you ever hear that expression 'Two can keep a secret if one is dead'?"

"No."

"Well, people can't keep secrets. Sometimes they don't even mean to reveal them, but they do accidentally. Lisa might have done that. She might have told other girls about the things you told her."

"No, she wouldn't. She's told me her secrets, and I wouldn't tell anyone."

"Whatever. If someone asks you about it, though, you'd better be sure you don't say you made things up. Okay? I can't stress this enough."

She nodded. "I'll ask her if she told," she said.

"And she'll say no, because she doesn't want you to be angry at her, or she might admit that she thought she could trust someone just like you thought you could trust her. She might have another friend she thinks of as a best friend, right? But she might think you'll be jealous, so she might not even tell you that. It probably won't do any good to cross-examine her."

I could see she was thinking.

"Right?"

She nodded.

"All right. Don't worry about it. I'm here for you. I'll make sure nothing happens to you and, that way, nothing happens to your mother and my father. Okay? It's too late for us not to expect some trouble."

She stared at me, her eyes filling with panic. "When?"

"Relax, Allison. I said I would protect you, and you know I can do that, right?"

"Right," she said.

"I'm trusting that you're telling me the basic truth about all this, Allison, trusting you the way an older sister would trust a younger sister. You realize that?"

She nodded. Again, she looked like she was going to burst into tears. I had pushed her far enough, I thought.

"Okay. Just go to sleep, and don't say anything to anyone about this, especially your mother, because once you tell her, she'll be very disappointed in you and maybe get sick or something. And that will be entirely your fault. It's better if you don't ever tell her you and I talked about it, either. Can you promise not to do that?"

She nodded.

"I don't hear you."

"I promise," she said.

"Good. This time, we have a secret," I said. "And I don't tell anyone anything that I don't want them to know," I added sharply. "You know you can depend on me, and I want to believe I can depend on you. That's what sisters do for each other."

She looked sufficiently impressed that I had referred to her twice as my sister.

"Good night," I said, and started out, stopped, and then returned to touch her hand. I saw how much that pleased her.

"Thank you, Mayfair," she said in a loud whisper.

I looked at her and smiled. She didn't know it, but

it was I who should be thanking her for not only helping her but helping me.

Allison's depression was replaced with abject fear the following morning, but it had the same appearance as far as her mother was concerned. She was just as quiet as the day before, maybe more so, because she was afraid to say anything about school in case she would make some mistake. She looked to me every time her mother asked her a question. I tried to answer for her, but I could see Julie was getting very concerned now.

That was good.

That was perfect.

I would go directly to stage two of the plan. I felt confident that I could carry it all out for both of us.

After my third period in the morning, I went to Mr. Martin's office and told his secretary I had to see him. I tried to be as dramatic as I could, emphasizing how important it was. She was impressed and went quickly to his inner office. Seconds later, she was out, telling me he was finishing a phone call and would see me immediately. For her benefit, I tried to look as troubled as I could.

"Mayfair?" Mr. Martin said, coming to his door moments later. "Come in. Please."

"Thank you," I said, and entered his office.

"Have a seat," he said, closing the door. "How can I help you today?"

"It's not me," I said. "It's my stepsister."

"Oh?" He sat behind his desk.

"Mr. Martin, I'm going to tell you some very

personal things so you will understand why you have to protect me."

"Protect you?" He sat forward. "What's this about?"

I looked down for a moment and then pulled myself up more firmly in the chair. "I was never happy about my father's remarriage," I began. "Julie knew that from the start, and consequently, we've never had a good relationship. I do what I can to keep the peace for my father's sake, but as you saw when she came in to talk about my situation with the other girls and their families, she was not what you would call a real advocate for me."

He didn't respond, but he didn't have to. I saw his agreement in his face.

"I'm not here for that," I added quickly. "I'm here for my stepsister, Allison. What goes on between her mother and me is not her fault. I've tried to be as good an older sister to her as I can be with her mother running interference all the time. She simply doesn't trust me with Allison. Allison, however, would like an older sister and does turn to me for help, not only with her homework but with other things."

"Well, that's very good," he said. "I'm sure in time Mrs. Cummings will realize—"

"The point is, what I'm about to tell you can't come from me. It has to come from Allison, but she is understandably terrified, especially about talking to someone else."

"Terrified? Of what?"

"Mr. Taylor," I said after a long pause.

"Mr. Taylor? Good heavens, why?"

"Even her mother doesn't know any of this yet," I said. "Allison is too frightened now even to tell her, but I can see how much she is suffering emotionally and psychologically. This is why I decided to come to you."

"Even her mother doesn't know about what?"

"Allison, my stepsister, has been sexually abused," I said.

His mouth opened and closed and then opened as he sat there dumbly.

"I didn't find out the details myself until recently. I've given it lots of thought, of course. I questioned her closely, and I read what she wrote in her diary without her knowing I had read it. In my opinion, there's validity to her stories. They're more than just some young girl's fantasies. I thought that because you and I have a good relationship, I could trust you with the information, and you would know how to handle it. I want to repeat, however, that if you use me as the source here, it will create new and more difficult problems, not only for my father and me but also for Allison herself. Her mother might never believe her, and that would be tragic. There are too many similar situations we all read about every day," I added, emphasizing the word *situations*.

"I see," he said. He looked like he was having trouble breathing.

"I don't have to tell you how hard mothers and fathers try to avoid facing reality when it comes to their children being responsible for something unpleasant, and in this situation, Allison has been involved in something quite unpleasant. Like you, I've read many of the extracts on the psychology of parenthood, the protective instinct of mothers and fathers, whether they be birds or people."

"That's true," he said. I could see his mind was reeling with the possibilities, the bad publicity, and his own responsibilities. He wasn't even listening to what I was saying now.

"Mr. Martin!"

He snapped out of his thoughts and looked at me. "Yes, yes, I'm listening, Mayfair."

"In this case, my case, Allison's mother would spin on me and try to blame me as long as it would all go away. She would be blind to what is really happening, and Allison would be victimized twice. If you can appreciate that, I'll go on."

"I understand your problem," he said.

"This isn't going to be hard, Mr. Martin." I leaned forward. "My stepsister is a very young, impressionable teenage girl just entering adolescence."

He nodded.

"Naturally, she has a trusted girlfriend."

He continued to nod.

"When I questioned Allison, she revealed that she had told her friend things, too, and I'm afraid that girl might have told another girl, who would tell another. You know how that can explode into something that would create quite a scandal for this school."

"Yes, of course." The worry in his face was practically oozing out of his eyes now.

"However, this gives us an opportunity. If you called Allison in and told her you've heard some things involving her and Mr. Taylor, she might just tell you everything herself, and that would make it easier for you. And for me and my family," I said.

The reality of what I was suggesting landed with a thump in his brain. He widened his eyes. "This is a very, very serious thing, Mayfair. An accusation like this against a teacher . . ."

"That's why I came to you first. Might I suggest, Mr. Martin," I added with a look of firm determination, "that as serious as it might be for a teacher, it is twice as serious for a young girl like Allison. Her whole emotional life could be damaged here. Her parents, my father especially, would be very, very upset."

"Of course," he said. "But young girls like Allison often form crushes on their teachers, and they fantasize, too."

"Absolutely. It will be up to you and whoever else to investigate and determine whether it is true or not. At some point, you'll have to ask for her diary to read the details or, if and when it comes to it, inform the proper authorities to request it." Before he spoke, I added, "Please keep this as quiet as possible for now, until you and whoever do a proper investigation."

"Yes, that's very important."

"You can be assured I won't talk about it. I've already explained why."

"Good."

"Mr. Martin, if you betray me, I'll make sure my stepsister clams up, and things will go far worse for everyone, especially the school administration. There are too many examples almost daily now of young people being abused and authorities sweeping it all under the rug to keep from being embarrassed."

"I understand. I'll handle it," he said quickly, and stood up. "Thank you for your trust," he added.

I rose. "No. Thank you for helping us. I'm leaving it entirely in your hands," I said, my voice full of warnings.

He nodded, and I left his office.

I didn't think I'd ever felt stronger, taller, and more powerful than I did at that moment. Anyone seeing me walk down the corridor would think I had just taken over the school.

My timing was good. The bell rang for lunch, and I intercepted Allison on her way.

"Take a walk with me," I said, pulling her away from her friends.

"What is it?"

"Mr. Martin called me into his office to ask about you, about the stories he had just heard. He has a very high regard for me and has often asked my advice about things, but this is quite different and the most serious thing of all."

Blood rushed into her face.

"Don't worry. I handled it well, as I promised. When he calls you in, tell him the truth. Can you re-member some of the details you wrote in your diary?"

"I guess so."

"When you wrote in your diary, did you include dates so someone would understand when these things actually happened?"

"Yes."

"That's good, very smart of you, Allison. It's like proof when it's written like that. I'm proud of you. So just tell those things if you're asked. You can tell him what you told Lisa, too. Did you tell her everything you wrote in your diary?"

"Not everything."

"Then just start with what you told her exactly. He might call her in, and it's important that she tells him what you said just the way you said it."

Her eyes began to tear up. She bit her lower lip. I think she was actually shaking.

"It's all right to look frightened, but if you're told you could get into great trouble by making false accusations against Mr. Taylor, don't start crying and say you made it up. This is a big embarrassment for the school and especially for the administration. They'll be hoping you're lying. They'll try to pressure you to say you were, but I told you that you could hurt us all, because they wouldn't stop with you. They'd call in my father and your mother, and other people would know about everything, especially Mr. Taylor. Okay?"

"Yes."

"When Mr. Martin calls you in, come look for me afterward to tell me what happened. I'm in the library all day today. All right?"

She didn't answer.

I shook her arm. "All right, Allison?"

"Yes," she said.

"Good. Go eat lunch, and act as if nothing is wrong," I told her, and sent her on her way.

I watched her in the cafeteria. Her friends were their usual boisterous and dramatic selves around her, but she sat like someone made of stone. When the bell rang to return to classes, she looked like she would need help to stand, but she did. I saw her walk out talking with her friend Lisa. Maybe she was warning her.

Toward the end of the following period, she came into the library. She looked pale and fragile. I was keeping an eye on the door, so when she appeared, I got up quickly and indicated that she should go back out.

"Into the girls' room," I said, and she followed me in. "Okay. Tell me everything that went on. Don't leave anything out."

"It wasn't just Mr. Martin. Dr. Richards was there, too."

"Yes?"

Finally, she started to cry. It was as though the tears had been pushing on her eyelids like a wild river pressing on a dam. They streamed down her face. Her lips trembled, and her shoulders shook. I put my arm around her and took her into a stall, put the toilet seat down, and had her sit. Then I handed her tissues and waited.

"It was just like you said it would be. Mr. Martin said he heard I was spreading stories about Mr. Taylor. He said it was a very, very serious thing and I could get into very big trouble if I was saying things that weren't true about a teacher."

"And?"

"I didn't say anything. Dr. Richards was nicer. He

smiled at me and said I shouldn't be afraid. I should tell them anything I wanted. So I did what you said. I thought about my diary and told them some of the things I had written in it."

"What exactly? You never showed me the diary, remember?"

"Like when Mr. Taylor started touching me and when he asked me to help him with marking quizzes. I only had study hall, so I could do it."

"He gave you a pass out of study hall to come to him?"

"Yes."

"Well, they can check that out easily enough. Very good, Allison. That was good thinking."

She smiled through her tears.

"What then?"

"I couldn't say some of the other things. I told them I was too embarrassed to say them, so they took me in to see Mrs. Milligan."

"The nurse. Very good. I should have anticipated they would do that," I added, but more for myself than for her. "What did she do?"

"She asked me all kinds of stuff, like what was in the book you gave me."

"And you told her?"

"She saw I couldn't say it easily, so she said she would ask me a question, and if it was true, I should say yes or, if I couldn't talk, just nod."

"I didn't hear everything in the gossip. What sorts of things did you say yes to? Him touching you between your legs, under your panties? It's all right to tell that. Those things often happen when someone takes sexual advantage of a young girl. Well?"

She nodded. "Even more," she said.

"Good. What did she tell you to do now?"

"Go back to class."

"You don't have to go back to class," I said. "You're too upset. We'll return to Mrs. Milligan's office. Don't worry. I'll go with you now. You'll say you came to look for me. It's all right."

"I'm scared," she said.

I put my arm around her. It felt as surprising to me as I'm sure it did to her. I had never embraced her like this before, but in a way, I felt I was embracing myself, comforting myself. I even kissed her on her forehead the way my father might kiss me to give me a sense of security. "You don't have to be the one who's scared now, Allison. Besides, I'm with you. C'mon," I urged, and walked her out.

I brought her to the nurse's office and told Mrs. Milligan she had come to me and was too upset to return to class. I asked her to let Allison rest in one of the small rooms she had in her office area, and of course she did.

"Did she tell you any of this?" Mrs. Milligan asked me.

"I'd rather not talk about it now," I said. "Besides, it might be legally unwise to do so. You should have kept her here. How could you expect her just to carry on as if nothing unusual had occurred after you cross-examined her? This is a major emotional and psychological crisis for a girl her age."

She recoiled. My sharp tone was like a slap to her. She nodded and went about some clerical work without trying to defend herself. I looked in on Allison, held her hand for a few minutes, and told her to be brave.

"Remember, you're doing this for all of us, Allison, especially your mother and my father. You're okay?"

She nodded and squeaked out a tiny "Yes."

I returned to the library. It was better to keep busy and behave as though nothing unusual was going on.

Stage three was about to start.

It began right before the end of the day. Julie was called to the school, and my father soon followed. They were in Dr. Richards's office when the bell to end the day rang. Dr. Richards's secretary came looking for me and told me to report to his office. I waited in the outer office. When the door opened, Julie had her arm around Allison's shoulders. Allison had been crying again, but now that was fine. The more she cried, the better it was, in fact. She would get the credibility she needed.

My father looked at me and shook his head. "You know what's going on here?" he asked.

I nodded. "She came to me after she was called to the office, and I took her to the nurse's office because she was so upset." That was all true. I wasn't lying to him.

"Let's go," he said.

Since he had met Julie at the school, they had two cars. I was to ride home with him, and Allison rode with Julie.

"What a mess," he said as we drove off behind Julie and Allison. "When did you learn about this?"

"I had some suspicions, but mostly last night."

"Why didn't you say something to Julie about it?"

"I'm not exactly Julie's favorite person right now, Daddy. I wasn't going to be the one to start something like this. What if it's not true? It has to be handled correctly."

"It sure looks true. You know that old expression 'Where there's smoke, there's fire.'"

"Yes, Grandmother Lizzy always said that," I replied. He turned and saw me smiling at the memory.

"What a mess. I wouldn't mind having Lizzy around to help with it."

"Where are we going?" I asked when I saw Julie miss a turn that would take us home and he turned to follow.

"We've arranged for Dr. Baer to see her."

"What? Why?"

"Julie wants her checked out to see . . . you know, if she's been sexually violated."

"That's disgusting. That will make her even more upset. That could cause serious emotional damage, Daddy."

"It's got to be done. This is a criminal situation now."

"But she never said things went that far."

"Who knows what she'll tell and won't tell, Mayfair, even to you. She's a very frightened little girl."

I sat back. This shook me up a little, because I hadn't anticipated it, and I should have. I really did feel sorry for Allison. I would hate to have had something like this done to me after being with Alan Taylor.

At the doctor's office, we waited in the lobby while Allison and Julie were in the examining room. When they came out, Julie looked at my father and shook her head. For a moment, I wasn't sure what that meant. It occurred to me that Allison might have somehow lost her virginity without telling me about it. Girls could have their hymens broken in other ways, too. I was a prime example.

We stood up, and Julie stepped closer.

"She's still a virgin," she told my father but also for my benefit.

I looked at Allison. She seemed to be walking in a trance. My heart twisted with regret. I didn't want to see her in so much emotional pain, but my anger was directed fully at Alan Taylor for both our sakes now.

"Let's go home," my father said.

The fact that she was still a virgin didn't contradict what I had read in her diary. She had never described penetration, so I didn't let that fact detract from the validity of the rest of it. What I had read and how she had reacted to my questioning were convincing enough for me, especially when I added what my own experience had been with Alan Taylor.

The story began to spread that night. Julie's friends were on the phone with her for hours, each taking a turn. Allison was too upset to come to dinner. Something was brought to her room. At dinner, my father and Julie said they had decided that Allison should stay home from school the next day.

"I don't think that's wise," I told them. "It will only make things more difficult for her when she returns. They'll be talking about her all day tomorrow. Besides, it will give her more strength if she follows a normal routine."

"I won't have her behave as if nothing unusual is going on. It's too much to expect of her. She's not you!" Julie practically screamed at me. "She has real feelings."

"Well, she can't be taking after you, either, then."

"Mayfair," my father said softly.

I thought about what she had said. I had no trouble returning to school on the days following my tryst with Alan and trying to confront him. His attitude and avoidance were just as traumatic, but I didn't stray from my normal routine. Was Julie right? Did that mean I didn't have real feelings?

"I'm only trying to help. I've studied these sorts of traumatic events, Daddy. I know what has been found to be helpful and what has not. It's not a matter of feelings, Julie," I said, trying desperately to sound as if I did care about her and what she was going through, having her daughter involved in such a thing. "It's a matter of what's more effective. I'm only thinking of Allison."

"She's not going there tomorrow, and that's that," she said firmly.

I looked at my father and then finished eating without saying another word.

Julie mumbled through the remainder of dinner.

"I'm not burying my head in the sand, letting the school take any convenient way out of this. I'm going to make sure that justice is done. Those administrators know it."

I couldn't resist. "I hope it's better justice than what occurred after those bitches from *Macbeth* soiled *my* reputation," I said.

Julie bit down on her lower lip. My father shook his head.

"Maybe that was a terrible injustice," Julie confessed. "I was only trying to do what was best for you."

"She knows that now," my father said, looking at me pointedly.

I didn't have to say anything. Stage four had begun. Julie was going to charge ahead like a wild bull again, and Dr. Richards, unlike me, couldn't lock his door against her.

There was nothing left for me to do but wait.

In the morning, I saw that a substitute was replacing Alan Taylor. It would remain that way until the matter was resolved, but it became very clear that no matter how it was resolved, his future at the school was in jeopardy. Julie and her friends were simply too powerful for anyone, even if he were innocent, to overcome them. This was, after all, a private school that was dependent on tuition and donations from wealthy parents and friends of the school.

Of course, in my mind, no matter what he did or didn't exactly do with Allison, he was not innocent.

Perhaps I was more of a victim. It didn't matter now. It was better this way. Julie was taken down more than a peg or two. I was getting two birds with one stone.

I did have moments of self-doubt and even moments when I thought I had gone too far for justice and revenge, but I always overcame those feelings with cold logic, convincing myself that I was surely not the first or the last high-school girl he had victimized, and Allison wasn't the first young teenager.

Before the week was over, Alan Taylor and his counsel appeared at the school for a meeting in the principal's office. The moment he was spotted, the news flowed like an electric current through the halls, classrooms, and offices. How he found out I was alone in the laboratory, I didn't know, but when I looked up from some slides I was studying under the microscope, he was in the doorway. For a long moment, we just looked at each other.

"You put her up to it, didn't you?" he asked.

"Did I? Or did you?"

"You can't believe that."

"I believe in what I can prove and what I know from my own experiences. Nothing else."

He nodded. "You don't have to admit to it. I know. I didn't treat you well. I'm sorry." Then he surprised me by smiling. "What was it William Congreve wrote?"

"'Hell hath no fury like a woman scorned,'" I answered.

"Exactly. I guess I should have remembered that.

Well, have a good and interesting life," he added, and walked away.

I returned to my slides, but I wasn't focusing on anything. My vision was too cloudy. I had my victories, but I was disappointed in my reaction.

I had trouble seeing through the tears.

17

The famous moments of the calm before a storm followed. It was especially dark and silent in our house. Dinners were like funerals. The clanking of silverware and dishes had never sounded as loud. Even the maids seemed to be tiptoeing wherever they went and speaking in whispers. Allison was forbidden to use her phone. She had been told to speak to no one about any of this now that an actual criminal trial was looming. Julie didn't even want her to mention it in the house. In fact, thinking about all this, Julie was so disturbed one day that she charged up the stairway and disconnected Allison's phone so it wouldn't ring, practically ripping the wire out of the wall. She was constantly laying down threats. I thought she was close to having a nervous breakdown.

Whether he had to or was just looking for some relief from the heavy atmosphere in our home, my father worked longer hours and took three overnight trips during the week. Julie went to dinner with friends all three nights, soaking up waves of sympathy, I was sure. In my mind, despite the act she put on in the house for us, she probably enjoyed the extra attention she was receiving from her friends.

And then, just as there was an opportunity to take a deep breath, another crisis exploded.

The district attorney informed Julie that he had to have Allison's diary. Just as I had advised her to do, Allison had revealed to Mr. Martin that she had written everything that had gone on between her and Alan Taylor in it, along with the dates. He had informed the district attorney. When the assistant district attorney arrived at our home a day later to get the diary, my father wasn't home, but I was downstairs. Julie had been at her wit's end about it because Allison wouldn't let her read it first. She had hidden it in a better place, which amused me at first and then, when I gave it more thought, worried me.

Was she simply embarrassed or afraid of her mother's reaction to the things she had written? Even though I had never written anything I didn't want anyone else to read, I realized that especially for a girl like Allison, someone else, even a mother, reading her intimate thoughts was truly like exposing herself, parading naked and revealing every blemish. Everyone needed some sort of privacy. If you couldn't even protect the sanctity of your thoughts, what did you have left? On top of everything else that had been done to her, especially the vaginal exam, Allison could easily have a nervous breakdown herself, and who knew what the result of that would be?

"Once we have it, we'll have to turn it over to Mr.

Taylor's attorney," the assistant district attorney told Julie.

She looked absolutely shocked. "What? How many people will read this? I won't permit it."

"We can't withhold evidence from the defense attorney," he explained calmly. "And that diary has now become evidence, Mrs. Cummings."

Of course, Allison didn't want to hand over the diary. She cried, and Julie made the assistant district attorney promise her that only the people who absolutely had to read it would be permitted to read it. Allison wanted to rip out the pages that had nothing to do with Alan Taylor, but the assistant DA said that would not go over too well.

"I haven't even read it," Julie said, and she looked angrily at Allison. "She's hidden it from everyone."

I was sure Julie was wondering what Allison had written about *her*.

"I'm sorry," the assistant DA said. "We'll ask the judge to restrict access to the document. That's the best we can do."

That didn't make Julie any happier, but there was nothing she could do about it. I was surprised when she looked to me for help.

I shook my head. "If the district attorney believes it will help make the case stronger, Julie, you shouldn't resist turning it over," I told her. "We want Allison to have all the support she can get."

She glared at Allison. "She never kept so many secrets from me. I never knew she had been writing in such a diary."

"Didn't you?" I asked.

I thought she had hit all the stops on her way to female adulthood. How many times did she describe the dances she had gone to, the boyfriends lining up, the proms, the clothes, the hairdos, all of it spun not only to rub it in my face, I thought, but also to convince Allison that her mother was some sort of a star?

"Didn't you have a diary when you were Allison's age?"

"It wasn't something I expected would end up in a courtroom," she snapped back. Her eyes quickly cooled because of the assistant DA, who now looked uncomfortable. Then she added, "But none of us expected any of this, I suppose. Go get the damn thing," she told Allison. "Now!"

Allison brought it down, fear and trepidation vivid in her eyes.

"I promise you'll get it back when it's no longer needed," the assistant DA told her when he took it from her reluctant fingers.

"We won't want it back. We'll want it burned," Julie told him.

Two days later, I waited in the living room for my father and Julie, because I knew the district attorney had called them to his offices to discuss the case. From the looks on both their faces, I could tell something wasn't right. Allison was up in her room doing her homework. I had just helped her understand some of her new math and explained some grammar problems. I was truly feeling sorry for her, but I also wanted her to be strong for what was to come, strong for both of us.

"I need a drink," Julie said almost the moment she stepped into the house.

My father glanced at me, shook his head, and went to the bar. Julie sat on a stool and lowered her head to her hands. Neither spoke. Watching them, I felt the tension building in me, too.

"What's happening?" I asked. "Why are you both so upset?"

Julie turned to look at me. I had been reading a book on child psychology and was still holding it. A crazed smile broke across her face, twisting her lips. One thing I had to say for her, she rarely looked ugly. Even when she was in a rage, she had the sort of beauty that was even more striking. Right now, she looked like someone suffering from Bell's palsy, a form of facial nerve weakness, with half her face distorted.

"That might be the right book for all of us to read now," she muttered. "I guess I'll have to borrow it when you're finished."

"What? What's going on?" I asked my father as he served her a Cosmopolitan, the vodka drink she favored.

He stood back and watched her drink half of it in one gulp.

"Daddy?"

"They've recorded the events and dates that Allison entered in her diary and continued their investigation based on that. Lisa Morris was interviewed yesterday, and the date that Allison claimed to be at her home when Mr. Taylor came by to pick her up is not right. Lisa's mother had taken her to the orthodontist that day. Allison couldn't have been there."

"What's the big deal? Maybe she just got the dates confused," I said.

"This is a criminal case, Mayfair. It goes to court. You can't claim dates and events that don't prove true and undermine Allison's credibility. It makes the diary nearly worthless."

"Didn't Lisa describe the things Allison had told her, though?"

"The assistant DA said she did describe some of those things but in a very vague and confused way. He said she isn't going to be a good witness. She is in Allison's class, and when she was asked if she had seen any of the things Allison claimed were happening in the classroom between her and Mr. Taylor, she said no. Apparently, they've quietly questioned some of the other students and have yet to find one who corroborates any of the things Allison claimed. It doesn't seem like he singled her out."

"But they had the pass he wrote for her to get her out of study hall, didn't they?" I asked. "Allison told me about that just the other day," I quickly added.

"Yes, but that only confirms that she helped him correct quizzes. Apparently, he did that with other students in his class, many of them boys. It's not something no other teacher in your school does, anyway, Mayfair."

Julie sucked back a sob and drank the rest of her Cosmopolitan. "Make me another, Roger," she commanded.

"What else did the district attorney say?" I asked. I could feel my stomach tightening into a knotted ball of rubber bands.

My father sighed. Julie uttered a small moan. He prepared another drink for her. "In light of this," he said, "but something he probably would have done anyway, Taylor's attorney, who saw a wide hole to drive through, asked the court to assign a child psychologist to interview Allison."

Maybe they'd assign Dr. Burns, I wanted to say, but any attempt at humor to lighten the moment would surely go over like a lead balloon.

"A girl as young as Allison, under such pressure and emotional tension, is easily capable of getting some facts confused," I offered.

Julie turned to me. "You think so?"

As if I had it underlined in the book I held, I lifted the volume for emphasis. "Of course. All those young girls are under great pressure. They're afraid to say anything that would involve them in any way with what's happening. Many might have been warned by their parents to keep their mouths shut. If the district attorney is good, he'll know how to navigate and build his case."

Julie looked a little relieved, but my father only offered a knowing smile, like someone who realized I was humoring a desperately worried person.

I left them.

I wanted to go right into her room and ask Allison more about Lisa from what I knew she had written, but I was still reluctant to reveal that I had read her diary, and my father had already asked me to try to help calm things down by avoiding any conversations about what had occurred.

The only thing I did discuss with Allison, a few days later, was her upcoming session with a court-appointed psychologist. She knew I had gone to Dr. Burns, of course, so she relied on my experience.

"It's just a lot of talking, Allison," I told her. "He's not going to make you feel bad. Tell him the truth, and tell him what makes you feel better to tell someone. Just the way you revealed everything to me, in fact."

She told my father and Julie that I had given her older-sisterly advice about her upcoming interview, and my father came to my room to let me know how proud he was of what I was doing to make the situation easier for Allison.

"Julie just said that it's at times like this when she really appreciates how mature and bright you are, Mayfair. I think she wanted me to express that to you, too."

"Did she?"

"Yes, she did."

He hugged and kissed me on the cheek before leaving. Secretly, of course, I was very frightened for Allison, as I was for myself.

The proverbial other shoe dropped two days after Allison's session. The district attorney called Julie and my father in again, this time to tell them the psychologist's report was going to be devastating to any prosecution. The heavy depression that had fallen over the house only seemed to get thicker.

"This is getting to look more and more like a disaster for all of us," my father declared.

"He's just got a very good lawyer," I told him and Julie. "Lawyers would defend Satan if they were paid enough."

Neither of them cared to argue or had much more to say about it.

One night soon after, my father came to my bedroom to tell me the school board was requesting that he and Julie attend a special closed session to discuss the matter. Julie said she felt like someone who had stuck her head out the window of a 747 jet. Previously, she had gathered a half dozen of her friends, mothers of other students at the school, and they had demanded a special session with the school board and administrators. The big question was how something like this could occur at a school as small as ours and right under the eyes of other teachers and staff. The conclusion the parents came to was that someone obviously was not supervising properly. My father attended the meeting, too, and I heard them discussing it afterward at home. The promise was made to conduct a vigorous investigation. But there was also the big possibility that some heads would roll.

This time, things went quite differently. I heard them arrive back home and waited in my room. Allison was already asleep. I think she had fled to bed out of fear more than anything. I went downstairs. They were both in the living room. My father was having a Scotch and soda, and Julie was sitting on the settee looking stunned.

"What's happened now?" I asked.

"It wasn't pretty," my father said.

Julie cried, "How can I ever look my friends in the face?"

"There'll be a story in the paper," my father said. "Of course, Allison's name won't be mentioned."

"But everyone will know what's happened and who it's happened to," Julie moaned.

"I don't understand. What went on?" I asked.

"Alan Taylor's lawyer was present," my father said. He could easily start a lawsuit, but Mr. Taylor's not interested in prolonging this. Under the circumstances, everyone else was quite relieved."

Alan Taylor was going to act like he was doing everyone a favor, but I was sure what he was really worried about was it going any longer and my coming forward. Allison's diary inaccuracies and fragility were one thing. If I were the witness, it would be a totally different situation. I could describe details of his apartment, where we got the pizza, even the wine he had served me, and both Julie and my father would remember that was an evening I did not call or come home for dinner. Maybe he'd be concerned that someone had seen us together. If the police really investigated, it could come to that. No psychologist or misdated diary was going to change it, good defense attorney or not.

Of course, there was the possibility that people would still think I was out to avenge my family, my stepsister, and anyway, I didn't think my father and Julie were up to another barrage of depositions, investigators, and public scrutiny.

"Damage is done to the school as it is. It will be mentioned in the stories, of course, and this sort of thing is not good for a private school always looking for potential new students with parents who have fat checkbooks," my father said.

"Mr. Taylor didn't ask for anything in return?"

"A good recommendation, apologies. He's already lined up a new job, apparently."

"You didn't apologize to him, did you, Daddy?"

"No."

Julie sobbed harder. She looked up at me. "You believed her," she asked with some note of hope in her voice. "Why?"

All of a sudden, my opinion was very important to her. Was this my time to make my case, start them at Alan Taylor again, and once more turn the school topsy-turvy?

I looked at my father. Should I do it? Should I tell them both exactly why?

"There's no point in doing this sort of thing to ourselves," my father said, sensing my reluctance. "Let's not go over it and over it. It's done. Over. Let's just work on our recuperation. Get things back to normal as quickly as we can." He looked to me for confirmation.

I said nothing. I turned and went up to my room.

In the days that followed, Julie seemed to wither right in front of me. Her arrogant posture and condescending tone were gone. She practically tiptoed, slouched over, and was unusually quiet at dinner. My father was upset and did the best he could to cheer her up, but she often broke into periods of sobbing.

This time, I took the opportunity to suggest that she go see Dr. Burns. "If there was ever a time when someone needed some therapy, Julie, it's now, and it's you."

After she flew out of the room, my father told me he didn't think that was funny.

"It's not meant to be funny, Daddy," I told him. "She's obviously in a bad depression and needs either some medication or counseling. She's not eating properly. She's spending too much time sleeping. Next thing you know, she'll abuse alcohol or drugs."

He frowned, but I could see he was taking me seriously and wondering if having her see someone for professional counseling wasn't indeed necessary.

Both he and Julie were worried about Allison, too, but oddly, when Allison returned to school, her friends treated her more like a heroine than a girl who had done something evil. Allison told me about their conversations. She claimed that many of her friends refused to believe it hadn't all been true. I understood that they could talk about Alan Taylor openly, since he wasn't in our school any longer. Now that they weren't in front of a district attorney or giving a deposition, they comfortably swore that Mr. Taylor did single Allison out and spent more time with her than he did with them. Some even claimed to have had similar experiences. It was like one of those mass-hypnosis situations. Maybe they thought it made them look older or more sophisticated to have been titillated, teased, and inappropriately touched. So Allison had gone a little too far with her accusations. So what? She did what she had to do, didn't she?

I stood back and watched her in school and laughed to myself when I saw how popular she had become. It made me feel a little better about the outcome. Everyone wanted to know the details about her being questioned by the district attorney and a psychologist and about the things she had said. She got away with it by admitting that she had exaggerated a little, but saying Mr. Taylor had still been after her "bod." In any case, after a while, I thought she had outdone her mother when it came to being a little arrogant. She was the one strutting around the house, not Julie. Her phone was always ringing, and invitations for parties and dinners with friends were constantly being offered to her.

I was the one who had new troubles in school. I had forgotten about the bitches of *Macbeth*. They boiled their venom and came at me whenever they could with their snide remarks about how bad an influence I was on Allison. Most of the time, I ignored them, but one afternoon outside the library, I decided enough was enough.

"Your little stepsister is quite the liar, isn't she?" Joyce Brooker asked me. She practically put her face right up against mine. "I guess you trained her well."

"Afraid she's competition for you?" I replied, not backing up a step.

"Just whose fantasies were they?" Cora Addison asked, stepping up beside her with her hands on her hips. "Yours or hers?"

I spun around on her and smiled. "I think she told me she overheard you dreaming out loud and got her ideas from that."

"That was a silly question, Cora," Denise Hartman said. "They can't possibly have been *her* fantasies. They involved someone with a penis."

They all laughed.

That brought some other students around to listen and watch, and then more gathered to see what was happening to cause such interest.

"From what I hear, you're the one around here who's involved with more penises than an urologist," I replied.

"A what?" Cora asked.

"Oh, I forgot. You're a little slow and need someone to translate English for you."

"You're such a freak," Denise said. "No wonder your stepsister is so screwed up. Who wouldn't be screwed up living with you?"

"What did your father do to have someone like you, take drugs?" Joyce said.

"No," Cora said over their laughter. "He has to take them now, now that he has to live with her and admit to being her father."

"Unlike your father, who's not sure he *is* your father, is that it?" I fired back.

"Bitch," she said.

"That's what I hear the boys around here call you, 'my bitch,'" I said.

Everyone howled, and Cora turned bright pink. She looked at her audience and then, without any warning, swung her pocketbook at me and caught me on the left side of my head. She must have had something heavy in it, because it dazed me. I stumbled and then lost my footing and slipped on the short step at the library door. When I fell, everyone took off in every possible direction.

I heard Mr. Martin call my name as I was struggling to my feet. "What's going on here?" he asked, helping me up. "My goodness, your head's bleeding, Mayfair. What happened?"

I felt my temple and looked at my fingers. The amount of blood didn't surprise me. "It's all right. Head wounds usually bleed like this," I told him.

"It's not all right. We'd better get you to the nurse. C'mon," he said, taking my arm. I was still a little dizzy. "What happened?" he asked again.

"The debate team lost control of itself," I said.

"Who hit you?"

"Does it matter?"

"Absolutely," he said.

We entered the nurse's office, and Mrs. Milligan sat me down immediately and hurried to get a wet cloth.

"Did she fall?"

"No, someone hit her."

"With what?"

"A pocketbook loaded with cement," I said.

She began to work on the wound.

Mr. Martin stood there staring at me. "Who did it? What was the argument about?"

"CSI will confirm Cora Addison," I replied. "I'm sure there's some of my DNA on her pocketbook."

"Was this about your stepsister?"

"It seemed to be more about Cora and her friends, but that's just my opinion."

"This is quite a deep cut," Mrs. Milligan said. "She might need stitches. We need to be concerned about a possible concussion."

"I'm not going to sleep, and there's nothing one could do about a minor concussion, anyway, Mrs. Milligan. I'll be fine."

"I don't know." She looked at Mr. Martin. "I'll clean it up and cover it, but I really think she needs stitches. I'll run her over to the urgent care. And I'd feel better if she had an X-ray."

"I don't need all that," I protested.

"You're not a doctor yet," Mr. Martin said. "Do what you have to, Lila," he told the nurse. "I'll inform her parents," he said, and left.

I tried to resist, but Mrs. Milligan was determined.

"It's out of your hands and mine," she said. "The insurance company would insist."

When we went out to her car, I could see students gaping at us from classroom windows. Mrs. Milligan saw them, too.

"You've attracted a crowd," she said.

"I'm glad I can provide them with desperately needed distraction from their boring classes," I told her, and she laughed, which surprised me. Could it be she liked me after all? Even after the things I said to her when I brought Allison to her office?

Less than an hour later, Julie arrived at the urgent care. I did require stitches, and an X-ray was taken. I had no concussion.

"How could such a thing happen now?" Julie asked Mrs. Milligan immediately. From the way she asked it, anyone would think she was blaming me, no matter what.

"I failed to duck, bob, and weave," I said.

Mrs. Milligan told her as much as she knew. The rest would come later.

"I guess we're going to have to seriously consider whether both of you should continue at this school," Julie told me on the way home.

I didn't say anything. My head was throbbing, and despite what I had told Mrs. Milligan and Mr. Martin, all I wanted to do was go to sleep.

My father was very upset when he heard about the incident. He came home as soon as he could and hurried up to my room.

"Hey, May," he said, sitting on my bed and taking my hand. He looked at my wound. "Nasty. I heard what you told Julie. I thought I taught you how to duck."

"I guess it was one of the few times I wasn't paying enough attention."

"You want to tell me how this happened?"

"It was the same girls who made those stupid accusations about me in the locker room, remember?"

"Oh."

"They were emboldened by the resolution of that situation, and now we're seeing the fruits of the politically correct compromise."

"I'll look into it myself this time," he promised. "This time, there'll be no politically convenient solution."

I shrugged skeptically, but he did look determined.

He went down to his home office to make some calls and returned in a little less than half an hour to report that Cora Addison had been called to the principal's office and suspended from school. Her parents would have to go in with her when she returned.

Although Mr. Martin and Dr. Richards saw this as just punishment because Cora had resorted to violence, I knew it would not do me any good with the rest of the student body, especially the other two bitches of *Macbeth*.

This was far from over.

18

If there had been anyone who would say hello, smile, or be in any way friendly to me before this at school, he or she was gone, probably forever. My academic achievements, my freedom in pursuing advanced studies, and my self-imposed isolation from school activities already had done much to single me out as someone too different. Now I was surely going to be not only too different but also too much trouble, someone never to be trusted. I knew I would feel like I was walking around school wearing not a scarlet A like Hester Prynne in *The Scarlet Letter* but a scarlet R for *rat*. Or a scarlet C for *creep*.

I didn't look forward to it.

Later, at dinner, when my father talked about my violent confrontation with the bitches of *Macbeth* again, Julie looked like she had always expected it and wondered why something like this had never happened before. I could squeeze as much sympathy out of her as I could squeeze water out of a rock.

However, Allison felt sorry for me, and after dinner, she came into my room to tell me so.

"That was very mean what they did to you," she said. "They ganged up on you."

"That's the way people like that are, Allison. They can't do anything unless they're part of a gang. They're really cowards."

"It's all my fault, isn't it?" she asked me.

"Why is it your fault, Allison?"

"I heard they were saying bad things about me, and you told them off."

"They were saying bad things about both of us, mostly me, Allison. Forget about them. They're not important. I could sketch out their entire lives for you. They'll end up eating their own hearts."

I didn't want to tell her they would probably become women just like her mother, but she brought up Julie herself. "I told my mother how you defended me, how you tried to help me with everything," she said.

I put down my book and looked at her. "What do you mean, everything?"

"You know," she said. "When you told me what to do and what to say and what not to say when Mr. Martin called me into his office that day."

"But you and I had a secret," I said. "You made me a promise you would never tell anyone, not even your mother, about our conversations."

"I wanted her to know how much you helped me," she said, raising her arms. "I wanted her to know how we were becoming real sisters and that she should feel sorry for you about what those girls did."

"Okay," I said.

What else could I say? But it was like sitting there listening to the ticking of a time bomb.

Allison returned to her own room. I closed my eyes. The throbbing had stopped but now suddenly began again. This time, it wasn't coming from the wound. It was coming from my anticipation.

After nearly an hour passed, I thought nothing more would occur this particular evening, but I was wrong. I heard the knock on my door, and before I could say "Come in," my father opened it, stepped in, and closed it behind him. The look on his face was enough. I didn't need to hear anything.

He stood there looking at me for a moment. Then he shook his head and came closer. "Let me begin by telling you that Julie is quite hysterical downstairs."

"Inordinately so?"

"No, King's English this time, Mayfair, and no sarcasm. I'm warning you. I'm trying to understand this. You went to Allison and told her that the stories she had told her best friend about Mr. Taylor were being spread around in the school?"

"So?"

"Did you do that?"

"I did, after she was so upset about overhearing him say he was going to get engaged. You saw how depressed she was during those days, how she hardly ate and wouldn't talk."

"Yes, I did. Julie tried to talk to her about it. We both assumed it was boy trouble at worst but certainly not man trouble."

I looked away. Why was he so sensitive to Allison's emotional pain and so insensitive to mine? When was the last time he looked at me and wondered if I was happy or if something had upset me? Was it my fault? Because I was so intelligent, with an off-the-charts IQ, he believed I would always be smarter at solving my own problems than he would be? Did my brilliance make my father feel unnecessary?

Or had Julie turned him away from me completely so that all his fatherly attention and concern were directed at Allison? Whenever I had been alone with them, Julie's conversation was usually centered on Allison. There was never any time to talk about me, ask about me, and care about me, unless it somehow supported her beliefs about who I was and what I needed on her terms and her terms only. She was the sun in this house, and I was barely just another planet.

I sincerely felt bad about it all, but another part of me was smart enough to ask if I wasn't simply trying to rationalize and excuse my bad behavior. The bottom line was that I shouldn't have used Allison to get my revenge on Alan Taylor and punish Julie at the same time, even though I still thought Allison had also been abused.

"According to what Julie is saying Allison told her, you advised her to tell Mr. Martin and Dr. Richards these fantasies and warned her not to say that any of it was a lie, no matter what. You told her to tell them what she had written in her diary. You pushed her into this situation, this confrontation, Mayfair. Is this true?"

"I gave her the best advice I could," I said.

"You know that's not true, Mayfair. The best advice was not to tell her to deny that anything was untrue but instead to only tell the truth. Did you know that what she was saying was untrue from the start?"

"I did not and I still do not know that to be a fact, just because she confused a date in her diary and her friend, who's probably a young airhead, can't remember details. Any psychologist can twist a girl like Allison into knots and get the district attorney to back off, especially if there's a smart lawyer involved."

"But . . . you didn't know any of this to be a fact, and you're the one who's always preaching facts first, feelings second. I can't believe this, Mayfair. What about this poor guy? You could have destroyed his career, his life. You nearly ruined him forever and, no question, put the school in a terrible position. Why did you take such an active role in this and manipulate Allison, and not only her but us? Me?"

I turned my gaze sharply on him, my eyes burning with the pain I felt inside. My father was betraying me, but he did not know why he shouldn't. Maybe I was too smart for my own good; maybe I was my own worst enemy. "Don't worry about him. He wasn't lily-white pure, Daddy."

"How would you know that?"

"I know," I said firmly. "Personally."

He flinched and then looked stunned. "What are you saying?"

"I have factual, positive proof that he took advantage of a student besides Allison."

"What? Who? What are you saying now?"

I stared at him.

His eyes washed over me, and then it was almost as if I could see a cartoon light bulb go off above his head. "Let me understand this, Mayfair. Are you now saying that you were the one sexually abused by Mr. Taylor?"

I turned away. "I have trouble thinking of it as sexual abuse, Daddy. I'm old enough both chronologically and mentally to know what I was doing. It's the aftermath that I consider abuse, and that's why I was so easily convinced that Allison might have been another victim," I said. I didn't want to mention any other motive, especially my chance to expose Julie so he would see her for what she was.

"I can't believe this. Why wouldn't you come to me if that was true?"

"As I told you, I didn't see myself as a victim then, and when I did, I felt more foolish than violated. We know who would enjoy seeing me embarrassed the most."

"You don't mean Julie."

I didn't reply. Then I thought and said, "Among others, especially the bitches from *Macbeth*."

"You're not eighteen," he said. "Of course you are a victim."

I smirked. "You know my opinion of chronological age versus mental age, Daddy."

"Your opinion isn't important in such a situation. There are legal opinions here." He shook his head. "This is too much. I don't understand what you did here or why. You hid what happened to you and decided instead to use what Allison told you to get back at this man? Is this the gist of what you're telling me?"

"I guess so," I said.

"You guess so?"

"Yes! That's the gist of it!" I felt my eyes flooding with tears, something I hadn't felt for some time. "Yes, yes!" I cried. "That's exactly what I did."

He sat for a moment, stunned. "Why, Mayfair? You're so much brighter than most people, brighter than anyone I know. This wasn't the right way to handle things."

I wiped tears off my cheeks. "Maybe intelligence isn't everything after all, Daddy. Maybe we underestimate the power of feelings. I was hurt, and logic didn't make it any better this time."

"What exactly happened between you and him?"

I sat for a moment looking out the window, wishing I were like a cloud that could be blown toward the horizon and not have to linger in one place.

"Mayfair?"

"What usually happens between men and women?"

"When?"

"The day Julie sold me out in school, that day, that afternoon and evening."

He thought a moment. "The time you said you were at the library?"

"I guess it qualifies as research now and nothing more." I turned to him. "I don't want you doing anything about it now. It's too late."

"You should have come to me. You shouldn't have tried to get revenge or justice this way, Mayfair."

"Should have and could have are probably the most used concepts since the invention of the wheel."

He nodded. "Well, Julie is rightfully upset, Mayfair. My marriage is in real jeopardy here."

He knew my feelings about his marriage. He didn't have to hear it. "I wouldn't call that jeopardy," I muttered nevertheless.

"She makes me happy, Mayfair. It's not up to you to judge that. I have a life to live, too. I mourned your mother's passing. I suffered. I was ready to give everything up and not care, but I wanted to be strong for you until you could be strong for yourself, and when I thought you were, I looked after myself somewhat, too. I don't feel guilty about it, and you will never make me feel guilty about it.

"No father could ever be prouder of a daughter than I was of you. I was right there for all your amazing awards. I bragged about you until my business associates wanted to take me out to be shot. My office walls are covered with your plaques, citations, and letters from every respected institution that involves academic accomplishment.

"During those early years after your mother's death, I tried to be your mother and father. I did the best I could. You've gone way too far this time, Mayfair. Not this school and certainly not Julie and I are capable of giving you what you need, apparently."

He lowered his head and sat quietly for a long moment. The tears that burned inside my eyes boiled over. I turned away quickly, and then he rose and left my room.

When I was very young, reading books that college-age kids were struggling with and doing math problems that high-school teachers wouldn't attempt, much less try to teach to seniors, I used to wonder if I had really been born like other children. The possibility occurred to me, especially after reading *Frankenstein*, that I might have been created in some laboratory. I asked my mother.

At first, she laughed, but then she saw that I was really thinking it might be so.

"Oh, no, no, Mayfair," she cried, and hugged me. "You were born on a very sunny morning. I was dreaming of giving birth to you and woke up when my water broke. Your father was so nervous and excited that he was very funny. He put on two completely different shoes and never realized it until he was at the hospital.

"It was only five fifteen in the morning, but on the way there, he stopped at that traffic light at the base of our road, the one everyone complains about because there's so little traffic that it barely needs a stop sign, and he just stayed there waiting for it to change while I was moaning. He suddenly realized how silly and nervous he was acting and shot ahead. These were wonderful memories for us after you were born.

"The moment I looked at your face, I knew you were going to be something special. Two days old, and you looked at me and listened as if you were already two years old. You were the favorite of the maternity nurses, too.

"No, my darling, wonderful little girl, you were

not created in a laboratory, unless you want to call my womb a laboratory."

She held me and laughed.

I could hear her melodic laugh now. I hadn't heard it for so long. It had been buried under too much in my brain, maybe, but when I remembered it now, it didn't make me smile. It made me cry.

I held myself and curled up in my bed, wishing I had someone who loved me holding me instead. I rocked and cried like a little girl.

Finally, sleep caught up with me, but I welcomed it. Thankfully, it was the weekend, and I didn't have to get up early and go to school. My father had decided yesterday that he was going to take us all for a ride to the Fashion Plaza in Newport Beach, where Julie could enjoy some shopping. We were all to go to lunch in Laguna Beach, but I didn't feel like getting up, much less going for a ride and spending a day with Julie and Allison now. I was anticipating her look of disgust and condemnation, even though she had probably promised my father she would not mention anything. When I didn't go down for breakfast, my father came up.

"Are you sick?" he asked. "Are you in pain from that cut on your head or anything?"

"No."

"Well, are you going with us today?"

"I'm tired," I said.

"Suit yourself," he replied, and left quickly. He had no patience for me and no forgiveness yet. I wondered if he ever would.

Later, I rose and had a little to eat. I wasn't happy being alone in the house this time. Normally, I could distract myself with reading or research, but I couldn't concentrate on anything. Impulsively, I dressed and called for a taxi to take me to Santa Monica. I had no idea why until I got out and walked on the beach. It took me only moments to realize I wanted to relive what had been the most exciting day and night of my life. It was the first time I could really say that I felt more like a young woman than a super-brilliant prodigy.

I took off my shoes, folded my arms under my breasts, and walked down the beach, sometimes stepping into the water and remembering how it had felt that afternoon when I was walking with Alan Taylor and how we had laughed about it. I recalled how I had begun to relax and become more and more fascinated with him, with how he opened up to talk about himself, which only encouraged me to do the same. I was telling him things I hadn't told anyone else, some things, in fact, that I had never told my father.

I remembered thinking, *I can do this. I can have a relationship with him secretly but intensely.* He was complimenting me in ways I had never been complimented and touching me in places that longed to be touched. As we walked, it really seemed like we passed through an invisible wall into a new world of possibilities. What he was back at school, what I was back at school, drifted behind us, blown away by our smiles and laughter. We were simply a man and a woman enjoying each other's conversation, each other's company, and the beauty surrounding us.

I had no idea how long I had been walking now. I suddenly stopped and realized I was close to Alan Taylor's apartment building. For a moment, I just stood there staring at it, the sea breeze threading through my hair. I turned off from the beach and stopped at a bench along the walkway to put on my shoes. I sat there thinking, remembering. The images and feelings were as vivid as ever, especially since I was so close.

Just as I was about to get up, walk back a little, and then call for a taxi home, I saw Alan coming up the sidewalk. He was holding hands with a very attractive strawberry-blond-haired woman who was only about an inch shorter than he was. She wore a pair of designer jeans, with glittering jeweled patterns on the sides of the legs, and a pink short-sleeved blouse. She had the svelte figure of a model and wore a pair of very fashionable sunglasses.

I froze and watched them. They were laughing at something and looked very happy. Perhaps he was telling the truth about becoming engaged, I thought. I didn't wait for them to enter his building. I turned quickly and headed down the walkway. The sight of him looking so fresh and young, in his dark blue jeans and tailored white shirt, seemed to rattle my brain. I hated feeling the excitement rush through my body. I felt like some lovesick teenage girl, more like Allison, and I wanted to pound my legs with my closed fists. I was walking quickly but slowed down to catch my breath.

For a few moments, I stood looking down and

then raised my head to look out at the ocean, just as I heard him call my name. Had I imagined it, wished for it so much that I convinced myself I really had heard it? Very slowly, I turned and saw him standing there alone.

"Why did you come down here?" he asked.

"Oh, is this private property? I hadn't realized it," I said.

"You know what I mean, Mayfair."

"I had to get out of my house for a while, and I wanted the sea air. I haven't been spying on you, if that's what you think."

"It did occur to me."

"Yes, I imagine it would. Your ego has enough room for all favorable possibilities."

He nodded, looked back at his apartment building, and stepped closer. "You're right to hate me, and I deserve your wrath and all that happened as a result. I did feel sorry for your stepsister. But she's not any more impressionable than any of them."

"Them?"

"Girls her age. I did consider the possibility that you might have believed I abused her, but I never intended to abuse you."

"What would you call it?"

"A man's weakness, I suppose. And you're right about my ego. I rationalized that I was giving you something special, too. What I told you is still true, Mayfair. You're a beautiful young woman with an amazing mind. You fascinated me, and for a while, I did fool myself into believing it was possible for us to carry on, but as difficult as it might be for you to believe, the mature man in me finally got control. I should have handled it differently. I was a coward."

I looked away. As much as I wanted to, I couldn't hate him.

"Why didn't you turn me in instead of using Allison?"

I didn't answer.

"I'll tell you why," he said, and I turned to him.

"Oh, you will? Tell me."

"Pride. That's going to be your one weakness, Mayfair, your *hubris*. See, I know my classic tragedy, even though I only teach junior-high English. You're constantly told how high up you are. You can't let yourself admit to being human, because that's what having a weakness means, being human."

My eyes felt as if the tears that had been building up were frozen.

"Don't judge every man you'll meet by what happened between us, by what I did and didn't do. Be kind. Be forgiving. You don't want to be with a man who is your equal. You want someone who will need you and whom you'll need, Mayfair. It's not a sin to need someone. I wish you luck," he said. "I really do." He smiled and walked away.

My chest ached. I couldn't swallow. I watched him disappear, and then I turned and walked for another hour before I called a taxi.

I wasn't prepared for the depth of depression I fell into that night. My father called from the freeway to tell me they were staying longer than anticipated and would stop for dinner before returning to Los Angeles. When I didn't even utter a grunt to acknowledge him, he asked if I had heard him.

"I heard you."

"What have you been doing all day, Mayfair?" he asked suspiciously. For a moment, I wondered if he had decided to have me watched or something.

"Nothing out of the ordinary for me," I said, which was cryptic enough.

"All right. Tell Martha what you would like for dinner," he said.

"Okay," I replied to end the call.

I didn't tell our maid anything. I took an apple upstairs with me and, after sitting and thinking for a while, went to sleep early. I didn't even hear them come home. If my father checked on me, I never noticed that, either. I was up before everyone the next morning, however. I had some coffee and buttered toast and went for a walk before sitting at the pool. It was nearly an hour and a half later when my father walked out to see what I was up to.

"How's your head?" he asked.

I laughed.

"What's so funny, Mayfair?"

"That's probably always been the most important part of me in your eyes and everyone else's," I said, which clearly upset him.

"You're acting like a girl half your age, and I don't mean chronological," he replied. "I'm taking Julie and Allison to the movies this afternoon to see the new Nick Razor blockbuster. Would you like to join us?"

Nick Razor was a detective in the future who was nostalgic for the past. The films were filled with special effects and nonstop action, what my father called popcorn movies. When I was a little girl, I did go to those sorts of movies with him and my mother, but I hadn't for some time.

"No, thanks," I said.

"Everyone's trying, Mayfair, but if you don't, this will go nowhere."

"I'm already there," I said.

He nodded, bit down on his lower lip, and turned and walked back to the house, his shoulders slumped. I closed my eyes and nearly fell asleep again. I knew my depression was continuing even more intensely after confronting Alan Taylor the day before, but I felt helpless, really helpless, for the first time in a long time. When I returned to the house, everyone already had left for lunch and the movies. I went up to my room and tried to do some reading, but my mind wouldn't absorb anything. I couldn't even watch television. Nothing held my attention. I went out again, walked again, and remembered that I hadn't eaten anything since my coffee and toast. It was only the realization that drove me to eat anything. I wasn't really hungry.

Afterward, I went up to my room and dozed until I heard my father, Julie, and Allison return. No one bothered me until just before dinner, when my father sent Allison to my room to tell me to come down to eat.

Reluctantly, I did. Everyone else seemed nervous. I was too numb to be nervous. They talked incessantly, it seemed to me, about the movie. I ate mechanically and then announced that I had a headache and was going up to rest.

"Maybe we should take you to a doctor for that," my father said.

"It's not from the injury," I replied.

"She would know," Julie quipped.

I didn't bother to respond.

When I went up this time, I was drawn to my closet to look in the carton that contained some photo albums, birthday cards, and old report cards. I sat on the floor and looked at everything slowly. The pictures of my mother and me, all three of us, brought back some of my warmest memories. I didn't cry, but I pretended I was back there and wished that I could magically turn back time. I wasn't one to fantasize or dwell in my imagination long, unless I was trying to project what something might be like after more technological advances.

When I was the little girl in those pictures, I wondered why I didn't react to toys in a similar way to how other girls my age did. I knew I wasn't much fun for them, and after a while, none really asked for me. I went to their birthday parties, but I guess I never looked like I was having fun. I was smart enough already to know that other girls' mothers considered me quite strange. Some were even worried about their daughters playing with me. I probably said things to them that confused and maybe shocked them, things they told their mothers. I recalled how hard my mother had tried to get me to enjoy myself. She would even say, "Remember, Mayfair, they are just little girls," as if she thought I might be more understanding and gentler with them, something only someone much older would do.

It never occurred to me back then that my mother might be sad or unhappy about me, maybe even disappointed. She probably feared that I wasn't going to be the young daughter she'd dreamed of having, the one she could dress up and slowly guide into a wonderful adolescence filled with new discoveries about myself almost daily, discoveries she remembered having and was so determined that I would enjoy. Mothers relived their own youth through their daughters, and even the short time we had together could have been something more wonderful for her.

How my heart ached now, for so many reasons.

I closed the albums and put everything back into the cartons and then the closet. I prepared for sleep and went to bed wishing I needed to suck my thumb or something. I curled up in the fetal position and hugged my oversize pillow, but nothing helped me sleep. I dozed and woke, dozed and woke, until the morning light slipped around my curtains like fingers of gold searching for a way to touch me.

Everything on me ached. I guessed I had been too flippant about the head injury. My neck was sore. I moaned and just fell asleep again. I never heard Allison come into my room, but I did sense her presence and opened my eyes.

"What?"

"Mom wants to know if you're going to school today. You'll have to hurry."

"Mom? Tell her no. You just go on without me."

"Are you sick?"

"Sick of."

"What's that mean?"

"Forget it, Allison. Tell her I'm taking the day off."

"Daddy had to leave early."

"Lucky him," I said, and turned over.

I thought that was it for the day, but a little more than an hour later, my phone rang. It was my father.

"What?" I said. "Don't worry. I don't need to go to a doctor."

"I'm not taking you to a doctor. I'd like you to get dressed and be ready to go to the school with me in about an hour. We have a meeting with Mr. Martin."

"Mr. Martin? What about?"

I imagined I was to make some sort of confession, but he surprised me.

"Your educational future," he said.

"What, is he a fortune-teller now, too?"

"Mayfair."

"Okay, Daddy," I said. "I'll be ready."

"Good."

I got dressed. Julie was nowhere to be found, which didn't make me unhappy. I wondered if she would be with my father when he came for me, but her car was gone, and she didn't return before he arrived.

I stepped out just as he opened his door, and I ran around to get in.

"What is this really all about, Daddy?" I asked as he backed out of the driveway.

"A solution," he said. "For all of us."

19

Mr. Martin handed my father and me copies of the Spindrift School brochure.

"It looks more like an old mansion than a school," I said. "An eclectic Queen Anne. How can it be a school?"

"Everything about it is unorthodox. You'll see as you read," he said.

I glanced at my father to show him my skepticism. Not that I was afraid of going to a school away from home, but a part of me was hoping he would say, "It won't be that long before she's completely away from us. Why rush it?"

"As you can see, the grounds are beautiful," Mr. Martin continued in a seller's tone, as if he were getting a commission.

It occurred to me that maybe he was. Maybe I was being exploited and victimized once again.

"It's fenced and walled in, a very private place with the most sophisticated technological security.

As you will see, it has most anything any really good school or college would. Turn the page. See that modern laboratory, that computer room, and look at that library. There are a thousand volumes, covering law, science, literature, anything you can possibly think of researching, plus the most up-to-date internet access, of course."

"Impressive," my father said.

"This is actually a specially designed school for students like you, Mayfair. It's a school at which you live and work in a totally unorthodox learning environment. The principal is a renowned child psychologist, Dr. Jessie Marlowe. You might have already read some of her studies."

"Yes, I think I have. I have some questions about some of her conclusions."

"I'm sure you have," he said, smiling. "Anyway, they take in only fifteen students."

"Only fifteen?" Daddy asked. "All this for only fifteen?" Now he sounded like the one getting a commission.

"Exactly. Frankly, there are not many students who would meet the criteria, Mr. Cummings, and Spindrift is very selective about choosing from the list of those who do. However," he added, "I already know that Mayfair would be very welcome. I took the liberty of getting them some preliminary information. No sense in wasting your time or theirs, right?"

"Where is Piñon Pine Grove?" I asked.

"It's in the Coachella Valley, not more than two hours from Los Angeles. Not that far from home."

"Maybe it's not far enough away," I muttered, and glanced at my father.

"How long has this school been in existence?" he asked Mr. Martin, ignoring my comment.

"It was started ten years ago as the brainchild of someone who would have benefited greatly from it, Dr. Norman Lazarus, now one of the world's most renowned biochemists."

"Lazarus? Did he rise from the dead?" I asked.

Mr. Martin smiled. "Maybe his ancestor did."

"I think we should be a little more serious about this, Mayfair," my father said. He looked at the brochure and read some more. "You're right, Mr. Martin. These students are very protected, apparently. There is a great deal of security. No one can just walk in on them. I like that."

"Exactly. The philosophy is that their students are very valuable national assets. The graduates of Spindrift have gone on to do wonderful things in all fields. A number of them work for NASA. Many are doing things that are kept top secret."

He turned to me. "The big point here is that you'd be studying and researching with students at your level of learning, students equipped the way you're equipped, Mayfair. I don't think it's much of a secret that your skills and intellect are not being challenged here.

"This recent incident you had with some of the other girls is characteristic of what happens with gifted students everywhere," he continued, talking more to my father. "Other students either resent them or see them as . . ."

"Weird, freaky," I finished for him.

He smiled. "I was just going to say unusual."

"It's not cheap," I said, noting the tuition. "Are all the other unusual students from wealthy families, too?"

"Most are. They do give out one scholarship a year to a candidate who fits the criteria but whose family can't afford to send her or him. One of the former graduates, who wants to remain anonymous, donates the tuition."

"Walled in, high security, guards at the gate—probably makes it quite a curiosity to the locals. Piñon Pine Grove sounds like an exciting little city," I said, reading from the description on the last page of the brochure. "Twenty-five thousand people, a few home building supply companies, other small factories, a mall and movie complex, and a senior citizens gated-home community with four thousand people. Wow. It's overwhelming."

"The students at Spindrift don't have much, if anything, to do with the people in Piñon Pine Grove. There's a sizable entertainment area in the school, with a big-screen movie theater and all the music you or anyone there would want. There's a gym and an indoor pool. As you see, they even have an impressive telescope for astronomy. You probably wouldn't want to leave."

"You sure this really isn't a mental institution?" I asked.

"Hardly, unless you call a place for developing your mind to even higher levels a mental institution," Mr. Martin said.

"Very good. How do you just happen to know so much about it, Mr. Martin?" I asked.

"I have a good friend in the state education department who told me about it."

"After you told him about me?"

"Exactly," he said, and smiled. "No sense trying to put one over on Mayfair," he told my father.

My father nodded and turned to me. "Well, what do you think?"

"Do I have a choice?"

There was no doubt in my mind that Julie was waiting for his call, waiting to hear that I was headed out of the house and especially away from Allison.

"Do you want a choice? Do you want to stay here in this school?"

I looked again at the brochure. "Spindrift," I said. "From where we can look down on everyone else."

"Which is exactly what you've been doing here," my father said.

It stung.

I closed the brochure and looked out the window.

There were graduates of our school who had returned for visits from colleges they attended. They often gravitated to me because they could have a more intelligent conversation than they could have with other juniors and even seniors, not to mention many of their former teachers. We talked about the courses they were taking, the books they were reading, and the demands on their time for study and research. All of them always commented on how much they respected me for being so far ahead that when I went to college, it would seem like kindergarten. But many of them, especially the ones who were college freshmen, voiced some nostalgia.

"I wish I was a carefree high-school student again," they might say. They'd look around and add, "I never thought I would miss this place, but I do. I had some happy times here."

I didn't, but I wanted to very much. I wanted to miss this place someday, too. Would I ever be nostalgic for anything anymore?

It was going to be easy to walk out of this building, out of this school world, but ironically, that didn't make me happy. It made me feel empty. Oh, there were a few teachers I would miss because we had some good discussions, but those talks were too few and far between to amount to much, not enough to give me that sense of nostalgia those returning college students showed.

I had joined no clubs, had been on no teams, and had never been in a school show or the school band. I had no good memories of any social event. Probably, in weeks or even days after I left, I would be forgotten, and if I weren't, I'd be remembered as some sort of freak or monster to which students could compare each other when insulting each other.

"You want to be another Mayfair?" they might say.

Or they might turn my name into a verb. "You're Mayfairing me" or, simply, "You're Mayfairing."

Poor Allison. If she weren't taken out of this school, she might suffer because of that, despite her current status as a little heroine. I hoped Julie wouldn't go back on seriously considering finding her another school even though it might alienate her from some of her precious lunch friends. She could very well think that because I was gone from the school, Allison would be fine.

Maybe she would be, I thought. What did I really know?

"Well, then," Mr. Martin said. "I'll contact Dr. Marlowe today and get things arranged. They don't have semesters like ordinary schools, so it doesn't really make any difference when you enroll her," he told my father. "I'll call you tomorrow, and most probably you can head up there this weekend. It'll be no problem getting the rest of her academic history to them."

"Very good. Mayfair, any more questions for Mr. Martin?"

I looked at him. He wasn't exactly riding me out of here on a rail, but he wasn't wasting any time, either. "Will you miss me when I'm gone?"

He laughed. "You know I will," he said.

We rose to go. He followed us out to the hallway and extended his hand to me.

"I want to wish you the best of luck, Mayfair. I know that people would say luck hasn't anything to do with it in your case, but I don't see the harm in wishing only the best for you."

"Thank you. I wish you the same, Mr. Martin. You have your challenges, too."

He smiled and watched us walk away.

"Is there anything here you might want, anything in a locker or something?" my father asked me.

"There's nothing here I might want," I said.

"This is for the best," he said.

To me, he sounded more like someone who was trying to convince himself.

I didn't have to be present to see Julie's face when my father told her about the arrangements. I could easily imagine her look of joy, her beaming smile of relief. At dinner, she already showed a renewal of energy. She was back at gossip, opinions on some new vacation places, and thoughts about some home renovation work she was convinced they should now do.

I hated it, but even my father looked happier, like a weight had been lifted from his shoulders. He laughed and smiled at many of the things Julie said. *He really does like her*, I thought. I'd study all sorts of insects and animals in my life, analyze human history from the caveman until now, but I might never come to understand men.

Too bad for me.

After dinner, I started to think about what clothing I wanted to take with me and what else I would bring. When I looked at the clothes Julie had bought me on that shopping spree, I thought about how my improved appearance had attracted male interest. Of course I was curious about what the boys at Spindrift would be like. They'd have to be very intelligent, obviously. Maybe there would be someone who was attracted to me, and I'd be attracted to him, and we'd enjoy challenging each other in many different ways. I decided I would take those outfits after all.

That I was actually leaving didn't hit Allison until

she saw my suitcases being taken out. Julie, trying to look like the good, concerned stepmother, had had my father find out what the school expected me to bring in the way of toiletries and the like. She'd then gone out and bought the items and packed them all for me.

I thought she was like a dog on a leash, panting with excitement. Soon she'd be released and could charge forward.

"Let's have something special for dinner the night before," she suggested to my father.

"Yes," I said, "like a last meal on death row."

She never enjoyed my sense of humor, and she certainly wasn't going to enjoy it now.

Nevertheless, my father had live lobsters delivered. It was one of Allison's favorite meals, not mine. Julie would eat only the tails, because it was simply too messy to get into the rest of it. She had gone ahead and ordered a chocolate cake with "Good Luck at Your New School" written in strawberries on the top.

What hypocrisy, I thought. She hated the idea of spending so much money on this new school, but she couldn't come right out and say that now, especially in front of my father. She didn't want anything to prevent me from leaving. Somehow, even though I was leaving before my senior year had technically begun, she was making it seem as if I were going off to college. That was the way she wanted Allison to see it, but to her credit, Allison did not see it that way.

After everything that had happened, Allison appeared to be the one who was most upset and disturbed by my being sent away, even though both her mother and my father tried their best to explain how much better off I would be and how wonderful this opportunity was for me.

Allison came to my bedroom after dinner. I was sifting through my research papers, deciding what might be of any value at Spindrift, when she knocked and entered. She looked like she might actually begin crying.

"What's wrong?"

"This is all my fault," she said. "It is. I shouldn't have broken my promise and told my mother things."

"It's not your fault. This would have happened eventually anyway, Allison."

I saw that this wasn't making her feel any better.

"Look, Allison, when you first showed me how upset you were after hearing Mr. Taylor talk about his engagement, I really believed he might have taken advantage of you, abused you."

She shrugged. I still didn't want to confess to reading her diary, but I thought she deserved to know more, to know enough to judge me more objectively in the years to come, when she was old enough to look back and understand more fully.

"The reason I would have believed it is that he took advantage of me."

She lifted her head and widened her eyes. "Really?"

"Yes, really, but I blame myself more than I blame him now. I was vulnerable. You know what that means?"

She shook her head.

"I was in a state of mental and emotional turmoil

that made me weak and blind, and he pounced like some fox that had the good fortune to have a plump chicken wander into his den. I didn't watch out for myself. I could have prevented it all from happening, no matter how good-looking and sophisticated he thought he was. Anyway, when I saw the opportunity to hurt him back, I took advantage of it. I took advantage of you, used you. So don't feel so sorry for me."

I looked away and added, "You won't understand how I could say this, but I don't blame him now as much as I did. I'm not saying he was right or anything. I'm just . . . more understanding. When you're older, you might understand what I mean."

I turned back to her. "I didn't do right by you. I'm sorry."

"I thought we were really getting to be like sisters," she said.

"We were. As much as I can be anyone's sister. None of this is your fault. Okay?"

She nodded. "Can I give you a hug?" she asked.

As nice a gesture as that would be, she probably couldn't have said anything that would have made me sadder. I nodded, and she came over and hugged me.

"I hope you'll be happy there, Mayfair," she said. "I won't do as well in math, though."

"You'll do fine," I said. "Really, Allison, you're going to be all right now."

She liked that, and so did I.

Afterward, I didn't read. I didn't go on my computer. I didn't watch television or write anything. I just sat looking out the window at the stars and the occasional clouds that seemed to be tiptoeing across them.

I went to bed thinking of my mother again, picturing her face when she tucked me in or sat reading to me. I knew those images were always trying to come back, fighting to get on the screen of my memory, but I kept them from doing so because I knew what they would bring.

They would bring tears, and I always hated tears.

They reminded me that I was once, for a short while, at least, a little girl, and when I was a little girl, my mother died and left me frightened.

I vowed never to be frightened again.

Right now, try as hard as I could, lie to myself as best I could, put on the best face of bravery I could, I couldn't help but admit that I was afraid of tomorrow.

And so, despite my hard attitude, I was trembling inside on Sunday when we set out for Spindrift. As we drove away, Allison stood at the living room's front window. She waved quickly, as if she was afraid her mother might see her. I waved back, and she and the house disappeared behind a turn.

When the sign indicating that we were finally entering the city of Piñon Pine Grove appeared, Julie exclaimed, "Thank God!"

I couldn't help but laugh.

She turned to defend herself. "Well, it was a difficult drive. Despite the way you explained it, who knew it would be like this on the freeway on a Sunday?"

"Most anyone else who lives in the state of California would know," I said dryly.

"You didn't think it would be this bad, did you, Roger?" she asked my father.

He just looked at her and smiled. She glared at everything out the window.

"It is pretty here," my father said. "Sort of rustic, don't you think, Mayfair?"

"Back to nature," I said. "There's your piñon pine," I pointed out as we approached the hill. This route avoided the actual city of Piñon Pine Grove. "It grows well here because it requires little water. The nuts are edible."

Julie glanced at me with her expression of surprise and amazement. *She's going to miss me, miss learning stuff*, I thought.

The GPS took us to the road that led up to Spindrift. For a while, we could see only the very top of the building. As we drew closer, it seemed to rise out of the ground. The area around it was fenced in, just the way it was shown in the brochure. The long driveway led us to an iron gate at least ten feet high. Beside it was a security booth, and when we approached, a tall, stout man in a gray uniform stepped out, a clipboard in his hand. My father pulled to a stop and lowered his window.

"Mr. and Mrs. Cummings and Mayfair," he told the security guard.

The guard's top jacket pocket had a name tag that read "Edwards." He nodded and tried to smile, but he had one of those sun-worn faces that looked leathery, with deep wrinkles, and eyes that suggested that he was much younger than he appeared. "May I see your license, please?"

"He's kidding," I muttered, but my father took it out to show him.

"Welcome," he said after copying down my father's license number. "You can park right up close to the entrance."

He handed my father a blue plastic card with a black strip across the top.

"This is coded. Just insert it in the front door, and she'll unlock for you. Give the card to Dr. Marlowe after you're finished bringing in your luggage and things."

"Thank you," my father said.

Edwards returned to his booth and pressed a button that opened the gate.

"You have to prove who you are? Gates, special key cards. This isn't what I call protected. It's what I call locked away," I muttered.

"Safety's important in today's world," my father said. "Like Mr. Martin told us, there's a lot of valuable property here, and I don't mean just the equipment, books, and furniture."

He drove us through and up to the building.

"What an interesting house," Julie said. "I'm sure you can tell us about it."

"It's a Queen Anne, an architectural style popular in the 1880s and '90s. Victorian. They're not usually this big. It looks like a lot's been added to it over the years, maybe recently, but it has the typical bay windows, balconies, stained glass, that turret, and the porch."

"Maybe you should become a detective," Julie

said, smiling. She was so happy now she could burst, and she didn't mind lavishing compliments on me.

"Any good student is a detective," I said.

My father turned off the engine. He glanced at me and got out. I followed him around to the trunk to get some of my luggage. Julie even hurried to take a bag. She was that enthusiastic about getting me settled in and gone.

Perhaps I shouldn't hate her so much after all, I thought. Maybe she and my father needed their space. She suddenly seemed more desperate and pathetic to me. I looked at both of them in a new way as I headed with them to my new home, my new world. My father had lost the love of his life and did struggle to keep us both afloat. Julie, for whatever reason, had a miserable start in her life, too.

Leave them be, I thought. *Get on with your own life*. Whatever that was.

My father inserted the key card in the front door, and we heard a click. He turned the handle and opened the door. The outside of Spindrift looked like an authentic old Victorian house, but inside we found an entrance lobby with very modern decor, beautifully laid cocoa-shaded tile floors, rich wood walls, and leather chairs and sofas.

A door was opened toward the rear, and an elegant-looking woman, with graying dark brown hair styled neatly around her face with well-trimmed bangs, entered the lobby. She looked about fifty, I thought, had a very nice figure, and, surprisingly, was dressed in a pair of jeans, a dark blue blouse, and a pair of sandals.

"Mr. and Mrs. Cummings," she said. "I'm Dr. Marlowe. Welcome."

"Thank you," my father said, taking her hand. "My wife, Julie, and my daughter, Mayfair."

Dr. Marlowe nodded at Julie and then turned quickly to me. She had intelligent blue-green eyes, and although she didn't wear any makeup, not even lipstick, she was attractive. I sensed a quiet contentment about her, none of the tension, defensiveness, or caution that was common in the school administrators I knew.

"Hello, Mayfair. I'm sure you'll have a million questions, so let's get you settled in. While you're unpacking your things, I'll meet with your father and mother and get our paperwork completed. I'll give your parents a tour of the school, too."

I looked at Julie. She could finally be known as my mother if she wanted.

"Do you need help with Mayfair's things, Mr. Cummings?"

"No, I think we can manage."

"We're going up a flight," she warned. "I can call for help. I have two maintenance personnel."

"I think we can do it," he said, looking at Julie. She nodded.

"Okay. Follow me, then."

"Oh, here's that coded card," he told her.

"Yes. We record all comings and goings."

"No one escapes?" I said.

"No one wants to," she countered with a smile. "So, trip from Los Angeles okay?"

"Longer than I expected," Julie said.

Dr. Marlowe smiled at her. "Well, the good thing about being here is that once you're here, there isn't much traffic with which to contend."

The stairway with its mahogany banister had obviously been rebuilt. It felt solid beneath us.

At the top, we paused.

"I have you in that section that faces the lake behind us," Dr. Marlowe explained to me. "The rooms are small, actually not much different from the way they were when the house was first built. There are two other girls in your section. They both arrived this year, too." She turned to my father. "We had three openings occur."

"Why?" Julie asked. "It's not graduation time, is it?"

"Our students have a different school year," Dr. Marlowe said, looking at me with a twinkle in her eyes. "It's built-in."

"Built into what?" Julie asked.

"Whoever they are," Dr. Marlowe said, smiling.

"What?"

I laughed. Maybe I would like it here, I thought.

My room was spartan. It had a double bed with a small side table, a dresser, a desk, a mirror on the closet door, and a closet half the size of one of our hall closets at home. I was glad I didn't bring all that much.

Julie, despite trying desperately not to say anything negative that might turn me around, couldn't contain herself. "Oh, how small."

"Our students don't spend very much time in their rooms," Dr. Marlowe said. She looked at me.

"It's more than enough," I said, and she smiled.

My father put my suitcases down. "You want any help unpacking?"

"No. Why don't you do the paperwork and take your tour? I'll be fine," I told him.

We heard someone laugh in the hallway. Dr. Marlowe looked out and said, "Oh, great, Corliss and Donna, your neighbors. Hi, girls. Mayfair Cummings has arrived."

The two came to my doorway.

"This is Corliss Simon," Dr. Marlowe said, putting her hand on the shoulder of an African American girl with a slim figure. Her hair was cut rather short. She had almond-shaped ebony eyes and an arrogant tightness in her mouth.

"And this is Donna Ramanez," Dr. Marlowe said as she turned to the light-brown-haired shorter girl beside her.

They both wore gray sweatshirts and jeans. Neither spoke. They stood in the doorway, looking in at us. We looked at each other like gunslingers sizing up the competition.

"Why don't we go to my office and let them get to know each other?" Dr. Marlowe told my father and Julie.

"Very good," he said, and they followed her out.

I turned to my suitcases.

"Need any help?" Corliss asked.

"Offering?"

"She wouldn't have asked otherwise, genius," Donna said.

I turned back to them and smiled. "What are you wearing, the school uniform?"

They looked at each other as if they had just realized they were wearing the same thing. Then they both laughed.

"Where are you from?" I asked Corliss.

"Nigeria. Originally," she added. "West LA. You?"

"Garden of Eden originally. Beverly Hills."

She laughed. I looked at Donna.

"My mother is from Ireland, and my father is from Costa Rica, but I was born in Arizona."

"What are the others here like?" I asked.

"You have a good imagination?" Corliss asked.

"Yes, why?"

"After you meet them, you'll need it," Donna said.

"Great," I said, and began to unpack.

They started to help. We worked quietly. Neither of them commented on anything I had brought. I watched them out of the corner of my eye and then stopped and turned to them.

They paused, too.

"What?" Donna asked.

"Neither of you especially wanted to be here, either?"

"I won the scholarship," Corliss said, "but it wasn't what I set out to do. It's supposed to save my life."

"My choice was either to come here or go to Alcatraz," Donna said.

"Alcatraz was closed a long time ago," I said.

"So I had no choice," she replied.

I laughed and then looked at them more intently.

"What?" Corliss asked.

"I was just thinking. You're the welcoming committee. This didn't all just happen."

They smiled.

"Nothing here just happens," Donna said. "If you belong, you'll know that, and you'll like it."

I nodded.

It didn't take long to size me up.

Maybe, just maybe, I had found a new home.

Epilogue

I stood outside with my father and Julie after they had returned from their tour of Spindrift and it was time for them to leave.

Since my mother's death, my father and I really had only been separated a few times, including for a little more than a week during his honeymoon with Julie. Most of the other times, his business trips took two or maybe three days.

I could see that this fact was occurring to him, too, as he stood looking out at the beautiful grounds and the fence that surrounded Spindrift.

"This is quite an educational institution," he said, still not looking at me. "We met all of the teachers you'll have, and they are all very impressive. I think you'll finally feel challenged. One thing's for sure," he added, turning to me and smiling, "you won't be bored."

"I saw a couple of very good-looking boys, too," Julie added.

"Don't worry. It's all right," I said.

"What's all right?" Julie asked.

"Your leaving me here. It's all right. Don't worry about it. You don't have to say anything more."

"Well, I didn't mean . . . I mean . . ."

"You can get into the car, Julie," my father said, surprisingly firmly. "I'll just take a few minutes with Mayfair, and we'll be off."

"Okay. Good luck, Mayfair," she said, and went to the car. She knew that if she hugged me or kissed me good-bye, it would feel like she had hugged or kissed a tree.

"Let's take a little walk," my father said.

We stepped down and went to the right, where there was a small pond. We stood next to it, looking into the water and at the colorful rocks.

"I know you need this place or something like it," he began, "but I hope you don't believe I failed you, Mayfair, even though I believe that."

"We failed each other, Daddy. I'm not as smart as you think, and anyway, Julie's right. Brains aren't everything. I don't want to be just a brilliant student. I want to be a brilliant person, too. I have a ways to go. Maybe I'll find my way here."

"I bet you will," he said, smiling. He put his arm around me. "I love you, May. I'll never stop loving you."

"I know, Daddy."

"I have something more to leave with you," he said, taking my hand.

We walked back to the car, and he opened the trunk to give me a package tied with a cord.

"I'm not good at making it look fancy."

I started to open it, and he stopped me.

"No," he said. "Open it when we leave." He kissed me again and opened his car door. "I'll call, or you call us whenever you need anything or just want to talk, okay?"

"Okay, Daddy."

"See you soon," he said. "Show them what a real genius can do, will you?"

"I will."

He smiled his winning smile and got into the car. I stood and watched them drive down to the gate. It opened, they drove out, and the gate closed.

I was about to feel very bad, but then I began to open the package.

I didn't have to open it all the way to know what it was.

He had brought me something I had forgotten, my special teddy bear, the first gift he and my mother had ever given me.